Wish Club

Wish Club

A NOVEL

Kim Strickland

THREE RIVERS PRESS • NEW YORK

This is a work of fiction. Names, characters, places, and incidents either
are the product of the author's imagination or are used fictitiously.
Any resemblance to actual persons, living or dead, events,
or locales is entirely coincidental.

Copyright © 2007 by Kim Strickland-Sargent

All rights reserved.
Published in the United States by Three Rivers Press, an imprint of the
Crown Publishing Group, a division of Random House, Inc., New York.
www.crownpublishing.com

THREE RIVERS PRESS and the Tugboat design are registered
trademarks of Random House, Inc.

Library of Congress Cataloging-in-Publication Data
Strickland, Kim.
Wish club : a novel / Kim Strickland.—1st ed.
p.   cm.
1. Book clubs (Discussion groups)—Fiction.   2. Female friendship—
Fiction.   I. Title.
PS3619.T749W57 2007
813'.6–dc22   2006037079

ISBN 978-0-307-35282-8

Printed in the United States of America

Design by Lauren Dong

10 9 8 7 6 5 4 3 2 1

First Edition

*This book is dedicated to my husband Jeff,
for helping me earn my wings*

Wish Club

The air felt parched, like a scorched puff of desert. Even though the night was cold, the air seemed to be burning its way into Greta's nose. She stuck her head farther out the window, sniffing, searching for any signs of moisture, and before she realized it, she was standing outside on the fire escape.

The orange Chicago streetlights traveled away below her to the horizon, and her eyes followed them, beginning a scan of the western sky for a different kind of sign, a clue to what was troubling her. Her concentrated expression deepened the furrows in her forehead, the fine lines in the corners of her eyes, the thin ridges around her mouth where lipstick sometimes crept. The late November wind whipped her long gray hair wildly around her face. She raised a veined hand to her forehead and kept on sniffing, but instead of sensing snow on the horizon or a storm a few days off, all she could sense was that something was not as it should be.

The air felt wrong, wrung out and dried, as if something or someone had thrown it out of balance. She brought her hand back down to match the other one on her hip and, after one final look, turned to step back inside, shaking her head.

Just one more thing to try to put right, she thought. Just one more thing in this world in need of fixing.

Chapter One

——✦——

C*laudia* climbed the uneven wooden steps to Gail's Victorian wondering if anyone else would show up, wondering if maybe, from now on, Book Club might be just herself and Gail. She pressed the doorbell and waited, staring at the sorry-looking ears of Indian corn hanging on the door.

A harsh wind blew in from the lake, which was visible during the day at the end of Gail's Edgewater street. It would be cool, Claudia thought, to live this close to the water. Although Claudia suspected the real reason Gail loved this neighborhood was because it reminded her of her edgier days. Tonight the lake at the end of the street was invisible, a black void, and Claudia hugged herself against the chill.

"Hey! We were beginning to wonder if you were going to show up." It wasn't Gail, but Lindsay, who opened the door.

"Am I late?" Claudia looked at her watch as she stepped inside. It was only a quarter past seven. Her eyes met Lindsay's. "You mean everyone's here?"

Lindsay closed the door and stepped around Claudia. "Everyone," she said, popping her eyebrows as if to say, *I told you so.* She reached out her hand for Claudia's coat, which Claudia took off and handed over, staring past Lindsay into Gail's living room.

All five Book Club members were there. Everyone.

W*ith* wineglasses in hand, they took their seats on the two couches in Gail's front parlor, Lindsay managing to snag the high-backed,

Queen Anne chair in between them. Claudia suppressed a smile; even subconsciously Lindsay thought she was the queen bee. And it was, of course, Lindsay's voice that quickly broke through their chatter. "I'm so excited about what happened last time. I think this group has a lot of positive energy."

Well, that took less than thirty seconds, Claudia thought.

Gail set a tray of vegetables, fruit, and cheese down on the coffee table and stood her nearly six-foot frame up to full height. She ruffed her spiky white-blond hair with one hand, her dark roots showing, almost as long as the blond ends. "Tonight," Gail gave Lindsay a look before she turned toward the kitchen, "I think we should try to focus our energy on the book we've all come here to discuss."

As she watched Gail, Claudia twirled the ends of her own dull brown hair, the same color as Gail's roots. Although she had to admit the idea of being able to work magic had its appeal—like maybe it could give her the courage to do something new with her boring hair—Claudia wasn't sure she wanted Book Club to change. She thought, as Gail obviously did, that Book Club should probably continue to be Book Club and that the previous month's digression into the occult should remain an anomaly.

"Oh, I loved the book." Mara hugged her copy of *Home* to her chest. "I just cried and cried at the end." She shook her head and sniffed when she said this, as if she were going to reenact her tears. Mara had a large face, a fat-woman's face. Claudia was always a little surprised whenever she noticed the tiny body beneath it. "It was so lovely," Mara continued, sniffing, her cheeks flushed. "Sad, but lovely."

"What about his wife and that other woman—they stay friends?" Jill asked from her seat on the couch next to Mara, the two of them contrasting against each other like fire and ice: Jill's cool elegance, Mara's warm frumpiness.

Jill was fabulously turned out tonight in her trademark black Prada. Combined with her long black hair and fair skin, the outfit made her blue eyes leap out, the effect of which, Claudia was certain, Jill was not unaware.

"I find it hard to believe they stay friends," Jill continued, "especially after all that."

"They were friends for a long time." Gail walked back into the room carrying another tray, this one full of pastries and chocolates. "They were friends since way before he came along." She put the tray on the table and took a seat on the couch next to Claudia.

"Well, I hope I don't have any friends like that," Jill said, biting the head off of a broccoli floret.

Claudia pushed her glasses up higher on her nose before she spoke. "She doesn't leave Joseph in the end, because Joseph is her home. She came home and he was there, where she was at home, and so, she decided to stay . . . where she felt at home and comfortable . . . you know, at home. With him."

"That's just the kind of insight we expect from our English teacher." Lindsay's sarcastic comment got a laugh from the group.

Claudia made a face at her. *Thanks a lot.*

"Well, there's no place like home." Mara giggled.

Lindsay used a wicked-witch voice to add, "And your little dog, too," and it made Claudia realize just how much Lindsay resembled not the Wicked Witch of the West, but the Good Witch, Glinda, with her heart-shaped face and her perfectly curled shoulder-length blond hair. It wasn't hard to imagine Lindsay with the gold crown, either, enveloped in a cloud of taffeta. She even had a proclivity for pink.

"I was hoping it would take longer than this before we started quoting witches." Gail rolled her eyes and tossed her copy of *Home* down onto the coffee table.

"I got some books about witchcraft." Mara watched for their reactions as she spoke, her eyes rapidly moving from face to face. "I've been reading them since—well, since, you know. Maybe I shouldn't admit this, but I really think there is something to it, something to what we did last time."

Lindsay clapped her hands together. "See? See? I'm telling you, there is."

"I need a drink." Gail got up and walked to the dining room, where the bar was set up.

"Gail, now, come on." Lindsay sat with perfect posture at the edge of her chair. She turned her entire body to face Gail. "You know we really should talk about this. It's unhealthy to keep things inside and all repressed."

Claudia watched Gail's face contort as she repressed a comment, probably one concerning the healthiness of too much therapy.

"I just don't think we should put any weight on what happened last time." Gail paused. Wine burbled into her glass in the silence. "I think we all had a little too much to drink and we got all caught up in ghost stories and witchcraft and whatnot."

"I'm with you," Jill said. "I don't think we can take credit for stopping the rain or putting out that candle. It was just a coincidence. All that chanting was just silliness. I mean, honestly."

Gail nodded her head and flipped the palm of her free hand up to the ceiling. *Exactly*, her face said as she walked back from the dining room to join them.

"But what if we did do it?" Mara asked. "Wouldn't it be a shame if we just stopped and never found out if that chant or spell or whatever it was actually *had* worked some magic?"

Mara could be like a terrier at times. It was a feature about her they all found simultaneously annoying and endearing. Mara could belabor a plot point or character trait to death, like that time at a previous meeting, when she'd kept insisting Ignatius Reilly from *A Confederacy of Dunces* was *not* crazy. When Mara argued, Claudia could almost imagine her teeth grinding into the book jacket while she thrashed it around in her mouth, an image reinforced by the fact that Mara's curly black hair was turning to salt and pepper: in other words, terrier gray.

"Don't you want to explore this at all?" Mara continued. "I can't believe you'd just let it drop, forget about it as if it had never happened. Think about what it could mean if it *did* happen. I think we need to look into this, just a little bit. To make sure. Wouldn't it be magnificent if we really could use our energy to make changes? And I'm not just talking about clearing the skies for the squash festival like in *The Kitchen Witches*, either. I'm talking about helping each other.

"These witchcraft books I've been reading, they talk a lot about controlling your reality—and your destiny—and it doesn't have as much to do with eye of newt and hemlock as it does with harnessing and controlling your own energy and using it for good."

Hmmm. Working magic. Controlling your destiny. The idea was beginning to grow on Claudia. Perhaps bringing Mara into this group would turn out to be one of her better ideas.

"I've read about this before, too," Claudia said, adjusting her glasses again. "It's in a lot of New Age literature. They talk about how women used to always meet for healings and to pray for good fortune, and to celebrate, but how, as our society became male-dominated, this stopped, and the women who did this became labeled as witches—because the men were afraid of their power as a group." Claudia, happy she'd found her voice again, pressed on. "It's why thirteen is an unlucky number. It's the number of moon cycles and women's cycles in a year. It's all related."

"Well, the book I read," Gail said, "was written by some crackpot from the sixties. He said you could use lemon and salt to break the effects of a negative psychic attack, you know, like the evil eye."

The women looked at Gail.

"What?"

No one said anything.

"What?" Gail asked again. "I don't get to go out and buy a book on witchcraft? I just wanted more information, that's all." She stopped. "It was a *used* book. It's not like I'm buying into this or anything."

"Who else bought a book about witchcraft this month?" Lindsay had her hands on her hips, her ringleader pose. She looked first at Claudia, who shook her head "no," and then Jill, who did the same. She reached down into the large Vuitton bag next to her chair and pulled out two books of her own. Mara took three books out of her tote bag. Lindsay looked up at Gail. "Well?"

Gail sighed, then got up and went to get her used 1960s crackpot book.

Lindsay set a huge *Benton's Grimoire* on the coffee table. "I am absolutely intrigued by witchcraft." She started flipping through the grimoire's glossy pages.

Gail's eyes met Claudia's. *Here we go again.*

"Lindsay," Gail said, "I don't think I have the patience or energy to endure another one of your trendy obsessions. Remember that Japanese tea ceremony? And I don't have the time to sit through whatever the witches equivalent might be."

"But this is different," Lindsay said, pulling the grimoire off the table and onto her lap, sinking back into the wings of her chair. She looked over the book, her chin lifted slightly off to one side.

Claudia could tell Lindsay wasn't really reading. In fact, she was pretty sure Lindsay's eyes couldn't even see the pages, the way her eyebrows had pulled together in a look of bemusement. Everything about her seemed to ask, *That tea ceremony wasn't so long, was it?*

"What I think Gail means is," Claudia raised her eyebrows at Gail, "she's not ready to buy into witchcraft or any whole new belief system, based on one controversial night and some anecdotal stories in some books." For all of Lindsay's bravado, Claudia knew that inside lay an extremely sensitive soul. "Gail? Am I right?"

Lindsay flipped a page of the grimoire.

Claudia clenched her jaw and thrust her chin toward Gail, widening her eyes.

"Right," Gail said.

"It's not like I'm trying to convert anybody." Lindsay looked up from the pages. "I just find the whole subject fascinating, that's all. I think this is something I want to explore for myself. If some people want to do it with me," she looked at Mara, "well maybe that would be fun, too. I'm not trying to change anyone's belief systems or anything. I'd never force someone into doing something they didn't want to do."

Claudia and Gail exchanged a glance again and this time Lindsay caught them. "Would you two quit doing that?"

"What?" Gail feigned innocence, and Lindsay glared at her, angry, but then she rolled her eyes and shook her head. "I don't know why I put up with the two of you."

"Because we put up with you, dear," Gail said. "You know we love you, Linds, it's just—"

"—we're not always as open to trying new things as you are," Claudia finished. "That's all."

"How about this," Mara said. "Why don't we try it one more time and see what happens. If it doesn't work, then the subject is closed and we never bring it up again."

"Oh, I don't think that's such a good idea." Jill's blue eyes were wide. "I think I'd really rather we didn't."

"I think we need to settle this." Lindsay leaned back into her chair, crossing her arms and legs.

"But it's not even raining." Jill looked pained.

"Not a rain spell." Mara shook her head. "Just any other spell. To see if it works."

"And what if it does work?" Jill asked. "What then?"

Mara looked surprised at the idea, then giggled. "I guess I never thought of that."

"What exactly is it you want to try in my house?" Gail asked.

"Well, I was thinking we could try one more spell, just like the last time—only this time we do it for something else." Mara looked hopefully at Gail.

"My kids are upstairs. I don't think I really want this to—"

"It's not like we're going to sacrifice a goat in your living room," Lindsay said.

Mara flashed a horrified *you're-not-helping* look at Lindsay before turning back to Gail. "I just thought we could try a chanting spell again. You know, light a candle, hold hands, say a few words."

Gail looked around the room. "In that nineteen-sixties nutcase book I read, the guy *really believed* he was under psychic attack from evil forces all the time."

She looked at Claudia as if she were expecting some support, but Claudia shrugged. She'd liked what Mara had said about harnessing their energy, about using it to help each other. What if this group did have some magic in it? Like Mara said, it would be a shame to waste it. And what if they could use it to help each other? What could be the harm in that?

Gail persevered. "The guy said he knew it was an evil spirit that put a thought into his head telling him to drive his car off the road. He said he had to race home for his lemon and salt."

But no one said anything. Gail was outnumbered. She looked at Jill, who shook her head and rolled her eyes.

"Oh jeez-o-pete," Gail said. "Fine. If this is what it's going to take to get this nonsense out of your systems, then fine. We'll try it. I'm going to make sure the little ones are asleep." She started walking toward the stairway, then turned back around with an afterthought. "By the way, what exactly is it you want to chant about tonight?"

Mara looked sheepish. "Well . . . I was thinking maybe we could chant for Tippy."

"Tippy?"

"My cat."

Gail sniffed in a big breath as if she were about to say something, but instead, she turned around and headed up the stairs.

A Christmas tree candle, the only green candle Gail could find, burned in the center of the coffee table. The top couple of tiers had melted down and now it leaned a little to one side, making it look more like a Christmas bush than a Christmas tree. In the dark of Gail's living room, the women stood in a circle around it, holding hands and an image of Tippy in their minds' eyes, bathing him in a healing circle of white light.

Tippy was a long-haired black cat recently diagnosed with diabetes. He couldn't jump anymore, and sometimes he walked as if he were in acute pain, although the veterinarian had assured Mara he wasn't, that he walked on the backs of his footpads because of some neurological condition brought about by the diabetes. This weird walk always seemed to miraculously disappear when it came time for his daily shot of insulin. After six weeks of chasing him around the kitchen with a syringe in her hand, Mara was willing to try anything else.

In the same way they had the last time, Mara and Lindsay worked up a short chant. They used the novel they'd read for their

October meeting, *The Kitchen Witches*, as a sort of template for their spell, copying the structure and phrases, changing a few words here and there to fit their specific, diabetic-cat needs.

The plan was to psychically bathe Tippy in white protective light, then douse him with green, the color of healing, then follow up with some red, the color of blood, since they couldn't find, in any of their books, a color that corresponded to the pancreas.

"Now change the light to a green healing light." Lindsay directed the group visualization as they held hands around the grotesquely morphing Christmas tree candle. "Okay, now change it to red, the color of energy and strength."

After a minute or so, they began the chant, hesitantly at first, then as they repeated it, gradually stronger.

> *We call upon the ancient power, in this time and in this hour.*
> *We ask please heal the cat, Tippy.*
> *It is our will, so mote it be.*

Gail started popping her eyebrows up and down every time they said "Tippy" and "it be," accentuating the ridiculousness of the rhyme. After a couple of times through, a laugh she'd apparently been trying to suppress escaped out of her nose as a snort, which caused the giggles to infect Jill, too. Both of them tried to conceal their mirth, which was only made harder by an angry terrier glare from Mara.

They finished chanting just as they had at the last meeting, with their arms up over their heads and heat pulsing through their connected palms.

After they dropped their arms down, Claudia bent over the table to blow out the candle.

"Wait!" Lindsay waved her hands. "Don't blow it out. Remember we need to let the candle burn all the way down. To help ensure the spell will work."

"Oops." Claudia stood back up. "I forgot. Sorry."

"Thank you, everyone." The light freckles on Mara's translucent skin ran together, covering her nose and cheeks, and she had bright red blotches on her face and neck as well. "I really appreciate you indulging me today. I hope I didn't embarrass you too much." She gave a nervous giggle. "Thanks."

"You'll have to let us know how Tippy does," Lindsay said.

"Oh, I will. At the next Book Club."

"Speaking of which . . ." Gail picked her copy of *Home* up off the table. "Is there anyone here that still wants to talk about the book?"

The group let out a groan.

"Then maybe we should pick out a book for next time," she said. "That is, if you still want to pretend this is a book club."

Gail finished cleaning up in the living room after everyone left. There were a few crumbs on the carpet and on the dark green damask of one of the couches, but that would have to wait until morning. She was tired and Emily, her early riser, would be up at six.

The blob that had been the Christmas tree candle burned alone in the center of the coffee table. She leaned over it to blow it out, then stopped herself and stood back up.

She went to get a plate from the kitchen and returned to the living room, cautiously picking up the candle to slip it underneath. There was so much melted wax it almost sloshed out the weak flame, but the flame survived, a tiny circle of light burning courageously in the center of the darkened room.

Chapter Two

✦

The thermometer beeped at Claudia, sounding exactly like her alarm clock, and she wondered if somebody had made it that way on purpose: to remind her, every morning, that her clock was ticking.

Holding the thermometer at the end of her outstretched arm, she read her temperature through blurry eyes: 97.4°. Damn. It had been up all week, and she'd allowed herself some hope. A positive pregnancy test would have made such a nice Christmas present, a happy ending to a long year of trying. She sank her head back onto her pillow and closed her eyes.

The ongoing effort to start a family, and its ineffectiveness, was starting to wear on her, and on Dan—and on their marriage. They seemed to be bickering more and more lately and they weren't bickerers. Old people were bickerers. They weren't even old people, either. At least, that's what Claudia had thought until they started trying to get pregnant. Everything she read on the subject made it sound as if she'd be washed up in two years, at the ripe old age of thirty-five.

She'd watched with envy as Gail and John had seemed to effortlessly pop out a new kid every few years. Probably she and Dan should have started trying sooner, but they'd been so preoccupied with their careers. Well, Dan had been preoccupied, anyway. Now that Gail and John had their third, little Emily, on the scene, Claudia was pretty sure they were finished. It was still odd, sometimes, to watch Gail being a mom, especially such a good one. Claudia never could have envisioned *that* when a tall, red-haired, dressed-all-in-black Gail had darkened the door to her dorm room that first time, simultaneously lighting a cigarette and striking awe, and a little fear, into Claudia's heart.

It was Lindsay whom Claudia had pegged to start having babies right away, with her mother-hen ways and high-school love of babysitting. After all, it wasn't as if she needed the extra money, unlike Claudia, who looked at all the snot-nosed kids she babysat for as just a way to put herself into a new pair of Calvin Klein jeans. Claudia wondered if maybe all those years of thinking of kids as snot-nosed was karmically blocking her from having a snot-nosed one of her own now.

But Lindsay and James didn't have any kids yet, either. Claudia figured that was because Lindsay was too obsessed with, well, with Lindsay. All her causes and trendy activities—had Lindsay really thought she could talk her and Gail into fencing lessons?

"What are you stewing about so early in the morning?" Dan reached an arm over Claudia's stomach, giving her a little hug.

She rolled sideways to face him, his arm now encircling her waist. He slid his other arm underneath her and pulled her closer.

"We're just having . . . it's just taking us so long to have a baby," Claudia spoke into the warm curve of his shoulder. "It makes me wonder, sometimes . . ." She let her voice trail off.

He brushed the hair off the side of her face. "I wonder too, sometimes, why it's not happening for us yet, but we haven't even talked about scientific intervention. I know conceiving a baby in a petri dish isn't very romantic, but—"

"It's not really that. It's the fact that it's not happening that makes me wonder why, if it's not some kind of . . . I don't know, sign. That we're not supposed to have kids. Or that we're not ready to."

"It's pretty natural, don't you think? To not feel ready?" Dan rolled onto his back, his arm still pinned underneath her. "But we've talked about this. Why we want kids—why we should start a family now."

It occurred to her then, as she studied the side of his face, the way he held his eyes on the ceiling when he spoke, that maybe he wasn't as on-board with the whole baby idea as she'd previously thought.

He turned to look at her. "You're just discouraged because you don't like it when things don't go your way."

Claudia propped herself up on her elbow. "What's that supposed to mean?"

"It's true, though. You get very . . ." He paused, as if he wanted to choose the perfect word. "*Pouty,* when things don't go your way."

"Pouty?"

"Uh-huh. See? You're doing it now."

Claudia took a breath in, ready to deny it, when she realized her lower lip had already jutted out.

"Can't argue with the truth, huh? You're just lucky your little pout drives me mad, mad, mad." He rolled over on top of her, wrestling with her, gently crushing her with his weight.

Tears popped into her eyes. The back of her throat ached with them. She remembered when sex used to be like this—impulsive and fun. Not goal-oriented. She loved Dan so much and she wanted to have his children. Their children. She wanted to watch him be a father and she knew he'd be great at it, the way kids always seemed to seek him out, to watch him make his funny faces and let him pull quarters out from behind their ears.

More than anything, Claudia wanted Dan to want to be a father himself.

He slid back down onto the bed and faced her. "Don't worry so much." He said it with a lightness in his voice that, had she wanted to look for trouble, could have been mistaken for indifference. She pressed her forehead against his chest to hide her tear-filled eyes and he hugged her close again, patting her back, rhythmically, absently, the way one might burp a baby.

Snow fell in clumps from the sky. The flakes joined together in the air as if through togetherness their fall to the earth would be easier to bear. The grass was already coated with them, and the sidewalks and streets were starting to lose their battle, changing over from wet to lightly frosted with snow. Gail could not believe her luck.

For the past six weeks, ever since the October Book Club meeting and their first witchy spell, there hadn't been a single drop of moisture from the sky, but today—with just ten shopping days left until Christmas—it looked like a damned blizzard outside her window.

The rosebush next to the garage still had leaves on it, and it was now blanketed with snow, which seemed odd, somehow. Wrong. She looked over into the neighbor's yard, where all the rosebushes had been lovingly mulched and covered with Styrofoam protectors months earlier.

Gail's eyes returned to her poor, miserable rosebush. *Oh well, too late now.* It had survived plenty of other winters without her interference, and it looked like it was going to have to survive at least one more.

Emily was banging something in the other room. Gail wished the babysitter, Ellen, would get her to stop. Gail had been counting the minutes until Ellen's arrival and now that she was finally here, all Gail wanted to do was go back into the other room and continue taking care of Emily. But she needed to do her shopping and she couldn't be Santa with Emily around. *What is Emily hitting?*

Gail wondered if maybe she were sometimes being unfair to Emily, if all her patience for dealing with two-year-olds had been used up on Will and Andrew. The previous week, when Gail had run into the living room and caught Emily banging a potato against the window, she'd screamed, "No banging potatoes on the window!"

Gail was not a yeller, but she'd been so ferociously mad. Now she had a hard time deciding what was more ridiculous: what she'd yelled, or how angry she'd been when she'd yelled it.

For the better part of her life, Gail hadn't been able to imagine herself yelling at all—except for maybe lines on a stage. But the safer choice had been business school and a degree in advertising, not drama and a degree in the fine arts. Besides, advertising appealed to her creative and avant-garde side. And she did it her way, as unconventionally as she could, choosing to study abroad for a year in Argentina, which was, ironically, where she met John, the beginning of the end of her unconventional ways.

She loved her life now, she really did. But still, there were days when she wished she were back in her brief advertising career, when she still had the chrome desk at Foote, Cone, an admin at her disposal, great suits she could wear. At the very least, she'd settle for being addressed with a little respect—and maybe, just once in a while, a few hours to herself.

The snow was coming down even harder now. Gail couldn't get over it. The boys had been playing in their sandbox up until yesterday, and now it was nearly buried under a carpet of white. The highway was going to be a mess because of it, and she didn't dare drive downtown in this. Maybe she should take the El, she thought, but she hadn't started her shopping yet and she knew she wouldn't be able to carry everything back on the train, especially not the barrage of large plastic things from China she needed to buy at Toys "Я" Us. She held her coffee mug up to her chin and curled her lip at the inconvenience descending outside her window.

At least her kids would be thrilled. They might get a white Christmas after all, something they'd been worried about this whole flakeless season: *If there isn't any snow, how will Santa land his sleigh?*

Yeah, Gail thought, but now, thanks to the snow, Santa's sleigh might be empty. She set her mug on the counter and took out her shopping list again to decide on her next move. Gail laughed at herself; she'd made a list and was checking it twice.

"Okay, Mrs. Claus," she said to herself, stuffing the list back into her purse, "just get into your car and go to the mall like all the rest of the poor Santas out there." This was shopping. Since when had she ever let a little bad weather stand between herself and *that*?

Jill unlocked the door to her studio and turned on the lights. The overhead fluorescents flickered, then came on, brightening slowly. It was a frigid December day inside as well as out, and she hugged herself as she walked across the room to turn up the heat. The silver globe of the thermostat felt icy against her fingers. Everything felt cold-soaked. She hadn't been there in a few days.

Floor-to-ceiling windows lined her studio on two sides. One set looked out to the west, the other to the north, and from those she could see the self-storage facility across the street and also, just to the east, the Metra train tracks—raised on a berm of earth, rocks, and garbage, all of which was now buried under an inch of snow.

Jill leaned against the window's brick frame and looked out, her arms still crossed on her chest, and watched a Metra train glide by, making far less noise than the El, almost silent in comparison. The El tracks, raised on a stout metal trestle, passed right next to the west windows. The gray paint on the El's bridge peeled back in more places than it clung, revealing rusted swaths of metal.

There's beauty in those ugly train tracks, she thought. She admired their strength, the way they gave an industrial feel to the neighborhood—a reminder that this was still the City of Big Shoulders, and not just a yuppie-filled City of Little Cubicles. The sound of the train hurtling by, rhythmically, every ten minutes, soothed her when she worked, gave her comfort to know that the outside world was still carrying on around her, even as she felt time stand still.

Jill turned back to the inside of her studio. She'd been avoiding this place, trying not to think of the dark turn her paintings had taken lately. She'd found herself mixing darker and darker colors, straying farther and farther from the cool color palette until, at the end of the day, she would step back and look at the two or three paintings she'd been working on, only to see how angrily the tarry, black-red colors had been swirled together.

She'd been feeling more lost in her work than ever before. She would get so caught up, so into flow, that the hours would fly by like the trains outside, almost without notice. Yet when she looked at her recent works, she was depressed by the results. They weren't meant to be happy paintings, but they weren't meant to be so dark or full of angst, either. That wasn't her thing. And with her opening coming up in March, she didn't want to give the impression that it was.

It had something to do with all that witchy nonsense going on at Book Club, of that she was certain. *Casting spells.* Of all the crazy things for Lindsay to drag her into, this one took the cake, even worse than her insane freshman-year plan to start the first sorority at the School of the Art Institute. Still, she had to admire Lindsay's chutzpah. But witchcraft?

It wasn't that she was a terribly religious person, she wasn't, at least not anymore, but the whole idea of witchcraft made her very uneasy. It must play upon the part of her the Catholic church had inculcated at an early age—the part deep inside that, although she *said* she didn't fear fire and brimstone, still did. It was too bad she was hosting the next meeting or she could just refuse to go. Well, with any luck, Mara's cat was already dead and that would be the end of that.

She took off her coat and put on her painting smock, a Northwestern Hospital lab coat she had borrowed from a med-student boyfriend years ago and never returned. She took an elastic ponytail holder out of the pocket and pulled back her glossy black hair.

Jill sat on her table and rubbed her hands together, looking around the room, trying to decide which painting she would work on today. She shook with a small chill. *Why isn't this room warming up?* She sipped the coffee she'd brought with her. It was cold now, too.

She removed one of her paintings from its easel and leaned it against the wall, then carried the empty easel over closer to the north windows. Today, she was going to start something new. It was time for a change.

The bright white of the fresh canvas contrasted with the paint-splattered frame of the easel as she tightened it into place. She opened her jar of gesso after a brief struggle with the lid and stirred it patiently. With her three-inch brush, she applied the white gesso to the virgin white of the canvas and began to think about what she would paint there.

She worked for hours, not even stopping for a cigarette. Jill purposefully concentrated on using only the cool color palette, putting big globs of blue and green on her mahogany board, and only tiny dabs of red and yellow, to remind herself to use them sparingly. She was painting with the knife today, something she hadn't done in a while. It seemed somehow right. It shouldn't get too detailed, too small. It was going to be an abstract, of course, and for right now it was okay that it was aimless. She could make a point later. Right now, the most important thing was to get back into it. To have fun—something that, she had noticed lately, seemed to be missing.

She and Michael had broken up recently, but that wasn't it. No, she was fairly certain *that* was a good thing. And she'd been dating plenty in the few months since then, but God, where had the fun gone? It seemed like all these guys were out wife shopping. Wasn't it supposed to be women over thirty who were desperate? To his credit, at least Michael had started out fun.

Jill stepped back from her painting. Something about the sea, that's where this was going. Waves washing on the shore, retreating, pushing forward again, the endless give and take. The irregular rhythm of it seemed to her an enigma. Shouldn't the uneven beat of the waves make you uneasy? Shouldn't they be annoying, the way they unpredictably crash and pause, then crash again? Yet it was one of the most sought-after sounds in the world. Machines were made that tried to duplicate it.

Her painting was starting to capture both the calm of the ocean and the struggle of the waves. The blues and greens and tans and browns smoothed into each other, blending first one way then back, changing with each stroke of the knife, not unlike the sand on a beach each time a wave passed over it. She stepped back once again to assess her work and was happy with what she saw. It was cool and calming. Cleansing. She let out a deep sigh. Finally. She had conquered some demons today.

Jill looked up at the clock; it was after five. She stretched and arched her back. With a craving for a cigarette welling up in her chest, she turned to look out the window and was startled to see, instead of dreary train tracks and snow-filled skies, that it was now nighttime. She couldn't see past the glass. She only saw her reflection staring back at her, closer than she had realized and darker than the rest of the room, the light from which surrounded her like a bright white halo.

———✦———

$\int weat$ trickled steadily into Lindsay's right eye while she knelt on the ground with her butt in the air and her hands gripping her ankles. Bikram yoga had seemed so much more invigorating when she'd read about it on the Web site.

With Christmas behind her and less than a week left of the old year, Lindsay wasn't about to wait around to start her New Year's resolutions. Then again, when it came to starting new things, Lindsay wasn't much of one for waiting around, ever. She couldn't believe all of the other Book Club members wanted to wait until January for their next meeting. She'd tried to talk them into forsaking tradition this year by having a meeting in December, but when she spoke with Claudia, she knew it would be impossible. "We just met, Linds, and everyone's so busy with the holidays. Let's just wait." She probably shouldn't have called Claudia—the member of Book Club with the greatest aversion to new things—first.

Savasana. That was rapidly becoming Lindsay's favorite new thing about Bikram yoga. She lay in dead-body pose, rest position, her "kind" eyes unfocused on the ceiling.

The spells, the chants, and all the possibilities they implied—it was all so exciting. That first night, when they had put that candle out, she'd felt so empowered. Like nothing she'd ever felt before. How could these women not want to keep feeling that? Gail was still convinced the candle had gone out of its own accord, but Lindsay had been watching it. The flame had collapsed straight down the wick and disappeared, just a thin wisp of black smoke drifting up after it had gone out. No breeze, no sloshing of wax had done that. They had.

Double-exhale and sit up. Lindsay watched the man next to her expel two forceful breaths to her two meager ones. He had to be almost seventy. More than twice her age. How come he wasn't suffering? Lindsay turned around for a second set of Rabbit Pose.

If only Mara would call, tell them Tippy was better, then they would see, then they would know what it was they'd stumbled into. A way to make everyone's life better. They could heal their friends, heal themselves, make all their dreams come true. Well, most of their dreams anyway.

The next Savasana seemed to end before it had started. Lindsay forced herself up. Only two more poses, the instructor promised, but throughout the class Lindsay had begun to question his mathematical abilities, the way his five-second counts seemed to stretch for fifteen.

The next Book Club meeting was in less than two weeks. Lindsay would have to wait until then to try to convince them of the worthiness of this pursuit. Which brought her mind back into the room, where it belonged, but where it began to question the pursuit of Bikram Yoga. Maybe this wasn't for her after all. Drenched from head to toe, with rivulets of sweat dripping from both elbows, she looked around the room at her classmates of every shape, size, age, and gender. How could anyone ever come to love something as painful as this?

Lindsay brought her head down for the final Head to Knee Pose, but instead of keeping her eyes open as the instructor directed, she crunched them closed. Saltwater filled both eyes anyway. Maybe someday she'd figure out what it was she was supposed to be doing. Maybe someday she'd find a place to belong.

Tippy jumped on Mara's stomach and let out a beseeching yowl. *Play with me!* it said. Mara, not fully awake, turned and looked at the clock. It was 3:42 a.m.

"Tippy, get down." Mara turned over on her side, her mind already descending back into sleep. She'd been having that dream again, the one with the yacht, the one in which she wore a sequined ball gown and sang "My Way" for a crowd of her champagne-drinking friends. She loved that dream. It was so far from her reality.

Tippy kneaded into Mara with his paws, his claws snagging the blanket with a snap, snap, snap. "Tippy, it's not time to play." She pulled the blanket in more tightly around her shoulders, trying to hide.

Then Mara rolled abruptly onto her back again.

"Tippy?" she whispered.

Tippy hadn't jumped onto her bed in months. He hadn't jumped on anything in months. "How did you get up here? Did you jump up here? All by yourself?"

He looked at her, his green eyes glowing while he purred, kneading his paws into her stomach as she scratched behind his ear.

Her husband Henry's deep snorky breathing meant he was still asleep—Tippy hadn't gotten any help onto the bed from him.

It *must* be the spell from Book Club. What other explanation could there be? Mara stared at the ceiling in the dim light, absently petting her purring cat, ruminating on all the many possibilities, all the things this could mean, long after Tippy had fallen asleep.

Chapter Three

———✦———

The veterinarian's waiting room always had the same smell: antiseptic, cedar chips, and cat piss. Mara sat on a bench near the window and waited. It wasn't supposed to be like this. This was going to be her year, a year with the power of witchcraft behind it. And yet, less than two weeks into it—with Book Club meeting tonight—all indications were that now, like her baseball team, she'd once again have to wait till next year.

Tippy had been doing so much better since they'd chanted for him—ever since that night he'd first jumped onto her bed. Mara had been beside herself. She couldn't wait to get to tonight's meeting to tell everyone, especially Jill, that their spell had helped. That was, until last Friday.

Mara had come home from work in the afternoon and found Tippy lethargic, his food from the morning still in his bowl. He'd looked up at her with sad green eyes. No hopping up today. She'd brought him straight to the vet in a panic and they had started him on IV fluids right away, just to keep him alive. It had been a terrible relapse. Mara had been stunned to realize that her poor cat might not make it—and what did that say about the chanting?

The veterinarian, Dr. Effingham, had kept Tippy over the weekend. Now, as she sat in his waiting room, after being told he wanted to speak with her, Mara figured this was not good. He might even recommend she put Tippy to sleep, as if it were really only a nap she would be considering.

"He's had a good life," she could imagine him saying, "but there comes a point where keeping him alive is going to cause more suffering than putting him down." She didn't want Tippy to suffer, and if the vet told her it was the best thing, she would listen to him. Mara felt the beginnings of a sob climb up her throat. She turned to look out the window behind her in the waiting room, not really wanting to think about it.

Dr. Seeley, her boss, had seemed displeased that Mara was going to be late to work today because she had to go to the veterinarian's. But then, Dr. Seeley always seemed displeased.

Henry kept telling her she should just quit, that he hated to see her so unhappy, but with their son Alan starting college next year and Marty only a couple of years behind, she didn't see how they would manage. Henry called it the "work force," the invisible force that pulled a person to a job she hated day after day, making her forget it could be any different. She supposed she could start looking for another job *before* she quit, but when was she supposed to find time for that? And it wasn't as if any new job she would find was going to put her in that sequined dress singing "My Way" on a yacht. It was just easier for her to stay where she was than to go off trying to make any big changes.

Suddenly an assistant called Mara's name and ushered her into one of the veterinary examining rooms, but Dr. Effingham wasn't there yet and neither was Tippy.

Oh my God, Mara thought, what if Tippy's already dead? What if he died over the weekend and they didn't want to tell me over the phone? I didn't even get to say good-bye. She imagined him alone in his cage, afraid and lonely, missing her, all those cold metal wires and no one to comfort him. Oh, what had she done?

"Meeowow." Mara's heart lifted as she heard Tippy's howl of protest coming from down the hall, getting louder as the assistant brought him into the room. He set Tippy's kennel on the stainless-steel examining table.

"Here you go," he said. "Dr. Effingham will be right in."

Mara stood up and crossed the room, saying "Thank you," without even looking at him. Her hands hurried to unlock the door to Tippy's cage and she scooped him up into her arms. He felt smaller. She sat down in the chair holding him to her chest, and

Tippy rested his head on her shoulder, snuggling her. He started purring loudly.

"Well, well, well." Dr. Effingham entered the room, taking Tippy's file from the mailbox on the door. "I just don't know what's going on with your cat."

"He's lost weight."

"Mmm . . . hmm." Dr. Effingham looked down at the file, "Yes, he has," he paused, silently calculating the weight loss, "eight ounces. But the strange thing is, we had to stop giving him the insulin, because he wasn't eating, and it was making him lethargic. Now his blood sugar is back to normal, and he's resumed a normal diet."

Mara stared back at him.

"I've heard about these cases, where the diabetes just spontaneously disappears for no apparent reason. I just have never seen an actual case of it." He gave her a perplexed smile.

Mara didn't say anything. She stared straight ahead, patting Tippy and stroking his fur over and over, not really feeling it.

When Mara didn't respond, Dr. Effingham's smile faded and he became immediately more clinical. "At any rate," he said, "I guess what I'm telling you is, the diabetes is gone."

January was supposed to denote a fresh start, a new beginning, a clean slate. But it was a mere one and a half weeks into the new year, and all of Jill's resolutions had already been thrown to the wayside in the same way the laundry she was now picking up had been cast to the floor. She'd tried to cut back on the drinking, but had given that up after she'd been invited to two great parties the first weekend of the new year. She'd thought she might like to try being a warmer, more compassionate person, but when she'd tried smiling at a little girl in line in front of her at Barney's, it had made her teeth ache. And the girl hadn't seemed to appreciate it anyway; her eyes hadn't followed Jill with the wide stare that her good looks usually evoked. So forget that. As for the smoking, she hadn't even made an attempt to quit. She still liked it too much.

Walking around her condo, Jill picked up shoes and magazines and mail and socks. Book Club was just plain bad timing. They always met on a Monday night, but her cleaning lady came on Tuesdays, and that always meant her apartment would be in its worst possible shape. She dumped her ashtrays into the kitchen garbage, then threw the rather large armful of clothes she'd picked up into the laundry room hamper, filling it.

Jill looked into her bedroom. Her bed was unmade, the blanket and comforter kicked all the way down to the floor, where they had been since last Wednesday morning. Clothes sat in mountainous piles on the floor. Her nightstand held another overflowing ashtray and an assortment of glassware representing all of her many bed-time moods of the previous week: martini in a martini glass, martini in a juice glass, coffee cup, juice in a juice glass, and one nearly empty bottle of Evian water. Jill cringed. Maybe she could just keep the door to her bedroom closed. These were her friends, after all. Surely they would understand a little mess. Although Lindsay's standard for cleanliness was off the charts: they'd shared a Printer's Row apartment during their last year at the Art Institute and it had almost ended their friendship.

When she'd first met Lindsay, during the second week of classes, Jill had been walking through the lobby of the Sharp Building and Lindsay had stopped her, saying that since they were in the same Research Studio section they would probably end up friends. Jill's immediate reaction had been to think, *probably not.* Lindsay had been so intense. But she'd had an earnestness about her, too, a kind of innocence, really, and a way of looking at you—as if she could see down to the core. In spite of Jill's initial aversion, Lindsay had been right. They had ended up friends.

Jill sighed and got to work making the bed. There might be no pleasing Lindsay, but she would make an attempt for the rest of them. She wanted to please them. Go figure. It was weird, this close-ness she felt for these Book Club women. Jill still couldn't under-stand it even after five years of being in Book Club. They were so not like her. Mara and Claudia were practically borderline nerds.

It was no surprise that Claudia had been the one to bring Mara, the wife of one of her schoolteacher friends, into the group. Jill had always thought Mara was a strange addition. Initially, she had tried to explain it away as a result of Mara joining Book Club after they'd already been meeting for a year. But that wasn't it. Now, Jill suspected it was because even though Mara was only a couple years older than the rest of them, she *seemed* so much older. It was as if she reveled in her dowdiness.

Then there was Gail, who always seemed to have such potential. She was far from dowdy, and Jill suspected underneath it all Gail was a kindred soul. Regardless, when Lindsay had introduced them, Gail's acceptance of her—and Claudia's for that matter— had been instant. And warm, like *Any friend of Lindsay's is a friend of ours.* Which Jill found even more weird.

She finished making the bed and cleared off the nightstand, then removed the laundry mountains from the floor. The place was actually starting to look better.

And all she had to do in the bathroom was make it *look* clean. Actually *getting* it clean, that was Loma's job. She thought of canceling Loma for the next day. She was going to do the whole place tonight; why should she pay Loma to do it all over again tomorrow? And how could she be sure that Loma *really* cleaned anything in the first place? Instead of using the heavy-duty stuff, like Ajax or Soft Scrub and some elbow grease, Loma could very well be pouring measured amounts of cleaning products down the drain each week and running through the house with paper towels and spray cleaners, like Jill was doing now, just making it *look* clean.

She looked down at the toilet next to her. No, she would continue to put her faith in Loma. It was going to be bad enough having to clean the outside of the bowl herself; she would be damned if she actually got in there and *cleaned* the inside as well.

After she finished, Jill washed up, changed out of her cleaning clothes, and freshened her makeup. They would arrive in less than thirty minutes and she still had to get the food set up. She paused with her hand on the door to the refrigerator for a moment before changing her mind and opening the freezer. She pulled out a bottle of Grey Goose vodka and set it on the counter, her fingertips leaving five melted imprints on the frosted glass. She blew off using a shaker and mixed her martini right in the glass, scooping out the ice cubes with a fork.

Jill sucked on an olive while she put all the veggie and finger-sandwich platters out. The caterer had delivered almost everything ready to go; all she had to do was pull off the shrink-wrap. One tray of hot hors d'oeuvres needed to go in the oven, which she started preheating.

She scanned the apartment from the kitchen. If she said so herself, it looked pretty damned good. The food was sitting on the dining room table and she had a little mini-bar set up on the small granite-topped island, which had high glass-fronted cabinets overhead that divided the kitchen from the living and dining room. Scented candles burned here and there, which, she hoped, would cover up some of the cigarette smell. *Eat your heart out, Martha Stewart.*

Jill took her drink and her cigarettes and went out to the balcony for a quick smoke. The cold air seemed to give the lights an extra sparkle—or maybe it was just the icy chill watering her eyes. The lights spread out below her. It was why she had bought this condo: the view and this balcony. It was a rare kind of city balcony. Private. High up and enclosed on three sides. It didn't stick out precariously from the side of the building like an afterthought. From here, the city looked like a much better place. The altitude had a cleansing effect; no visible dirt or crime or homeless people—just tiny lights in all the windows spread out for miles. Beautiful.

At least tonight it wasn't snowing or raining. No precipitation for them to chant about. God, she hoped this witchcraft thing would just go away. That first night they'd tried it, she'd thought she'd made it pretty clear she didn't want to participate. But Lindsay could be so pushy, and Mara, too. The only choice they had given her had been between going along or leaving in the middle of a thunderstorm.

Everyone had stayed late because of the rain. Making the best of the situation, they drank more wine. And then the power had gone out.

After they had lit several candles, their conversation turned to ghost stories and Halloween and, coincidentally enough, the book they'd read for the meeting. It was Mara who'd suggested they try a spell from *The Kitchen Witches* to stop the rain, and Lindsay had jumped all over the idea. Gail sarcastically said they should probably begin their first foray into the occult by trying to tackle something a little smaller, like using their brain waves to put out a candle. She'd rubbed her temples and closed her eyes when she said it, making fun of the whole idea. But Gail's scorn had only seemed to motivate Lindsay.

Jill had hoped the chanting was over for good when Gail told them it was obvious a draft had blown out the candle—not their crazy chanting. But Lindsay, of course, would have none of it. "It just went out. Didn't you see? It didn't bend beforehand like it would have if it had been blown out by a draft." Lindsay had tipped to one side, with her hands on her hips, to demonstrate what the candle should have looked like had it succumbed to a breeze. She'd insisted they try it again.

When they'd finished the rain chant, they were all acting so silly—laughing and giggling and falling on the couches—that Jill had assumed that was going to be the end of that. It was going to be one isolated, drunken night.

And then the power came back on.

Everyone stopped their giggling. They looked up at the lights with awe on their faces and wineglasses held frozen in midair.

"Oh, my." Lindsay started hopping up and down. "Oh my God. Do you believe this? Do you believe it?"

"You honestly think we had something to do with this?" Gail looked at Lindsay with utter disbelief on her face.

"The rain stopped, too." Mara, over at the window already, turned around to face them, holding the curtain back for everyone to see. "There's no more rain."

"Wow. I can't believe this. This is so amazing. We did it! We really, really did it." Lindsay was apoplectic.

"This is so neat." Mara looked outside the window again, up at the sky, as if she were trying to make sure the rain had really stopped.

"Please. It was just a coincidence." Jill tried to brush off the idea their spell had done it with a wave of her hand.

"A coincidence? It was *not*." Lindsay sounded as if she were taking Jill's doubt personally. "You can't explain away the power coming on *and* the rain stopping right after we finished our spell as just a coincidence. You can't. Just like with the candle, it was our spell. I know it was. It wasn't a coincidence. There's no other way to explain it."

"Cold frontal passage," Gail had said, before resolutely taking a sip of her wine.

Jill smiled, remembering Gail's quip. Jill liked Gail. And she found herself liking her more and more lately, as Gail joined her in voicing anti-witchcraft opinions. Jill looked out over the city lights and took another drag off her cigarette. She cupped her opposite elbow with her free hand and exhaled an exaggerated cloud of smoke, most of it formed of steam as her warm breath hit the cold air. Jill pushed out her cigarette before it was finished, in the not-so-overflowing outside ashtray, before heading inside.

It reeked inside her apartment. Something stank—badly. Something was burning. Jill took a quick inventory of all the candles. No, she couldn't see any smoke anywhere; there was just that god-awful burning smell. The oven! She walked over and opened the door and was hit with a blast of smoke and the greasy-diner smell of burning cheese.

"Damn it, Loma, could you just ever clean this sometimes?" The cheese that had slid from some long-ago frozen pizza was a smoking black crust on the bottom of her oven. Jill closed the door and turned it off, unable to use it now. She opened windows, hoping to get most of the smell out, then took the tray of mini quiches and slid them into the trash. She picked up some of the paper towels at the bottom of the garbage and stuffed them on top. If no one saw the little veggie quiches, they wouldn't be missed. *That will teach me to take Martha Stewart's name in vain.*

Jill lit another cigarette (what difference could it make now?) and sat down on one of the bar stools at the kitchen counter. She crossed her perfectly shaped legs and sat smoking and drinking at the bar as though she were at one of her clubs, waiting for a pick-up line just so she could rebuff it.

Her copy of this month's book, *Only the Lonely,* her suggestion, was sitting out, and she paged through it, cigarette in hand, eventually landing at the inside of the back dust jacket. The perfectly coifed and airbrushed photo of the author smiled back at her. *What has she got to be so smug about? Anyone could write some dumb book about depressed single people. Anyone.* A fan was blowing the author's hair back. *Why?* Jill took a final drag off her cigarette and closed the book.

She got up and started closing the windows. Jill wasn't afraid of heights, but every now and then, when only a flimsy screen stood between her and a thirty-story drop, she would look down and feel the world start to spin beneath her. A quick glance at something solid—the skyline, her couch—would anchor her safely back in the room and the spinning sensation would stop. It was curious, she thought, and probably not a bad reaction. Human beings were never meant to live this high off the ground.

Chapter Four

———✦———

Claudia wrestled open the heavy glass door to Jill's North Lake Shore Drive building and presented herself to the doorman, who remained seated behind his mahogany podium. He gave her what she considered to be a rude once-over before he slid his thumb and forefinger along his mustache slowly several times while looking down at some papers on his desk.

Pretty bold arrogance, Claudia thought, for someone oblivious to the irony of his own existence.

"Miss Trebelmeier is expecting you." He pointed her to the elevators, seeming somehow surprised by this.

Claudia tried tossing her head when she said "Thank you," as if to say, "of course Miss Trebelmeier is expecting me," but all the action succeeded in accomplishing was to drop her glasses farther down her nose.

After an ear-popping elevator ride, Claudia stepped into Jill's condo and was struck by two things: the amazing view of downtown, and the overpowering smell of burnt cheese.

As if it were merely a frame for the view, Jill's home was spartanly decorated, with lots of white and a few pieces of expensive-looking artwork and furniture. Claudia hurried over to the kitchen counter and poured herself a glass of wine. Once again, she'd been the last to arrive.

Claudia took a sip of wine and gave the table a quick scan for whatever had made Jill's condo smell like the Billy Goat. Not finding anything, she walked over to stand with Mara and Gail.

"I totally do not buy into the fact that they're gay. No way," Mara was saying.

"I don't know," Gail answered. "There might be some truth to it." Gail's hair was gelled and stylized tonight, slicked back on her head. She wore slim-cut black slacks and a green silk blouse. With her height and model's figure, she looked like someone who *belonged* in Jill's apartment.

"They were married for five years. They had three kids," Mara argued.

"Three *adopted* kids," Gail said. "Why didn't they have any of their own kids?"

"Maybe they couldn't. Maybe she didn't want to ruin her figure. She is a movie star after all."

"Hollywood gossip?" Lindsay came up to join them. "Is this what we're discussing?" She rolled her eyes upward. "I can't believe it's come to this. Tabloids at Book Club."

"Sorry, dear girl." Gail spoke without moving her jaw, using the affected, not quite British accent of the very rich. "I didn't mean to offend you with such banal topics. What say we move on to more stimulating subject matter—the stock market, perhaps?"

Lindsay tilted her chin up and rolled her eyes again. The brave face. But Claudia could tell that Gail's Thurston Howell impression had struck a nerve. It was weird, Claudia thought, how uncomfortable Lindsay was with her money. All the other rich people Claudia knew—like Jill, for instance—didn't seem to mind flaunting it, but Lindsay, more often than not, acted ashamed of it, as if she thought it somehow made her less of a person.

"I honestly don't know what's more dull, the tabloids or the stock market," Lindsay said.

"Oh, definitely the stock market." Mara looked as if she couldn't believe anyone could possibly think otherwise. "I think the tabloids are fun." She giggled. "Oh dear, I can't believe I admitted to that." She pressed her lips together into a flat smile and thrust her chin forward. "What if I said I only read them at the grocery check-out?"

"Nope." Jill had come over from the kitchen to join them, martini in hand.

"Too late," Gail said.

"Our opinion of you is ruined forever," Claudia added.

"Hey, how's Tippy?" Gail put her hand on her hip. "You know I think about him every time I look at my coffee table. There's a stain on it from that Christmas tree candle. John was very suspicious of that melted green blob."

Mara hesitated, as if for effect, then said, "He's cured."

It was like a scene from a soap opera, where everyone stops talking at once and the music gets switched off.

All of the women stared at Mara.

"You are kidding me." Gail ran a hand through her hair, apparently forgetting she had slicked it back.

"No. Honest. I was at the vet this morning, and he said he'd never seen anything like it in his practice. He said he'd heard about cases where the diabetes goes into remission, but he'd never actually had it happen to one of his patients."

"Oh my Goddess." Lindsay looked around the room, methodically making eye contact with everyone.

Here we go, Claudia thought.

"Look at what we've done. Will you think about what we've done?" Lindsay closed her eyes, took in a deep breath, and shook her head with an ecstatic shiver, then smiled. She opened her eyes. "Ladies, I think we're on to something here."

"What is it you think we're on to?" Gail's hair stuck together in a big clump on one side.

"Witchcraft! The power of women in a group! The power to work magic!" Lindsay held her arms straight in front of her, palms up, and moved them in a circle, gesturing around the room, her eyes wide.

Jill rolled her eyes at Lindsay's theatrics. "I know that's what this may look like, but I think there's still the possibility of coincidence."

"Yeah," Gail gestured at Mara. "She said her vet had heard of this happening before . . ." She paused. "I just have a hard time imagining . . . It could still be . . ."

It sounded like Gail was having a hard time convincing herself. She stopped talking and looked down at the ground, crossing her arms over the front of her silk shirt. She started to kick a little path against the nap of the carpet with the pointed toe of her shoe.

Claudia watched the narrow line in the carpet darken under Gail's foot. No cold front would explain this.

"I'm with Lindsay," Mara said. "I think we have magic in this group. We stopped the rain and now we healed Tippy."

"Don't forget the candle." Lindsay bounced in place. "We put out that candle with our chant." She hunched her shoulders up and shivered her head again, her blonde curls bouncing. "Oh, just imagine the possibilities."

"For what?" Gail asked. "Getting jobs with the fire department?"

Lindsay's shoulders dropped. She glared at Gail, her happy expression completely deflated.

Claudia decided to step in. "Here's the thing, guys. I don't think we know *what* we're doing. We just stumbled into something. If what we did do was really magic, then I think we just got incredibly lucky."

"I think we got lucky too. I'm not denying that." Lindsay stopped all her bouncing and hand waving and held very still, her voice quiet. "But imagine what we could accomplish if we did our homework—if we prepared. Think about it. We could heal sick people or help poor people. We could help someone find true love, the meaning of life—whatever. Maybe we could even remove cellulite from our butts." Lindsay laughed, an uncharacteristic Mara-like giggle.

Gail gave Lindsay a *whoa* gesture. "I don't think we should let ourselves get so carried away. I don't like that this whole thing started in a bad way. Under the influence of alcohol and a rotten novel. Those chants and spells—they came from a work of fiction, for Pete's sake. It's probably not even real witchcraft.

"It's all been sort of a fun diversion, you know, kind of like the Victorians and their Ouija boards and table-tipping, but I don't think I want to take it any farther. I don't want to get involved in the formation of some sort of amateur coven."

"Who said anything about covens?" Mara said.

"Well, isn't that what you're talking about?" Jill's fingertips had ceased all capillary action and pressed white into her martini glass. "That's what it sounds like—you want to turn Book Club into a coven."

"Oh please, that's just a little too . . . that's just so *Rosemary's Baby*," Mara said.

"Coven is wrong anyway." Lindsay shook her head, already acting the expert. "It's called a 'circle.' That's what the Wiccans would call it, 'circle,' and I think it's a lovely idea, getting together and working magic to help one another. I think it's just lovely."

"'Circle' is what the *who* would call it?" Jill asked.

"The Wiccans. The modern-day witches. I read about them in my book. They get together and form circles to work magic. Just like we did."

Convincing Lindsay not to pursue this witchcraft thing was going to prove impossible, Claudia knew from experience. Especially now that she could see in Lindsay's eyes a look that suggested she was already dreaming about her new size-six, cellulite-free butt.

"Who else thinks we should keep going? Who else thinks we should pursue this newfound power—raise your hands." Lindsay raised her hand high.

"Can't we just think about it for a while?" Claudia asked.

"Why? What's to think about? You either believe or you don't believe. You're either for us or against us."

"You can count me in." Mara raised her hand.

Claudia looked at her friends as if she hardly recognized them. Why was it she always managed to feel backed into outrageous situations in Lindsay's presence? Now her Book Club was voting on whether or not they would become witches. At least it would be a democratic coven. She shook her head and put her hand up slowly, holding it at about shoulder height, watching it move to the vertical as if it were something unattached to her.

Gail was looking off to one side, her arms still crossed over her chest. She tilted her head up and inhaled. "God, I don't know, you guys. This just goes against my better judgment." She exhaled, looking back toward her friends. She paused for a few moments, then raised her right hand up without uncrossing her arms.

They all looked at Jill, the lone holdout. "Do I have to decide right this minute?" She looked a little panicked, her eyes darting from person to person, her mouth slightly parted. "I really don't like it—the idea of witchcraft. I was raised Catholic. I just get a bad feeling about all this."

"One of the primary beliefs of Wicca," Lindsay offered, "is that there are many different paths, and just because you follow Wicca doesn't mean you can't still be Catholic."

"Well, that's fine," Jill said. "It's just that most Catholics aren't that understanding."

Lindsay had been holding her hand up the entire time. She finally took it down. "Well. I guess there isn't any *real* reason anyone needs to decide right this minute."

"I hate to be the party pooper," Jill said. "I guess maybe if you weren't raised Catholic, then you wouldn't understand." She looked around at them as if she were trying to see if anyone else might "understand," but no one spoke up.

"I guess there's no real reason we need to have everyone on board," Lindsay began. "I suppose just those of us who were truly interested in pursuing it could, well . . . be the ones to pursue it, you know, separately." She looked pointedly at Mara.

Jill glared at Lindsay for a moment before she abruptly turned around. She stood in front of the dining room table and started fussing with the food, rearranging platters and dusting crumbs off the tablecloth.

The silence was weird. Awkward. They usually made so much noise when they got together.

Was this going to be the end? Claudia thought. Would they split up over this? Because of some homespun spells and a freshly healed cat named Tippy? What an ignominious way for her book club to die. She would not let this happen. She loved this group so much. They were her friends, her best friends. Outwardly she knew they must look like any other book group, a bunch of thirty-something women who got together to socialize and talk about books. But Claudia had a sense of what this group really meant to each of them. She'd practically grown up with Lindsay, had spent college with Gail, and even though she hadn't known Jill and Mara during any formative years, she'd learned enough about them during the past several to know each of them shared one thing in common: a sense that Book Club was the one place they *really* fit in, where they fit perfectly. It was a place where they all could just be themselves. And Claudia wasn't about to sit back and watch that come to an end.

But which way to go? It would be cool to be able to cast spells and heal people. But then again, this was *witchcraft* they were talking about. What if her school found out? Their neighbors? Would they understand—or be understandably afraid? *You're either for us or against us.* Claudia looked at Lindsay and Mara, the pro-Wicca juggernaut on one side of the room—and at Jill, her back still to them, dead set against it, on the other.

"You know, Jill, I don't think this thing is as sinister as you seem to think." Claudia kept her voice soft, as gentle as she could. "I think it's more along the lines of that slumber party finger-lifting thing, you know, 'light as a feather, stiff as a board,' where as a group you have a power, an energy to do cool things you can't do all on your own. If we really did heal Tippy, it might be a shame if we never tried to see what else we could do. Maybe it will be like Lindsay says, we could really make some great changes. Changes for good."

Jill had stopped her fussing and was standing very still. But she hadn't turned around.

"Besides," Claudia continued, "with Lindsay as the driving force behind us, how long do you think she'll stay with it before she decides we all really need to be learning how to free-dive instead?"

Jill's head dropped and her shoulders shook. A laugh. She turned around, shaking her head, smiling with her eyes closed. "Oh, all right."

She walked back from the table to the center of the room. "What the hell. Since when have I ever been accused of being a scaredy-cat party pooper? But can we not call it 'witchcraft'? Can we call it that, um, Wicca circle thing from now on? Okay? Then I guess I'll be in." She raised her hand and waved it lamely next to her shoulder, her face saying, *I'm going along with this, but remember that I think it's dumb.*

Lindsay clapped her hands together and did her little hopping thing. Everyone started talking at once, enjoying a brief moment of relief from the tension of the past few minutes.

"Well, Glinda Good Witch," Gail had a hand on her hip as she turned to Lindsay. "What do we do now?"

"Me?" Lindsay asked. "Why me?"

"This whole thing was your idea," Claudia said. "This is your show, Linds."

"I . . ." Lindsay stopped, and then continued. "There's really nothing to qualify me here to know what to do next . . ."

"When has that ever stopped you?"

Lindsay pursed her lips at Claudia, then recovered quickly. "What I think we should do is—get a book." She raised her eyebrows and continued with a laugh, "Just like a book club. We should get a witchcraft—uh, Wicca how-to book, if you will."

Gail looked at her incredulously. "Oh sure, you mean like *A Complete Idiot's Guide to Witchcraft*?"

"Ha!" Mara giggled. "*Wicca for Dummies.*"

"Ohhh." Lindsay rolled her eyes. "No. A *real* book. I saw one at Borders called *The Sacredness of the Wiccan Way*. I just skimmed through it, and I don't remember the author's name, but I can find out. We should all get a copy of it and read it and then maybe take it from there. It was pretty big, but it explained the basics of how to practice witchcraft and went into all the rituals and terminology—"

"Terminology?" Mara looked worried now.

"The names of holidays and deities and things."

"Deities?" Jill emphasized the "s" at the end, letting it hiss between her teeth. "There are deities?"

"It's the neatest thing," Lindsay said. "You get to choose your own gods."

Jill widened her eyes again. "There are *gods* involved with this?" She closed her eyes for a moment and exhaled a huge breath. "If I ever make it to confession again, I'm going to have a lot of explaining to do."

"You have to pick your own gods?" Claudia asked. "But how do you know? I mean, how do you choose?"

"The book talks about all the different pantheons you can choose from. Roman, Egyptian, Celtic—there're a lot of them. Then you study up on them and find one you feel you belong to, one that you can align with."

"Can you mix and match?" Mara cracked. "Hey, what if you pick gods that don't get along with each other? What then?"

"Do they make pantheon Garanimals?"

"Gail, I think you should really start to take this more seriously—"

A horrible thought occurred to Claudia. She interrupted, "I just don't want to have to be naked when we chant. We don't have to be naked, do we?"

"Oh, of course not." Lindsay rolled her eyes again. "All right, all right. Before we get too far ahead of ourselves, why don't we just see if we agree to buy this book and start studying it and start collecting the things we'll need for our magical toolboxes?"

"Toolboxes too?" Jill asked. "We need *tools* for this, too?" She looked around at the women in her living room, as if she were trying to find some support. She held her eyes on Gail.

"I guess we can't keep using Christmas candles forever." Gail looked up, as if she were writing a mental shopping list. "We'll need incense and herbs, probably lemon and salt, too."

"Listen to you," Claudia said.

Gail shrugged. "It's shopping. I get excited about shopping."

"Let's see a show of hands to see if everyone is agreed—that this is how we should proceed." Lindsay had her hand up again. "Who thinks we should get this book and start learning more about it?"

All the women raised their hands, holding them up more confidently this time, not too high, just even with their heads. Lindsay's was waving excitedly in place. Jill's palm flopped up to face the ceiling.

Claudia tried to hold her hand steady, but she felt her palm buzzing with an inexplicable energy, like an electric cloud, like static that builds up in your body when you walk across a rug in winter, just waiting to give you a shock when you touch something.

Chapter Five

Claudia moved the eraser over the Dry Erase board in her classroom in large sweeping motions. *What was so wrong with chalkboards?* Oh yeah, dangerous dust. Good grief. At least chalk never ran dry. She hated these dumb markers. They took away a small part of why she wanted to be a teacher. The pleasant way chalk pressed onto the board, the dust that fell, the smooth, creamy way it erased. Claudia sighed, then began plotting the rest of her day while she finished erasing the board.

Classes were over and she had a lot to accomplish in the remainder of her afternoon. She needed to get to a bookstore. There was a Borders right around the corner from school, and earlier she'd thought about stopping there on her lunch hour to pick up Lindsay's recommended *Sacredness of the Wiccan Way*, but she had been afraid she might run into some of her sophomore English students there. They hung out in its café, tossing back espresso drinks with not just the feigned sophistication of Claudia's adolescence, but with actual worldliness. They possessed the real poise and confidence that accompanied a childhood of affluence.

It was hard at times not to be intimidated by them, as they, supposedly going through their most awkward stage, seemed to have it more together than Claudia did. She imagined being called over to their table and asked to show them her literary selection. And why shouldn't she? She was their English teacher, after all. In the process she would stammer and stutter, break into a sweat, drop her purchase, and then one of the girls would reach down and pick her *witchcraft* book up off of the floor with perfectly manicured fingernails, showing it around the table for all to see. "Look, Ms. Dubois is reading *The Sacredness of the Wiccan Way.*"

No. It would definitely be better all around if she went out of her way and stopped at the Barnes & Noble on Clybourn on her way home.

So after school it would be the bookstore first, and if she could manage to get in and out of there in less than half an hour (something akin to a miracle), she could still make it home before rush hour and in time to run by the dry cleaner's to pick up something to wear for tomorrow, her available wardrobe getting dangerously thin. And then she had a lot of papers to grade tonight. The students were getting antsy because she hadn't finished their latest essay exam yet. It had been three days.

"Ms. Dubois?" Claudia recognized the voice at her door instantly. Her shoulders fell, the eraser coming to rest at her side.

"Hello, April."

Claudia turned to see April Sibley flipping her long hair over her shoulder with one hand. "I was wondering if you had a chance to grade my test yet."

"I, uh . . ."

"I really need to know, because, as you know, I'm going for valedictorian and I really would like to," she flipped her hair back over her shoulder again, even though it hadn't budged, "see if I'm still on target for it, or if, on the off chance that I'm not," April gave an *as if* laugh, "then maybe there's some extra credit I could do to make up the grade." She looked imploringly at Claudia, flipped her hair over her shoulder again, sniffed, and waited for an answer.

Perhaps on a different day, Claudia would have told April that she'd graded her test the previous night and that she'd gotten an A, but today Claudia wasn't feeling generous. April always approached Claudia with a conspiratorial, us-against-them attitude, as if it were the two of them versus all the rest of the students, the ones April dubbed "slackers and wanna-bes," those who failed to achieve April's level of shining brilliance. Part of that might be because she was the headmaster's niece, which made her feel she was more on the side of the teachers than the rest of the student body. Part of it was because April was a chatterbox and a suck-up.

Claudia wondered how much of what came out of April's mouth was attributable to April, and how much of what she said was really the opinion of Headmaster Peterson. "I know you have to put up with it too, Ms. Dubois," April had once confided. "Believe you me. I know what it's like to have to deal with lazy slackers and their little jealousies."

"The essay tests . . ." Claudia said it as if she were really thinking about them and not about how much she wanted to be rid of April. She turned to put the eraser on the ledge, and then back around to face April, who had already started talking again, as if her words could chase away any possibility of hearing she'd gotten a grade as mortifying as a B.

Claudia collected the papers on her desk, stacked them, and put them into her shoulder bag. April started saying something disparaging about her classmates' ability to competently complete essay exams, and Claudia looked at April with astonishment. *How is it possible to have such an unwaveringly high opinion of oneself?* "I just don't know where they think they're going to get in life," April said with a flip of her hair. "They won't get very far, believe you me." Claudia wanted to tell April she should be grateful for the lackadaisical tendencies of her peers, for without them she wouldn't be *in the running for valedictorian.*

April droned on, something about the importance of being valedictorian and her ability to become an Ivy Leaguer, which, to Claudia, made it sound as if April thought the whole process was like joining a country club.

Claudia tuned out. She hung her head down and then, because it felt so good, stretched her neck down farther, rolling it gently from side to side while staring down at her desk. Quite possibly, this desk had been in this classroom more years than the tree used to build it had been alive. Initials and dates had been carved into it by kids trying to make their mark, preserve a memento of themselves for posterity. Maybe even a few teachers had caved to the temptation. "Aldo was here" was Claudia's favorite, written in the upper right-hand corner of the desk, angled in such a way as to fill the corner. "Aldo." Claudia wondered at the poor child named Aldo, or was he really so deserving of her pity, being a child prone to arrogantly pronouncing his presence on other people's furniture? Whatever. Aldo *was* here. April *was still* here and that was something she needed to fix.

"April," Claudia interrupted. April had been saying something about her plans to apply to some schools just for the pleasure of turning them down. "April, I really am in a bit of a hurry today. I kind of have to get going."

"Well. I just wanted to find out if you'd gotten to my test yet."

"No, not yet," Claudia lied.

"Do you think you'll get to it tonight? It's been three—"

"I'm sorry, but I don't think I'm going to be able to do any grading tonight. I'm afraid I have some personal business to attend to and I don't think I'll be able to get to those tests until, at the earliest, tomorrow night. But they should all be done by Friday."

"Friday?" April looked as if she'd been slapped.

"Hopefully by Friday."

"Hopefully?" April looked as if the wait would kill her. "But I really need to know my grade, because if I didn't get an A and Gretchen Delaney gets an A on the Trig test then she'll be ahead of me—"

"April, I'm sorry, but I can't tell you your grade because I haven't graded your test yet. Even if I had, it wouldn't be fair to the other kids. If you must know, I haven't gotten around to grading any of them yet. I've had quite a lot going on this week and I'm afraid I've been quite a *slacker* as far as my classwork goes. I wish I could tell you otherwise, *believe you me*—"

Claudia had gone too far. April looked as if she'd been slapped again.

Claudia cleared her throat. "Anyway, I do need to get going now."

April's eyes, which had momentarily clouded over in what could have been the precursor to tears, had now tensed into a look of pity, as if to say, *I should have known you were no better than the rest. I should have known not to trust you.*

Christ, Claudia thought, *leave it to me to piss off the headmaster's niece. Leave it to me to bring her to tears. Shit.* Claudia put on what she hoped would look like an understanding smile.

"I'm sure you did fine, April. You always do. Regardless, we're going to have to wait to see until Friday."

Claudia swung her shoulder bag off the desk. "Try not to sweat it." She walked over to the door and opened it, the smile still on her face. She held it open for April.

April flipped her hair over her shoulder one last time and laughed through her nose as she walked through the door, apparently her way of telling Claudia that slackers like her couldn't understand the importance of these things.

Claudia stood there holding the door open to an empty room, watching April's back as she walked away. *Shit,* was all she could think.

A flash of white light caught Lindsay's eye as she passed Bergenstorm's. She stopped on the sidewalk and took a step backward and it flashed at her again, a beam from the display window's overhead spotlight hitting the mirrored surface of some jewelry. Initially, she'd thought the light had been a reflection of the sun, because it was such a bright day, a midwinter treat. The nice weather had brought a lot of people outside. Lindsay stepped out of the foot traffic on Michigan Avenue and up to the jewelry store's window, her breath misting it in the January chill. A locket had signaled her.

It was very similar to her great-great-grandmother's, handed down through the generations, which now waited in her mother's anxious hands. And it would have to keep waiting.

The heart-shaped locket was displayed on a bed of rumpled black velvet, meticulously arranged to look casually thrown there. Even the design on its surface was eerily familiar. Her family's heirloom probably was Bergenstorm's silver. Established in 1885, the marquee proudly declared on the awning over her head, not unlike Tate's Pharmacy and Apothecary, proudly established in 1872.

She wondered if her great-great-grandfather Tate had ever imagined that his little store that sold ointments—and probably snake oil—would become the Tate's drug empire it was today. Probably he did. Tates were notoriously motivated.

Lindsay watched the rush of people behind her via the reflection in the window. She really should get going, too. She had a four-o'clock meeting at the Women's Foundation headquarters. Their spring fundraiser, the Spring Fashion Show Extravaganza, was coming up in March, and Lindsay was on the committee, responsible for luncheon and flowers.

Lindsay watched with perplexed curiosity as all these society women at the Foundation planned their luncheons. It was as if they didn't get it. They had all this money, all this power, and they used it to *have lunch*. Of course they were raising money for all sorts of causes, and she supposed it wasn't everyone who could go off and join the Peace Corps, but ever since she was a little girl she had found herself looking around her and wondering at the unfairness of it all.

How come she was born an heiress to the Tate's Drugstore fortune, and little girls her same age were going to bed hungry each night in India? "What can you do?" had been her mother's refrain as she tucked Lindsay into her canopied bed, but that was exactly Lindsay's question: what can you do? More than lunch. More than fashion shows. Her mother had always said that trying to change the whole world was folly, that the best you could do was to try to change your own little corner of it, but Lindsay didn't believe that was necessarily true.

But it wasn't so easy. Trying to get these women to change their minds about how they did their good deeds was like trying to turn a fast-moving barge. And Lindsay, despite her family name, never felt she carried enough influence. She always felt that somehow, when she spoke up, people looked at her as if to say, *why are you talking?* Whether it was all in her imagination—as Claudia said— or not, she still felt victimized. It still hurt.

Lindsay wondered if she'd be more popular and influential if maybe she were prettier, or thinner—but she watched other women at the Foundation, plain women, chubby women, and they seemed to have plenty of influence. And she knew it wasn't about the money. Even Claudia, who always seemed to be so in awe of the Tate fortune, had more influence than Lindsay. At Book Club, the women soaked up her words every time she spoke. Not that Claudia could see it. She always focused on how she'd tripped over her words, instead of how much what she said was valued by the group. And then there was Mara, who seemed to think that having money would solve everything, that it was the means to happiness. Lindsay pictured Mara's two big beautiful sons and wanted to give her a thump on the head.

Lindsay clenched the front of her coat, pulling it more tightly over her chest. She held her hand over her heart for a moment, over the place a locket might go. She looked down at the locket in the store window, so similar to the one meant for her, for her children. The one she most likely would never have.

When Claudia pulled into the parking lot at Barnes & Noble she was still thinking about April Sibley, annoyed with April for being April and with herself for letting April get to her. Why had she snipped like that at a student?

The poor girl had very few friends, and even though the reasons for that seemed obvious, Claudia thought if any student was worthy of some pity and a little sympathy from a teacher, it was probably April Sibley. Then again, like Aldo, maybe her deservedness was deceptive.

Claudia walked into the bookstore and sighed: instant relief. She just loved it here. All these books. She ran her hand lovingly along the covers of the books on the front table as she made her way over to the escalator. As she rose up to the second floor, Claudia scanned the tables of bargain books, stacks of fiction on sale for more than half off. It was scary to think of all these writers, writing all these novels, working so hard, finally getting published, getting their books in print, only to have them end up here, in obscurity, their titles and names never heard of or forgotten, lost in a sea of bargain books. She mourned for them. It took a lot to write a book, a lot of time, a lot of courage, things she had always thought she had. Or would have. She'd envisioned herself writing her novels over the summer breaks and then editing and refining at night during the school year.

Claudia got off the escalator and stood in front of another display. She picked up a copy of a best-selling hardcover book and looked at the cover. She ran a hand over the jacket, creaked it open. God, how she had wanted this. How many books had she started? Three? Four? It didn't matter. It was an idea she had given up on.

She'd abandoned it shortly after buying a *Writer's Market* guide. "Over 4.3 Million Sold," it boasted on the cover. Four-point-three million. That was a lot of people writing, and they were all probably working on their novels, the pinnacle of prose, what the marathon was to runners. The look on the clerk's face when he'd rung up her purchase was what had stopped her writing cold, had given her a writer's block that to date had lasted for two years. In one brief glance, his look had mocked her. It was as if he'd said, *Oh yeah, sweetie, you too. Isn't everyone writing their novel?* Of course, she realized, everyone was. Four-point-three million copies sold.

Now, Claudia resigned herself to just reading books. It was much less frustrating for her, and she felt free to criticize and critique without fear of any future karmic repercussions. It also made her feel a little less like a character in someone else's novel—the English-teacher/aspiring writer.

Claudia turned the corner and arrived at the New Age section and began scanning for *The Sacredness of the Wiccan Way*. She could have called ahead to see if they had it, but then they always ask if they can hold a copy for you. Claudia could visualize the book behind the counter with "Dubois" emblazoned on the spine, right there in front of the main check-out counter. Ms. Dubois, teacher at the prestigious Strawn Academy of Arts and Sciences, a heathen. Blatant paganism right there for all to see. She couldn't take the chance, even if this store was out of the way, even if her school was always professing its desire to "embrace individualism."

If only she could be more bold. Yeah, well. Claudia always managed to find a way to stop herself when it came to acting more bold. She couldn't even shoo away one of her students without worrying about getting fired.

Claudia started looking for the book. The New Age Wicca section wasn't too big, which was a good thing, since Lindsay had never gotten back to her with the author's name.

A woman came around the corner and stood next to her, pulling a book off the shelf and flipping through it slowly. *Bell's Complete Astrologer and Ephemeris.* She had long gray hair and was wearing a long skirt, down to her ankles, and sandals with socks—an edgy, bohemian look but, judging from the skirt, the sandals and the jewelry, one that didn't come cheap. The woman smelled vaguely of sandalwood incense.

Great, Claudia thought. *That's how I'm going to end up. A crazy old New Age woman browsing astrology books and looking all eccentric. I'll bet she has twenty cats at home.*

Claudia glanced from the shoes to the shelf and found herself staring directly at the store's only copy of *The Sacredness of the Wiccan Way.* She crouched down and began flipping through it. It seemed to be everything Lindsay had said it would be. It was big, but it wasn't terribly expensive. Claudia's knees started to ache. She sat down cross-legged on the floor and flicked through the book, resting it on her lap. The woman reached for another book, this time pulling out a copy of *Past Lives, Past Loves,* skimming it, then putting it quickly back on the shelf.

The woman ran her hands slowly along a row of books on crystals, and the motion was so fluid it gave Claudia a chill to watch her do it, the little hairs on her scalp tingling every time the woman's hands switched direction. She found the woman's presence so calming. Claudia felt herself relaxing, turning the pages of her book more slowly, becoming completely intrigued with the woman standing next to her. Claudia watched her covertly until she bent down to reach for a book on the shelf in front of where Claudia was sitting, a book on the tarot.

"Oh, I'm sorry." Claudia hated to break the quiet. "Am I in your way?"

"No, dear. You're fine." Even her voice was calming, ethereal, and the familiar way she had called Claudia "dear." It gave Claudia the most pleasant goose bumps.

"Don't apologize, either," she spoke again. "Women do way too much apologizing." She smiled down at Claudia.

Claudia had read something to that effect, a study that said women were apologizing too much—at least way more than men were—saying they were sorry for all sorts of little things, things that weren't even their fault: "Sorry about the rain"; "I'm sorry traffic was so bad." Right after she'd read it, Claudia had started noticing how often she did say "sorry." *I'm sorry you had a bad day. I'm sorry I didn't grade your paper. I'm sorry I irritated you by wanting to be a writer.* At the time she'd made a conscious effort to stop saying "sorry," but somewhere along the line she'd forgotten all about it. She should try again. She was sorry she had stopped.

"That's a wonderful book," the woman next to her said, gesturing to *The Sacredness of the Wiccan Way* in Claudia's lap. "I read it many years ago. Excellent."

"Oh, this, I—" Claudia stammered. "I'm just browsing through it. I'm not . . . I guess . . . it looks okay."

The woman smiled back at her and then returned to her tarot book. Claudia was sorry the conversation was over. *Why am I always such a dork?*

The woman grabbed another book from the shelf and, without looking at it, stacked it on top of the tarot book and the astrology book she had chosen. She started to leave, then turned back around before she walked away. "I really don't much care for cats. I think I might be allergic." She smiled very kindly when she said this.

Cats? I didn't say anything about cats, Claudia thought. What an odd thing to say. She sat there a moment, shaking her head. *There sure are a lot of nuts in this world.*

Then Claudia jolted up, remembering her thought about the house full of cats. Had she said it out loud? No. She was certain she hadn't. Claudia walked out into the main aisle, expecting to see the back of the woman strolling slowly away, but she was nowhere in sight. She walked over to the railing and looked down at the empty escalators. She even crouched down and looked at the cash register line, but the woman was gone.

How could she have heard her thought? Claudia asked herself, breathing hard as she walked back to where she had been sitting. Or was it just a lucky guess? Maybe when you hang around the New Age section looking as eccentric as she did, a lot of people assumed you had twenty cats at home. Maybe the woman was finally taking the offensive, boldly pronouncing her dislike of cats to anyone who would listen.

The Sacredness of the Wiccan Way still lay open on the floor, and Claudia's huge purse, likewise wide open, was still sitting next to it. *Oh good grief. How could I have left my purse here?* She looked into its gaping top and took a quick inventory; everything was there. She sighed. *I need to quit the caffeine. I need to chill out. Maybe some form of New Age meditation* would *be in order.* She reached down to pick up her book and saw a small crystal that lay on the ground near where the woman had been standing.

Claudia picked it up and turned it in her hand. A thin piece of quartz, icicle shaped, about two inches long. It must have belonged to the woman; she must have dropped it. Although anyone visiting this section could have dropped it. Claudia hadn't noticed it earlier, though. She grabbed her purse and the copy of *The Sacredness of the Wiccan Way.* Maybe the woman was still on the first floor, and Claudia had missed her when she'd looked. She hurried to the escalator and walked down, doubling her pace. She scanned the large room as she descended, but the woman wasn't there.

Two people stood in line ahead of Claudia at the register. On the sale table next to her, she saw, under a sign that declared, "Buy This Book!," the stack of three books the woman had been carrying when she'd walked away. Claudia picked them up, then looked at the door.

"Next please." The annoyed tone in the cashier's voice indicated to her that it wasn't the first time he had called to her.

"I just—" Claudia walked over, carrying the stack of books with her. "Did you see the woman who put these here? She was . . . I think I found something of hers and—"

The clerk was the same man who had intimidated her into two years of writer's block.

"I think she left this." Claudia held up the crystal.

"Do you want those or not?" He nodded at the pile of books in her arms.

Claudia looked down at her stack, now made up of four books. "Yes," she said.

Chapter Six

Claudia walked into her kitchen and put the bag of books on the counter. *What was I thinking?* She put both hands on top of the bag and blew out through her lips, letting the air flutter through them with a sound of flatulent disgust. One hundred and thirty-two dollars. What had possessed her to buy all of these books? Dan was going to kill her.

The Sacredness of the Wiccan Way was on top, *Bell's Complete Astrologer and Ephemeris* was in there, as was a book called *The Modern Witches' Grimoire* and then last, a small, hardcover book called *A Beginner's Guide to the Tarot.*

Claudia pulled out the tarot book and scanned the cover. Three cards were fanned out on it, number VIII, the Strength card, on top. The woman on the card stared back at her with fierce black eyes, her image drawn in several shades of dark ink, cross-hatched in a manner that made it look very old and somewhat childish. Claudia flipped through the pages, the color templates of the cards flashing past. They looked mysterious, complicated, and scary.

"The Suit of Cups, Hearts in a conventional card deck, represents water and emotions," she read. "It is a feminine suit, with the properties of the water signs Cancer, Scorpio, and Pisces." *Water signs? There are water signs? What am I getting myself into?*

Claudia set the tarot book down on her kitchen countertop. Their coffee cups from this morning were still sitting out, hers with an imprint of her lipstick on the rim, his with an inch of cold coffee still in the bottom.

He'd had to leave a little earlier than usual this morning—some big meeting about a new project at his firm. Dan tended to keep irregular hours at the architectural offices of Taylor, Glickman, Bleeker and Associates. When he told her he would be home at the regular time tonight, she'd had to ask, "And what time would that be?"

"Six"—he'd pulled up one side of his mouth—"ish?"

Claudia had smiled at him doubtfully. *Really?*

Dan had ignored her skeptical look. "Hey, how about I make my famous stir-fried beef and broccoli for dinner? What do you think? I'll pick up everything on the way home. You won't have to lift a finger." He picked her hand up off the counter and kissed the back of it, raising his eyebrows up into the boyish brown hair that curled over them.

She had smiled. "Sounds like an offer I can't refuse."

Claudia walked the coffee cups over to the sink. Dan would be home in less than an hour. She could start getting things ready for him. Get the wok out, slice some onions.

The light went on in her neighbor's kitchen across the gangway and Claudia turned in time to catch a glimpse of him walking out of the room. Their third-floor windows were less than ten feet apart and at night they wouldn't make eye contact before closing their blinds, a city dweller's way of showing respect for each other's privacy.

Claudia twisted her mini-blinds shut. A city dweller. How weird was that now, to have that thought about herself? When Dan had suggested they move to the north side after school, Claudia hadn't been too thrilled by the idea.

"Don't people get mugged in the city?"

"People get mugged in the suburbs, too. The difference is, in the city they just take your money and run. In the suburbs, they chop you into little bits and hide you in a Hefty bag in their crawlspace."

"Is that meant to be comforting?"

The first time she'd come to the apartment alone, a few days before they had moved in, everything had tested her nerves: the parking, the creepy people on the street, all the keys and locks. It had irritated her thoroughly. It wasn't until she'd been cleaning the bathtub and had heard the singing that she'd known Dan had been right.

The bathroom window had been cracked open and she'd heard someone singing opera—not playing it, but *singing* opera. She sat back on her heels and listened, her yellow rubber gloves resting over the side of the tub. The woman's voice was incredible. She'd never heard anything like it before, at least not *live*, and definitely not in her bathroom.

Claudia sat there for several minutes listening, amazed. *This is what he meant.* This is what he'd wanted, for himself *and* for her. The city burbled with creative inspiration, creative people and places. Its own muse. A place that, in spite of its constrictions on space, ironically offered its occupants more privacy—and more freedom.

Claudia had slowly returned to scrubbing the tub, her shoulders a little less tense, her jaw a little less clenched, the cleanser on the sponge quietly scouring away. Hearing live opera while scrubbing your bathtub was, she presumed, an experience unique to the city, and the intimacy of it made her feel all at once at home.

Now, she couldn't imagine living anywhere else. She loved it here—the activity, the energy, the *life*. Dan had a way of ending up being right about things.

Claudia turned from the window and once again faced the pile of books on her counter. *Good grief.* She imagined the activity, the energy, the *danger* to her life that would occur when Dan came home and saw them. They'd just had a big talk about saving money. *Maybe it wouldn't be such a bad idea to hide them for a while, pull them out one at a time later, over the course of the next few—*

"Hi. I'm home," Dan called from the living room.

"In here." *Shit.*

Claudia put the books in a stack. The front door thumped closed. She picked up the books, then put them back down. She put the plastic shopping bag they'd been inside over the top of them; then, thinking that looked too obvious, she rested it against the pile, trying to disguise the height of the stack. Claudia came around the other side of the counter and stood in front of them.

"What, no martini waiting?" Dan was coming down the hall. "No cocktail dress or one-heel-kicked-in-the-air hug?" He put the grocery bags he was carrying on the counter next to her.

"Didn't want you to think you'd walked into the wrong apartment." Claudia reached up and wrapped her arms around his neck. She kicked a heel up behind her, but it wasn't her sarcasm he noticed.

"Do a little shopping today?"

"Umm."

Dan pulled back, crossed his arms in front of him, and arched his eyebrows.

"I bought a few books for Book Club."

"Book Club? Since when does Book Club read four books in a month?"

Claudia made no comment, busying herself with folding the bag and taking it over to the recycling bin.

"How much were they?"

"I kind of got carried away, but there was this woman there who—"

"How much was it, Claude?"

"—and she left this stack, so when I got to the register and the guy asked me, I—"

"How much was it, Claude?" Dan paused ever so briefly between each word, the way she often did with her students when they failed to respond to a question.

"A hundred and thirty-two."

"A hun—" he ran his hand through his hair, "a hundred and thirty-two? Claudia, I thought we talked about this."

"I know. I'm sorry. It's just that—"

"We *just* talked about this. We've got to start saving more money. I thought we were agreed. Until I can get a business off the ground, we've got to really cut back. A hundred—" He couldn't bring himself to say it. "And you want to have a baby? You can't even be responsible with a credit card and you want to—"

Claudia could feel the ache in the back of her throat that always preceded her tears. "Sorry. I'm sorry. I—"

"Sorry isn't going to pay the bills. Jesus Christ. A hundred and thirty bucks is not cutting back." Dan turned around and walked back down the hall to his office.

"I can return the—"

He shut the door hard and Claudia could feel the pressure change, a tangible thump that took the warmth out of the room and sucked the air from her chest.

The apartment smelled of onions. On the living room couch, Claudia kept her head down grading essay tests, even though she could sense Dan's presence at the end of the hall. He'd been in the kitchen for the past hour, silently preparing dinner.

"We lost the Atkinson bid," he said finally. He walked over, taking a seat on the arm of the couch. "That's what the big meeting was all about."

Claudia sucked in a breath, her hands crinkling an essay test on her lap. She should have figured it was something like that. It was pretty rare that Dan acted like such an asshole, but when he did, it usually had something to do with money. It seemed to her they had plenty saved up, but she wondered what it was going to take for him to feel secure and not worry about every nickel.

"Oh, Dan. I'm sorry. What happened?"

"They said they wanted a bigger firm, one with *more depth* is how they put it. I guess our bid was okay. They said it wasn't *out of line.*" He exhaled a short laugh. "We were all counting on this. I don't know what's going to happen now."

Taylor, Glickman, Bleeker and Associates had hired Dan right after his internship there. He knew he had to pay his dues, but he was getting tired of designing restrooms for schools and hospitals. He'd been a project architect for three years now, but it wasn't what he had in mind for himself. The Atkinson bid, on a Loop mixed-use commercial and residential mid-rise building, had given the more junior people at Taylor, Glickman, Bleeker and Associates hope. Hope that they'd get to do some meatier projects, which was just the kind of experience Dan wanted before leaving to hang out his own shingle. With most of the nine-part licensing exam behind him, except for the dreaded structures sections, he'd planned to start up his own firm as soon as the following year. Now those plans would most likely be put on hold.

"Wasn't Atkinson kind of a jerk anyway?"

"A jerk with deep pockets."

"It's probably just as well. Maybe he could have turned out to be such a tyrant, he could have ruined the firm's reputation. He could have set your own plans back even farther."

Dan gave her a look.

"Well, maybe that wouldn't have happened but . . ."

He was still giving her the look.

"Oh, come on. You know you're a great architect. The best one I've ever been married to." Some of the essays slid off the couch onto the floor as she moved closer to Dan, putting her arms around him.

"Everything's going to be fine," she said. "Just fine. You'll see. Everything happens for a reason. Maybe the reason this happened is because tomorrow something better is going to come along and now they'll be able to—"

"—that's my Claudia. The glass is always half-full and everything happens for a reason." Dan disentangled himself from her and patted her thigh, then stood up and walked into the kitchen.

Claudia sank back into the couch. She stared down at her thigh where he'd patted it. It practically stung. *Jeez.* She'd only been trying to make him feel better.

The door to their liquor cabinet creaked open and she heard a bottle being set down on the kitchen counter. What sounded like one of their Scotch glasses clunked down next.

Claudia heard Dan's footsteps come down the hall. "Will you be joining me?"

"For dinner or Scotch?" She leaned over and picked up the essay tests off the floor.

"Right now, Scotch."

"Not on a school night." Claudia smoothed out a wrinkled essay, running her hand over it a couple of times, maybe a little too loudly. A car hissed by on the street.

"Hey, about earlier . . ."

The test rustled as she flipped a page. Dan waited in the doorway.

"Forget it." Her voice was quiet. "It's no big deal." She didn't look up at him, even though she was already starting to forgive him.

"Well, how about some dinner, then. Should be ready in about ten." He paused. "Hey, I saw some Merlot in there."

Claudia flipped another page. More gently this time. "Okay," she said, but when she looked over at him, he was already back in the kitchen.

When she heard the wine bottle thud onto the counter, Claudia closed her eyes and pressed her lips together. By the time she heard the dull pop of the cork, she was already crying. It didn't seem right, that the making-up could sometimes hurt more than the fighting.

The weather was perfect: crisp and cold, but not too cold, in the mid-forties, mild for mid-January in Chicago. Jill tugged down the sleeves of her jacket and looked out at the skyline from her perch in the Ferris wheel basket, then down at Darrin far below her on the walkway, eating popcorn from a box and looking out over the water. She groaned out loud. The basket of the Ferris wheel was on its way down but its movement was so slow as to be barely detectible. The problem was, it wasn't slow enough.

He'd been too afraid to go up with her. She hadn't even wanted to go up in the first place—too touristy, not her type of thing—but he'd been so insistent that she'd finally just gone along, figuring it would be easier than trying to talk him out of it. At that point, she would have done anything to accelerate this date to its conclusion.

What had happened between dinner and now? All through dinner he'd seemed so cool and smart and witty, but sometime during coffee and before the check, he had gone off on a verbal excursion, a rant about himself and his dull job as a suit somewhere downtown. He'd kept talking and talking, on and on, and at one point when she'd tried to interject something about herself he'd said, "Well, I don't know art, but I know what I like." She had decided right then that there would never be a second date with the moron Darrin.

The line for the Ferris wheel hadn't been too long, made up mostly of a large tour group of Korean men. Jill couldn't help thinking, *Who comes to Chicago on a tour—in January?* When their turn had come, Darrin had said he wasn't feeling well, that maybe the shrimp scampi he'd eaten for dinner wasn't agreeing with him—but she'd noticed the way he had looked fearfully at the top of the huge wheel. "Just go on ahead," he'd said. "I don't want to ruin your fun."

This was never my idea of fun.

"I'll wait for you over there." He pointed toward the carousel.

More your speed? Little horsies and ponies and only two axes? "Oh please. It's okay," she told him. He had no idea *how* okay it really was. "Let's just forget about it." But she'd started to think it might be a good opportunity to get away from him for a while.

"No really. You should just do it. I'll be fine. Besides, we've already paid for the tickets."

Yes they had. Split them fifty-fifty, just like dinner. It had been partly her doing anyway; she'd offered to pay her half and in spite of wanting to believe she was a modern woman living in a modern age, she had been a bit miffed that he'd taken her up on it. Jill supposed she couldn't blame him for wanting to share the cost of the date: it sounded like he was going through a rough patch of first dates like she was, and for a while there she almost felt sorry for him. She couldn't really fault him for not wanting to invest any more of his money on a date that, more than likely, would lead nowhere. Dating must be as miserable for him as it was for her.

Michael had been her last semi-serious boyfriend; they'd dated for nearly six months, the previous summer and autumn. Jill had started noticing signs of trouble with him early in the fall, when he'd begun talking about "their" future, and had developed a new possessiveness. It was such a difference; in the beginning, he had seemed so *not* looking for a wife. It was precisely his lack of clinginess that had attracted her to him in the first place, the fact that he didn't need to know where she was every hour of the day that they weren't together.

Jill had rebelled against this change in him, playing little head games: not returning his calls promptly, being unnecessarily vague in telling him her whereabouts. In truth, she'd been working long hours at the studio, but her capriciousness had of course caused him to suspect all sorts of things, and she'd never done anything to assuage his fears. When he'd asked her to lunch in November, she knew. He must have thought he was being so smart, so coy—but she knew. They'd never met for lunch before.

He'd told her he didn't want to see her anymore, that the relationship wasn't "going in the right direction," whatever that meant. Jill hadn't put up a fight. She never did in this situation. She had worn a bored expression, acting not the least bit affected. It was a trick she'd learned from her mother, the first time her father had left.

"But you didn't say *anything*. You just let him go." Jill had been confounded.

"What do you think would hurt him more," her mother had asked, "acting like I cared, or acting like I didn't?"

When Michael had slid his chair back from the table at the restaurant, the legs had made an excruciatingly loud noise as they scraped over the hardwood floor. He stood up, looking around nervously to see if anyone had noticed. After all, that had been the entire point of coming there: to avoid a scene.

A crisp one-hundred-dollar bill lay balancing on its side on the table. He'd chosen not to wait around for the check. Instead he pulled the bill out of his gold money clip, saying, "This should cover it."

Jill watched him slide the chair back under the table more carefully after he stood. He gave her a parting half-smile, which faded quickly under her calm stare. Then he walked away down the long aisle of the restaurant and disappeared around the corner without looking back.

After Michael had left, Jill sipped at her martini alone. Michael's plan had been effective. To all outward appearances, her date had left lunch early to get back to work. She had known he'd chosen to meet over lunch because he didn't want any complications. It was a jerky thing to do, a way to avoid any real conversation about why the relationship had failed, avoid any discussion of real feelings. He obviously hadn't understood Jill enough to know she didn't care much for the discussion of feelings.

Jill had left the martini unfinished, next to the one-hundred-dollar bill, still standing on its side on the table. It was too bad. Michael's plot wasn't necessary. Jill wouldn't have caused a scene over him anywhere.

Her basket hit the bottom and a Navy Pier worker opened the gate. She stepped out onto the platform, the wheel never stopping, continuing its slow-motion turn.

She looked around for Darrin, walking over to the side of the carousel near the water where she'd spotted him last, then walking all around it. She made a wider search of the area, but he was nowhere to be found. It took a while before it dawned on her, but once it did, she exhaled sharply in disbelief. She'd been ditched in the middle of her date—by a man afraid of Ferris wheels.

As she walked back down the pier, the city lights sparkled on the lake. She passed couples holding hands, or with their arms wrapped around one another, or fighting, with tight expressions of disagreement on their faces—the full relationship spectrum. Jill tried to ignore them as she made her way down to the cab stand at the front of the pier, where she could get a taxi home.

Candlelight flickered burgundy through the wineglass sitting on her nightstand, Dan's empty Scotch glass beside it. He was asleep already, his breathing steady and deep. Claudia was always thirsty after sex. Tonight her mouth felt especially cottony from the wine, but she didn't want to get out of bed. The radiators had started their nighttime schedule and the air in their bedroom was growing cool; she could feel the chill on the tip of her nose.

Instead she lay there, letting her worries whipsaw through her head. It shouldn't be any big deal if they had to wait another year or two for Dan to start his business. But what if Dan now thought they should wait to have a baby? It seemed like she'd already waited too long. It had taken forever to convince him to start trying in the first place. Besides, they could fit a baby in the apartment, a lot of people did that—little babies didn't take up that much room. They could wait to get a condo or bigger place when they had their second one. If that was really the issue. Money.

Claudia rolled over onto her side, away from Dan, and pulled the blanket up, covering her mouth and nose. She knew she would probably go along with him, end up back on the Pill for another year. But if they weren't trying to have a baby, if they didn't have a baby, then she'd have no excuse for not writing. *Was that the real reason she wanted to get pregnant? To have an excuse?* Claudia shut her eyes tight.

That's not it, she told herself. Pregnant or not, writing or not, the real issue was that she was worried about Dan. He was so talented and she hated watching him get discouraged—especially when he took it out on her. All those years in school, "archi-torture" school they called it and for good reason, and he didn't have anything very exciting to show for it. Not what he'd envisioned, anyway. Not like Howard Roark.

He had a stack of drawings in their office, his "noodlings" he called them, and Claudia was pretty sure he didn't think she knew how very serious he was about them. They were drawings of houses. His houses. Various floor plans and elevations. It was brilliant stuff—the stuff of his dreams. And now those dreams would be postponed again. They both had known going into it that it was going to take some time for him to realize his dream. It just got harder and harder each time they thought they were close to watch it slip a little farther away.

The air under the covers was getting too stuffy. Claudia slid the blanket off her nose and opened her eyes. She was still thirsty and she eyed her wineglass on the nightstand, the light from the candle glimmering faintly behind it.

Dan stirred next to her. "Are you going to blow that out? I can't sleep with it."

Claudia smiled. She slid the comforter down and got up, pulling it back over her place on the bed.

"Where are you going?"

"To the bathroom, if that's okay with you." She laughed. As if she would just get up and leave him right now, as if he thought she might be off to run naked errands in the middle of the night.

Claudia drank two glasses of water before filling one to take back to Dan. She'd only had one glass of wine, but it felt like the beginning of a hangover coming on. When she opened the medicine cabinet for some aspirin, the smell of their sex rose up off of her and she could feel the warm trickle of its aftermath start down her leg, making it all the way to her ankle before she could grab a tissue.

Dan's lovemaking had been different tonight—not aggressive, not really . . . just, not gentle. He had held her so tightly while he thrusted that she had thought she might stop breathing. It was as though all the rage and fear of the day were coming through him and he needed to hold her tight to ground himself, to keep himself from flying apart in a million directions.

It had been wonderful.

She drank a sip of Dan's water with her aspirin, then refilled the glass before taking it back with her to the bedroom. He was asleep again by the time she returned. Claudia blew out the candle and crawled under the covers, her place still as warm as when she had left it.

Chapter Seven

———✦———

Claudia pushed the miniature shopping cart down the produce aisle at the Wild Prairie Market, wondering if the size of the basket was one of those mind tricks, like in dieting: if you put your food on a smaller plate, it tricks your mind into thinking you've eaten more. If you put two hundred dollars' worth of groceries in a Lilliputian cart, it tricks your wallet into thinking you've gotten your money's worth.

The February Book Club meeting was at her house tonight. She probably should have just gone to Jewel, it would have been faster, but she wanted the food to be extra nice. She wanted pretentious, trendy little snacks and fruit tortes, and she'd come to the right store, since there was no place more pretentious than the place she was in now, "Where Everything is Alimentary!" Even Claudia thought she could have written a better tag line than that. And she knew Gail certainly could have. Back in the day, when Gail was a climber at Foote, Cone and Belding, she'd been the copywriter on the Sunshine Orange Juice campaign. The jingle "Happy Days Start with Happy Rays!" was a phrase that, at the time, was as kitschy-popular as Wendy's "Where's the Beef?" or "I've fallen and I can't get up." Gail kept her Clio in the office at her house.

Claudia had been proud of her friend, but to tell the truth, Gail sure seemed a lot happier now. In the few short years she'd been at Foote, Cone, each time Claudia had seen her it had seemed like a little bit more of the life had been sucked out of her, like watching the colored syrup get drained out of a snow cone.

Claudia put a small basket of grape tomatoes in her cart and turned the corner, nearly hitting a braless woman reading the ingredients on a hummus container. The woman flashed annoyance at Claudia before quickly collecting herself, putting on a thin smile, and going back to reading her label. Jeez, Claudia thought, people here are so pretentious, they even pretend not to be mad at you.

She wove her way through the narrow aisles, picking up miniature melba toasts and sun-dried tomato cream cheese, dodging shoppers reading labels or trying to decide which type of bland organic canned goods they should buy. She got biscotti for the coffee, a fruit torte, and some cookies from the bakery counter. The food she had in her cart would scarcely fill one paper shopping bag and she knew it would cost over a hundred dollars. Dan's going to shit, she thought. She glanced at her watch while standing in line. She still had time to run down to Sam's Wines and Spirits; he couldn't be mad at her for shopping there. And they had to have wine.

The man in front of her pulled out a pile of dirty cloth grocery bags from under his cart and sanctimoniously laid them on the conveyor belt with his groceries. He glanced sideways at Claudia's cart in the not very discreet way men have of checking something out, and Claudia just knew he was disapproving of her ecoterrorist ways, of her destroying the world one disposable grocery bag at a time.

She folded her arms across her chest and pretended to be interested in something on the far side of the store, near the juice bar. She scanned over the menu written in chalk above the counter. Sitting at one of the little tables, reading a book, was a woman with gray hair. Claudia could only see the top of her head and forehead, but she was certain it was the woman from the bookstore, the woman whose books she'd ended up buying. Could it really be her?

"Hell-o," the cashier greeted Claudia with what sounded to her like barely concealed disdain, and she felt as though he were eyeing her food as if it were a competition entry. She turned around again to see if the woman was still in the juice bar. It would be cool to talk to her again, Claudia thought, maybe ask her about the books she'd left. Or how she had managed to disappear from a bookstore in broad daylight. When Claudia turned around, the bagger was staring at her, waiting with his pierced eyebrows arched.

"I'm sorry, what?" Claudia asked.

"Paper or plastic?"

"Oh, um, paper I guess."

"One-o-three ninety-six," the cashier said. She handed him her debit card and he pointed to the electronic box in front of her. *Amateur*, Claudia could hear him think. She swiped her card and waited for the cashier input, the familiar sound of the receipt printing out.

"It's not going through for some reason. Try swiping it again."

Claudia felt heat rise up from her neck to her face and ears as she swiped the card through again. *Oh God, please let this go through. Did Dan mail that Visa bill? I told him not to. . . .*

"It's not going through. It's saying insufficient funds in your account." Claudia stared at him for a moment, then shrugged. "I don't know what the problem is. I just took out an ATM this morning, maybe that's the trouble—I took out too much money this morning." She smiled at him, but she could tell he didn't believe it either. "Well anyway." She handed him her regular Visa card. "Try this."

He pointed back at the electronic control pad in front of her. "You need to swipe it through." His tone was sympathetic. She hadn't been expecting that.

They waited. She stared at the keypad, willing the word *approved* to appear. She tried a glance at the woman behind her in line, but instead of the smile Claudia had been hoping for, the woman just looked quickly away, shifting her weight from one foot to the other. Claudia wiped some sweat from her upper lip.

The register receipt started printing out. Claudia waved the front panel of her jacket back and forth a couple of times. *Thank God.* A cloud of relief enveloped all of them.

The cashier handed her the receipt. "Sign please," he said, the low-level disdain returning to his voice.

She signed and got behind her cart while watching the juice bar, wanting to put this scene behind her. The woman was still sitting there, her brows knitted together over her reading glasses, as if she were very concerned about what she was reading. Her hair was pulled back into a bun today, taking away her hippie-like aura, making her seem almost professorial.

Claudia turned her cart in that direction. *I'll just park it outside and pretend I'm getting a drink to take with me and then she'll either notice me or I can pretend to notice her and . . .*

"You forgot your receipt," the cashier called after her, the words *you idiot* hanging unsaid in the air. Claudia turned back with a laugh, shaking her head at herself. "Oh. Thanks," she said. She made a face. *Silly me.* "Don't want to forget that."

She smiled at him, but he just looked at her, his initial coldness returning in its entirety. Claudia could just feel him exchange a look with the bagger after she'd turned around. "Hell-o." He greeted the woman that had been behind her in line.

The woman in the café was still sitting at her table reading when Claudia approached the juice bar. She left her cart outside the railing that separated the small restaurant from the grocery store, worrying about the sun-dried tomato cream cheese that needed to get to a refrigerator.

Claudia scanned the overhead menu, careful to stand in the woman's line of sight, but the woman didn't look up. *The crystal.* Claudia started searching her purse for the crystal the woman had dropped at the bookstore. She'd been carrying it around in her pockets, hoping it would bring her good luck or answers or something. That was up until the previous week, when she'd found it on the floor of her classroom next to her desk and decided that, since it was such a slippery little thing, she'd be better off keeping it at home. She'd dropped it into her purse.

Claudia held her head close to the top of her bag while she searched. *Where is it? It's got to be in here—I don't remember taking it out. I guess I must have. Damn. It would have been the perfect ice-breaker.*

The little café was almost full. It only had four tables; each one could seat two, maybe three people. Claudia thought it might work out, if the couple in front of her took the last table, that she could ask the woman to share hers—although the woman might think it strange that Claudia would sit down and drink a cup of coffee while she watched her cart of groceries defrost.

She ordered a small latte and glanced back while the espresso machine steamed her milk. A juice machine whirred in the background, too. It was not the most serene place to read a book, Claudia thought. Maybe that's what the woman had been frowning about.

Claudia didn't understand why she felt so drawn to her, why she felt compelled to talk to her. It was true the woman had a calming presence; Claudia remembered the chills she'd felt when she'd watched her run her hands over the books at the bookstore. She seemed so confident and poised. "Don't apologize," she'd said. She was like the anti-Claudia.

When her coffee was ready she took it from the counter and turned around to look at the woman, who had just stood up with her back to Claudia. She was wearing a thick black turtleneck sweater over black slacks and she looked thinner than Claudia remembered. It must be the black, or maybe the skirt she'd been wearing the last time had made her look bigger.

Claudia had an awful revelation. *What if all the long skirts I wear make me look fatter?* She couldn't deny that the woman was not shaped as much like an avocado as she remembered. Claudia quickly checked that thought, for fear of provoking another comment along the lines of "I don't much care for avocados."

The title of the book the woman had been reading was visible under her hand: *A Prayer for Owen Meany.*

"That's a wonderful book," Claudia blurted, happy at having found a way to break into conversation with her. "Do you like Irving?"

The woman turned toward Claudia, assessing her over the rims of her black reading glasses.

"Do I know you?" she asked, and Claudia wanted to die. *Okay, maybe this wasn't such a great idea.*

The woman seemed to sense her consternation. "No, dear. I meant, have we met before? I feel like I know you from somewhere."

"I met you at the bookstore. Barnes and Noble? We weren't properly introduced, but," Claudia laughed nervously, "I mean, we never exchanged names, but we spoke briefly. You picked out some books, a stack and—I think you dropped your crystal. I still have it . . . just not with me, but if you want I could get it to you."

"Well," the woman paused, as if she were enjoying the refreshing moment of silence, "I've always believed that crystals come to you when they're meant to be yours and leave you when they've done all they can for you."

Claudia nodded in agreement, as if she understood this.

"What kind of crystal was it? What did it look like?"

Claudia held her thumb and forefinger about two inches apart. "Quartz, about this long, and very thin. I found it on the floor right after you left."

"Hmm," she paused, "I don't think I . . . No. Wait. I did have a crystal like that once . . . I thought I'd lost it ages ago." The woman thought for a long moment. "Maybe it had been in that skirt pocket all along. I hadn't worn *that* skirt in ages. Ha! Well, either way, I think you should keep it."

"Really? I can keep it? Oh. Well, thank you."

The woman put her book into a black leather handbag even larger than the one Claudia carried. She took her coat, a black cape with a velvet collar and velvet trim around the pockets, and swung it around her shoulders. She started buttoning the large round buttons that went down the front.

"I'd better go, too." Claudia nodded at her parked cart. "Got a cart full of groceries I need to get home." She laughed. "Just needed a little afternoon pick-me-up." She held her latte up to eye level and gave a little shrug.

The woman watched Claudia, a good-natured smile in her eyes.

Claudia tried to settle back down into herself. No more acting the goof. "You know," Claudia took a deep breath, "I was wondering, since you're an Irving fan and all, I mean this will probably sound strange just having met you, but if you like to read, I'm having a—"

Beethoven's "Ode to Joy" blared loudly from the gaping top of the woman's handbag. "Excuse me, dear." She reached into her bag and pulled out her phone. "Hello . . . Mmm. Hmm."

Claudia stood for a moment, waiting for the woman to finish her call, but she didn't want to appear to be eavesdropping so she stepped back a few paces and looked politely away. But that felt totally awkward, so she decided to leave, slowly, so the woman could catch up to her if she wanted to, if it were a short call. Claudia waved a timid good-bye at her and pointed toward the exit. The woman nodded and smiled without pausing her conversation. "No, no—don't do that," she said and Claudia stopped her departure, before realizing the woman had been talking into her phone.

Claudia nodded and waved again and watched the woman sit back down into the chair she had just vacated, her gigantic purse now resting on her lap.

Claudia put the grocery bags into the trunk of her car and walked the cart the whole way back to the store, putting her cart back into the queue—pushing it all the way in snug. She gave one last look into the store and then walked back to her car. When it started up, the clock on the dash said 4:30 p.m. *Damn it.* It would really be pushing it to try to get all the way down to Sam's and back, especially since rush hour had begun. She'd have to pick up the wine at Rick and Dave's Lakeview Liquors now and hope Dan didn't have a cow about the price.

Chapter Eight

✦

Claudia carried a glass of wine and a chair over from her dining room. She clunked the chair down between Gail and Jill, who scooched theirs over to make room. Lindsay followed Claudia into the now overcrowded living room and settled onto the couch next to Mara.

"How's Tippy doing?" Lindsay took a sip of her wine, eyeing Mara over her glass.

She's like an attorney, Claudia thought, asking a question she already knows the answer to.

"Just great." Mara smiled her wide grin. "He's back to his old self. He's gained back almost all his weight."

Lindsay sank more deeply into the couch, a look of satisfaction on her face as she took another sip of her wine. "Does anyone," Lindsay said, still swallowing, "have any doubts about what we've done?"

"It just can't be this simple," Gail said, "wishing for something you want, chanting about it, throwing a few herbs into a bucket or lighting a candle and—voilà, magic."

"Well, it's not just throwing a few herbs into a bucket." Lindsay frowned at her. "You have to use your energy, focus your energy onto your wish, into the herbs. I think that's the hardest part, the concentrating. When I used to meditate at home, I always felt so scattered when I tried to focus my mind. Most of the time, I found myself thinking about everything else except what I wanted to be thinking about. I think that's why this works in a group; we help each other focus and concentrate."

Lindsay meditated? I never knew that. Huh. Claudia marveled at
Lindsay, always so fearless in her willingness to try everything, the
way she dove into her causes and trends with voracious abandon.
It was admirable—even if she did end up abandoning most of her
new things before too long. In fact, it was too bad Lindsay had quit
meditating, because if anyone could use some focus, it was Lindsay. Then again, who was she to talk. If anyone could use more Zen
moments, it was Claudia.

"I've always been curious about stuff like meditation," Claudia
said. "The supernatural, the metaphysical, all that New Age thought.
The thing I never realized until I started reading this book we got is
that all the things I thought were cool, that held some truth in
them—ESP, numerology . . . astrology, herbology. What I didn't
know is that all these things, these *'ologies,* are actually part of one
ancient religion. I mean, I think it's really neat that they are, but on
the other hand I think the fact that witchcraft *is* a religion makes
me . . . I don't know, uncomfortable, I guess. I mean, I don't think
I could ever publicly call myself a witch, or even a Wiccan. It's just
too, I don't know," she waved her hand in circles at the end of her
outstretched arm, "too, out there."

There were nods of agreement around the room.

"Everyone just thinks witchcraft is satanic," Mara said, "but they
have no idea. It's so totally *not* that. There's no devil in Wicca at all.
And if you were to call yourself a witch, people would either think
you were nuts or a devil-worshipper—and they'd lock up their pets
and small children." She sank back into the couch and crossed her
arms over her chest, shaking her head.

"Maybe . . ." Lindsay paused and looked up for a long moment,
then made her *getting an idea* face. She brought her eyes back down
to the group. "Maybe we could just call what we're doing 'wishing.'
It's obvious we don't want to be a witch club, but I don't think
we're just a book club anymore, either. Maybe we could be a 'wish
club.' Then we wouldn't have to get all caught up in the religion
thing *or* the witchcraft thing." Lindsay nodded her head in agreement with herself.

"We *should* just call it 'wishing.'" Even though Lindsay was still sitting on the couch, she started doing her little hopping thing, bouncing up and down in the cushions. "That *is* what it is. And we've had such huge success I certainly don't want to have to stop—and this way we won't have to worry about what we tell other people, or about reading all these witchcraft books or consecrating circles and all that other stuff. If we could, like . . . say, after we're done with our book discussions . . . make *wishes* for people. If we happen to use some herbs or a candle or some scented oil, well then, that's just our New Age way of focusing our energy. It'll just be our way of pulling it together."

Lindsay was bouncing so hard on the couch now, that Claudia thought it a wonder she hadn't catapulted Mara to the other side of the room.

"Oh come on, this is perfect." Lindsay was in her groove now. "This is it. It may sound a little weird, maybe, but it certainly isn't terribly 'out there,' and it isn't going to get us run out of town or hung by a rope in the town square."

"I think it's a great idea!" Mara was nodding her head in agreement, or maybe it was just an aftershock from the vibrating couch.

Gail was nodding her head too, although more slowly. Even Jill seemed to be considering Lindsay's idea.

Wishing. Hmm. Claudia liked the idea of *wishing* much better. Truly, what could be the harm in making a few wishes and burning some candles?

"Besides," Mara said, "who doesn't have a million things they want to wish for?"

"Of course," Lindsay said. "See? We can make this work. We can still do this thing—we'll just do it our way."

They all started talking at once, as though a huge underlying tension had been broken. Their beloved Book Club wasn't going to turn into some freaky coven. They were even still going to read books. Regular books. And then afterward they were going to make wishes. *Wishes.* Even the word had a simple, uplifting quality to it. Childlike and innocent. Wishes.

Everyone seemed happy. They were all talking and drinking their wine, discussing all the things they were going to wish for.

As Claudia listened to the discussion, she felt a lingering uneasiness. There was something she didn't like about it, even though she couldn't put her finger on it. Something about all of it that still gave her pause. Could it be that it was just semantics? Weren't they really talking about practicing witchcraft without *calling* it practicing witchcraft?

"I've got a million things I'd like to wish for." Mara's face was flush with excitement.

Claudia swallowed a large gulp of wine and said out loud, to no one in particular, "Well, you know what they say about being careful what you wish for." She was trying to be funny, but no one had laughed. It seemed her comment had gone unheard above the din.

$\mathcal{A}$ little black cauldron full of wishes hovered above Mara's head, the hopeful paper scraps bouncing up and down like popcorn every time she shook it. The women had decided the most democratic way of choosing the wishes was for everyone to write one down on a piece of paper and then draw them out of a bowl. Mara had been given the honor of drawing them out. Claudia had been given the honor of choosing the bowl and she'd picked her cauldron-like potpourri cooker. She enjoyed the irony.

Mara raised the bowl up over her head, closed her eyes tight, then reached her hand in, and pulled the first one out. "Okay, here we go." She unfolded the small slip and looked around the room, trying to heighten the anticipation as if she were an announcer at the Academy Awards. "It says . . . 'I want to have a baby.' It's Claudia's wish."

The women gushed out an "aww" in unison.

"Oh Claudia, that's wonderful, honey," Gail said. "Kids are great. Have you been trying?"

"Yeah, we have. A year or so—it hasn't been . . ." She blinked and looked up, on the verge of tears.

"Well, don't worry about what hasn't been, my dear," Lindsay came to her rescue. "Start worrying about how to decorate the nursery, because we are going to make this happen for you."

Mara consulted Claudia's copy of *The Modern Witches' Grimoire.* Its celestial cover design was a throwback to another era, something from a 1950s textbook, and it gave the impression that any witches pictured on the inside would, along with the pointy hat, be wearing a frilly apron and holding a tray of fresh-baked muffins.

For a fertility spell, *The Modern Witches' Grimoire* suggested a green candle, a handful of dirt, and some sage leaves. Gail was put in charge of procuring the dirt, which meant she had to walk down three flights of stairs and dig under the snow in the front yard, using one of Claudia's serving spoons, because Claudia didn't own a shovel. She dumped several spoonfuls of dirt into a bowl and when she got back inside, Gail told them that a man out walking his dog had asked her, as he passed, if she'd gotten his ex-wife's recipe for soup.

Jill's effort to find a green candle in the drawer of the dining room's built-in hutch was much less farcical. Mara and Lindsay stayed on the couch and consulted their books to write the chant and work out how to do the spell. And Claudia went to find the sage.

In the kitchen, she opened the door to her spice cabinet and was assaulted by a cacophony of smells. *What had she been thinking?* Her nerves were raw, and for a minute she'd thought she was going to burst into tears back there. She had never told anyone that she and Dan were trying to have a baby—not even Lindsay or Gail— and now she'd just spilled to the whole room. Sure, they were all her friends, but suddenly she felt so vulnerable. *We don't have to be naked when we chant, do we?*

The red-topped McCormick spice bottles kept falling over inside the overcrowded cabinet and a few bounced down onto the counter as she searched for the sage. Claudia hurried to stand them back up, stuff them back in. They kept falling over. Another one fell out. She was all thumbs. *Good grief.*

She should just run back into the living room and call it off. *Just kidding. Never mind. Let's forget this whole thing.* Maybe the toppling spices were a sign.

Where was the sage? Maybe she didn't have any. Her stomach fell, and Claudia was struck at how much that thought had scared her, way more than going through with casting the spell did.

She moved a tall canister of sea salt. Aha! The sage. She put the chili powder and garlic salt back on their shelf. And they stayed.

From their circle, Claudia stepped into the center and sprinkled dirt around the softly glowing green candle. Then she shook some of the dried sage leaves on top of the dirt. She stepped back into her place and they rejoined hands, beginning their chant.

> *Oh Great Goddess hear our plea,*
> *Bless our Claudia with a baby.*
> *No more waiting, no more strife,*
> *Bring to her a brand new life.*

They finished like they always did, with their clasped hands raised up over their heads, looking like the scalloped edges of a big-top tent at the circus.

"Well, thanks everyone," Claudia said.

"No problem, sweetie," Mara said. "But if it's a girl, you have to name her after us—or at least me." Mara giggled and thrust out her chin before taking a sip of her wine.

"Okay," Lindsay asked. "Who's next?" She nodded to Mara, who quickly, guiltily put her wineglass back on the coffee table and picked up the bowl, getting back to duty.

Mara shook the bowl again, tossing the paper wishes up and down. She raised her eyebrows up and down in synchronization with her tosses, then held the bowl up over her head, closed her eyes, reached in, and plucked one out.

"Okay, here we go . . ." She unfolded the little slip in her hand and her face exploded. "Oh my. Oh! I've picked my own. I've picked out my wish."

"Well, are you going to share it with us?" Gail asked.

"Oh. Ha." Mara's face turned red. "I guess that would help the process. Of course. It says, 'I would like more abundance in my life.'" She looked up at them with a wicked grin on her face. "In other words, ladies, I'd like to win the lottery!"

And with that the wish-making process began to fall into a routine. Mara looked for the spell they needed, or a similar one, in the grimoire, and then the others were sent off on a scavenger hunt to find the necessary supplies and ingredients. Meanwhile, Lindsay and Mara sat on the couch and wrote the chant, reworking what the books said—to make it more *wishy*.

When everyone returned to the living room, wish-making supplies in hand, they took their places in the circle, went over the chant, and then joined their hands together again. They began their wish for Mara.

> *Oh Great Goddess hear our prayer,*
> *Bring great abundance to our Mara.*
> *May abundance grow for her and Henry,*
> *It is our will so mote it be.*

"The next meeting at my house will be held in the ballroom," Mara laughed, holding her wineglass up to them in a toast. They all toasted back, before taking sips of their own.

They wished for Lindsay, who wanted to lose weight and obtain the perfect body. Her wish required an orange candle, rosemary, and a waning moon—the one ingredient they couldn't control, but since they were just *wishing*, they figured it wouldn't matter. Besides, Lindsay said she thought it actually was a waning moon anyway.

They wished for Gail, who wanted some time for herself, to help her feel as if she still had a life of her own. Her wish called for one brown and one white candle, and some lavender—which Claudia didn't have, so they substituted some lavender massage oil they found in the bathroom.

One wish remained in the cauldron.

"Well, I don't think I need to close my eyes for this one." Mara reached in and pulled it out. She unfolded it in the same melodramatic way she'd done with the others. Her face screwed up, puzzled. She flipped it over. Twice. "It's blank."

Everyone's eyes went to Jill. "I just couldn't think of anything I wanted to wish for."

"Not one single thing?" Mara asked.

"No, not really. I guess I never realized how contented I am."

There was a long pause.

"Well maybe," Lindsay said, "if you can't think of anything for yourself—you could wish for someone else. You know, like food for the hungry or peace on earth."

"I think before we start asking our little group of novice wishers here to change the world," Gail said, "we need to find out exactly what it is our girl Jill over here is doing to achieve such contentedness."

"*I'll have what she's having,*" Mara giggled.

Jill allowed one corner of her voluptuous lips to curl up.

In all the years she'd known Jill, Claudia had always suspected that underneath her calm, poised, and beautiful exterior, something was missing, as if a smooth veneer had been glued over chipped porcelain. Jill may try to ooze an aura of calm contentedness, but a sadness was hinted at sometimes—in the way she tilted her head, the lilt of her voice. Claudia was certain it indicated a hidden cavern full of wishes unspoken.

Claudia decided to call her on it. "I'm not buying it. I think you're afraid."

Jill turned her ice-blue eyes to Claudia. "Afraid?"

"Yeah." Claudia tried not to be intimidated. "I think you're afraid to admit to us what it is you really want."

"I'm not afraid of anything." Jill flipped her wrist at Claudia in dismissal. "I can't think of anything that I want right now, that's all."

Gail narrowed her eyes at Jill. "You know . . . I don't think I'm buying this either."

"Not one single thing?" Mara appeared to be having a hard time wrapping her mind around the idea of not wanting for anything.

"There's got to be something," Gail said, "that if you had it—it would make you *more* content."

Jill gave her a look. *Et tu, Brute?*

"If I can admit to everyone that I haven't been able to conceive a baby—and Lindsay can admit she's always wanted a size-six butt—then the least you can do is throw us a bone."

Lindsay gave Claudia a look, which caused a flicker of a smile to pass across Jill's face. Jill crossed her arms over her chest, then shook her head, rolling her eyes. "All right. I suppose I can come up with something." She pushed her lips out, thinking, eyes tilted up. "I guess I wouldn't mind dating someone normal for once."

"Aha."

"I knew it."

"There had to be something."

"Define normal," Gail said, at the same time Claudia asked, "Was that so hard?"

Claudia meant the question to be a flip, *See, wasn't that easy?* but somehow it had come out wrong. She and Jill exchanged a look, which silently acknowledged just how hard it was to confess what it was you really wished for.

"I keep finding these real losers." Jill pulled her eyes from Claudia and turned them back to the group. "I would just like to meet a guy who doesn't want to get married on the second date, doesn't expect me to be his mother and who doesn't have any . . . any weird traits—like a toe fetish or a phobia that appears suddenly in the middle of a date."

"Oh no, no, nooo." Lindsay waved her hands back and forth, as if she were sweeping Jill's silly idea away. "I don't think so. We are not going to waste the energies of this group finding a guy for you that's just plain old *normal*. Come on. We are going to attract for you the hottest, most gorgeous, sexiest man we can find. Huh? What do you think?" Lindsay nodded her head at all of them in turn. "Ladies? Am I right?"

They all laughed and began nodding and smiling, too. Even Jill allowed herself a rare full-out grin.

A circle of dried rose petals (Gail picked them out of an old bag of potpourri) surrounded a pink candle on the coffee table. Several strands of Jill's long black hair were intertwined with the petals. With everything and everyone in place, they began their chant to find Jill her perfect man.

> *Oh Great Goddess grant our request,*
> *Help our Jill to end her quest.*
> *Attract to her an amazing guy—gorgeous, smart, sexy and fun*
> *Please make sure to send "the one."*
> *Oh Great Goddess hear our plea,*
> *It is our will, so mote it be.*

They brought their hands down to their sides. Jill put hers on her hips. "Well, I guess we'll see what happens."

Five multicolored candles now burned on Claudia's coffee table, flickering at various heights. The little black cauldron sat empty next to them.

"Shit." Gail was looking at her watch. "How did it get to be midnight?"

"Midnight?" Lindsay asked.

"Damn, I gotta go," Mara said.

"Me too." Lindsay took one last sip of her wine, bending over with the glass still at her lips before she set it on the table.

With a bustle of coats and scarves and gloves and kisses they were gone, swirling out the door into the night like water draining from a tub after a bubble bath. Claudia felt like a toy forgotten in the suds as she closed the door behind them.

Her living room was a disaster: bags of potpourri and spice bottles sat on the floor; food and extra candles and holders cluttered both end tables. The coffee table was covered with candles and wineglasses, herbs, spices, and dirt. *What a mess.* Of course they'd offered to help clean up, but as much as she would have appreciated some help, she'd sent them on their way.

The mantel clock said 12:04. *Where was Dan?* He had said he was going to work late tonight—but midnight? *He's probably been at the Tap since six.* She started to clean up, carrying as many wine-glasses as she could into the kitchen. When she returned to the living room she plopped onto the couch, suddenly exhausted.

Claudia frowned at the burning candles. She had to get up for school in the morning, but she probably should wait for the candles to burn out. How long would that take? *I could just go to bed. They'll be fine. They'll burn out soon enough.*

Claudia had seen too many Smokey Bear public-service announcements as a child to just leave them unattended. *Why not just blow them out? Who would know the difference?* Claudia leaned forward. The flames on the candles all bent in unison in response to the breeze her movement created. The green candle at the far end of the table contained a deep pool of wax. Her candle. It was almost done.

She leaned back on the couch and watched their gentle flickering. Gradually her gaze blurred, smearing the small flames into a single patch of light. She sat and listened to the clock tick, a lonely sound, like so many tiny popping bubbles.

Chapter Nine

When Claudia woke up on the couch, Dan was bending over, inhaling a deep breath above the candles.

"No!" Claudia was immediately on her feet.

"What the—?" He tottered backward, startled. "I was just trying to—It's not like I was gonna pee on them."

"I know. I know. It's just. I'm sorry. It's okay. I was watching them. I—just leave them."

Claudia walked around the table, checking the candles, making sure none of them had been unnaturally snuffed out. Two of them had burned out already—the gold and the green one. Three were still weakly flickering. She came up to Dan and put her arms around his neck. He smelled like the Tap: cigarettes, grease, and formaldehyde—the aftermath of plenty of beer.

He kissed her on her forehead, then grabbed her more tightly, his hands dropping down onto her butt. His mouth started groping for hers.

Claudia turned her head away, smiling. "You're funny. You need to go straight to bed."

"And you need to come with me." He grabbed at her waist again.

"Dan. Knock it off." Claudia dropped her arms from his neck and held her palms against his chest. "Are you nuts? It's the middle of the night."

He made his pouty little-boy face—the one she found hard to resist.

"You started it. Coming up and throwing yourself all over me— all the candlelight and the wine." He removed a hand from her waist and gestured at the coffee table, then looked down at it, but now it seemed he was seeing it for the first time. He cocked his head back up at his wife, his face saying, *this Book Club shit keeps getting weirder and weirder.*

"I didn't *start* anything," Claudia said. "I was just greeting my husband after a hard day at the *office.*" She folded her arms across her chest, grinning.

"Why, I ought to—" He lunged for her, laughing, grabbing her at the thighs and throwing her over his shoulder.

"Dan! Put me down! Stop it this minute—I mean it! You're going to drop me!"

But he held her steady, ignoring her protests, and hauled her off to the bedroom, where he, albeit a little clumsily, transformed her protests into moans.

Ancient blinds covered the window opposite Claudia's bed. They had wide metal slats that two yellowed strips of canvas held together. Only tiny slits of light crept through in the morning because the buildings were so close together. Claudia liked to play a little game each day. She liked to guess if it was cloudy or sunny based on how much light was shining through. It wasn't so easy. When she guessed right, she thought it was a sign it would be a good day. This morning, she was betting on sunny.

She reached for the thermometer and stuck it in her mouth. What a Book Club meeting last night. All those wishes they made. She replayed the night's events, up to and including Dan's arrival—both of them. He was still passed out next to her. She put the thermometer back on her nightstand, then swung her legs onto the floor, reached for the graph paper, and put a dot on February third at 98.9°.

Claudia was dressed and in the kitchen drinking coffee when she heard Dan get up and go into the bathroom. His pee hit the water forcefully and she listened until she heard the last few splashes followed by the flush. She didn't hear the toilet seat drop down and she hoped today wouldn't be a bickering day, a distinct possibility since they'd both been up so late the previous night.

Today she'd tried to achieve a put-together look by wearing a long-skirted suit, an attempt to counteract feeling exhausted and a little hung over. Dan, in contrast, walked into the kitchen still half asleep. His bathrobe was tied crookedly around him, with one cuff of his pajamas hanging a full foot higher up his calf than the other, stuck on a ruff of hair on his leg.

"You look nice." He reached around her into the cabinet for a mug. "Thanks for making coffee."

"Don't mention it." She loved the way he smelled in the morning, a smell that was just all him, no perfumed deodorants or shampoo or aftershave, just the androgenic smell of slept-in pajamas and unwashed hair. Although this morning, she could have done without the formaldehyde reek of yesterday's beer.

"I'm getting pretty suspicious of your Book Club, Claude." He grinned at her sleepily. "All these late hours and burning candles and expensive books on the occult." He leaned his back against the sink and took a sip of his coffee.

"Oh, you know—" Claudia stopped, then started again. "Lindsay's kind of started this thing—this wishing thing? Well, it's not just her . . . I mean everyone is going along . . ."

Dan just looked at her.

"Where we wish for things? We say a chant and light a candle and it seems like . . . Well, before we were able to make some things happen." Claudia tucked her hair behind her ear and pushed her glasses up her nose.

"You wish for things?"

"Yeah. Like once we made a wish for Tippy."

"Tippy?"

"Mara's cat."

Dan took a long drink of coffee and brought the cup back down, his eyes never leaving Claudia. He waited a moment, then took another sip.

"We made one wish to stop the rain, and I think we may have done it. We made a whole bunch of wishes last night."

"It wasn't raining last night."

"No, we make wishes for other things, too." He wasn't getting it. "It's mostly all Lindsay's idea. I mean, you know how she is."

Dan nodded, slowly. "Is this like that feng shui thing?"

Lindsay had hired a feng shui specialist for their apartment when they'd first moved in, in spite of their protests. "It's my treat," she'd said. "My housewarming present to you." Dan hadn't been there for the specialist's assessment, but the paper lantern she'd hung inside the front door had hit him in the head every day for a week, until he finally had insisted they take it down. No terrible twists of fate had befallen them after that, so when he found the goldfish they were supposed to keep on the coffee table floating dead in its bowl, he was able to persuade Claudia they could get rid of that, too.

"So what, exactly, is it? This idea of Lindsay's?" he asked.

"It's Wish Club." Claudia paused. "Where we sort of pool our energy together and wish for things. It sounds really weird, I know, but it actually seems to be working."

Dan took another sip of coffee and didn't say anything.

"I wished for us to have a baby."

Now Dan smiled at her, his demeanor softening. He nodded. "I see. So this is just more of Lindsay's New Age foolishness. And now her new thing is to get everyone together to wish for cats and babies?"

"Umm, yeah, something like that."

"Well. Okay. As long as it doesn't involve anymore dead gold-fish."

Claudia laughed, as if to say, *Dead goldfish! Ha ha!* But she really wasn't completely sure that it wouldn't. She sidled up close to him to empty her coffee mug in the sink. "I think I'd better get going or I'm gonna be late."

"I'll make you late." He shot her a wicked grin.

"Are you kidding?" She walked away as if she'd been at the corral breaking horses all day. "After last night?" Claudia's mock cowboy gait slowed and her walk returned to normal as she hit the end of the hall and approached the coffee table in the living room.

Claudia groaned. "What a mess."

Dan came up behind her with his coffee mug in his hand. "Don't worry about it. I can clean up after your *Wish Club*. Say, maybe next time you ladies could wish for a housekeeper."

He was smiling, laughing at his joke, as he bent over to clear a small patch of space on the table to set his mug down.

God, I love him, she thought. The way his wavy brown hair was always a little too long. The way the dimples creased more deeply around his mouth when he was genuinely happy. When he stood back up, Claudia reached in and gave him a hug.

Dan wrapped his arms around her, squeezing her tight before loosening his grip a little and rubbing a hand over the small of her back. They started a gentle sway back and forth, moving together, dancing with no music, the way they always used to.

"It's been a while," she said.

"Hmm?"

Claudia regretted pulling his thoughts back from wherever they'd been. "It's been a while, since we danced like this—with no music. You know, before we realized we were doing it."

Dan bent his head down, nuzzled his face into her hair. "Mmm. Hmm."

They danced for another moment before Dan leaned back, one hand still on her waist, the other reaching up to stroke her hair, brushing it with his fingertips off to one side of her face. "You're all the music I need."

"Awww." Claudia closed her eyes and tilted her head down. "I love you."

"I love you, too." He pulled her close again.

Claudia pulled out of the hug and gave him a teasing smile. "Well, you've made me late now anyway."

She looked back down at the disaster-strewn coffee table.

"Well, get going then." He gave her a quick kiss. "And don't worry about this. I've got it covered."

Claudia put on her coat with a final glance down at the table, at the wineglasses and candles, the little black bowl. "Thanks, hon."

"No pro-blem-o."

Claudia hurried down the three flights of stairs and stepped out of her building into the day. She looked up at the asphalt-gray sky and wondered if today it would rain or snow.

Claudia rubbed her temples as she walked into the cafeteria, still feeling the bleary after-effects of the Book Club meeting. Of all the days to pull lunchroom duty. She'd groaned when she'd seen the reminder in her mailbox earlier in the morning. At least she was sharing the chore with Henry O'Connor, Mara's husband. On the off chance they would actually get a moment to speak to each other, he could always make her laugh.

The cafeteria at the Arthur G. Strawn Academy of Arts and Sciences was unlike any school cafeteria Claudia had ever eaten in when she was a student, and it wasn't just the menu selection—her high school cafeteria had never served pesto—but the sanitized newness of it all. The seating consisted of booths along the walls and tables and chairs in the center of the room. It looked like a restaurant. Her old cafeteria had all-in-one picnic-style benches, which were all the same, in that they'd been covered with graffiti and smelled faintly of sour milk.

In Claudia's high school lunchroom, the popular girls had sat at the table in the corner by the window, across from the table of popular boys, and at Strawn the popular girls sat at the table by the door. On the days she had lunchroom duty, she could watch the complex inner workings of the popular girls' clique, the way they subjectively dismissed and added to their circle of friends, allowing a "guest" the occasional honor of a seat at their table of eight. Invariably, when Claudia returned to lunchroom duty a few weeks later, that "guest" would either be back at her old table or, worse, shunned by her old friends for desertion and sitting at the table with the leftovers—the misfits who either had been cast off by old friends too, or had never fit in anywhere in the first place.

When Claudia's family had moved during the second semester of her freshman year of high school, the only place she'd been allowed to sit that first day was at the leftover table. She remembered walking with her tray through the cafeteria looking for a seat. She'd gotten the lunch special—some sort of scary meatloaf with potatoes and gravy—not knowing that no one ever got the lunch special, but she'd felt pressured into making a quick choice by the bored woman behind the lunch counter and the kids behind her in line. She was embarrassed by her meatloaf as she walked past the tables, noticing all the pizza slices and grilled cheese sandwiches. No one invited her to sit down. She knew they couldn't risk lowering their social standing by letting her sit at their table, because she was an unknown quantity. They couldn't be sure. She wasn't wearing terribly fashionable or expensive clothing, and she *had* gotten the meatloaf.

The leftover table was the only table with seats, where no one threw a hand across an empty space and said, "Sorry, that's saved." It was understood when the girls looked up at her from the other tables; she could see it in their eyes—some of their eyes, anyway—that they did feel sorry for her and wanted to help, but they just couldn't take the chance. So Claudia took her seat with the leftovers. She drank her Coke and moved her mashed potatoes around her meatloaf with her fork.

Then Molly Bonner had walked over from the popular table and introduced herself. Claudia couldn't believe her luck. She could tell from her hair and clothes and confidant demeanor that Molly was, quite possibly, the most popular girl in the freshman class; she had that certain queen-bee-like aura about her. Molly smiled and welcomed Claudia to the school and said if there was ever anything Claudia needed she should just ask her, or one of her friends, and she gestured to her table. Most of the girls at Molly's table had turned around to watch them.

Claudia stuttered out a thank you.

"Where are you from, Claudia?" Molly asked, and Claudia told her Addison. Immediately Claudia knew it would have been better if she'd lied, made up a small town or picked someplace out of state, rather than name the working-class western suburb of Addison. Molly closed her lips, flattening her smile into a grimace.

"And where do you live now?" Molly asked, and when Claudia told her Forest Hills, Molly's demeanor immediately became frosty.

"I'm from Forest *Woods*." Molly eyed Claudia's tray. "Tell me," she paused, "do they eat a lot of meatloaf in Addison?"

Claudia swallowed hard. "No, not really."

"Do you *like* meatloaf?"

"No, not really." Claudia knew she was doomed.

"Then why did you get the meatloaf if you don't like it? That doesn't seem very smart." She paused. "Or are you lying to me?" Molly's demeanor had quickly changed from frosty to mean.

"You wouldn't lie to me, would you? I think maybe you really like meatloaf."

Molly glanced over to her table; her friends were smiling at her in encouragement. A large portion of the lunchroom was paying attention to them by now. Claudia glanced up and met the eyes of her new classmates. They looked hungry for carnage.

"I think you need to eat your meatloaf," Molly said, "just like you did back home in Addison."

Claudia looked down at her cold plate. The gray meat looked as menacing as Molly's green eyes. "I guess I'm just not very hungry."

"Oh, I think you are. I think you'd better eat your meatloaf, Cloddia."

And so Claudia's new nickname was born, accompanied by a rumble of laughter from her peers, from which the word *Cloddia* could be heard repeated several times.

"You better eat your meatloaf, or no one here is going to be your friend."

Claudia looked down at her plate. She could sense the room holding its breath, waiting to see if she might actually try it.

"I'm not hungry." Claudia said it with more strength than she felt. There came a point on the downward spiral where you had nothing more left to lose.

"I think you are. I think you need to eat your meatloaf like you did in Addison." Molly smiled and looked over at her table of friends again. "If you don't eat your meatloaf, you won't have any friends. You won't have a single friend at this school."

Claudia couldn't imagine that eating her meatloaf would help her in any way. With more hostility this time, while simultaneously managing to stare down Molly Bonner, she said, "I'm not hungry."

The standoff had captured the attention of the entire room and, to Claudia, there seemed to be no escape. She looked down at her plate, then up at Molly again, this time with calm defiance. "Maybe you're the one who isn't very smart, because I've had to tell you I'm not hungry three times."

A silent yet palpable gasp permeated the room.

Claudia held Molly's gaze. Clearly, this was not the response Molly had been expecting. She'd obviously been hoping for tears or pleas for mercy, or maybe even to see someone sample the meatloaf and gravy for the first time in the history of Forest Woods High School.

Something along those lines would have been the response Claudia would have normally expected from herself as well. Instead she continued down her newfound course. "So let me see if I've got this straight. If I eat this crap, then I can have a bitch like you for a friend. Hmm. What's behind door number two—"

"I'll be your friend," she heard a girl's voice say. It had come from the next table over.

The voice had belonged to Lindsay Tate.

Watching the social dramas unfold in the Strawn Academy cafeteria brought Claudia back to her adolescence every time, like a lesson in social hindsight. The students interacted in their assigned hierarchies and she wondered which friendships would last. It wasn't predictable.

People sometimes decided you would be their friend, and it was as though you weren't given any choice in the matter. Lindsay had chosen her that day because of the way Claudia had stood up to Molly Bonner. In both situations, Claudia felt her choice had been made for her. It hadn't been a conscious decision to stand up to Molly. It had just happened.

And as far as Lindsay's overture of friendship went, Claudia saw no choice there either. She saw no other possibility in a lunchroom full of people, everyone waiting to see if the two of them would unite to deflate Molly Bonner. And so, for nearly twenty years, Lindsay Tate-McDermott had been Claudia's friend.

Later, other friends, like Gail, would comment on how odd their pairing was, what improbable friends Claudia and Lindsay seemed. Unlike most friendships between women, theirs was never warm and girly, based on a mutual affection for each other. It was a friendship that merely persevered. But, like an arranged marriage in which the man and woman eventually fall in love and become happy growing old together, time gradually softened the hard edges of their friendship. Shared experience formed a common bond. They were friends now, real friends, but occasionally Claudia could sense a cold undertow, just below the surface—that sometimes made its presence known with a vicious comment or an angry look. Claudia had never thought much about it until recently, not until she watched the trickle-down economics of social status play out in the high-school cafeteria at Strawn, seeing it through her thirty-three-year-old eyes.

At Strawn the cliques were divided along strictly fiscal lines, with the most popular girls belonging to either old money or really big-name new-money families. Fame also helped, and the scions of famous actors or sports stars could be accepted.

It had been the same at Forest Woods High School but it hadn't been quite so apparent to Claudia at the time. Everyone had had more money than her family did, and she had known nothing about society and its striations; she had only known she fell at the bottom.

She had learned that Lindsay Tate was the granddaughter of one of the heirs to Tate Drugs and that her family was extremely wealthy—wealthier than Molly Bonner's family and most of the families of the girls who sat at the popular table. But Lindsay had cultivated her own clique, eschewing Molly's kind of gumball popularity—sweet on the outside, hollow on the inside, with a flavor that didn't last for very long.

At that time, Claudia had thought Lindsay had decided to stand apart, refusing to fit into the place society had carved out for her—her own little form of rebellion, a striking out against her birthright—and that Lindsay's independence had garnered her her own following. It wasn't until much later, when they were grown and living in the city, that a different truth had occurred to Claudia: that maybe it hadn't been Lindsay who'd done the eschewing after all.

The adult Lindsay seemed so hungry to be accepted by society— and not just by the other rich people who lived around her, but by *real society*. The big names, with mentions on the society page. Ann Gerber's column, the Women's Foundation annual spring fashion show. All of it. Claudia watched Lindsay visibly wince whenever someone mentioned being asked to do that fashion show—the brass ring, an invitation Lindsay had yet to receive.

Her independent clique in high school had seemed to be Lindsay's way of making the best of her situation, and Claudia's angry "I'm not hungry" in the cafeteria that day was what had probably made Lindsay decide Claudia would be an asset to her little group. But it had been so out of character for Claudia to behave that way and she was later able to sense Lindsay's frustration with her every time she refused to stand up for herself.

A spit-wad fight was breaking out at Strawn's popular boys' table. Claudia had been watching it brew for several minutes now, waiting for it to die down. It wouldn't. She scanned the room for Henry, but he was over on the other side of the room with the second-graders, breaking up an argument—probably over a poorly traded Twinkie.

The boys at the popular table were now starting to target other tables, namely the popular girls' table and the leftovers, who looked ready to fight back. Claudia started walking over and she could see the boys nudging and elbowing each other. She hoped that just walking by the tables would be enough.

One of the boys at the popular boys' table, with his back to her, was readying a spit wad in his straw. The boy directly across from him was talking to him, leaning in, without taking his eyes from Claudia, obviously telling him she was on her way. The boy fired the spit wad through the straw anyway—landing it on a backpack at the leftover table.

"Hey," Claudia said to him. "I think you need to st—"

A spit wad fired from the leftovers hit Claudia squarely in the forehead. Laughter erupted at both tables as Claudia wiped it away.

"Just knock it off," she said as she walked away, even though the fight had already ended. A common enemy was one way to unite would-be rivals.

Chapter Ten

The 10 duck was fighting back. The fabric was just so cumbersome and heavy. Not what she was used to, and Jill was starting to lose patience. This canvas was going to be the centerpiece, the pièce de résistance of her show. And she wanted to make it huge—literally. She'd never built a canvas this large before, and she barely had room for it on the floor of her studio. All the furniture in the room was pushed up against the walls. When the canvas was finished, Jill would have to hang it on the back wall in order to paint it.

Kneeling over the canvas, Jill gave the 10 duck one more perfunctory tug before sinking back and sitting cross-legged on the floor, the stretching pliers in her hand hanging over her thigh, still holding the edge of the heavy canvas in its grip.

She really needed someone to help her with this. Stretching a canvas this size wasn't a job for just one person, even though Jill would have liked it to be. *I should just ask someone on the floor to help me.* It would only take a few minutes—just until she could get a few main anchor points stapled in. Why was it so hard for her to ask for help? She looked down at the rumpled 10 duck. If she kept at it like this, it was going to look like a first-grader had built it. Jill let go of the pliers and stood up.

In the hall outside her studio, most of the other doors were closed. It was a luxury, she knew, for her to be here during the day. Most everyone in the building had a day job—except the husband and wife sculptors who shared the big studio on the first floor. They made their living with their art. Jill made her living with her art, too. She just *lived* off her trust fund. A luxury. She half-heartedly knocked on a few doors with a preconceived notion of futility, not expecting any answers.

Jill went down the back stairs to the first floor, worrying now that she might not find anyone around. She really wanted to get the canvas stretched and primed today so she could start working on it. Something this size was going to take some time to complete. It was only the first week in February and her show wasn't opening until the third week in March, springtime, which seemed such a long way off—but in reality it was not much more than six weeks.

Greta, the owner of the Eleventh House Gallery, which represented Jill, never agreed to a show unless her artists already had a fair amount of pieces ready, which Jill did, but they both wanted more. If she could pull it off, she knew Greta would let her use the entire floor. Greta was generous that way. Jill envisioned the giant canvas hanging on the back wall of the gallery, imposing, stunning, anchoring the rest of the pieces in the show, a sun around which they could orbit.

It was cold in the hallway of the first-floor studios, a chill breeze gliding through. When Jill turned the corner, she saw boxes stacked up outside a doorway in the front hall, in front of the studio directly below hers. Someone was finally moving into 1W. Great. She'd found signs of life, but what life form would be willing to help her stretch canvas on its own moving day?

The front door was being held open with the cinder block they usually kept just inside of it for that purpose. A tall stack of boxes rounded the corner and came through the door, the stack held up by muscular forearms that attached to equally muscular biceps that attached to the profile of an amazing-looking man.

Wow. Jill stopped, frozen to her spot in the hallway. *Wow.*

"Hey." He greeted her as he went into the studio, the word breathy and clipped with exertion.

Dark black hair hung over his face in sweaty strands. Brown eyes; unbelievable face. Smooth muscular skin. Gorgeous.

Jill heard the boxes being set down inside with a gentle thud, then footsteps heading back toward her. Involuntarily, Jill licked her lips.

"That was it." He gave a quick glance in her direction before he went to close the front door, wiping the side of his face on a raised bicep as he passed. As he walked away, Jill couldn't help but admire his tall physique, the broad shoulders, the narrow waist. He bent over and picked up the cinder block and set it back down inside the door. Cute butt, too. The door-closer hissed as the door swung shut behind him, muffling the sound of the El running by outside.

"Well, I guess *this* is really it." He gestured at the stack of boxes outside the studio door, one hand on a hip. He looked up then and reached the other one out to her. "I'm Marc. Marc with a 'c.'"

He's so young. Mid-twenties at most. Gorgeous, though. And the way he moved, smooth and graceful, like a big cat. Sexy. He had a calm demeanor, so confident. It made him seem older. But now that she studied his face more closely, she noticed he had a little strip of beard down the center of his chin, a sort of bunny-wax for the face. *Okay, still a kid.*

"I'm Jill." She took his hand. "I'm right on top of you."

He held her hand in his grip for maybe a second longer than was necessary, his smile growing wider, revealing beautiful white teeth.

"I meant my studio is . . . up there." She pointed to the ceiling. "On—above yours."

"You know," he said, his eyes laughing, "I had a feeling I was going to like it here."

Lindsay worked out in her downstairs exercise room on the treadmill, race-walking to a 1980s hair band. She pumped her fists back and forth, the song "I Ran So Far Away" blaring over the rumble of the treadmill, upon which she ran exactly nowhere.

She felt great today, as if she could keep going forever. She punched up the speed with her index finger, increasing the pace a few tenths of a mile. She punched up the incline a half of a percentage, too.

It had only been two weeks since the last Book Club meeting, when she'd made her wish to lose weight, and she'd already lost six pounds. It was unbelievable. Three pounds a week! At this rate . . . Lindsay smiled at herself in the mirror.

Her whole life she had struggled with her weight. She had never been fat—not really. She was just never thin. *Pleasantly plump* was how one high-school boyfriend had put it. Ouch.

But now—and she hadn't been doing anything any differently, nothing she could think of anyway—now, with the power of Wish Club behind her, she was on track to be thin in a matter of months. Just months. Lindsay smiled at herself in the mirror again, reflexively bringing her right index finger up to touch her nose.

The signal. Lindsay laughed out loud. It had been years since she'd done that—used the signal. It had been years since she'd even thought of it. What a funny reflex. It was as though for a moment something outside herself had taken over—like channeling her inner child. Or maybe a muscle memory. The signal: an index finger touching the tip of the nose. To her clique of high school girlfriends it had meant something was cool. It had meant, *Isn't this great?* Or *Oh my God, he's so cute.* Or *I totally agree with this.*

Lindsay had tapped her finger on the tip of her nose and held it there when she had heard Claudia tell Molly Bonner, "I'm not hungry," in the Forest Woods High School cafeteria. The girls around her table had all brought their index fingers to their noses in agreement, their eyes locked together, wide with excitement, as they listened to the argument unfold. When Claudia had coolly stated, "If I eat this crap, then I can have a bitch like you for a friend," Lindsay had excitedly tapped her nose twice before announcing, "I'll be your friend."

Her treadmill flashed numbers at her in red, 37:34. The time was flying by; she was almost finished with her workout. Lindsay slowed the speed on the treadmill and its rumble lessened, as if she had turned the volume down. She wiped her face with the hand towel and scooched her headband up a bit higher on her forehead. She frowned at her reflection. *This headband is hideous—so retro—so eighties.* Struck by another memory, she brought her thumb and forefinger up to tug at her right ear. The other signal, the opposite of the nose tap. They used to tug their ears whenever they wanted to leave a bad party, or when they needed help with a situation, and every time Molly or one of her henchwomen walked by.

That was a long time ago—the day she and Claudia met. And to think they'd been friends all these years (Lindsay refused to do the math). Claudia had been so sweet, so innocent really. Even now she was sweet, but it was infuriating how she could still be such a wuss sometimes. It was like dealing with two different people.

After the showdown with Molly Bonner, the girls had slid closer together at their lunch table to make room for Claudia to sit down. As Claudia had walked over, Lindsay remembered thinking she was such a pretty girl, something that hadn't been apparent at first glance. Claudia was still the kind of pretty that took a while to notice. Sometimes Lindsay would make little hints about some makeup or maybe a change of wardrobe, but Claudia, to date, had never taken a single hint. In fact, her hairstyle hadn't changed since high school: long and straight, a nondescript shade of light brown. And those glasses!

Back then Claudia had taken a seat at the end of the table, across from Lindsay, as the rest of the lunchroom had settled down around them, the sound level ratcheting back up, returning to its usual boisterous hum.

"I'm Lindsay Tate."

"I'm Claudia—" and in what they'd learn was typical Claudia fashion, she'd hesitated before saying, "—Podzednik."

They had gone around the table introducing themselves.

"Thanks for the rescue," Claudia Podzednik had said, lowering her eyes. Her voice had grown soft, as if she were trying to show them she wasn't usually so controversial.

"Way to go, standing up to Molly like that," Lindsay said, beginning to wonder if maybe she'd been wrong about this girl.

And Claudia went all fumbly the way she did, stammering and shrugging—she probably dropped something, too. She pushed her glasses up her nose before saying, "I'm not usually so bitchy, but—"

Lindsay's eyes bored into her. Had she made a mistake? Who was *this* girl?

Somehow, Claudia must have sensed her consternation, because, with a nervous glance at Lindsay, she changed her tack. "But . . . but that girl. Molly? Fight fire with fire, huh?"

"You were great."

"Did you see the look on Molly's face?"

With a *welcome to our club* camaraderie, the girl next to Claudia congenially picked something off Claudia's shoulder while Lindsay watched.

"Am I perfect now?" Claudia quipped without missing a beat.

"Sassy," said one of the girls from the other side of the table.

Lindsay's gaze softened. Maybe Claudia wasn't exactly who she'd thought she was, but she had some spunk. "You'll do," she said.

"I brought this down for you." Lindsay's husband, James, walked through the open door of the exercise room, holding a wheat-grass shake in his hand. He turned the stereo off, silencing the New Wave music.

"Thank you, sweetie. Could you set it over there? I want to keep going for a few more minutes. I'm feeling really good today." Lindsay realized as she spoke that she didn't even have any shortness of breath.

He set the shake down on the window ledge and looked around the workout room. "One of these days, I'm going to get around to putting those up." He nodded at the stack of shelves in the far corner.

"You should have just bought a free-standing unit." Lindsay's fists continued to pump back and forth.

James had bought adjustable shelves that fastened to the wall with metal runners. It was going to be a place for her to store her exercise books and videos and rest her yoga mat and ankle weights, and all the other forgotten by-products of her past fitness crazes.

He shrugged. "It seems like an easy project. I just haven't found the time."

"I don't know why," Lindsay was breathing a little harder, "you want to bother with it. You get so little free time as it is . . . you should relax when you get home . . . pay someone else to do that kind of stuff."

James nodded as if in agreement, but Lindsay was fairly certain he pictured himself walking around with a huge tool belt around his waist grunting like Tim Allen. That vision of her husband, with his thinning hair and paunchy belly, made her smile.

He walked over to inspect the pile of shelving supplies and stared at it for a while, in the male take-charge position. Hands on hips. Then he passed her, heading toward the weight bench. James's eyes popped when he saw the timer on her treadmill: it read 44:47. "How long were you planning on going at it?"

"I don't know—maybe forever. I just feel great today."

James gave her a look. *Don't overdo it.*

Lindsay ignored it. "I'm finally, finally starting to lose some weight."

"You look fabulous, just the way you are." He gave her a meaningful look in the mirror, then leaned over and peeked at her rear end.

"You're fresh."

He grinned, pleased.

"I think it's Wish Club," Lindsay said.

"Wish Club?"

"Well, actually, Wish Club is the same as Book Club, but we've started working together to make wishes, so now I'm starting to think of it more as Wish Club."

"Wish Club."

"We're using the energy of our group, the strength of women working together to empower our wishes and make things happen. I think it's why I'm losing weight now, when I could never do it before. I made a wish for it."

James looked skeptical.

"I can tell what you're thinking," Lindsay said. "You're thinking it's just a coincidence."

"No. It's . . . I'm just trying to understand. What is it you're doing, exactly?"

"Well," Lindsay was getting more winded. "Everyone gets to make a wish. We get in a circle . . . and hold hands around a candle . . . with herbs and maybe some scented oil or something—you know, to add the right energy. Then we chant for the wish to come true. It works. Look." She waved a hand up and down her waist. "I've lost six pounds already."

James watched her for a minute. "What you're doing sort of sounds like witchcraft to me."

Lindsay pressed her lips together. "It's not . . . witchcraft." Her words came out in puffs. "It's wish . . . *ing*. It's different."

"I don't know, Linds. What I know about witchcraft could fit in a thimble, but this wishing thing you're telling me about doesn't sound too different. I think people might . . . I think people could misconstrue what it is you gals are up to."

Gals? Ick. She hated "gals." Lindsay turned the treadmill off. Its rumbling stopped immediately, creating a startling silence.

"Oh come on. What's to misconstrue? We're making wishes. It's fun."

Lindsay toweled her face and neck. She slid the white terry-cloth headband up even farther. Blond streaks of hair puffed out on the top of her head, standing out in contrast with the rest of her damp head. Her own hair-band hairstyle.

James still hadn't said anything.

"Look at you. C'mon, it's not like we've formed a coven or anything." She picked up the wheat-grass shake and took a drink.

A dark look passed across James's face. He was probably all worried about what rumors of a witchy wife would do to the burgeoning new-construction branch of his already lucrative real estate brokerage.

"Ohh," she grunted and flipped her wrist down at him. "You worry too much. What's the worst that could happen?" She laughed, before taking another drink of the shake. "Thanks for this." She held the glass up an inch higher, her mouth full of wheat grass. She swallowed and started to head out of the room. "I need to hit the shower right away. I've got lunch at the Women's Foundation today."

Mara put the bills into the blue mouth of the mailbox and hoisted its bottom ledge up. The big hinge squeaked, twice, because she had to peek in again and make sure all the envelopes had dropped down. That done, she turned back down the block toward home. Normally she didn't make a special trip out just for the mail, but some of the bills were late.

She retraced her steps down the sidewalk, which was covered in a slushy snow, making a game of finding her old footprints going in the opposite direction. She could recognize the tread of her boots in some of the footprints. Others were just a foot-shaped impression in the slush.

Something caught her eye on the sidewalk, partially buried in a boot print—maybe hers. It was unmistakable, what it was—but whenever she discovered it on the ground unattended, there was always that hesitation. As if she weren't sure it could be hers. And then of course the thrill when she picked it up. *It is. And it's mine. And I just* found *it*. Money.

Mara reached down and pulled the bill out of the slush, the tips of her wool gloves getting drenched in the process. A one-hundred-dollar bill. She giggled. *A one-hundred-dollar bill!* The bill was wet and folded in half. It had been partially buried under the icy muck. Mara looked around to see if anyone had dropped it, or was around to claim it, or had seen her pick it up. She must have walked right over it earlier, missing it completely. No one else was on the street.

How cool was this? She'd just found one hundred dollars. How lucky was that?

But then, maybe luck had nothing to do with it. Maybe it was abundance already heading her way. Mara smoothed out the bill, wiping some slush from the back of it. This was her wish from Wish Club starting to manifest. It must be. You don't just find one-hundred-dollar bills lying around every day.

Mara folded the bill and put it in the pocket of her coat with a smile. She started walking back home, a new spring in her step. She would take the bill home and let it dry.

Chapter Eleven

✦

The light had gone all wrong. Or that's what Jill told herself. It really only happened around this time of the year, when the sun was so low in the sky that the blinds couldn't quite keep all the light out. It had been cloudy all day, the sky in keeping with the slush on the ground, but the sun had just burst through a few minutes earlier, and now it was blaring through the window of her studio, ruining everything.

Jill had been working, rather half-heartedly, for the previous hour or so, but her mind had kept straying to the portrait artist downstairs. She hadn't seen him since that day a couple of weeks earlier when he had moved in, but she couldn't stop thinking about him. His eyes, his smile, his cute butt as it bent over to move the cinder block when he closed the door. Marc with a "c." *He's gay*, she remembered thinking when he had introduced himself—that whole "with a 'c' " thing. But then he'd really flirted with her: the way he held her eyes, her hand. But he still could be gay, because gay men sometimes did that, flirted with straight women.

Coffee. That's what I need. Just a quick little break. Jill looked at the painting she'd been working on and grunted with disapproval. Any excuse to get out of here for a little while. *Maybe I should ask Marc to join me for coffee. He probably doesn't even know about Sally's yet, the way it's hidden under the El tracks.* Sally's coffee shop looked like such a dump from the street, like the kind of place where every head turns to see who's walked in and where the welcome isn't warm if you're not a regular. Judging from the outside, anyone who didn't know better would be afraid to venture in there.

Jill took off her smock. She thought about stopping to freshen her makeup, but then she might look as if she were trying too hard, showing up at his door with fresh lipstick. But every single morning since she'd last seen him, she'd been showing up at the 4400 North Studios with fresh lipstick. Fresh lipstick in the morning was normal. *Would a straight man be observant enough to question fresh lipstick during the day?*

She was dying for another glimpse of him. He was so unbelievably gorgeous. She'd walked away from the studios that first day convinced that her wish for the perfect man was coming true. Look who'd just moved into the studio below hers! Just what the Wish Club ordered.

But now she was starting to have doubts. If this was the man of her dreams, shouldn't he make an appearance in her reality, too? One morning earlier in the week, the light in his studio had been on when she'd come up the sidewalk, and her heart had jumped. But when she had gotten inside the building his door had been closed and instead of knocking, she'd just walked past, disappointed.

He'd dropped everything, almost literally, on that first day to come up to her studio and help her with the big canvas and she'd thought that was so sweet. He'd seemed really *into* her, as if he couldn't imagine a better thing to do right then, than help a damsel in distress stretch some canvas—even though, obviously, he had a ton of things to do himself.

She'd had to get in close to him while he held the 10 duck taut so she could staple it onto the stretcher bars. She'd been afraid she was going to miss the canvas—send a staple shooting across the room—because she hadn't been able to take her eyes off of his flexed bicep holding the stretching pliers. She'd never met an artist that *cut* before. Standing so close, she'd had a hard time controlling her breath. She'd had to force herself to make it smooth, a problem not unlike what happened whenever she thought about blinking her eyes; the more she thought about it, the less natural it became. And he hadn't been making it easy on her, not really moving far enough out of the way for her to get in and staple. She'd suspected he was doing it on purpose.

Jill walked down the stairs and along the front hall of 4400 North. The light was on in 1W. *Okay, just do this. Just knock on his door. What do those ads say, "It's only lunch?" Well, this is only coffee.* This was so not like her. She couldn't believe how fast her heart was racing.

Jill beat her knuckles on the door and waited, committed now. No answer. She waited, almost walked away, then knocked a little harder—too hard. The door latch clicked and the door swung open of its own accord, revealing the naked back of a woman, seated on top of his model's platform. Her legs were spread wide, and pockets of cellulite rippled in the back of her thighs each time he thrust into her.

Marc looked up and the model turned to look over her right shoulder when Jill gasped.

Neither of them seemed terribly embarrassed about the interruption. Marc had even put forth a couple of perfunctory thrusts as he looked up at Jill, as though he'd been going at it so fast he needed a few seconds to spool himself down.

"Sorry!" Jill closed the door so quickly it was almost a slam. *Okay. So definitely not gay.* She cupped her hand over her mouth as she hurried out the front door of the building and down the sidewalk, trying to muffle the horrified laughs that were burbling out of her cheeks, pressing against the palm of her hand. Halfway down the block she let them free, cracking up by herself like a lunatic, one of those crazy people you see walking down the street. Some wish-come-true this was.

Jill tried to regain her composure. What had come over her, anyway, running away, giggling, acting like such a kid? She was behaving like Mara. And why was she laughing? She sure hadn't felt happy or thought it was funny. What a weird, nervous reaction. Especially for her. Jill wasn't used to laughing much at anything.

She took a deep breath and kept walking down the block toward Sally's. As she pulled her gloves out of her pockets and put them on, the picture of Marc and his model burned in her mind's eye: the waves of her long black hair cascading down her back, her face in profile, his serene expression as he stared bare-chested over her white shoulder. She was almost at Sally's when she had an interesting thought: What a nice portrait they would have made.

"So, um, I guess I could come back tomorrow—you know, if you need me."

Gail held the phone to her ear, fighting the urge to pull it away and check the caller ID again. This was her babysitter, Ellen, on the phone—wasn't it? Saying she'd be able to return to work—*sooner?*

Ellen worked for Gail three mornings a week. That was, up until three weeks ago, when Ellen had dropped a stapler on her big toe and broken it. Only Ellen could find a way to break her toe with a stapler—well no, actually, Claudia probably could too, but only Ellen would turn it into an opportunity to get so much time off work. "Six weeks *minimum* is, like, what the doctor's saying."

Gail and the kids had gone to visit her, and the cast went all the way up to her knee. Gail wouldn't have believed it if she hadn't seen it for herself. The whole odd situation sounded like the kind of story Gail might have concocted in order to get some time off of work, adding that one bizarre detail—a stapler—to make it sound like a story you couldn't possibly make up.

"Sooner?" Gail asked.

"Yeah. The doctor says it's healing well and I don't have to stay off my feet so much anymore, so, you know, I could work, like, maybe one day to try it out and then, if that was okay, then do, like, one day a week—or something."

"How soon can you get here?"

How awesome was this? Unexpected free time. What was she going to do? She had tons of errands to run—she really needed to take the minivan in. No. Wait. She should stop that line of thinking. This was a bonus. A free gift. She shouldn't squander something like this on *need to's* and *have to's*. She should *enjoy* the day tomorrow. Do something fun—just for her—

The wish. *Is that what this was? Was this her wish from Wish Club?*

Gail had had something more substantial in mind than just one day when she'd made her wish. But this single day could turn into more, *like, you know, if everything went okay.* Guiltily, secretly, Gail had just recently allowed herself to start thinking about maybe going back to work. About writing the next big jingle. Well, so what if her wish wasn't going to give her the big chunks of time she'd envisioned. Maybe it was just one day—but she'd take it. And tomorrow she would spend the day at a coffee shop with a book, or maybe the newspaper, maybe looking at want ads, just for fun.

Someone tapped on the door to Jill's studio. "Door's open," she called.

"Hey."

"Well, if it isn't Marc with a 'c.' " Jill tried to remain calm, keep her cool exterior cool. She smiled at him. He smiled back. *Ooof.* She could feel the effect in her solar plexus.

He continued smiling, being coy, his hands jammed into his front pockets, seemingly trying to use his smile to say all the things it would be hard to use words to say about what had happened two days earlier when she'd seen him with his model.

Employing his boyish mannerisms, he looked even younger than she remembered. Still cute, though. Very.

"I haven't heard you up here in a couple of days." Marc ran a finger down his thin goatee. "Thought maybe someone was breakin' in or something. Decided I'd better have a look-see."

Jill hadn't been at the studio since Wednesday; she'd been avoiding him. She tried to get the picture of him in action out of her head. "Nope, it's just me up here rattling around, trying to get the creative juices flowing."

He nodded his head and flashed her an understanding look, as if to say *I know the feeling.* He looked around the studio. "Wow, I like this one. Is it new?"

"Yeah." Jill hated that one; the colors were off. She'd just decided it wouldn't make the show.

His eyes continued to scan her studio, checking it out. He was wearing a pookah-shell necklace. *Kids,* Jill thought. She wondered if he'd ever heard of David Cassidy.

Marc looked back at her, gave her a penetrating smile. It seemed clear his smile was something he was used to falling back on when words failed him.

Cute, and knows it, too. But what, really, is the harm in that?

"Well, just wanted to make sure everything was kosh up here." He smiled at her again, stuffed his hands back into the pockets of his jeans.

Had he intended for it to be a double entendre? No hard feelings between us, no one up here breaking in? Probably not. He looked nervous, like he was struggling.

"Everything's kosh," Jill said, then, uncharacteristically, decided to show him some mercy. "Say, I'm up for a break. You want to go grab some coffee or something?"

Marc locked his eyes on hers, giving her a sly smile when she said, "or something," and she could tell he'd almost said something naughty but had decided better of it. "Sure, that'd be great," he said. "We can go to my place."

"Your place?"

"Yeah, Sally's—the coffee shop under the El. Not many people know about it—the sign's mostly hidden under the tracks."

"Right."

Sally's was a small diner that served up breakfast and lunch and closed at two in the afternoon. It hadn't been redecorated since sometime in the 1970s, and it featured a décor with lots of brown, gold, and orange. No lattes here. Sally's served plain old Superior Coffee, roasted and packaged down on Elston Avenue. When the wind was right, the Superior Coffee factory could make the whole north side smell like Colombian roast.

Marc opened the door to Sally's and stood aside to let Jill pass through in front of him. He did it naturally, without ceremony, as if he were used to being polite. He paid for both their coffees. Jill thought that was sweet, too, the way he'd insisted, with a gentle wave of his hand as he pulled out his money, especially since Jill had been the one to suggest they go get coffee.

"So why portraits?" Jill asked him after they'd sat down at their booth.

"Portraits let me get inside people's heads." He looked away from her, his eyes roving through Sally's, as if maybe he were scouting for subjects, heads to get inside of. "You know how when you paint something, you *know* it." He fixed his eyes on her now. "I mean you really, really *know it*. It's like that with people, too. Maybe even more so. A series of portraits on one person and, BAM, you're inside their head." He slammed his hand down on the table, Emeril-like, when he said "bam," and Jill jumped. The coffee quivered in her mug.

Marc continued, not noticing that he'd startled her. "People walk around their whole lives and they never let you *in*. They're closed-off, shut down, isolated. I hate that. I like to *get inside*, take a peek." His eyes had been wandering again, and now he turned back to Jill, holding them on hers. "After I do someone's portrait, it's like I've been inside their head for so long . . . It's like I really know them, maybe even better than they wanted me to. I love that—I *live* for that. The portraits I do—well, they're not usually the interpretation people expect, that's for sure. But that's *why portraits*." He smiled his smile. "With most people, the experience is pretty cool." He paused. "Sometimes . . ." He shrugged. His smile turned wicked, finishing his thought . . . *it isn't.*

People's heads weren't the only thing he got *inside of* when he did their portraits, Jill thought.

"Maybe you'd let me paint you sometime." That smile again. *Damn he is beautiful.*

"Maybe I would."

Claudia sat in one of the stuffed chairs in the faculty break room, wading her way through a stack of essays on *The Old Man and the Sea*, even though she hadn't gone in there to grade them. She had wanted to call Gail, to find out if her wish was coming true the way everyone else's appeared to be, but people kept wandering in and out, putting lunches in the fridge, getting a cup of coffee, grabbing a doughnut left over from the morning.

It was against school policy to use cellular phones inside the school, except in the common area at the main entrance—and she couldn't talk openly there. Teachers were expected to abide by school policy, so Claudia bided her time in the break room, waiting for it to clear out, annoyed because it was usually so deserted at this hour.

Finally the room emptied and Claudia had Gail's phone ringing before the door had shut.

"C'mon, c'mon, pick up," she whispered. Claudia knew that at 1:45 p.m. Gail ought to be home alone with Emily. Finally, Gail answered.

"Hi, it's me," Claudia said. "Did Mara call you?"

"Yeah. Can you make it on Monday?"

"Yeah, I can but—Mara says everybody's wishes are starting to come true but I . . ."

"Oh aargh." Gail sounded completely exasperated, pissed off.

Crap. I shouldn't have called.

"Emily!"

Oh, Claudia thought. *She's mad at Emily.*

"She just pulled all the clothes off the hangers in her closet. Are you sure you want to have kids?"

"That's why I—"

"This is going to take me an hour. Emily, honey, we don't pull clothes off the hangers. It makes a mess." Gail had this sweet-mommy voice she used when she talked to her kids—it almost always took Claudia by surprise.

"You are not going to believe this," Gail's voice had grown a little fainter and Claudia could envision the phone tucked under her chin as she, presumably, put little pink outfits back on little pink hangers, "but Ellen called and she was able to come back early. Emily, I said no. The clothes have to *stay* on the hangers. She was here yesterday and she said if her foot wasn't bothering her too much today she could start up again one day a week. Emily, do *not* do that. No!"

Emily's tantrum was starting to mount in the background and it grated on Claudia's nerves.

Gail continued, seemingly oblivious to it. "So will you be there on Monday?"

"Well, I'm planning on it but—"

Claudia heard a *whummphf* from Gail's end of the line.

Marion Chutterman, the school nurse, walked into the break room and started fixing herself some coffee.

"Oh man," Gail whined. "She pulled the whole shelf down—John is going to . . ."

Emily started to cry. "You're all right honey. You're okay. Claudia, I gotta go."

Claudia could hear Gail say, "Emily Anne—" in her sweet-mommy voice, before she hung up.

Claudia frowned as she turned off her phone, staring at it in the palm of her hand for a while. She probably should have known better than to try to call Gail in the middle of the day.

"Everything okay on the home front?" Marion asked her, always on the alert for some gossip. Her Minnesota accent stretched and rounded out her Os.

"Oh," Claudia said, unintentionally imitating her. "Everything is fine. Actually, that wa—"

"Oh, I know what it's like sometimes," Marion interrupted. "Everyone gets so busy they just don't take the time for one another, but when you're in a relationship, time together is the most important thing. It'll be even more important when you start your family." Marion bobbed her head on the word *family*, a presumptuous, get-going kind of gesture. It couldn't have been more rude if she'd tapped her finger on her watch.

Claudia wanted to jump over the table and wrap her hands around Marion's neck. She gave Marion a fake smile instead, as if to thank her for her unsolicited advice.

"I need to get back in time for class." Claudia shuffled her still ungraded *Old Man and the Sea* essays into a pile. April Sibley was going to have another hissy fit. Claudia stopped at the side table and filled her mug, eyeing the Dunkin' Donut munchkins still sitting out. She grabbed one and popped it in her mouth.

"Oh, I envy you young ladies," Marion started in again. "You can eat whatever you like and it never stays with you. I used to be like that myself, but once you hit thirty-five, well, then the free ride is over and the doughnuts just stick to your thighs like dried oatmeal to a bowl."

Claudia gave her another weak smile, her cheeks full of chocolate munchkin—which she could no longer enjoy, thanks to an uninvited visual of Marion Chutterman's oatmealy thighs.

She gave Marion a stilted good-bye wave with the free fingers she had on the handle of her coffee mug while she juggled with her papers and the handle to the door. Her parting gesture went unnoticed; Marion was already preoccupied with ripping open a packet of artificial sweetener. Claudia's wiggling fingers jostled her full cup of coffee, splashing some on the *Old Man and the Sea* essays, the indoor-outdoor carpeting in the hallway, and the toe of her gray suede boot.

Chapter Twelve

———✦———

Mara lugged groceries up the salt-encrusted front steps to her framed northwest-side bungalow. "Saint Ben's" is what they'd always called their neighborhood, but as more and more yuppies and dinks started moving in, she'd noticed a slow transition to the trendier "North Center" label. If only their tax increases had made such a slow transition.

She tried to lift her keys to the lock on the front door but the grocery bags were too heavy and she didn't have the arm strength, so she ended up setting everything down on the salt, exactly what she'd been trying to avoid.

Once the groceries were in the kitchen, she walked back across the hardwood floor, which she would now have to mop again, to close the front door.

Tippy had his nose sticking out and around the partially opened screen door, which never closed completely without some brute force. He darted back in when he heard her footsteps getting close, his body low to the ground as he hurried away.

"No Hills Science Diet or radiators out there," Mara said to his backside. "The life of an alley cat is not what it's cracked up to be."

Tippy ran into the kitchen and sat by the grocery bags on the floor, his tail wrapped around him where he sat. He flipped the tip of it onto the linoleum as if he were a woman tapping a manicured nail on a countertop. His green eyes stared at Mara.

"Oh, sure." Mara started putting the groceries away. "Sure, it sounds all glamorous—the freedom, the grass between your toes, the tomcatting around. But, I tell you what, getting your dinner out of a garbage can every night like a common gray squirrel, well, that is a fate much too undignified for my precious Tippy."

With everything that needed to be put in the refrigerator safely inside, she left the rest of the groceries where they were and scooped Tippy up on her way to the living room. He squirmed in her arms, then gave her a low meow, as if he were trying to protest yet another assault on his dignity. "Oh, hush now. You've got nothing to complain about." Mara sat down in the armchair by the window.

She was hosting an impromptu meeting of Book Club tonight. It had only been two weeks since the last meeting, and it was all happening very last minute—but Mara didn't mind. Everyone was having such good luck with their wishes that they all wanted to make more right away, and Mara was certainly in favor of that.

At Dr. Seeley's office this morning, she'd been staring at the sailboat print that hung on the wall opposite her desk when she'd decided to take the afternoon off work, burn up half of a personal day. Sail away. When she'd asked Dr. Seeley, he'd of course acted displeased that an employee of his would have to attend to anything "personal," but he'd agreed to it, "Fine, fine. If you feel you must." And he'd seemed to be waiting for an explanation, which Mara gleefully hadn't given. *Let him stew on this one.*

Mara knew Seeley would hate it if she spent her time idly, which was why she thought right now, the right thing to do was to take a little personal time and relax. She sat in Henry's La-Z-Boy by the window, petted her cat, and enjoyed the afternoon sun. Tippy circled her lap several times before curling up in it. The sun warmed her face and when she closed her eyes, she could pretend she was someplace tropical; something worth wishing for in Chicago in February, when it was cold and snowy and the sun was making its first appearance in nearly a week. But then, there were so many things to wish for.

Her wish for abundance seemed to be humming along. It had started with that hundred-dollar bill and, while she hadn't found anything quite so dramatic since then, she kept finding coins lying on the ground, a quarter, a few pennies. Two days ago she'd found a twenty in the pocket of a laundered pair of jeans. *This counts,* she'd thought. Well, she was going to need all of it when Henry found out it was her turn to host Book Club. The wine and noshes always seemed to break their budget for the month. She could hear Henry now: *"Precious snacks for all the precious ladies."*

Precious was Henry's word for any fabulously-well-put-together woman of means, with perfect hair and skin and clothes and, of course, manicured nails. Mara adapted the term as well, adding a criterion—any woman whose dark wool coat never, not ever, had a speck of lint on it. They had a mutual understanding of who fell into the category of *precious:* anyone who might fear lint or poverty.

While Mara might have, at first, prejudiciously dumped Lindsay and Jill into that category, she certainly couldn't have done that to Claudia or Gail. And it was Claudia whom Mara had met first, at some boring Strawn faculty function. Claudia had invited her to join Book Club that same night, since they'd spent the whole evening off in a corner talking about books while Dan and Henry had mourned their Cubs. During the first few Book Club meetings she attended, Mara had felt a little out of place—surrounded by more preciousness than she was used to—but she had stuck it out. They picked such interesting books.

Now, Mara thought all the Book Club women were precious, but in the true sense of the word. She adored every one of them—well, except for maybe Jill, but even she was okay when she stopped being so self-absorbed, when she got over herself and actually showed some emotion, which seemed to be happening a little more often now, ever since the wishing had started.

Mara petted Tippy and sighed as she looked out at her living room. Jill had such a designed apartment; every detail had the touch of an interior decorator written all over it. Very under con-trol. Mara's house had been designed by life. And she wished she had a coffee table. Tippy, Henry, and the boys had done some redecorating of their own during one of the previous season's Sunday-afternoon football games.

Mara had discovered their misdeed while driving home. She'd shortcutted down the alley and as she'd driven past her garage, she'd stopped and stared at what she'd been sure was her coffee table in the garbage can in front of it, two of its three remaining legs sticking out of it like a body with rigor mortis.

"Tippy has been jumping on that coffee table for twelve years," she'd said to Henry when she'd gone inside. "I don't see how he could manage to tip the glass top over *and* break a metal leg off. "

Henry had just shrugged, refusing to get defensive. The boys had nodded their heads in support. Mara had been fairly certain the demise of the table had had less to do with Tippy and more to do with the Bears' defensive line and their loss to the Green Bay Packers on that same Sunday.

The old beat-up coffee table had been better than no coffee table and today, she wished she had something. She had a vision of the Book Club women balancing plates on their knees and setting wineglasses at their feet. *Maybe I could run out and get one now?* Mara pulled her arm out from under Tippy and checked her watch, disturbing him. He arched up in irritation for a moment before settling back down. No time. Oh well, she thought, sometimes you imagine you absolutely have to have something that you really don't need. She could just make do with what she had. Her friends wouldn't mind.

Mara rubbed Tippy's ears and started to hum, *A sailboat in the moonlight and you, Wouldn't that be heaven.*

An old Billie Holiday song. Mara had a lovely voice; people often compared it to Billie Holiday's. It was something she had once thought she might make a career out of, but that was a long time ago. Her dream had given way to Henry, and then her boys and then hygienist school to help pay the bills. In retrospect, her dream had always seemed a little far-fetched, anyway.

Mara started singing the song out loud, softly.

A heaven just for two, a soft breeze on a June night and you.

Tippy continued to purr in her lap.

But now. Now, maybe her dream wasn't as far-fetched as all that. Mara allowed herself to think of it—just for a minute or two.

What a perfect setting for letting dreams come true.

+

The Book Club women sat on the floor in Mara's living room, having given up on the couches. Without the cofee table, it was easier this way. More like a picnic.

One white origami wish rested on its side in a Tupperware bowl, looking sadly like a bird with a broken wing. The bowl was with them on the floor, which was now covered with candles and herbs and magical ingredients and wineglasses, along with a few empty bottles. Everyone else's wishes had been cast, with only Claudia's to go.

I should let everybody off the hook, Claudia thought, *just tell them to forget it so we can all go home.*

She watched her friends as they relaxed between wishes. She was happy for them, truly. She *loved* them, but she couldn't help feeling sorry for herself. She'd been so certain it was going to finally happen for her, that she would finally get pregnant. Even the timing had been right. According to her temperature, she'd ovulated the day after the last meeting, the day after she and Dan had had sex. The way everyone's wishes had been going, Claudia thought her pregnancy was practically a given. Over the course of the past couple of weeks she kept putting her hand on her belly, hoping it, willing it. What an idiot. She'd gotten her period three days earlier. It had happened the previous Friday morning, right before she called Gail from school.

Everyone had been very consoling about her wish's lack of success. *Your wish is different. It needs a little time. It's only been two weeks.* Only Lindsay found a way to be irritating when she said, *You can't rush Mother Nature.* You can't rush Mother Nature? *Good grief.*

Tonight, they'd done Jill's wish first. She'd shown up late and then said she couldn't stay for very long because she had plans with her new boyfriend later.

"Creative inspiration?" Gail asked when she pulled Jill's wish out of the Tupperware. "You think you need more creativity? I think your work is amazing as it is."

"Thanks, but . . . I'm ready to break out, you know? I want that flash, that brilliant creative insight to help me make a huge splash with my show. I guess I'm just getting tired of futzing along."

It seemed to Claudia that during this round of wishes, no one held back—everyone was completely honest.

Lindsay finally admitted she wanted to be completely and totally accepted in Chicago society, and not just skirt around the edges, as she felt she'd been doing her whole life, being accepted in some minimal way because of her family name.

Finally, Claudia thought, *she admits it!*

Whenever the subject of society had come up in the past, Lindsay had shrugged it off, trying to make a point that she didn't care much about it. Her independent clique in high school was supposed to be proof, but Claudia wasn't buying it anymore. Not after what she saw every day at Strawn. All of Lindsay's charity work and fads and fitness crazes—Claudia had always suspected that they were just Lindsay's attempts to be friends, to fit in, *to belong*. In some way, it was as though Lindsay were trying to make up for high school, trying to recover from some unrequited longing to be accepted by the Molly Bonners of the world.

So, they'd helped Lindsay with her wish to find her place in society.

When Gail's turn came, Claudia expected she would ask to go back to work, which she did in a way, but in a way that had surprised all of them. Gail wished to return to the theater.

Claudia had forgotten. She'd gone to see Gail in countless plays down at school, her favorite being *Bleacher Bums*, in which Gail played the part of the hottie, Melody. Gail was a great actor. She radiated on stage and off, whenever she was in a play. Claudia looked over at Gail now, her short blond hair all that remained of the artsy girl she'd known in college. Gail's hair used to change color every few months and her clothes were always so cool, nothing Claudia could ever pull off. It was as if Gail had been made for the theater. It was weird, and sad, that she hadn't remembered this aspect of her friend. It might be even more sad, Claudia thought, that Gail had almost forgotten about this aspect of herself.

"You know, on the way here, I must have changed my mind about it a hundred times." Gail said. "I kept thinking I'd like to go back to work, to Foote, Cone, pick up somewhere close to where I left off. Do the next Sunshine Orange Juice jingle. But even though I could see myself back in the office, in the power suit, doing the presentations, the brainstorming sessions, all of it—something just . . . It just didn't seem *true*." Gail paused, her face asking, *you know what I mean?*

"It just got me thinking about what I'd *really* like to be doing—what was in my heart. And then it came to me: the theater. Back in college, I'd given up on the idea of a professional acting career by the time I was a junior, because I'd convinced myself that if I pursued it in any way, I would surely starve to death, and I grew up without much, so I knew I didn't want that. But over the past few weeks I started thinking, why couldn't I try again now? There are lots of small local theater companies I could get involved with—or maybe a talent agency, to do commercials or something. I don't know—as long as I'm *wishing*, I might as well wish for something that would really be a dream."

"I was so relieved," Mara said when her wish was pulled, "to hear Gail talk about always wanting to go back to the theater. You see," Mara's normally gregarious demeanor was subdued, "I used to sing." She paused. No one had had any idea. "Well, I still sing, but only to my cat." Mara giggled, back to her old self. "I had a scholarship, a voice scholarship to Indiana University, but I didn't go."

All the women exchanged looks. This was news to them. "The summer after high school, I . . . well, I got pregnant with Alan. Henry and I did the whole shotgun wedding thing and I ended up at married student housing at Purdue instead of IU. It was hard being on campus and being a mom. There weren't many of us, and I always felt so out of place walking around with a baby—being the same age as the students. But I don't regret it. I wouldn't change anything. I love Henry and the boys and, who knows, music is such a . . . well, it's hard. I probably wouldn't have been the next Barbra Streisand or Billie Holliday, but would have ended up teaching music somewhere." Mara sighed. Her face looked wistful. "But still . . ."

"But still," Gail continued for her, "teaching music to a bunch of uninterested brats, on a dwindling public-school budget, would still beat the crap out of picking tartar out of gums in Dr. Seeley's office?"

Mara nodded back with a sad smile.

And so they made a wish to help Mara find her voice again.

"You know, guys. I'm pretty tired." Claudia pulled her eyes from her wish in the Tupperware bowl. "If you want to just call it a night, we can always start with me the next time."

Mara looked open-mouthed at Claudia. "Not a chance."

"Are you kidding?" Gail picked up the bowl from the floor. "What's this about," she held the broken-bird wish up and out toward Claudia, "that you don't want your girlfriends to know anymore?" She started unfolding the wish.

"No, it's not that. It's just . . . well, everyone's wishes are all going so well," Claudia pushed her glasses up her nose, "and, mine . . ." Her voice trailed off.

"—are going to go just fine, too," Lindsay said. "You just picked a hard one for the first time around."

"Don't be discouraged, Claude." Gail was using her sweet-mommy voice. "I have a feeling about you." She opened up Claudia's wish and looked at it, her face puzzled. "I can't read it . . . you scribbled out part of the—" She handed the wish over to Claudia. "Here. You'll have to tell us what it says."

Claudia looked down at the scrap of paper. She'd scribbled out her wish about writing a novel. *I changed my mind*, she'd told herself. *I don't really care about writing novels anymore.* Even though she knew that wasn't particularly true. Instead, she'd made a wish for Dan. She wished that he would find happiness with his career— whatever that might entail. Whether it would mean he would finally start up his own firm or make more money at his current job, she didn't know. She only knew she wanted him to be happy. On some level, she knew it wasn't a completely selfless wish; if Dan felt more comfortable with his career, he would feel more comfortable having a child.

Claudia had scribbled out her old wish and scrunched her words together trying to make her new wish for Dan fit at the bottom of the paper. No wonder Gail couldn't read it. It was a mess.

"I wished for Dan. That he find some happiness in his job." Claudia looked up at them, hoping they would buy it. "I wasn't sure how to phrase it." She pushed her glasses up her nose again. "Whether I should ask for him to make more money—because I think that would make him happier—or whether I should wish he could start his own firm. So, I decided to make it more general and just wish that he finds more happiness in his career. That's why it's so scribbly."

"Well, what was so hard about that?" Mara asked, picking up one of the spell books without waiting for Claudia to answer. "C'mon everyone, let's make a wish for Claudia—or for Dan, rather, and his happy career."

It occurred to Claudia then, that maybe the only thing more sad than forgetting about a dream, was being too afraid to ask for one to come true.

Chapter Thirteen

———✦———

Henry had fallen asleep again in his La-Z-Boy recliner, watching whatever sport had been showing on TV. The chair was back in the full recline position, and Henry lay supine, mouth open, his exhalations sounding like someone fogging a mirror. His left hand, flung over the left armrest, was nearly resting on the floor. His right hand still clutched the remote control to his chest, and Mara wanted it so she could shut up the post-game sports announcers who were still bantering on the screen, loudly, because Henry had the volume up too high.

Mara had just returned home from picking up her son, Alan, from wrestling practice. He'd already raided the refrigerator, forgoing the fancy snacks left over from last night's Book Club meeting for two hastily thrown-together peanut butter and jelly sandwiches, one of which he still carried with him as he ran out the front door to a friend's house. On her way back from closing the door behind him, Mara wondered how Henry could possibly sleep through all the commotion, especially with the TV volume up that loud.

She reached down over Henry and grabbed the remote, sliding it easily out of his hand. As she stood up, she got a good look at the top of Henry's head. At six feet one inch, he was a full foot taller than she was, so this was a pretty rare view. And now hair was sprouting there. Right there in what used to be the middle of his rather large, shiny bald spot. True, sometimes it did look different—in the winter, it would get dry and a little dull and flaky. Mara would urge him to put something on it, but Henry would get indignant. *I am not rubbing lotion on my head, Mara.*

But this was something else, a soft downy little patch of brown hair sprouting out of his scalp. *You'd think he would have noticed this,* she thought, *the way he runs his hand back over his scalp constantly, as if checking to see if this exact sort of thing might have happened.*

She rubbed her hand over it to check, to confirm that her eyes weren't playing tricks on her. They were there, sure enough, like the fine hairs on a newborn baby's head. Henry sighed in his sleep, closed his mouth as if to swallow, and then opened it again to continue his foggy-mirror breathing. Mara put the remote down and grabbed the reading lamp, tilting it toward Henry's head a little, leaning in close to inspect his scalp.

Suddenly Henry woke with a start, jolting his head upright, right into Mara's nose. She reeled back, grabbing her nose with a yelp, letting the lamp drop to the floor where it first bounced, then shattered, sending broken glass scattering everywhere.

"What the . . . ?" Henry asked.

Mara was doubled at the waist, her hand over her nose, bobbing up and down and moaning. A trickle of blood started down her fingers. "It's bleeding. My nose is bleeding!"

Henry sat open-mouthed in his chair, his feet thrown over the side. He blinked.

"Henry, I think id's bwoken. Oh, my nose is bwoken." She could hear the congestion in her voice. *Not my nose!* She had the cutest little nose—it was her best feature. Blood continued to trickle between her fingers.

"Let me get you a towel." Henry rose from his chair. "And some ice." He put his arm around her shoulders, guiding her along with him as he started toward the kitchen, circling around the broken glass in his stocking feet. "What happened?"

She whimpered. "Ow ow ow," was all she could manage until she was seated in a kitchen chair, and Henry reached into the drawer next to the sink.

"Don'd use the good towels." She pointed to a bottom drawer next to the refrigerator with her free hand. Henry bent down and took two of the old dish rags out, handing her one, filling the other with ice. "What happened?" he asked her again.

"I was looking at the tob of your head when you jumbed up and your head hid me in the nose."

"Why were y—Never mind." He made a face at her, as if he'd caught her trying to sneak some lotion on his head while he slept. "Let me see it." He winced when she removed her hand.

Her eyes welled up at his reaction. "It's bad? Oh, I know it's bad . . . Oh Henry, it hurds."

He gently wiped blood off her upper lip and chin with a damp towel, giving it to her when he finished so she could clean her hands. He gave her the towel filled with ice and she gingerly put it over the bridge of her nose, peering at him over it.

Henry stood in front of her with one hand on his hip, the other holding the bloodied rag. "I think we need to get you to a doctor, hon."

"Id's bwoken. You think id's bwoken?"

Henry inhaled deeply through his nose as he reached a hand up and ran it over his scalp. His eyes snapped open as if just now he'd fully awakened from his nap. He brought his hand down in front of his face and examined the palm, as if maybe the hair he'd felt had come from there. He reached up again and ran his hand over his former bald spot.

"Mara! I've got hair on my head!"

"Thad's whad I've been trying to tell you."

From the living room they could hear the voice of a sportscaster yelling, "It's un-be-leev-able."

The class hunched over their tests, ran fingers through hair, bit lips, coughed, and occasionally sent her a dirty look. And occasionally, Claudia caught a dirty look when she glanced up from sipping her coffee and reading her *New Yorker*, as she made sure that the casual glances at the ceiling were only that and not attempts to *casually* find out what someone else had answered.

Claudia enjoyed test days; all the work being done, she could relax and catch up on her reading. The only problem she had with test day was that she couldn't leave the room if she needed to and, after sipping so much coffee, Claudia needed to leave the room.

She thought about putting April Sibley in charge while she went to the bathroom. Claudia looked over at April. She saw her face contort as she hunched over the exam, her head down low to the page and her knuckles white as she gripped her pen. It was unusual to see April struggling with a test. Claudia looked around to see if there was anyone else she could trust to stop the slackers and wanna-bes from cheating while she was gone, and decided that it was just coffee pee anyway, which always seemed to be more urgent than it really was. Claudia turned her attention back to her magazine.

"Ms. Dubois? I need to use the bathroom." It was April.

Claudia eyed her a little suspiciously, but after imagining the repercussions of refusing the headmaster's niece permission to pee, Claudia just said "sure."

After April left, Claudia flipped through her magazine, still looking up once in a while to make sure no one was cheating. There were several kids looking up at the ceiling now, and she looked up at it herself, to make sure no one had written answers there when she hadn't been looking.

"Guys? I don't think the answers are going to appear up there, so maybe we could focus our eyes on our own papers?" She got a couple of embarrassed smiles, several more confused ones, and one dagger-like stare of irritation for the interruption.

Claudia took a sip of coffee and returned to her magazine with a sigh. She was deep into an article when April returned from the bathroom, and Claudia silently reprimanded herself for forgetting for so long that she'd been gone.

Class always ran over on test days and today was no different. She allowed the students who needed more time to use the ten minutes they were allotted between classes to finish up their essays. Today, one of them was April. When she collected the last of the tests, Claudia locked them in her file cabinet, grabbed her purse, and hurried for the door. She did not want to get into a discussion with April, or anyone else for that matter, about when the tests would be graded. Even though the next period was her free period, today Claudia really did have personal business to attend to.

It wasn't a long walk to the bathroom, but the urgency of her mission seemed to increase the closer she came to her destination. It was empty when she got there and she rushed into a stall.

While the toilet was flushing, Claudia swore she heard a cat's muffled yowling and she stepped out of the stall, cocking her head to listen, but heard nothing more and walked over to the sinks, her chunky heels echoing on the floor.

As soon as the water was on, she heard it again. She turned the water back off.

The sound had come from her left side. She walked over to the large red garbage can and looked behind it. The mewling sound came again—this time from inside the can. *How could a kitten get inside . . . ?* Claudia lifted the lid off. Blood was smeared on the side and her hand slipped in it. Gross. She hurried her hand over to the sink to run it under water. These girls can be such pigs. She remembered one time she had entered a stall and sat down to see a bloody tampon hanging from its string on the hook on the back of the door.

The mewling sound came again, and she came back to the trashcan. Blood saturated some of the paper towels inside and Claudia's heart started thumping, afraid of what she would find in there if she dared to look. She heard it again, louder, and this time it didn't sound like a cat but a baby's cry. She dug through the bloodied paper towels and found a tiny, tiny baby at the bottom of the can, his eyes closed tight.

"OhmyGodOhmyGodOhmyGod." She reached in and picked up the baby and cradled him to her chest.

"Oh my God, my little one, what happened to you—what are you doing here?" She touched the side of his little red face. She pulled up the bottom of her sweater and wrapped it over him. He was still wet and gooey, with a strange white paste on his skin. She paced back and forth, breathing hard. *Don't freak out. Don't freak out.* Claudia headed for the door. The baby started mewling.

"Ohh." Claudia walked toward the door then stopped. *I need to keep him warm. He needs to be warmer.* He was already wrapped in the bottom of her sweater, and she enveloped him now inside her suit jacket as well. She needed to get him to the nurse, to Marion. She needed to call an ambulance. Claudia raced out of the bathroom and hurried toward the stairwell. She went down the stairs carefully, holding the baby like a piece of crystal, keeping one hand on the handrail.

These sorts of things didn't happen at fine, upstanding private schools like Strawn. *This is going to cause a ruckus,* she thought. What was Peterson going to do? Of course they needed to find the mother right away. He would probably lock down the school, but she might already be gone. They had an open campus. Peterson would definitely want to keep this as under wraps as possible, try to avoid a scandal for the school.

The mother had to be one of the girls. Well, probably it was one of the girls, but there weren't any she knew of that had been pregnant, not in any of her classes or that she'd seen in passing down the halls—or heard about in the faculty break room.

The boy's little cries subsided and Claudia stopped halfway down the stairs, opening her jacket in a panic to make sure he hadn't stopped breathing. No. But he started crying again as soon as she'd stopped. Claudia covered him back up with her jacket and continued until she reached the first-floor hallway, where she ran as smoothly as she could to Marion's office, trying not to jostle the baby too much.

Henry O'Connor turned out of a doorway, his eyes down, reading some forms in his hand.

Henry O'Connor. Upper-grades math teacher. Boys' cross-country and baseball coach. Mara's husband.

"Henry!"

"Claudia?" He stared down at her blood-stained sweater. "What happened? Let me help you. Do you need to sit down?" He gestured back toward the office he'd just left.

Claudia kept up her pace down the hallway. "No, Henry. It's—I found a baby!"

"You what?" Henry fell into a slow jog next to her. His eyes widened when he looked down and noticed the bulge under her jacket. "Holy shit."

"He was in the girls' bathroom." Claudia was breathing hard. "I'm taking him to Marion. Call 9-1-1!"

Henry turned around and ran full-speed back down the hall to his office.

Claudia spun into Marion's waiting room. Two girls sat on the bench outside Marion's door. Their mouths gaped open. Claudia ran past without acknowledging them and tried the interior door. It was locked and she banged her fist on its smoked-glass panel so hard it vibrated in its frame.

"Marion! Marion open up, it's an emergency." She banged on the door again. "Marion! Please, it's—"

She could hear Marion muttering from the other side, *always an emergency.*

Marion opened the door with a pissy "What is it?" before looking down at Claudia's bloody front. Claudia pulled back part of her jacket to reveal the baby's slimy head and crying face.

Marion's eyes got huge as she sucked in a mouthful of air. "Oh!" she said, her Minnesota roots drenching the word.

"I found him. In the bathroom upstairs. Just now."

Marion reached her arms out for the baby. "We have to call 9-1-1. We need to get him to the hospital right away."

Claudia hesitated before handing him over, not sure if it was the baby she didn't want to give up, or Marion's starched white cotton she didn't want to see smeared with blood. Marion always wore the old-fashioned white cotton uniform, even though the trend in nursing fashion these days was toward cartoon animals and multi-colored scrubs. After she handed the baby over to Marion, her arms felt strangely empty.

"I saw Henry O'Connor in the hall. He's calling 9-1-1."

"Good." Marion gave the baby a quick once-over before she clamped down on his umbilical cord with her fingers. She turned to the boy on the examining table behind her, whom Claudia hadn't noticed until right then. "Sean, you're done," she said, nodding her head toward the door. "Tell Mr. Redding I said you can sit out gym today."

Sean was staring, red-nosed and open-mouthed, at the bloody baby in Marion's arms. A little trickle of snot seeped from one of his nostrils.

"Sean, I said you're done."

"Uh," Sean tore his eyes from the baby and looked up at Marion. "Uh, Mr. Redding said he wanted a node."

"Just tell him I SAID SO and go tell him NOW."

Sean stared at Marion with a stunned look for about a nanosecond before he tore out of her office.

Marion calmly pulled a sheet from a drawer under the examining table and wiped the baby off before pulling out another one and wrapping him up in it tightly.

She held him so naturally, pacing the room, her shoulders relaxed. Claudia knew she'd raised four children and the majority of them now had children of their own. She was accustomed to holding little babies, and she made it look as if it were the most natural thing in the world to be standing in the first-floor nurse's office at the Arthur G. Strawn Academy holding a baby that had just been pulled out of the trash.

The baby must have understood he was in good hands because he stopped his crying. "You are quite a little trooper." Marion's nose did Eskimo air kisses with the baby's nose. "We've got an ambulance on the way. They're going to take you to the hospital where you'll get some extra-special care."

Watching Marion pace the office, idly chatting and cooing over the newborn, Claudia could almost forgive her for all her nosey, boorish gossip and uninvited advice.

Well, the gossip this little incident was going to stir up would surely blow away anything Marion could dish out. The news vans would probably be rolling up shortly after—maybe even before— the ambulance did. Claudia didn't have to look outside the door to know the two girls sitting in the waiting area were long gone— discreetly text-messaging their friends while hiding behind locker doors, all symptoms of premenstrual cramping long forgotten.

"You found him in the trash can?" Marion looked up at her now.

"He sounded like a cat. I thought someone—I thought there was a cat, a kitten in there at first. But the blood. I couldn't believe it when I reached in and found him. I mean a baby! Who could do such a thing? To a baby?"

"Did you see the mother? Who was it?"

"There was no one else around. I have no idea where she is—or who she is."

"Call Charles's office. He needs to know about this. Let's get him down here. And we need to try to find the mother, too."

Claudia went over to Marion's desk and picked up the phone to call Headmaster Peterson.

It felt as if her whole body were vibrating, she was so angry—or sad. Maybe *betrayed* was the better word, because she didn't feel like crying. She felt like a part of her world had cracked. Like the vibration in her chest was the aftershock of the earthquake that had just rocked her foundation. Claudia had spent the better part of her life always trying to believe the best of people. She knew the world wasn't perfect; obviously bad things happened and bad people existed, but they all had the fictional quality of a media story, an intangible feeling of distance to them. The media turned events into stories. It's what they did. But the stories made it seem like bad things only happened far away, in bad places and in bad neighborhoods. Not here. Not in her world. Not at her school, in the bathroom she used every day.

Peterson's receptionist picked up the phone. "Is Charles there? It's Claudia Dubois."

"Headmaster Peterson is not available at the—"

"You need to tell him to get down to Marion's office right away."

"He's asked that he not be—"

"It's an emergency . . . You have to tell him. Interrupt whatever he's doing and just tell him." Claudia hung up the phone.

They could hear sirens approaching. Marion looked up from her cooing. "I think it would be best if we drew as little attention to ourselves as possible."

Claudia nodded. This was the Marion she knew. The one who would try, like Peterson, to avoid scandal for the school.

Marion looked down, frowning, at the front of Claudia's blood-stained sweater.

"Oh." Claudia quickly took her jacket off, pressed it to her stomach, and crossed her arms over it to hide most of the blood. "Better?"

Marion nodded, but one corner of her mouth was still turned down in a frown.

"I'm going to cover him as much as I can with the sheet. It's only a few steps to the front door, but . . . you should hold your arms just like that, but maybe you're in pain?" She looked pointedly at Claudia. "Maybe you slipped on the floor in the bathroom and hurt your arm. Something like that."

Claudia looked back at her for a moment, then decided it would be best to play along. "Okay, I get it, make it look like *I* got hurt."

Marion nodded. "Any loud murmurs from our little champ here and your pain immediately escalates. Kapeesh?"

"I—yeah, okay—but don't you think it might already be too late? That boy, Sean—and the two girls in the waiting room. Henry O'Connor."

Marion silenced her with a look.

"Okay, okay. My arm's hurt." Claudia didn't want any trouble with Marion, because she knew Marion and Peterson were close. Peterson had probably gotten an earful about Claudia's slacker tendencies from April. She didn't need trouble with Marion, too. Claudia would play along with the ruse for her own sake—if not for the sake of the fine reputation of their fine school.

The ambulance pulled into the circular drive in front and the paramedics were getting out when Claudia rotated out the door, meeting them on the sidewalk. They saw the blood on her sweater and she had to hold them off, telling them their patient was coming through the revolving door behind her.

With her arms wrapped around herself in an effort to keep warm now, instead of hiding blood, Claudia stood at the back door of the ambulance watching the two men check out the baby. They worked quickly, putting a clamp on his umbilical cord and taking his vital signs.

A handful of students had stepped outside the school lobby and gathered on the sidewalk next to the ambulance. They stayed several yards away from Claudia, but more students were coming up from the street on the front sidewalk.

"He's going to be okay, right?" Claudia asked, leaning in a little closer to the back door.

"These babies tend to be pretty resilient," one of the paramedics said without looking up.

She couldn't imagine how many of "these babies" he must have seen to make him so jaded by the time he got to this one.

"What's going to happen to him?"

He shrugged. "Social Services usually takes over at the hospital."

Claudia glanced at the small crowd that was gathering before looking at Marion. "Maybe I should go with."

Claudia couldn't decipher Marion's odd look—confused, her lips thrust out and eyebrows raised. Didn't she understand why Claudia wanted to follow this baby? Or was she pissed that she hadn't thought of it first, it being in keeping with the whole broken-arm ploy? Or maybe Marion was thinking it was typical of a teacher to try to play hooky in the middle of the day—just another slacker.

The driver shrugged at Claudia again. *Whatever.* It was obvious he didn't care if she stayed or went. "If you're comin'," he said, "you gotta come now." He shut the rear doors of the ambulance and pointed up front toward the passenger side, before disappearing around the back.

With a quick glance at Marion, Claudia walked over to the passenger side and climbed in. Before her door was shut the driver started pulling out of the drive, at the same time reaching over to the center console to press a button. The siren started.

From the rearview mirror outside her window, Claudia could see Peterson spinning out of the revolving door. He met Marion on the sidewalk and he reached out as if to touch her upper arm, but he pulled his hand back at the last second. They exchanged a few words and Peterson gestured his arm out at the ambulance as it rolled away.

Peterson was tall and always looked distinguished in his dark suits and gleaming black Salvatore Ferragamo oxford shoes, but he had a disheveled quality about him now. His face was flushed, his tie just ever so slightly askew.

Claudia watched them grow smaller in the mirror, then out of sight completely as the ambulance turned the corner and sped on its way. She stared at the mirror even after they'd disappeared, and she noticed that the usual admonition, "Objects in mirror are closer than they appear," was missing.

Chapter Fourteen

———✳———

The ambulance driver appeared nonchalant as he wove quickly in and out of traffic. Claudia couldn't tell if he was oblivious to her presence or, worse, showing off because of it. He picked up the radio from the center console and told whoever it was on the other end that Unit Eight was a "two-four" at Strawn and they were "five-out" from Mercy. Claudia assumed he would call Mercy next to give their ETA, like they did on TV, but he just put the mike back in its cradle.

They raced through the familiar streets faster than she'd ever gone down them before, and she wondered if the baby's condition was that critical or if the driver was just driving that fast because he could. Although there were a surprising number of assholes who wouldn't move out of the way for an ambulance. Maybe that was how the driver got his contempt for the road. Claudia could see one such asshole in her side mirror, a black Lexus following closely behind them, passing all the drivers who had pulled over, turning someone else's misfortune to his advantage—a real-life ambulance chaser.

What a world to be born into, she thought. A world in which it seemed no one gave a shit about anyone else, in which everyone seemed only to care about themselves: a world in which a young girl can give birth in the bathroom of a prestigious private school and literally throw her baby away. Why? Because it interfered with what? Her plans for herself? Other people's plans for her? What? There was not one single reason—not any combination of reasons—that Claudia could think of to excuse it.

It was so unfair. All the effort she and Dan had been putting into trying to have a baby, and here some teenager just effortlessly gives birth in a high school bathroom and, seemingly just as effortlessly, abandons it.

Claudia wondered why the girl had done it that way, why she hadn't gotten help from someone—a teacher or her parents— anyone. There were posters all over the place, on the buses and on the subway, asking "Pregnant? We can help." But Claudia realized the Strawn girls weren't exactly the public-transportation type.

That girl must have felt she was all alone.

How long would it take them to find her? And what about the father? This could become a huge, long-drawn-out mess. Peterson must be having a cow. The thought gave Claudia schadenfreude as she imagined him pacing up and down his office, wearing out his expensive shoes, worrying about the potential disgrace to the Strawn Academy.

Claudia wondered how anyone could have hidden an entire pregnancy. April Sibley had used the bathroom earlier during third period—maybe she had seen something. Claudia visualized the way April's forehead had furrowed while taking her test, the way her hand had gripped her pen with white knuckles. She'd seemed so agitated.

Oh my God. Maybe it was April.

No, of course not April. Even though this baby was small, he looked to Claudia's inexpert eye to be about full term, and April hadn't put on any weight—well, not that Claudia had noticed anyway. April had always been a little on the plump side. But certainly someone so hell-bent on becoming valedictorian wouldn't allow herself to get pregnant, wouldn't let something like this get in the way—

Oh my God. Peterson was really going to have a cow—or maybe a grandnephew. What kind of a mother would April be? She was so young.

Well, you never know. People can surprise you sometimes. Maybe April, or whoever it was, would rise to the occasion, but Claudia still thought it would be better to be raised by people who really wanted you in the first place, by people who loved children and who wanted nothing more than to have children.

People like her and Dan.

The idea came into focus in her mind the way a stereogram did. It crept into view like the 3-D image, appearing briefly only to quickly disappear, and finally reappearing for good when she focused on it the right way. Once she got it. She remembered how empty her arms had felt when she'd handed the baby over to Marion; how, after just a few short moments, they missed the weight and warmth of him. Maybe, just maybe, she was meant to find this child. Maybe, somehow, he was meant to be hers.

Oh that's crazy. No way. Not a baby that could be one of her student's. Maybe April's. Related to Peterson. No.

Claudia crossed her arms over her chest and looked out the window, trying to ignore the recklessness of the driver.

But maybe.

And then it hit her. Her wish. The chant from Wish Club.

The connection came barreling into her like a sucker punch. *No more waiting, no more strife, bring to her a brand new life.*

Had they done this? Could she be the one responsible for *this?* They'd wished that she get a baby *without delay* and here it was, one month later and she had found a baby. No one can deliver a baby more *without delay* than that.

She stared out the front window of the ambulance, numb and not seeing. Her head vibrated with thoughts of wishes and connections and fate and hope. She didn't notice they were near the hospital until the driver shut off the siren and it began to wind down.

The ambulance pulled up the ramp and stopped by the entrance to the emergency room.

Claudia thought it was something you'd probably never notice—how long it took for the sound of the siren to dissipate completely—unless you were actually inside the ambulance. The men took the baby from the back and slammed the doors.

She got out, too, and started to follow them, thinking it was a strange thing for her to be paying attention to right now—the long slow exhalation of a siren, a sigh that had become softer and softer until it faded out, as if all its air had been spent.

The playground music of squeaky swings and high voices filled the background while Jill sketched at the edge of the park. The mild, late-February weather had brought everyone out today, enjoying a reprieve from the cold and the snow, which still sat in huge gray piles from when it had been plowed.

Charcoal dust coated Jill's fingertips, making them look a little like the soot-coated piles of melting snow that surrounded her as she worked sketching the naked trees. She liked the way the catalpa trees looked in winter, their gnarled and confused limbs clinging to the seedpods, waiting for a real spring day to litter them down. She didn't like the way her drawing was going, however. Everything seemed just a little bit off—out of perspective or proportion. It was just a rough patch, that was all. "You can't be Picasso every day." *Who'd said that?* She couldn't remember where she'd heard it, but she figured whoever had said it must have been an artist, too.

Jill was taking a break from her studio, where her painting over the past few days had become more and more laborious. Taking advantage of the warm weather, Jill had come outside to try to shake off some of her tension or nerves or whatever it was that was making it so challenging to work. She really had put a lot of pressure on herself, trying to make this show her big, breakout show. And that big canvas. *Ugh.* It was good to get away, to work on something different to try to spur her creativity. Jill focused on the gnarled branches again, trying to bring them back into scale with the rest of the tree.

Every now and then a yell from the playground would rise above all the others, and she'd just now heard someone yell, "Mom?" Jill stopped her drawing and looked up, half expecting to find a bloody mess of a child in a heap by the slide.

Twenty-seven years ago, she'd been the bloody mess. The morning it had happened had started out like any other, with her nanny,

Sophie, waking her up, but during breakfast the day's planned course of events had changed and her mother had ended up being the one to get her dressed.

"I just bought those, Jilly," her mother had complained.

Jill's tights wouldn't come up all the way at the crotch. They hung suspended between her thighs, and she could feel the breeze through the fabric when she penguin-walked over to where her mother was standing.

A six-year-old Jill smiled into her mother's forehead while being jostled back and forth, her mother working the tights up, pulling the fabric up her legs in increments until the crotch of her tights hung only a couple of inches below her own. She pulled Jill's skirt down over them. "I suppose that will have to do."

Jill could still feel a breeze on her groin when she walked, and the way the elastic rested on her hips seemed precarious, but she didn't dare argue with her mother on an occasion like this. White tights and a skirt for the playground were bad choices, too, but Jill didn't dare tell her mother that either, for fear of jeopardizing this fortuitous turn of events. Besides, she knew from experience that nothing she could say about her outfit would change her mother's mind. Her mother's word on fashion was the last word. Period.

Her nanny, Sophie, had suggested during breakfast that they go for a walk in the park and feed the ducks in Lincoln Park Zoo, usually one of her favorite past times. But this morning Jill had caught sight of her mother getting coffee in the butler's pantry.

"I don't want to feed the ducks. We always have to go feed the stupid ducks," Jill had said, her fork in her fist, a piece of French toast still stuck in the tines. "I want to go to the playground. Why do I always have to feed the stupid ducks?"

"Okay," Sophie said, "we be going to playgroun' then. After breakfast, we can be going."

"Why can't Mommy go too?" Jill's voice started ratcheting up a little louder, a little whinier. "When can Mommy take me? I always have to go with you."

"You mom very busy. I be taking you to playgroun'." Sophie had spotted Mrs. Trebelmeier in the butler's pantry too, and a flicker of fear had passed across her face.

"She's always busy. What does she always got to do?" Jilly's sad, sad voice now. "How come she can't *ever* take me?"

Her mom had come around the corner with her coffee cup in her hand. "How come you can't ever take me anywhere?" Jill pouted, eyes brimming with just the right amount of water, even though *real* tears had not been an intentional part of this tantrum.

Her mother's blue eyes glared at her, and Jill's lower lip quivered, also quite unintentionally.

Sensing the danger, Sophie tried to intervene. "You mom very busy. After breakfast, I be taking you to park—"

"—the playground."

"—the playgroun'. You mom has lots things to do today." She stopped, apparently unable to explain what those things might be. Mrs. Trebelmeier glared at Sophie, raising the level of fear in her nanny's eyes. But then: "My schedule's not too full this morning, Sophie." Mrs. Trebelmeier had surprised them both. "I could take Jilly to the park for a little while."

It was a cold morning under an overcast sky, but Jill's face was radiant as she held her mother's hand on their walk to the playground. She had the most beautiful mother: refined, almost regal, and always perfectly turned out.

Jill's face fell as they approached the playground, though, when she saw that none of her friends were there. She and her mother had arrived a little earlier than usual because Jill hadn't performed her standard morning litany of tantrums; there had been none of the *I'm not wearing that, I don't want to brush my teeth, Ouch! Ouch! Ouch! You're pulling my hair*, You *tie my shoes*. Today, Jilly had been the perfect little lady.

She headed for the merry-go-round first, pushing one foot along the concrete. The hulking metal wheel ground to a squeaky start. She held on to the cold bar and smiled at her mom each time she circled past her bench. Her mom had a pleasant enough expression on her face, but her eyes were focused far away, not on her daughter going around and around.

The merry-go-round was hard for her to push all by herself and Jill quickly lost interest, never able to build up enough speed for her satisfaction. She abandoned it for the slide. The soles of her patent-leather Mary Janes slipped over the metal steps as she scrambled to the top. She slid down with her hands in the air and this time her mother did smile back before calling out, "Be careful not to get your new tights dirty."

Where could they be? Jill thought on her way up the steps again. Surely some other kids should be here by now. She scanned the playground as she slid down. She thought she spotted one of her friends outside the far gate and she reached up a hand to wave, but it was just a short blond woman walking by. The ground caught her by surprise and her feet stubbed into it, flipping her over and landing her head on the cement. There was a moment immediately after she hit, before it started to hurt, when she opened her eyes and stared into the ground without moving her head, a moment when she thought, "I'm okay." But then the pain started, and she peeled her head off the ground, reaching a hand up to find blood.

She couldn't breathe normally; she could only suck in tiny gasps of air. She got to her knees, but they'd been scraped and she sank back onto the ground. Still the tears wouldn't come, there was only her heart palpitating hard in her chest and the strange hyperventilating sensation. Blood soaked the hand she held to her forehead, and she looked through her hair for her mother, who was still seated on the same bench, with her gaze directed above and past Jill.

Her tongue explored the newly rough interior of her mouth, the cracked and chipped teeth, the metallic taste of blood. Tears started to fill her eyes. What was her mother looking at? And then, finally, she found her voice. "Mom?"

Her mother had turned to look at her, taking a moment to recognize the tangled and bloody mess as her daughter. "Jilly!"

As she'd come toward Jill, she searched in her pockets for her handkerchief, and then she bent at the waist in front of Jill. "Oh

Jilly," she said, holding out the handkerchief, "you've ruined your new tights."

As if it were yesterday, Jill remembered the sensation of peeling her forehead from the pavement, the initial relief that her skull was in one piece. She'd ended up with a pretty good-sized goose egg on her forehead, one missing and one chipped front tooth, and a couple of skinned knees. Her mother had held a constant wince on her face while she wiped the blood from Jill's face, but the look of horror that had appeared there when Jill had opened her mouth to reveal her damaged smile was entrenched in Jill's memory forever.

The dentist hadn't been much help, refusing to utilize any cosmetic dentistry on baby teeth, and Jill often wondered why her mother hadn't pursued it by going to another dentist with her checkbook in hand. Probably, at some point, her mother had become *too busy* to be caught up in her daughter's smile, perhaps consoling herself with the fact that Jill's missing teeth were in fact just baby teeth and that they, and therefore her smile, would grow back.

A cold breeze kicked up and the pages of Jill's sketchbook fought against the clips that were holding them down to her board. Jill blew the charcoal off of her cold fingers and continued to draw, but the tree branches she was sketching began to move, making them look to her like the grabby, gnarled fingers of an old woman—witch's fingers.

In spite of the apparent success of her first wish—for a perfect man, which, as she got to know him better, Marc was turning out to be—Jill couldn't shake a growing sense of uneasiness. No matter what they called it, wishing, energy raising, whatever—it was, she felt, on some level still witchcraft, and there was a part of her inculcated by her Catholic upbringing that still thought it was wrong.

But she couldn't quit now. Jill was waiting for her wish for creative inspiration to kick in. Her opening was in a month, and she still had the big canvas to do. She needed to get going on it, or, at the very least, on something else. But maybe she needed to be patient. If it turned out half as well as her first wish had . . .

And as for Marc, well. In all the years of dating and relationships, she couldn't understand now why she'd never tried dating a younger man before. She'd never met anyone like him. He was so fun. So free. So amazing in bed, unlike the pathetic fumblers of *her* early twenties. She loved that he was so *not* into the *where is this headed* routine. He was polite and funny and charming, and gorgeous beyond belief on top of it all. The way some women stared at him when they were out together—they ought to be ashamed of themselves. But it gave her a thrill. *That's right, ladies, he's with me.*

He left her short, meaningless messages on her voicemail. "*Grrrrr.*" How fun was that? She couldn't imagine uptight Michael ever leaving a message like that.

Marc had finally asked her to sit for some portraits and she'd agreed, pretending to be reluctant, but secretly thrilled. This was the way he preferred to connect with his girlfriends, and she thought it was great.

He'd certainly connected with his black-haired model. They'd both shared a laugh about Jill's interruption, later, when they could talk about it, although Jill's laughter had felt forced and hollow.

She and Marc hadn't had any exclusivity conversations about their relationship. Jill wasn't seeing anyone else, and she sort of assumed that he wasn't either, but for the first time she could remember, Jill felt like *she* wanted to ask *him* not to. It was as though she couldn't get enough of him—and she didn't want to share.

One night the previous week, she'd been on her way out of 4400 North when she'd seen the lights on in his studio. Jill had knocked, but he hadn't answered. She'd waited a long time before deciding he must have just forgotten the lights and left them on. She couldn't bring herself to think of any alternatives.

The cold breeze in the park was more constant now and it was clear to Jill and everyone else that their "spring break" was over. Jill put her charcoals in her art bin and snapped the lid down. After securing a cover sheet over her drawings, she stood up and folded her portable canvas stool, collected her things, and headed back through the park to the pedestrian tunnel that would take her under Lake Shore Drive and up across the street to her building. She passed the mothers and nannies hurrying their children along, all of them wearing coats too thin for the changing weather.

Winter had returned to Chicago like it always did—without fair warning.

Chapter Fifteen

"In my next life," Gail thought, "I'm going to have kids who sleep in the car."

The whole way back from Dominick's Emily had sung the *Caillou* song over and over. Of all the PBS cartoon soundtracks, the one from *Caillou* was the most insidiously evil, in that you really only needed to hear it once to have it stuck in your head all day. The way Emily was carrying on, Gail was fairly certain she wouldn't be able to get the *Caillou* song out of her head until sometime around the middle of next week.

Gail glanced in the rearview mirror. Emily was singing to the side window of the car. She had a thoughtful look on her face, an expression you might see on a ballad singer's face as he crooned "Dust in the Wind," which was made all the more humorous by the fact that she could only pronounce half of the words she was singing. "I'm just a kid who's four, each day I grow some more, I like exploring, I'm Caillou."

I need to learn to treasure these moments, she thought. I need to take Excedrin *before* I go to the grocery store.

"Fuu—uck."

Gail's eyes jumped to the rearview mirror. Emily had stopped her singing and her finger was pointing out the window. "Fuu—uck."

"Emily Anne—"

The sound of a fire truck's siren reached her ears. *Oh jeez-o-pete.*

"Say Figh-errrr truck, Emmy. Figh-errrrr."

Another fire truck came barreling down Foster, hurtling up behind Gail, and she pulled over to the side, her heart pounding. She'd been so caught up in Emily's suspected profanity she hadn't noticed its approach. Sad the way the Universe worked, she thought. At the time in your life when you wanted to be the safest driver possible, you were so distracted by your kids you turned into a menace. Every time she saw one of those crashed broomstick witches at Halloween, she'd tell her kids, "You know what happened here, don't you? That witch got distracted by the kids on the back of her broom."

Speaking of witches, Gail remembered she still needed to call Claudia back. Claudia had left another of her incomprehensible messages this morning, telling Gail to call her back right away, *It's urgent.* She'd sounded extremely upset.

Man, there sure were a lot of fire trucks. There must be a huge fire somewhere. A third truck sped by. This time Gail had pulled over to the side in a timelier manner.

"Where are all the fire trucks going, Emmy? There must be a big fire."

When she went through the intersection at Ashland, past the tall buildings on the corner, she could see black smoke rising from the west, a few blocks south. "Look at all that smoke . . ."

The smoke was near the boys' school.

No. It couldn't be. Worrywart. Worrywart. Stop it—just stop.

In spite of what her brain was trying to tell her was just paranoia, Gail turned south down a side street to pick up Burns Street westbound, forgoing her trip home to drop off the groceries. The air was foggy with smoke and people were standing on their front porches or in the street looking west. As Gail got closer and closer to the school, the smoke got thicker and thicker.

When she turned down Harcourt, she could see the flashing strobes of a squad car blocking the intersection farther down, at the northeast corner of the school. Her heart dropped in her chest. No. No!

The smoke was thickest here, and it smelled acrid, but also, oddly enough, it had the pleasant wintry smell of crackling hardwood. Cars jammed Harcourt and Gail couldn't drive any closer. She double-parked and got out, yanking Emily from the back seat, leaving her hat where it had dropped on the floor mat. The ding ding ding of the van's warning system, *You've left your lights on, The keys are still in the ignition,* faded behind her as she broke into a run down the sidewalk toward the school. Smoke billowed from the second floor and roof. Flames were still coming out of some windows on the east side of the building, despite the stream of water the firefighters had trained on it.

"You can't go down there, lady." A cop was shouting but Gail didn't turn around. In the noise and commotion she elected to pretend she hadn't heard him. Let him *try* to keep me from my kids, she thought.

It would take a bullet.

Kids milled around the edge of the parking lot in the smoke-fog, some of them crying, huddling close to teachers. One group was still wearing gym clothes, and stood shivering. Gail scanned for Will and Andrew. For Andrew's blue sweater, Will's maroon one. She looked for the junior kindergartners, the third-grade class. Their teachers, Mrs. Dwyer or Mrs. Mitchell. She circled the teachers' parking lot, heading toward the playground on the northwest corner, closer to where the kindergarten classrooms were. There were parents and kids and firefighters everywhere, cops running.

Two firemen ran by, heading toward the corner ahead of her. "They said about twenty still on the second floor," one was yelling into a radio. "Northwest stairway's blocked—they're going up the main stairway on the east—"

There are kids still inside? A short wail, an "ahh" escaped Gail's mouth, and Emily started chewing on the knuckle of the thumb she'd been sucking on.

Gail hurried to the edge of the playground, to a group of what appeared to be first- or second-graders standing together with their teacher.

"Where's the third grade?" Gail asked the teacher. "Mrs. Mitchell's class?"

"I don't know. I haven't seen them."

"Mrs. Dwyer—the junior kindergartners?"

The teacher shook her head and shrugged sympathetically.

"Mrs. Stone? Kayla fell over"—a boy started tugging on the teacher's arm—"and her eyes are all—" he rolled his eyes back into his head, apparently a simulation of Kayla, and Mrs. Stone hurried away from Gail.

A fireman yelled over a megaphone. "You have to stand back—get back, people. We need to get everyone back and out of the way so no one gets hurt." Gail left the playground and hurried out to the sidewalk, which was crowded with spectators. She jogged down toward the kindergarten entry.

Smoke poured from the second floor here, but no flames. On this side, the west side of the school, the sidewalk was deserted—no teachers or children—just emergency workers. Gail sensed that panic was close, waiting to take hold of her, like a bird of prey circling overhead.

Emily started sobbing and Gail pulled her tighter, closer, glad for something solid to hang on to.

"Everything's going to be okay, baby." Gail patted the back of Emily's coat while she held her. "Don't you worry. Everything's going to be fine."

The headquarters for the Chicago Women's Foundation were in a large Victorian house in Lincoln Park West. The house, in its heyday, must have really been something—inlaid wooden floors, mahogany woodwork, crystal chandeliers—and while it hadn't fallen into disrepair, it had taken on a more worn appearance. The Women's Foundation was, after all, a foundation based on charitable works and therefore, they couldn't be seen squandering too much money on something as unnecessary as appearances.

Lindsay hung up the phone in the first-floor office and consulted her notes. A member of the planning committee for the spring fashion show, Lindsay was working with the Metron Hotel, this week's trendiest, see-and-be-seen-at hotel. The fashion show was going to be held there three weeks from now, during the second week in March, and she'd just finished talking with the

Metron's events coordinator when Evelyn Cantwell stuck her head inside the door.

"Lindsay. Hello, love."

Evelyn had a way of calling all the Foundation women "love." It was always good to get one of Evelyn's "loves," because it usually meant you were in her favor, and since Evelyn was the president of the Chicago chapter of the Women's Foundation, and therefore the gatekeeper of Chicago society, it was good to be in her favor. The irony was, as often as Evelyn handed out the "loves," she was one of the least loving people Lindsay knew.

"Evelyn. Hi." Lindsay smiled.

"My goodness, Lindsay, you've been looking fabulous lately. What's your secret—have you lost weight?"

"Oh, well thank you." Lindsay's smile brightened naturally, warming to her favorite subject of late. "I've lost a little weight, yes. Thanks for noticing."

Evelyn stood in the doorway with her arms crossed over her chest officiously. "Well, everyone's talking about how great you look—and I have to agree, you're simply radiating." She continued to stare at Lindsay, her eyebrows pulled together ever so slightly.

Lindsay just smiled, speechless. After a brief moment, she got the feeling she shouldn't just be sitting there smiling, or *radiating*, so Lindsay got down to business. "I just got off the phone with the Metron. George wants to know if we want them to take care of the flowers using their house florist, or if we're going to be supplying them. He seemed rather intent on having us go with their in-house florist, but I don't think we should—"

"That is *so* George, now isn't it, love? I was at a Chamber Music board meeting last fall and I'm pretty sure his precious in-house florists had done the arrangements because they had carnations in them." Evelyn made a face as if to say, *can you believe it?* "Your instincts are correct. We should supply our own. Can we get Keiko's? On this late notice?"

"I'll call over there right now." Lindsay put her hand on the phone.

"Something orchidy, I think."

Lindsay nodded in agreement, smiling. *How perfect. I share your vision.*

"But not just Phalaenopsis, something more exotic. Keiko will know." Evelyn dropped her arms down onto her hips. "I'll let you get to it, then. Keep up the good work, love." She gave Lindsay another smile before turning to leave the room.

Lindsay picked up the phone and tried to dial, but it was difficult. She couldn't stop bouncing in her seat.

Emily kept squirming in Gail's arms as Gail ran along the west side of the school. The building was closer to the street here and it was quieter on this side, too, only a few firemen hurrying around. One stopped to yell at her, "You can't be over here. Get across the street." He waved her over to the other side.

Unable to pretend she hadn't heard him, Gail obeyed, crossing over and cutting in between two cars. The snow on the parkway near the curb was in a high mound and she climbed over, her right foot breaking through the frozen crust on top, sinking her down about a foot. She put her other foot down on the icy snow and it skidded out from under her. Gail fell. Emily slid from her arms and simultaneously Gail heard a snap, feeling a sharp pain in her right knee.

"Emmy!"

Gail climbed out of the snow bank and crawled over to where Emily was crying, lying on her side, a little pink bundle. "Are you okay, honey?" Gail's eyes widened at the splotches of blood on the front of Emily's coat. "Where does it hurt honey? Where—?"

Emmy's right thumb was bloody. Gail calmed slightly. It didn't look too bad.

Gail's eyes filled with tears; she had her daughter out here in the cold, running around in the snow, with no hat and no gloves, her coat unzipped. Gail hugged Emily close, wishing she could be holding her sons close as well. Her fingers shook as she zipped the front of Emily's pink parka.

God, let the boys be okay, Please let them be fine. Gail looked over Emily's shoulder. She could see people moving through the smoke, on the sidewalk farther down. *I want Will and Andrew to run up to me now. God, I'll do anything, anything if you just let them be okay.*

Gail lifted herself and Emily up out of the dirty snow, wincing as she put weight on her right leg. She made her way carefully over to the sidewalk, looking down, watching where she placed her boots on the ice. The sidewalk was dry, and she hurried down to the group of people, her right knee throbbing. There were older kids here, fifth- and sixth-graders. A few teachers.

"Has anyone seen the kindergartners? Or the third grade?" Gail shouted. Her eyes burned with tears and smoke.

People shook their heads.

Gail worked her way down the sidewalk, bumping into people, asking her question over and over.

"Mom!" It came from pretty far away.

Gail spun around. "Will?" but she didn't see him in the crowd, through the smoke. Had she mistaken another child's voice for her son's? It had happened to her before, in other places at other times, always driving a guilt-stake through her heart.

"Will? Will! Where are you?" Gail circled back down the sidewalk the way she'd just come, squinting her eyes against the smoke. Then she saw his back, his sandy brown hair, the maroon sweater he'd worn to school that morning. He was standing still, his head tilted up, watching the faces of people as they passed him by.

"Will!"

He turned around and, seeing her, ran, crashing into them with a thud rendered silent by the commotion around them. Gail teetered back with the impact, but didn't fall. She dropped to her knees and, with Emily still tight in her arms, hugged her son.

Mara sat at her desk, chewing her way through a box of Girl Scout Thin Mints while she filled out the previous week's paperwork. The elastic band on her pants kept digging into her waist, which was taking on a new, rounder shape. She had put on a few pounds. Well, quite a few pounds. In fact, she'd probably put on as much weight as Lindsay had lost.

Well so what? she tried to tell herself, *I can afford it.* Besides, she'd had to take a couple of days off work to let her nose heal. (*Personal days and sick days—Dr. Seeley must have done a slow burn.*) And it was easy to eat too much when you were just sitting around, what with the refrigerator so close and all.

But something had changed. Previously when she'd looked in the mirror, she had been repulsed by the little pooch her belly made, but not recently. *Finally, I've come to accept my body. To love it for what it is.*

Well, if she wanted to, this weight wasn't anything she couldn't exercise off. But the exercise would have to wait for a while. She touched a finger to the bandage over her nose. She wouldn't be allowed to jostle it around any time soon. Maybe she could wish the weight away at the next Wish Club the way Lindsay had.

Her greatest fear wearing the bandage around was that people would think she'd had plastic surgery on her nose. Imagine. She already had the perfect nose. Her other fear, and Henry's too, was that people were going to think he had hit her. She had two huge purple bruises under her eyes.

Mara had been at Tate's Drugs two days ago, and while she'd been checking out, the cashier kept glancing up at her face after she slid each item over the scanner. When the cashier, a young, extremely thin woman with long, unkempt hair, had handed Mara the receipt, she'd said, after another quick glance around, "You know there are people that can help you." She looked like someone who might *know*, and she'd kept her hand on the top of the receipt in Mara's hand for an extra moment until Mara had replied, "Help me what? Recover from plastic surgery?"

At least Dr. Seeley had refrained from any verbal comment this morning.

"There's a lot of filing backed up," he'd said to her when she walked in. When she had turned around after taking her coat off and he could see her face, his face had expressed surprise, but he hadn't said anything. Maybe he'd thought she'd had plastic surgery, too.

Before heading into his office he'd hesitated for a moment, in that manner of his that made it look like he was trying hard to think of something nice to say. Apparently unable to come up with anything, Dr. Seeley had pursed his giant lips again and left the room.

What a kind and considerate man I work for.

Mara bit into a Thin Mint and tore it away from her mouth, glaring at the tall stacks of files that lined the front edge of her desk. They were all uniformly two feet high, except for the pile farthest to the right, which was only about six inches tall. The most recent one—a work in progress. She leaned forward on her elbows and shoved the rest of the cookie in her mouth. With her bruised circles under her eyes, she felt like a raccoon peering out from inside a burrow.

She gave a deep sigh. The eleven-o'clock patient had canceled, and there was no time like the present to get started on these files. But maybe she should get lunch. She sure had been hungry lately. Hungry constantly, it seemed. If she hadn't known better she would have thought she was pregnant. *It's probably just middle age or hormones or something. Nothing extraordinary.*

What was extraordinary was the way Henry's hair had been growing. The downy hairs on his head kept spreading, filling in the bald spot. It looked as if he were using one of those hair-transplant-in-a-can products. He now had enough hair to hold down a comb-over if he wanted to have one. And then there was her discovery last night.

Mara had been reading when Henry had come to bed. He'd sunk down beside her, asking how much longer she was going to stay up.

"Just to the end of this chapter. Two more pages."

He'd smiled at her, "all right," and turned over.

She'd bent over and kissed his head, then started to stroke his back, when she'd noticed, after one pass, that there was more of that light brown, downy hair sprouting up. On his back. Was this another one of those middle-age things? Like hair growing out of noses and ears, or sprouting on chins? Henry had never had hair on his back before.

Mara'd run her hand over the hairs again. Henry nestled more deeply into the covers and made a little sighing noise. There were an abundance of hairs, mostly concentrated around his shoulder blades. She leaned in closer to inspect them, but not too close, lest Henry make any sudden moves.

"Henry. You've got hairs on your back!"

After some discussion and several minutes of watching Henry's elbows point off in odd directions as he tried to get his hands onto the hair, Mara had placed him in front of the bathroom mirror and given him her hand mirror so he could look at them.

There they were. Two small dark patches of fur growing in between his shoulder blades. Their eyes met in the mirror.

Of course there had to be a plausible explanation for spontaneous hair growth, but neither one of them had been able to think of any. Mara thought he should see a doctor.

"It's just hair, Mara, not open lesions. You're making such a big deal about this."

Of course he was happy with the hair on his head, and she wasn't totally displeased with it either. But the hair on his back— well, that was werewolfy. It had taken a while, but she'd finally convinced him he should call his doctor. "It's just coming in so fast—everywhere."

"Okay, okay. I'll make an appointment with Dr. Bernstein tomorrow."

Mara had raised her eyebrows at him.

"I promise. Really."

She should call Henry now, she thought, biting into another cookie, to remind him to make that appointment, because she knew he would put it off for as long as he could get away with it, hoping she would forget. A little sprinkle of dark crumbs landed on the file in front of her. She would call Henry right now, she decided. Mara absently pressed her fingers into the black crumbs and brought them to her mouth before reaching for the phone.

"*Some* kindergartners—stuck up on the second—science fair today." Gail caught fragments of a conversation as two people rushed by her, breathless as they yelled to each other. The words came at her, taking a moment to register, like a cut from an extremely sharp knife. She broke away from her hug and stood up, but the men were lost in the crowd behind her.

"Will." Gail put both of her hands on his small shoulders. "Have you seen Andrew? The kindergartners?"

"No." He shook his head. His eyes looked more worried than a nine-year-old's ever should as they turned to search the front of the school across the street.

"Was the science fair today?" she asked him. His science project wasn't due until next week—at least that's what he'd told her.

"Yeah, it started yesterday for six through eight. They said that's where the fire started."

Oh God no. No.

"Where was it? Did you go—did other classes go?"

Will wrinkled his forehead at his mom, like, *Why does she care about science projects at a time like this?* "We went yesterday."

"You went—Where? Where was the fair?"

"In the science lab. On the second floor."

Gail felt the dizziness rise up from her stomach, climbing inside her until it filled her head. She bent at the waist and reached out an arm, steadying herself on Will's shoulder. She managed a couple of breaths and just as she was about to stand up straight, she lurched to one side and threw up.

Chapter Sixteen

⟡

Greta held her hands loosely clasped behind her back as she followed the couple around her gallery, Eleventh House. She paused with them when they stopped to admire a painting and hurried past the works they elected to hurry past. Greta reached a thumb up to scratch her lower back through the purple velour shirt she was wearing, and her bracelets clattered. She knew they wouldn't buy today. They were just browsing, bored, wasting time after their lunch at D'Alliance or Savoury or one of the many other trendy restaurants in the River North neighborhood.

Greta watched them browse, bored herself. She really had a lot of things to do—calls to make, paperwork to catch up on. Normally she enjoyed these mindless tours of the gallery, but today Greta's mood was off; a nagging feeling was plaguing her, like the dream everyone had in college about signing up for a class and forgetting to go to that class until the night before the final exam. A feeling like she needed to be doing something—only what?

Last fall, she'd had the same sinking feeling when she'd sensed that weird dry spell, that unnatural lack of balance. It had felt as if something or someone had thrown Mother Nature out of whack. At least her rainmaking spell had worked. Well, it had made snow, anyway, since it had taken effect in December. But this time, she was sensing something dark, too. Something more like a cloud. Like trouble brewing.

Davis. The word slid into Greta's conscious the way quicksilver rolls down into a crack. As she trailed the couple, her first thought was, *Is Davis the trouble? It doesn't make sense.*

It occurred to her then that maybe *Davis* was unrelated to her nagging mood. *Davis* could just simply be the man's first name, or maybe it was the couple's last name.

Davis slipped in again, but this time with an image of the woman in her gallery pressing against a male figure that was taller and darker and definitely not the man in front of her. *That explains Davis*, Greta thought, betraying nothing of what she now knew with her face or her posture.

"Ooh, I like this one." The wife pointed to an abstract expressionist work in oils.

"Mmm." The husband was noncommittal.

Greta looked at them over the rim of her reading glasses. "I'm afraid I don't have too many abstracts on hand, but if they're what you truly enjoy, you may prefer to return in March."

The woman snapped her head around to look at Greta, her mouth slightly open, as if she'd forgotten Greta was there.

"I'm having an opening, the third Friday in March," Greta continued, "for a wonderful abstract artist, Jill Trebelmeier. She's really quite good, it might be worth checking out." Greta smiled pleasantly, pretending her comment hadn't been an attempt to rush them off, even though she really would have preferred to be rid of them.

The wife's mouth still hung open, only now with surprise. "We know Jill!" She looked at her husband, then back at Greta. "Is this her gallery then?"

"Well, it's my gallery. But I've been representing Jill for the past six years."

"How fascinating. What a small world." The woman's smile had a slightly dreamy quality to it. "I worked with her father—well, before he passed, naturally. I practically watched little Jilly grow up. I'd love to see her work. When is the opening? March you say?"

Greta nodded. "Yes, the sixteenth."

"Fabulous, then. I'll check my calendar—I do hope I can make it."

The husband already had his BlackBerry out. "Mmm. I'll be in Tokyo. I'm afraid you'll have to manage without me." He winked at Greta. "Usually not a problem for the Missus. I make it and she spends it—simultaneously." He gave his wife a congenial, just-kidding squeeze around her shoulders, and she grimaced, the dreamy look completely zapped out of her. "In this case, though," he continued, "I wouldn't mind having a piece of Jill's work on hand. Pretty little thing—I'll bet she's grown into quite a looker."

Greta nodded again. "Jill is indeed a lovely young woman." She looked at the wife. "I hope you can make it on the sixteenth."

This had turned out better than anticipated. The woman might even come back and buy something. Greta was relieved she hadn't tried to rush them off any more forcefully.

The couple began to meander slowly toward the front of the gallery, the woman's stiletto heels making astonishingly little sound on the hardwood floor. They were almost to the door when her husband paused to admire a glass sculpture.

It was exactly the shape made when you put index finger to index finger and thumb to thumb and stretched them as long as you could. The outside was green and from its opening unfolded many layered pink petals until at the very center there was a dark burgundy core. The woman drew down the corners of her mouth and widened her eyes when she came around to look at the front of the sculpture.

Greta had to control her face so as not to grin. The wife knew what she was looking at, and *Davis* probably would too, but the question was, did the husband?

𝒜 muffled whoosh—then flames shot from a first-floor window, sending glass onto the pavement below. Every head on Gail's side of the street snapped around to look. The glass sprinkled the pavement, making a tinkling sound, like wind chimes, a bright, happy noise that was horribly out of place.

"We've got to find Andrew, guys." Gail stood up, wincing at her sore knee, and wiped her mouth with the back of her hand the way she always told her children not to. She hoisted Emily back onto her hip and wiped the back of her hand on her jeans.

Will was staring at his mother's vomit in the snow. "Will, c'mon." She reached her hand out for him to hold and he hesitated only briefly—most likely because of the vomit, and not because he wanted a fight about being *too old*.

Gail walked favoring her right knee; something was definitely wrong there.

Something was definitely wrong everywhere. More sirens were approaching: ambulances. Gail reached the end of the block, across from the southwest corner of the school, and they started to cross the street. Two ambulances sped by, stopping on the south side of the school, joining two or three that were already there.

Two firemen hurried from the south entrance of the school, carrying two kids apiece. Three small kids straggled behind, coughing and looking disoriented when they stepped outside, eyes squinting. A paramedic ran up to the three of them and herded them toward the circle of ambulances where a triage area had been set up.

Gail quickened her pace—those kids were about the right size for kindergartners. She weaved in and out of the standing crowds and around the ambulances, irritated with all the gawkers getting in her way. When she came around the side of an ambulance, she saw Mrs. Dwyer leaning against it, an oxygen mask to her face, breathing into it hard. One of her cheeks was smudged black and her forehead was sweaty, despite the cold. Her eyes moved nervously from child to child, scattered all around her, as if she were reflexively taking a head count.

"Mrs. Dwyer, where's Andrew?"

Mrs. Dwyer pulled the mask down from her face, "I don't know—I couldn't—" Her eyes were red from smoke and tears. She coughed, brought the mask to her face and inhaled, blinked, and brought it back down to speak. "I think he's out, honey."

She *thinks?* Gail looked back toward the south door, the yellow coat of a fireman disappearing in smoke as he went inside. Gail kept searching the children, trying to find Andrew. Will's eyes scanned the crowd, too, looking worried. Every now and then he'd tug on her hand and stretch her arm out as he tried to identify a boy here or there, hidden behind oxygen masks and soot.

A movement at the south entrance caught Gail's attention and she turned to see a fireman running out the door, carrying a child in his arms. The boy's body was limp, bouncing as the fireman ran, his head and blond hair flopping gently with each step, shoes bobbling. Blue and white Shaq shoes. Andrew's shoes.

"Andrew!"

Gail ran to him. A paramedic met the fireman, hurrying Andrew to the ground in front of an ambulance. They looked about to shoo her away.

"That's my son," Gail said. "He's *my* son. Is he okay? Is he going to be okay?" No one answered in the rush of activity, the calls for oxygen and intubation. Andrew's beautiful straight blond hair splayed on the dirty asphalt. Gail started crying.

"Is he dead?" Will asked, his voice high, twisted.

"No." Gail snapped at him. Then, her sweet-mommy voice kicked in, "He's going to be okay. They're going to get him better and he's going to be fine."

And it was then, Gail decided to *know it*. She would tell her friends later it was as if a latent prizefighter inside her had punched a fist through a paper wall in her chest, and she decided right then that this was how it was going to be. She just chose a different future than the one that had started to unfold in front of her.

"I've got breath sounds," someone said, kneeling over Andrew.

"He's fine." Gail said it out loud, again—the words lending power, credence to her will. Andrew was going to be fine because that was the only way it could be, the only way she could ever imagine her future to be. *Andrew is okay now. And he will be okay and that is the only future for him and for me.* This is the way it is and always shall be. It was as if she were overcome with faith. She'd chosen her future and she decided to be certain that God would let her have it, the future that she wished for.

Andrew was fine and everything would be okay.

It was the only possible outcome.

✳

Coincidences, Dan thought, were just a nutty part of life. For him, running into someone he hadn't seen in twenty years was just that: nutty. It meant nothing more than an accident of chance. But he knew that for Claudia, the opposite was true. Such things were *meant* to happen; there was always *a reason* they happened. Dan knew that for Claudia, there was no such thing as a coincidence.

"You're reading way too much into this," he told her.

Claudia had been playing with her chopsticks, picking up the same piece of pickled ginger over and over again. She finally popped it into her mouth.

"This is not *just a coincidence*," she said, chewing. "There's more to it than that and I just—I want to look into it more, that's all. I think it might be a sign."

Dan didn't snort, but he wanted to. That was another thing; she was always getting signs. The last *really good* sign she'd gotten was on the side of a CTA bus, an ad that said, "Welcome Home for the Holidays." The previous fall, when interest rates had been at an all-time low, they'd been trying to decide whether or not they should buy a condo they'd just looked at, when a bus had pulled up with the ad plastered on the side while they were waiting to cross the street.

Claudia had immediately pounced on it as the sign they were looking for. "We have to do it. It's a sign. A really good sign. If we buy it now, we'll close in . . . in mid-November and see—we'll be home for the holidays."

She had been all smiles as she looked at him, happy, as if the decision had been made. Just then a bike messenger had flown by between the bus and the curb and had clipped Claudia's purse with the tube he was carrying under his arm, the same kind of tube Dan sometimes used for architectural drawings. Her huge purse had fallen to the sidewalk, where half of its contents had spilled from its gaping top, getting tossed onto the curb and sidewalk and into the street. Her wallet had ended up resting precariously on a sewer grate.

"And exactly what kind of sign was that?" he'd asked her.

They walked for about twenty minutes before she would talk to him again.

"Don't snort," she said after swallowing the ginger. "I hate your snort."

He stared her down. There were any number of examples he could give her from their past, examples of good signs gone bad.

"This time it's different," she said. "You have to agree with that. This is on a much bigger scale."

"I don't know, Claude. It just seems so far-fetched. Besides, what do you think the chances are that they would actually let *us* get in the middle of all of it—try to adopt it? There are all sorts of conflict-of-interest issues here. They could accuse you of having the mother plant it in the bathroom—"

"Oh, don't be ridiculous."

Dan leaned forward in his chair. "This thing is going to get really ugly, I'll bet. Do you know how many hearings and interviews you're going to have to go through just because you found that baby and now you want to cloud the situation up by trying to adopt it?"

"Him. By trying to adopt *him*."

"Him, then. You're too trusting, Claude. There's nothing wrong with that. I love that about you—your ability to believe the best in people—but it's just not realistic." He pointed his chopsticks out toward her and waved them back and forth, showing her a fake smile as he said, "There isn't always a happy ending."

"I know that. Don't condescend to me like that—like . . . like I'm a child." She lowered her voice, but there was gravel in it now. "I see plenty of ugliness every day. Every single day. Sometimes I swear this world is just one giant ugly pile of shit and that just about everyone in it sucks."

The waitress had started over to their table, but she passed them by discreetly, in the "save face" way of the Japanese, when she heard their heated discussion, apparently not wanting to get caught up in the middle of an argument about whether or not the world is one giant ugly pile of shit.

The outburst, the cloud of negativity surrounding his usually idealistic wife, took Dan aback. He looked around to see if anyone had noticed their argument and, still unable to look at Claudia, his eyes ended up resting on the wall of the booth, trying to take comfort in the familiarity of the photographs of peaceful fountains and pagodas.

They came here a lot. Although the staff gave no indication of it. They were treated pleasantly enough every time, but without any hint of recognition or preference for their status as regular customers. It always sat poorly with Dan, who thought they should employ more Western sales techniques in attracting and keeping their regular customers happy. Now he wondered if maybe there wasn't something to their sales technique after all, something that appealed to self-flagellating Midwesterners.

He looked at his wife, still flagellating her pickled ginger. Silently. Her cheeks were flushed and her lips made that subtle curve downward at the corners that indicated her displeasure, usually a precursor to her pout—when she wasn't so angry.

"How do you know there isn't something wrong? What if there's something wrong with it?" Dan asked.

"Him."

"Him. Did you ever consider that? Maybe there's a *reason* the mother threw him away. She might be on drugs or have HIV or who knows what."

"That baby is fine. I know it. I knew it the minute I held him. He's perfect."

Their eyes locked in impasse. Claudia was the first to look away, back down at her mutilated pile of ginger. They sat in silence for several long moments.

"To be honest, I don't really understand it myself," Claudia started, without looking up, her chopsticks back to worrying the ginger. "I just feel like I need to do something. I know we don't have much of a chance of actually getting this baby, all the red tape and that's not even considering the fact it could turn out to be April's. Peterson's grandnephew. But even if he isn't, and they do put him into foster care or up for adoption, there are people who have been on waiting lists for years.

"But I don't know . . . I just can't shake the thought that somehow I was the one that was meant to find him and that *I* was meant to try to help him, somehow, for some reason."

"Maybe it's April you were supposed to help."

Claudia eyes wrinkled, like, *Eeuw.* "Maybe," she said. She pushed her glasses up her nose and looked seriously at Dan, though, as if she were actually considering it. "Sure, maybe April needs my help. I think that baby does. I don't know—whatever it is I'm supposed to do, do you think you could just humor me for a while? Just go along until we see where this leads? Please?"

Dan sat back and crossed his arms with a sigh. He stared at his dish of soy sauce, green whorls of wasabi floating on top. Humoring her about buying a condo or a stack of books on witchcraft was one thing. Humoring her about a life-changing, a lifestyle-*threatening* event was quite another.

He'd never even held a baby before. He was still having some doubts about wanting one of his *own*, much less someone else's castoff. He thought about what he considered to be their already precarious financial situation and how much he wanted to get out on his own. He thought about smelly diapers and tripping over toys and never being able to go out, on the spur of the moment, to even a dismal place like this for sushi. Is that where all this would lead?

He thought of living with Claudia for any length of time when she was in one of her drowning moods—moods that could suck him right down with her into a dark, swirling cesspool of doom and gloom. He thought back to her silence just now after their fight, to her silence last fall during their twenty-minute walk from where her purse had spilled on the sewer, and it was just that kind of quiet he knew he'd have to live with, for what? A week? A month? Longer?

What *were* the chances this would lead to anything after all? Probably next to nothing. Surely they wouldn't let her have this baby, just because she'd found it. Maybe it was just best to humor his wife and avoid a painful coexistence that could last for some indeterminate amount of time.

Claudia was picking up a new piece of ginger and dropping it, over and over.

Dan reached out his hand and put it over hers. He squeezed, gently at first, then harder, until she set the chopsticks down onto the wood-block tray. One rolled down off the block and onto the table.

When he was holding nothing but her empty hand in his, he said, "Okay."

The crowds at Children's Memorial Hospital were gone and, at this hour of the night, Gail and John had the waiting area to themselves.

John sat in his chair and waited. After ten years of marriage and a total of twelve years together, he knew better than to say anything to Gail while she cried. It was best to let her purge her system uninterrupted.

His arm was resting on the back of Gail's chair and now that her sobbing had started to subside, he moved his arm down and enveloped her shoulder in his huge hand. He held some Kleenex in the other, and when she seemed ready, he handed it to her. She wiped her eyes and cheeks and blew her nose.

"You know he's going to be okay, right?" he asked, as if maybe she hadn't understood the doctor.

Gail shook her head. "I know. I know." She sniffed, then started shaking her head in the negative. "It's just that . . . that . . . ." She turned her blotched face up to him. She took a deep quivery breath in through her mouth. "I . . . I just . . . I feel like I shouldn't have . . . ."

"Shouldn't have what?"

Gail started sobbing again.

"Gail, what . . . ? You're acting like all this is your fault."

Fear popped into her eyes and stayed there.

"Gail? What is it? How could you be responsible?" He paused. Tried a smile. "What? Have you taken up a secret life as an arsonist or something?"

Gail didn't laugh. She exhaled a huge breath of air. "It's Book Club. I think Book Club did this."

"Your Book Club has taken up a secret life as arsonists?"

"No." She shook her head, and this time she did allow a smile to pass across her face, very briefly, before she said, "John, there's something I need to tell you."

A woman came into the waiting room with her young son while Gail explained to John, through her tears, the recent turn of events at Book Club.

The woman and her son sat in the opposite corner of the waiting room, as if they were trying to get as far away from the crazy crying lady as they could. The boy appeared to be about two and was astonishingly awake for this hour of the night. He tugged on the fringe of a pink blanket she had in her arms, within which, presumably, a baby sister slept.

"*Agua mami. Agua.*" The boy pulled and tugged at his mother and pointed to the drinking fountain. She whispered something quickly to him in Spanish and his face contorted into tears.

"So you think it's because you wanted more time to yourself," John pulled his eyes from the little boy and looked back down at Gail, "and you made this, er . . . *wish* and that's what caused the school to catch fire?" He shook his head, made a face as if to say, *that's goofy.* "I don't know anything about these types of things— psychics and fortune-tellers and—well, basically I think it's all just a crock. And these wishes you're talking about—the witchcraft stuff. I don't know, but if you're asking me, it's kind of a stretch, don't you think? Especially the part about wanting time to yourself causing the fire. Besides, the school burning down would have the opposite eff—"

And then he got it. *If the boys were dead . . .*

Tears started to stream down Gail's cheeks again. She put her face in her hands and sobbed. John rubbed circles on her back. He wanted to tell her he thought she was being crazy, that all this witchcraft and wishing stuff was just in their heads. But she was crying so uncontrollably. There were few times in their life together he'd ever seen her this upset.

John broke his own rule, leaned closer and tried talking to his wife while she cried. "Gail? Gail." He paused, then decided to stay the course even though she hadn't looked up. He stopped rubbing her back and took both of her shoulders in his hands. "I don't know a better mother in the world than you. Whatever you think you did . . . I just don't think anything like this could ever have come from you. I know you'd rather die than let anything happen to our kids."

John loosened the grip he had on her shoulders but didn't remove his hands. It took a long moment before Gail leaned into him, letting his big arms encircle her. She put her head on his chest and he held her.

Down the hall, Andrew had finally fallen asleep in his room. He'd fallen down some stairs evacuating the school and had broken his ankle. There had been a bit of a pile-up, with a few other children falling down as well, but they weren't hurt as seriously as Andrew and had managed to escape. Andrew had succumbed to the smoke.

A firefighter had found him unconscious on the landing near the south entrance and, while he'd regained consciousness fairly quickly after they put him on oxygen, it was still going to be a while before the doctors would know the extent of the damage to his lungs. They'd done a blood test and taken X-rays, and initial reports were good, but the doctors also wanted a bronchoscopy. They'd just finished the test and Gail and John were waiting to talk to the doctor about the results. After the procedure, Andrew had dozed off, which was when the tears Gail had been fighting back had begun to fall.

"Why don't we go back to the room," John said. "It's been at least twenty minutes by now."

Gail looked at her watch and nodded her head against his shoulder.

"If you want, I could run home in a little while," John continued, "see how Ellen's managing with the other two. I could grab some stuff for you, get your toothbrush, or a change of clothes." He ran his hand through her hair. Gail didn't look up, but she seemed to be considering it. "I'd be gone less than an hour." He stopped rubbing her hair. "Unless you want me to stay."

Gail shook her head. "No. That's a good idea. You should check on them. They had a rough day, too."

"Okay then." John gave her a squeeze before he stood up. "I'll walk you back to his room first. Can you think of anything else you need from—"

"Angélica Pérez?" The nurse had her head down, looking at her clipboard, when she stepped into the waiting room.

"—anything else you need from home?" John finished his sentence while Gail stood up, but she wasn't paying attention to him anymore.

The nurse looked directly at the woman in the corner, "Angélica Pérez?" she said again, more loudly.

The young mother was already trying to gather her things, but progress was slow. She stood up with the baby, the diaper bag slung over her forearm, and asked for her son to follow. They started toward the door, but all progress stopped when the little boy grabbed onto the drinking fountain as they passed it and started crying.

"*Portate bien. Vamanos a la doctor. ¡Date prisa!*" his mother said in a harsh whisper, but her son refused to let go. The woman smiled at the nurse, who gave her a wan, impatient smile back. The mother tugged at the arm of her son, but her hands were full and he wouldn't let go of the drinking fountain, both arms around it in an embrace.

Gail and John had walked as far as the doors to the patient rooms, and John held one of them open for Gail, but she turned and, with her new limp, walked away from him and over to the little boy.

She smiled at his mother. "*¿Con su permiso?*" Gail asked, putting her hands around the little boy's waist to lift him.

"*Sí,*" the mother said, and Gail hoisted him up for a drink, bending only her left knee, keeping her right leg out straight. She said, "*Aprieta el botón plateado,*" but he already knew what to do. After his drink he ran to grab his mother's hand and they went through the door on the other side of the waiting room, which the nurse was holding open.

Gail was still by the drinking fountain, watching them walk away. The mother stopped in the doorway and turned back toward Gail, giving her a shy smile and a slight nod, a silent *thank you* for another mother's understanding. No words necessary.

John stood watching his wife, marveling at her. It had been so many years since he'd heard her speak Spanish, he'd forgotten she could do it. It was like seeing her with new eyes. It reminded him of the girl he'd first met all those years ago in Buenos Aires—the mischief in her eyes, the artificially jet-black hair, the sultry way she moved.

Her gait was syncopated as she walked toward him now, with her red nose and puffy eyes. She gave him a weak smile and John realized he couldn't love her any more than he did right this minute.

He held the door open for her and Gail hobbled through without saying anything. No words necessary.

Chapter Seventeen

The incongruous country smell of a wood fire filled the air on the tony city street. Chichi boutiques, restaurants, and galleries lined either side. Greta lingered on the front steps of her gallery instead of going back inside to lock up, which had been her intention before she'd stepped out here.

It was the first week of March and the streetlights glowed, haloed by a foggy mist that made it feel even colder than it was. She looked up at the loft condos topping the storefronts to see if she could determine from which fireplace the smoke was coming. Greta inhaled another deep breath of the smoky air and closed her eyes, the smell summoning up images of buffalo plaid and s'mores, not the cashmere and saffron-infused polenta that filled this street.

The rich smoke reminded her of her mother and her first circle gatherings, taking her back to the woods of southern Wisconsin and all those kind, mysterious women preparing for their rituals. She'd been so nervous before the first one. All of her mother's comforting words had done nothing to stop the feeling that someone was jumping rope in her stomach. Her mother and her words of wisdom had, of course, been right. To Greta, going to circle had felt like coming home. At these gatherings of women with amazing gifts, no one thought anything of someone else hearing her thoughts, no one thought she was a weirdo for sensing things that other people, normal people, couldn't sense.

Greta took another big sniff of the smoky night air and stepped back inside Eleventh House.

Facing her gallery with her hands on her hips, she refocused her mind from the ancient past to the not-so-distant future. What was it going to be like having an opening with so little art? She could joke that Trebelmeier was a minimalist. Or perhaps she could stand, straight-faced, staring at an exposed expanse of brick wall and pretend *that* was the art. *"Don't you get it? It's so powerful."* Greta grinned, knowing for certain she would find someone that would agree with her, like those New York art critics who wrote rave reviews about a minimalist wood sculpture that was actually just the stand for a metallic piece of art that had been lost in transport.

Jill hadn't returned her latest phone calls. Her opening was in two weeks and still Greta only had the original handful of finished paintings. She'd been prodding Jill for months, telling her she'd like to see a few more works, that the amount she had was a little too thin. Greta had never had to think about canceling an opening before, although she knew it happened. But she didn't want it to happen to her next weekend. Everything was in place. Advertising was paid for, deposits on the catering were paid.

Advanced publicity had been good, too; Jill was generating quite a buzz and this could prove to be her breakout show. But when she'd mentioned that to Jill, Jill had responded with an unemotional, "Well, we'll see."

But that was Jill. In the years that Greta had known her, she'd never once been able to penetrate that exterior. The only things Greta could ascertain about Jill she'd had to learn the old-fashioned way, the way everybody else did—by observing her from the outside. Jill was so reserved and closed-off, as though she'd constructed a protective wall around herself. It made Greta sad. What was it that she was protecting herself from?

Greta locked the front door and took her nightly wander through her gallery, lingering in front of her favorite pieces, never knowing how much longer they would be in her care. When she got to the back she turned off the main lights and went down the hallway to her office. One of her mother's paintings hung on the brick wall just outside, and she remembered watching her mother paint it, up in her attic studio. As a child she'd loved to watch her mother paint, the quiet, fluid-like way she worked.

"There's beauty in just about everything," her mother had told her when she was working on this one. "You just have to stop and look for it." Greta remembered her putting a daub of paint on her brush, then pointing its newly rust-colored tip at her. "And usually," her mother had said, turning back to the painting, "if you know how to see the beauty"—she had dabbed at the painting, concentrating—"you'll know how to see the magic, too."

Greta stood in front of the painting for a long while, watching the smoke rise from the factory chimneys and the stars begin to twinkle in the darkened sky.

"Good night, Mama," she said, before turning out the light and heading back to her office to finish up the day's work.

Mara pulled the small paper bag out of her purse and set it on her kitchen table. Myrrh. If she'd known it was going to be that hard to find, she might have called off this whole project. She'd phoned every New Age store in the city trying to find some, but it seemed there recently had been a *run* on myrrh. Everyone was fresh out. She'd had to drive all the way out to a western suburb just to get it, fighting Friday-afternoon traffic and wasting the only half-day she got from Dr. Seeley each week.

She pulled a Hostess cupcake out of her purse too and took a bite. She'd had to stop for gas on the way back and she'd been kind of hungry, so she'd decided to pick up a snack as well.

Mara needed the myrrh for a cleansing spell, since she'd decided she would try to break that haywire abundance wish by herself. It shouldn't be too hard, she thought. She'd read how to do it in her books, and now she finally had all the necessary ingredients.

And there was no time like the present, because the boys and Henry had baseball practice after school today, which on Fridays was usually followed by pizza at Ranalli's. They wouldn't be home until after seven.

She hadn't told Henry about the wishing yet and she didn't think, in light of his newly hirsute condition, it was something she should tell him about *now*. At least her wish for a singing career hadn't begun to manifest. She couldn't take any more insanity.

Mara licked the last bit of cupcake off her fingers, set out the piece of paper with the new, improved spell she had written, and began collecting the rest of the ingredients she would need: cinnamon, lemon peel, salt, and bay leaves. She would do the wish reversal right there in the kitchen, at the table.

Mara lit a short green candle and turned off the lights. After a few deep breaths to relax her mind and focus, she reached into the bag to remove the tiny vial of myrrh essential oil, which had cost a fortune. If she hadn't chased all over town for it, she never would have bought it. Nineteen ninety-five for half of a fluid ounce!

The paper bag crinkled in the otherwise silent room when Mara tossed it down to the floor next to the table to get it out of the way. She dabbed some of the pricey oil on her index finger, then started drawing a circle around the candle with it, rewetting her finger with the oil several times to complete the circle. Mara sprinkled the cinnamon and salt on the oil, then rested the lemon peel in the concoction, chanting:

> Oh Great Goddess hear me pray,
> Please cleanse my abundance wish today.
> Eliminate extra hair from Henry,
> The weight from me, and do not tarry.
> I ask you with deep sincerity,
> To replace "Abundance" with "Prosperity."

Mara repeated the chant several times, as they had at Book Club, although during her third time through she'd had to pause to scold Tippy, because he'd started playing with the paper bag on the floor, climbing inside and making a racket.

When she finished, she sat at the table and watched the candle burn for a long while, listening to Tippy push the paper bag around the kitchen floor.

"I hope that does the trick," Mara said out loud, patting her hand on her poochy belly, which rumbled its request for the other cupcake.

Through the nursery window Claudia could see little baby Elliot in his incubator, sound asleep, an angel. Elliot Doe—that was his name now. She watched him through the shatterproof glass, absently tracing the wire design inside the glass with her fingers, her fingertips so close to the encased diamonds yet unable to touch them. He made an especially expressive exhale, his perfect bow-tie lips fluttering with it. He was every bit as beautiful as she remembered him.

It was almost noon on a Saturday, the first week in March, nearly one and a half weeks since she had found him. The day she'd brought him in, Claudia had asked if she could come back to visit. The supervisor, Nurse Galt, a gruff and serious African-American woman, had told her it might be possible, but she didn't think so. Their "cuddlers" went through extensive background checks that the hospital only ran twice a year. Claudia had left her information with them anyway.

Elliot would have to stay in the hospital for a while longer because he'd been, the doctors guessed, about a month premature, and he needed to gain some weight. His lungs were also slightly underdeveloped. Claudia couldn't have imagined she'd be pleased to hear he wasn't perfect, that there *might be something wrong with him*, but since he wasn't in any pain, she'd allowed herself to be happy that he was still at the hospital, having to stay longer than usual before being turned over to foster care.

Yesterday, Claudia had received the call from Nurse Galt, who had said, in her gruff manner, that since Claudia had found Elliot and possibly saved his life, they'd allow her special dispensation to come in and cuddle.

Pushing her luck, Claudia had asked if Dan could come, too. With an irritated sigh, Nurse Galt had told her she absolutely didn't think so, but she'd check.

She'd called Claudia back two hours later to say, just this once, if they remained accompanied by a nurse, the hospital would allow it, which seemed to make her even more irritable.

"May I help you?" A nurse had come up alongside Claudia.

"Oh, I . . ." Claudia brought her hand down from the glass. "I'm Claudia Dubois. I found . . . I was the one who found baby Elliot." She pushed her glasses up her nose, shrugged, and smiled. "I just wanted to see how he was doing, you know? They said—Nurse Galt, I mean—said it would be okay . . . that I could come in and see him. I called this morning and they said—He's going to be okay, right?"

The nurse's face softened. Apparently she knew the story. "Would you like to see for yourself?"

She guided Claudia to a small room outside the nursery and instructed her to wait there, then returned several minutes later with a blanketed bundle. "Would you like to hold him for a while?"

Claudia nodded.

"Well, wash your hands then." The nurse pointed at the sink, then continued talking while Claudia walked over to wash her hands. "Our little babies need so much holding—sometimes it gets so crazy around here, we just can't get to them all. It's nice you came in."

"Just be sure to support his head," she said, handing Elliot over to Claudia, adjusting his blanket a little in Claudia's arms, making sure she was leaving him in capable hands. "Go ahead, sit down. Take some time." She took a seat across from Claudia. "We heard you're going to try to adopt him—is that right?"

Claudia nodded again, not taking her eyes off of Elliot. "We're trying the foster route, first. I started the paperwork a few days ago. It's kind of a long shot and my school is—well, they're not being terribly supportive. But when I scheduled the interview with the social worker, she was encouraging. She said since I was the one who rescued him, I had a *vested interest* in him. She said it might help our case."

Claudia rubbed the downy hair that peeked from under his cap and ran the back of her hand over his cheek. The nurse watched her caresses and smiled, then checked her watch. "It's just about his feeding time. How about I get a bottle and you can give him his lunch?" She didn't wait for an answer before she started for the door. "He's finally beginning to get the hang of sucking," she said as she stepped into the next room.

Elliot felt a little thicker than he had the last time Claudia had held him, the day she found him in the bathroom. He opened his eyes and looked up at her. "Are they taking good care of you here? Are they giving you lots of tender care?" Her words got caught in her throat.

"You are so precious." Claudia fought back tears. She should have come here sooner.

But she'd been too afraid. Afraid of how it would feel if she kept visiting him, became attached, and then had to watch him get torn away. Now, after talking to the social worker, she had some hope. *A vested interest.* Although the amount of paperwork and interviews and background checks she and Dan were going to have to endure seemed insurmountable. They needed to get physicals, to make a fire-escape plan, give fingerprints, and even prove their pets had been vaccinated. At least, since their feng shui goldfish had died, they didn't have to vaccinate any fish.

Now that Claudia had set the gears in motion, Dan was starting to balk at the process, making it all seem so much more insurmountable. His *just-going-along-with-your-nutty-idea* attitude had given way to barely concealed surliness. Monosyllabic answers to her questions as she filled out forms. Moody silences that were out of character for him. And of course, she was sure he knew what she was really up to, suggesting the foster parenting route as a way to ease him into the adoption route.

It did seem hopeless. She couldn't do this without Dan on board, and it would probably take all of two seconds during the interview process before the social worker would know that Dan wasn't on board. It was ridiculous to even try. But still, now that she was finally here, holding this little baby, she knew this is what she was supposed to do. She knew that somehow, making sure Elliot was going to be fine was her responsibility.

And where was Dan anyway? He'd said he would be here twenty minutes ago. Saturday traffic could be brutal, but this might be just another of his passive-aggressive protests.

They'd run separate errands this morning. Claudia had bought groceries and stopped by the cleaner's. Dan had gone to get the oil changed in his car. He'd said he needed to run by his office to pick up some drawings he'd forgotten and that he also wanted to stop by Genesis Art Supply on the way back if he had time. Claudia was sure he'd make the time. Dan had said it would be easier if he just met her here, but now she was getting the sinking feeling he wasn't going to show at all.

Claudia looked down at Elliot and snuggled him a little closer, amazed at the warmth he gave off. He fell back asleep in her arms, so precious and trusting, and she had to wonder, as she looked at his face, what she'd ever been afraid of.

Mara was just getting to the good part of her book when she saw, from the corner of her eye, Henry climbing up the front steps. His key turned the front lock and Tippy hopped down off her lap in anticipation. She started reading more quickly, trying to get in as many words as she could before Henry got inside. She crammed in one more sentence while he shut the front door and walked over to her.

"Hi honey," she said, closing her book, at the same time that Henry bent down to kiss her.

Mara tilted her cheek up for him and when he bussed it, she recoiled as if he'd scraped her face with thirty-grade sandpaper.

"Henry!" she complained, turning her face up to look at him. Her eyes went wide.

"What?"

She stared back at him open-mouthed and pulled her legs up under herself on the chair. Mara crouched there, speechless, pointing at his face.

"Oh, this?" He rubbed the quarter inch of thick stubble that covered his chin and cheeks. "Yeah, I really need to shave. Didn't mean to scratch ya, hon. Sorry." He mussed her hair with his hand.

Mara sank back down in the chair with a sigh. He must not have shaved before going to the gym this morning—probably had overslept and been in a hurry. Mara shook her head with relief. She shouldn't let herself get spooked like that.

"I think I am going to call Dr. Bernstein today, though," Henry said, turning toward the kitchen. "This hair stuff is getting a little too weird."

She could see Henry rubbing his face with his hand again as he walked away.

"I shaved once this morning already."

 The truck had its trailer wedged securely underneath the viaduct, ironically right underneath the yellow and black sign that read, 13' 10", something, Dan imagined, the driver should have read before he tried driving underneath it. He tapped his hand on the steering wheel. Claudia was going to be pissed; he was already twenty minutes late.

The truck driver kept getting out of his cab, looking up at the viaduct and assessing his truck, then getting back in to talk on his radio. Dan watched from his car, penned in by traffic on all sides, positioned about six cars back from the scene of the accident. At one point, the man in the car directly behind the stuck truck had tried to wave it backward authoritatively, but the truck driver had just looked at him as if he were nuts. Now, the truck driver was hiding in his cab, apparently waiting for the police, or someone of authority, to arrive and untangle the mess.

Dan tried to call Claudia on her cell phone but she hadn't picked up, and that's when he figured she probably couldn't have it on at the hospital. He left her a message, telling her he was stuck in traffic, but it sounded like the kind of thing he wouldn't believe either. They both knew he didn't want to go to the hospital to see this baby, but he had promised.

He'd been hoping Claudia's idea that this was *going to lead to something* was just *going to go away,* but as the week had worn on, she'd only seemed more determined. He felt like the guy in the car behind the truck—tilting at windmills, trying to single-handedly unstick an impossibly stuck situation.

Two squad cars, a tow truck, and forty-five minutes later, Dan stood outside the nursery. The babies in the bassinettes all looked the same to him, with the exception of the one who was crying. Dan could hear his howls through the glass, his little red face screwed up under his blue cap. "That's probably him," Dan thought. He watched a nurse walk over and pick up the crying boy; she held him to her chest and patted his back. When she noticed Dan, she pointed off to his right and he went through the double doors to the nurses' station.

The woman sitting behind the desk didn't look up as he stood in front of her, ignoring him even after he'd cleared his throat. He was thinking there should be better security in a place like this, when the nurse he'd seen through the window came around the corner, no longer carrying the squalling boy, and asked if she could help him.

"I'm Daniel Dubois. I was supposed to meet my wife here a while ago, but—"

"About an hour ago, if I'm not mistaken." She smiled at him. "C'mon." She waved her hand for Dan to follow her. "I was just going to check on them. I think she was getting ready to leave pretty soon."

They walked down a short hallway and the nurse stopped outside a room next to the nursery. She put her index finger over her lips and then silently mouthed the words, "in there," while pointing inside. Dan could see Claudia in profile from the door; her hair was hanging down the side of her face, swaying back and forth as she rocked the baby in the glider, and she was humming Brahms's Lullaby. Dan could see Elliot asleep in her arms, his face the picture of contentment, a little arm thrown back next to his shoulder in complete relaxation.

It might have been less of a surprise to him if he'd watched her go through an entire pregnancy, instead of just all of a sudden one day acting like someone's mother. He stood watching silently, not wanting to interrupt this scene. He wished he could keep watching it indefinitely. She looked so relaxed, so confident—so oddly unlike Claudia. When she finally looked up and noticed him there, he could see that her face was the picture of contentment, too.

Chapter Eighteen

———✦———

"Whoa, whoa, whoa. Gimme that. Where'd you find this?" Gail grabbed the video out of Will's hand.

"Andrew wants to watch a video," Will said. "I was helping him get it—since he needs to take it easy." Will made big eyes at her—all innocence and light.

Andrew was on the couch, his expression a mirror image of his brother's.

"Well, I have no idea what's on this." Gail turned the unlabeled video over in her hand. "Why are you getting into these old video tapes? I had them in a bit of an order. What is it you wanted to see, Andrew?"

"Nokio."

"Well, this isn't Pinocchio. I don't know what's on this—old baby videos or vacation or something. Let me help you find Pinocchio." Gail rummaged through the stack of videos forced to the back of their entertainment cabinet, having given way over time to the stack of DVDs that had replaced them. "Here it is."

"Let me do it. I can do it."

"Okay, here you go." Gail gave the video to Will. "You guys got it under control now?"

"Yeah, we got it."

The VCR ingested the videotape with a high-pitched wheeze and Will nodded at her vigorously, his shaking head saying, *go away.* She looked over at Andrew on the couch, his new inhaler resting on the coffee table in front of him—just in case. She frowned at it, hating it. Andrew smiled at her, too, the same *go away* expression on his face. Gail smiled back and left the room, heading into the kitchen with the mystery video in her hand.

She flipped it over again, as if hoping a label might appear. They had so many old VHS tapes, and the labels had fallen off a bunch of them, if they even had had them in the first place. Another project for another day: cleaning out the old videos. Probably half of them were ancient episodes of *All My Children*, material she didn't want her children to see, but before she could get rid of any of them, she wanted to look through them all, catalogue them maybe, at least make sure they didn't contain anything important.

Back when Will was first born, they used to have a VHS recorder, and she didn't want to take the chance they'd accidentally throw away any VHS tapes of first steps or spaghetti dinners. It would take time to archive all those old tapes, figure out which ones she wanted to keep, and then she'd still have to take them in somewhere to have them converted to digital. It would take time she didn't know where she'd find. It had been on her list of things to do for a couple of years now at least. Well, in light of everything that had happened recently, she certainly wasn't going to *wish* for time to do something like that. She was still reeling from what she thought were the consequences of her last wish.

Andrew had had to stay in the hospital for two days and had been sent home with that inhaler. The doctor had said he would have to use it for as long a year, until his lungs had time to recover. Until then, no running, no sports: Andrew was to *take it easy*. Clearly, Gail thought, that woman had never tried to raise a five-year-old boy.

She sat down at her desk in the kitchen and booted up the computer, her fingers absently drumming the videocassette. A long, long time ago—back before the kids—she and John had used their video camera to make some home videos of their own. Gail smiled: their own private Paris Hilton–like "memoirs." Come to think of it, where was *that* video? Gail stopped tapping the one under her hand. *Oh man, what if? Maybe I dodged more than a racy episode of* All My Children. That would have been God-awful. Terrifyingly embarrassing. Lord only knows—well, maybe Lindsay did, too—how much therapy it would require to recover from an incident like that.

John entered the kitchen, walking past her and over to the fridge. "What are you grinning at?" he asked, opening the door and leaning inside. "You look like you're guilty of crimes."

"Do you remember that old, *old* video we made? Right after college? At our first apartment on Wellington?"

John turned around and grinned at her, his hand still on the open refrigerator door. Not much else besides sex could take his mind off food. "Why yee-esss I do. Why's that? Do you want to make another?" He gave her a mischievous grin.

Gail smirked back at him. "I was just wondering where it is. I haven't seen it in ages and now, with the kids getting older . . . Do you remember where we hid it?"

"In a safe place so we'd know where to find it?" John took out the mayonnaise and the bologna and cheese and shut the door to the fridge. "I remember hiding it." He laughed. "I just have no idea where."

Gail didn't say anything. She tapped the video under her hand again.

"Why? Did *you* want a *movie night* tonight?"

"No . . . I . . . That's not what this is about. The boys had this." She held up the tape. "And it's unlabeled and I don't know, it got me thinking. I guess I got a little concerned again—thinking about, you know, *what if*?"

John shrugged and pulled out the loaf of Wonder Bread from the breadbox, forgoing the Brownberry Whole Wheat. "I'm sure it's around here somewhere."

"Mmm."

"If you're worried about it, we can look. It's got to be up in our room—or buried in a box in the attic from one of the moves. We'll find it. I'm sure we didn't give it away."

"Give it away?" Gail's voice was higher than usual.

"I'm saying I don't think we gave it away."

"When would we have given it away?"

"I'm sure we didn't. All the stuff we've donated to the Brown Elephant has been clothes or books—albums and stuff. I don't think we ever unloaded any videos."

Gail did not feel comforted. She felt panicked.

John spread mayonnaise on both slices of bread before slapping his sandwich together. "If it'll make you feel better, I'll look around for it tonight. It's probably up in the attic."

Gail nodded. She ran her hand over the tape on the counter. Maybe this one was it; maybe it somehow got mixed in with the others during a move. Given away? Of course not.

John stuffed nearly half of his sandwich into his mouth in one bite.

"How can you be hungry? We just ate dinner."

John smiled at her while he chewed. He winked at her and said, through a mouthful of pasty white bread, "As you should know, I'm a man with large appetites."

The large white canvas stretched out in front of Jill like an arctic landscape, cold and foreboding, freezing every ounce of creativity in her psyche. She sat on a metal stool in front of the abominable seventy-two by one-hundred-two-inch canvas with her arms crossed over her chest, her feet flat on the floor and her legs spread wide. The canvas hung on the back wall of her studio. *The big canvas. The anchor for her show.* It was an anchor all right. Every time she looked at it, she could feel it dragging her down.

What had happened? Everything had been going so well. She'd been on quite a roll getting ready for her show, and then—poof—nothing. All inspiration and motivation had stopped cold.

The thought that this might be some problem with her wish for creative inspiration crossed her mind. Could it be that her wish had backfired? This badly? It didn't seem possible, because her first wish, the one that had brought her Marc, was going so well.

At least she had that going for her. And Marc was the best. It was ironic, she thought, how the less he pushed her for a commitment, the more she found herself thinking about one. The less he pushed her to *open up*, the less he tried to chip away at her shell, the more she felt compelled to crack it open.

So far, Marc had never once interrupted a comfortable moment of silence to ask, "What are you thinking about?" The *death sentence*, she called it. Whenever it came out of one of her boyfriends, Jill was tempted to run. And usually did. Marc didn't spend all his time trying to get to know her better; he seemed to be just letting the relationship unfold—and how wonderful was that?

He'd started her portrait a week ago, having her pose in an off-the-shoulder, red velvet dress in which her black hair framed an enticingly exposed décolletage. Marc hadn't let her see the painting while he worked, wanting her to wait, to see only the finished product. Although once, when he'd left the room, she'd stolen a peek.

Even though she'd already gone back to her side of the studio, and was stretching her neck and back, when he'd walked back into the room, he knew.

"You peeked." He stood behind the canvas again, holding his brush.

"No I didn't." Jill adjusted herself in her chair, returning to her pose.

He narrowed his eyes at her, staring. "You peeked."

"I did not."

"Don't lie to me, Jilly girl." He'd been smiling when he'd come over and sat on top of her, straddling her, pressing her down into the chair with his weight. "I have a way of dealing with models who lie to me."

"You don't scare me. I've seen the way you *deal* with your models, remember?"

And he'd dealt with her right then. On the modeling platform in the middle of the floor of his studio.

Today, during the five hours and forty-three minutes she'd been sitting in her studio, Jill had mulled that scene over and over in her mind. She'd mulled a lot of scenes over and over. She just hadn't *painted* any. She was starting to panic. The opening at Eleventh House was less than two weeks away and she didn't have anywhere near the amount of pieces she wanted—the amount of pieces she *needed* if she wanted to break out. She knew she should probably forgo this big canvas and just get on with some smaller ones; that had been her plan in the first place. Only one or two more would have done it, but she'd gotten all wrapped around the axle with this big one and now she wasn't going to be ready.

This had never happened before. Jill was always ready. Always prepared. Always professional. Sure, she had enough for a smaller show, but what had Greta said: that the finished pieces were *fine, but the quantity was a little thin?* She'd given Jill a judgmental, motherly look, a look that had torn her up more than she cared to admit. And now the pressure was really on, because she'd gotten a great preview in *Chicago* magazine, which meant there would probably be a crowd. She'd already sold one of the paintings to the City of Chicago, too, which was great, but now it meant that the quantity of available paintings was even more *thin.*

As her panic began to rise, so did her drinking. Each night she had a martini, and then, when it didn't make her feel any better, she had another, and then some nights, another. Falling asleep eventually, she would wake up two or three hours later and be unable to fall back asleep until just before dawn. It was then, between six and sometimes noon—when she finally emerged from bed—that she had the dreams.

Winter dreams. Snow dreams. Crawling though white shag carpeting dreams. One night she'd dreamt she'd stumbled upon two albinos having sex on a white sand beach.

No psychoanalysis was necessary for her to figure out where the dreams where coming from; she'd been staring at seven thousand, three hundred and forty-four square inches of pure unadulterated white space for six hours a day, every day, for the past two weeks.

This kind of thing, this loss for ideas, this "painter's block," had never happened to her before. She always had ideas. In fact, she always had too many ideas, so many ideas she never had time to execute them all. There were some she'd been meaning to get to for years. And now . . . well now, they all just seemed so dumb. This, too, had never happened to her before. Sure, a few times she'd gone back to an old idea, rethought it and then concluded it wasn't timely anymore, or maybe it just wasn't anything she was interested in doing anymore, but she had never thought of any of her old ideas as *dumb* before.

Jill squeezed her eyes shut and pressed her knuckles into them, then opened them onto the blank canvas, hoping the swirling colors burned into her retinas might inspire something on the great white canvas. They didn't.

She reached over to the side table, grabbed her palette knife, and began scraping the big globs of paint off of her mahogany board and into the trash.

Was this Wish Club's fault? Was this all because of her wish for creative inspiration? Her stomach twisted into a knot. She'd been against all the wishing, all the witchy nonsense, at the beginning. Maybe she should have stood by her original feelings, because now here she was staring at her big, blank canvas unable to paint a stroke. It seemed to her that the wish had stopped up her creativity with the worst case of imagination constipation she'd ever had.

Creative inspiration. Goddamn it, why had she done it?

Because of Marc. Because things with Marc had been going so great, that's why. Because everyone else in Book Club had done it, too. They'd all made wishes—for fame and fortune, success. Maybe she should call Lindsay, or Gail, to see if their second wishes were coming true. To see if their second wishes were going as badly as their first wishes had gone well.

Jill whacked away at her mahogany board, scraping it hard, trying to squeeze the paint out from between the minute grooves of wood the way you might try to squeeze the last bits of pulp out of a lemon. *It serves me right for letting it go as far as I did, for not staying with my gut.* Her stomach contorted again thinking about it. She should have walked out of that second witchy meeting when Lindsay and Mara had conned them all into wishing for Tippy. Tippy, the diabetic cat with the retarded name, for chrissakes.

Jill stopped her scraping. But what about Marc, then? It couldn't just be a coincidence that he'd turned up the next day, the day after she'd made a wish for a perfect man. He'd told her he'd signed the lease at 4400 North the night before he'd moved in—after having spent the day torn between this studio and one down in Bucktown. How could that be a coincidence? She'd *wished* for him the night before.

Jill craved a drink and a cigarette. She needed to call Greta—and Lindsay or Gail. She wanted to run downstairs to Marc. She felt pulled in so many directions she couldn't move at all. Glaring up at the big canvas, she fantasized about slashing at it, raging against the 10 duck with an X-acto knife until it hung in shreds. Jill shook, her heart pounding with the thought. She'd never let so much emotion boil up, come so close to boiling over. The hand she was using to scrape the paint was shaking. She tried a deep breath. When the anger faded, she thought for a moment she might start to cry, but then, what would that solve?

Another deep breath and then, suddenly, she knew what she had to do. She knew it as clearly as if she'd had a vision—the first creative flash she'd had in weeks. It was as if a ray of sunlight had broken through a hole in a layer of stratocumulus clouds and touched her forehead. Giving her a plan.

Jill wiped her hands on the Turpenoid-saturated rag she'd started to clean her board with and grabbed her jacket from the hook behind the door. She hurried out of her studio without turning down the heat or turning off the lights. She left without even making sure the lock on her door clicked shut behind her.

Chapter Nineteen

Minted berries with Grand Marnier sauce
Apple cake with preserved lemon and
  cinnamon streusel
Vanilla-bean crème brûlée
Tiramisù
Hazelnut gelato with raspberry reduction

Lindsay scanned her clipboard, stymied. She needed to choose the dessert for the Women's Foundation Spring Fashion Show Extravaganza from the list the Metron catering staff had given her, and she was terrified she would make the wrong choice. Her intuition was telling her to go with the minted berries. Certainly not the streusel—*yawn*. Same for tiramisù and crème brûlée. But the hazelnut gelato. Hmm.

It had to be perfect.

She picked up her clipboard and walked down the hall to Evelyn Cantwell's Foundation office. Evelyn's door was open, and Lindsay entered before realizing Evelyn had the phone to her ear and was nodding silently to whoever was on the other end of the line. Lindsay froze on the spot. *Damn.* She should have at least pretended to knock, rapped her knuckles on the door a couple of times as a courtesy to announce her presence and request permission to enter. *What a boneheaded mistake. Damn my nerves.*

Evelyn looked up and Lindsay silently mouthed *sorry* before starting to back herself out the door, but Evelyn waggled her hand at Lindsay, signaling it was okay for her to come in. Hugging the clipboard to her chest, Lindsay waited just inside the doorway while Evelyn talked on the phone.

"I am so sorry to hear that, love." Pause. "You know a lot may change between now and then. There's still a couple of weeks." Pause. "Well, we certainly are going to miss you, but of course we understand that family comes first." Pause. "Yes, love. Now you take care of yourself, too, and let us know when you get back to town. Don't worry about a thing, now. We'll get it covered." Pause. "Of course, love. Give Stafford my love, same to the girls. Buh-bye."

Evelyn clicked the phone off and set it down on her desk, her hand still holding it.

"I am so sorry I barged in—"

"Oh nonsense, nonsense, love." Evelyn held the phone out in her hand and gestured to Lindsay with it. "That was Nancy Blades. Her mother's taken ill in West Palm and she's had to extend her winter. She won't be back until May at the earliest."

"Oh. That's terrible. It must be serious."

"Well, shingles, which I hear can be awful, but then you know how melodramatic the Bladeses can be." Evelyn gave Lindsay a conspiratorial wink. It looked to Lindsay like the kind of wink Evelyn seemed accustomed to giving, although Lindsay had never received one before. Lindsay had to stop herself from bouncing up on her toes.

"What is it that you needed, love?" Evelyn glanced down at the clipboard Lindsay held over her chest.

"Dessert."

Evelyn raised an eyebrow.

"I'd like your opinion on which dessert to pick for the fashion show."

Evelyn smiled. "Well now, that makes more sense, because certainly, it seems that someone I know has been actively avoiding dessert lately."

"Oh, well. Yes." Lindsay looked down at her waist, tipping one heel off the ground in spite of herself.

"Let's see what we've got there." Evelyn motioned for Lindsay to show her the clipboard and Lindsay walked around to her side of the desk and leaned in, so they could look at the choices together.

"I was thinking the minted berries would be the best choice, but I wanted a second opinion."

Evelyn picked up a pen and ran it down the menu choices, tapping it against each selection.

"I just think tiramisù and crème brûlée are just, so—been there done that. And the streusel," Lindsay humphed her opinion on such a pedestrian dessert. "I like the sound of the berries, but the gelato could be nice."

Evelyn had stopped looking at the list. She held the pen in two fingers, touching the end to one side of her mouth. She was staring at Lindsay.

Which made Lindsay nervous. "But of course, anything you—I would imagine they're all good, of course, it being the Metron, after all." Lindsay laughed.

Evelyn stared.

"Of course," Evelyn said. "Why didn't I think of it sooner?" She pointed the pen at Lindsay while continuing to stare. "It makes perfect sense."

"The berries?"

Evelyn looked surprised. "The berr—? No, love. You."

"Me?"

"Yes, of course. You. *You* should take Nancy's place in the fashion show." Evelyn leaned back in her chair, one arm crossed under her bosom, the other holding out her pen as though it were a cigarette. "Without her we're out one model and I couldn't think of anyone better to take her place, at least not anyone we could get on such short notice. And, you *look fabulous.*" Evelyn's eyes dropped down to scan Lindsay's body, then came back up to meet Lindsay's.

Lindsay was speechless. Evelyn Cantwell had just asked her to model in the Women's Foundation Spring Fashion Show Extravaganza. This was her dream come true. She wanted to pinch herself. Laugh. Cry. Bounce up and down. This was *the* invitation, the welcome into *society.* Her lifelong dream was coming true right here, right now.

Or perhaps, she should say, this was her *wish* coming true. Lindsay's right hand started shaking and she tucked it under her other arm to hide it from Evelyn. *Don't act too eager. Don't blow this chance. Don't pull a Claudia.*

Lindsay had finally, finally lost the weight that had plagued her throughout her life. She was down nearly twenty pounds since she'd made the wish; was this all it took? Was her big butt the only thing that had been holding her back all these years? They hadn't wanted her because she was chubby? Her gut reaction to this thought was disgust—which must have played across her face because Evelyn asked, " What's wrong, love? Don't you want to do it?"

"No. I mean YES. I'd *love* to do it, Evelyn. This is like a dr—I mean, of course I'd love to be in the show. *Love* to. It would be an honor." Lindsay gave Evelyn what she hoped appeared to be a calm, pleased smile. "Anything I can do to help out."

"Well, plan on it then. Talk to Marla about what Nancy was going to wear; see if there needs to be any adjustments made, size-wise, that sort of thing. But I doubt it. Nancy's such a skinny-binny, and well, frankly, now you are too. You know, truly—now that I think of it—is everything okay, love? You have dropped an awful lot of weight lately, and so quickly. James is good? Everything with the two of you?"

"We're fine. No, everything is fine." Lindsay absently ran her hand over her flat stomach. This was diet and exercise. There was nothing wrong. This was a wish come true.

"Excellent then. And you're sure you don't mind taking on the extra responsibility—what with your organization of the luncheon and everything?"

"No." Lindsay thought she might have said it too suddenly. "The luncheon is completely under control. Being *in* the show would be fun—the icing on the cake."

"Well, excellent, love. Excellent. I'm thrilled you can help us out." Evelyn gave her a brief, knowing smile before turning back to the dessert menu. "And I think your choice of the minted berries is flawless. I couldn't think of a more perfect complement to the meal. Certainly not the streusel." Evelyn laughed and Lindsay joined in with her. *Ha. Ha. Streusel—how ridiculous.*

Lindsay bounced out of Evelyn's office, floating all the way back to her own. She was going to model in the show. Lindsay

Tate-McDermott and her brand-new size-six butt, walking down the runway at the Chicago Women's Foundation Spring Fashion Show Extravaganza. It was like the perfect cap to a wonderful day, like dessert after an excellent meal. The icing on the cake.

Jill knocked on the door to Marc's studio. When he didn't answer, she knocked a little harder, no longer afraid of it opening up on something she'd rather not see. She waited. If he didn't answer soon, Jill thought that she might lose her nerve, that she might not be able to go through with her plan—to ask him for help. Not for help lifting a heavy box or stretching a big canvas; she needed the kind of help she never asked for, the kind that was personal.

She tried the knob. It was locked. *Oh, this was stupid. It was a dumb plan, anyway. I don't need a shoulder to cry on, I should just—*

"Hang on, hang on. I'm coming," Marc yelled from the other side of the door.

When he opened it, she could see his model putting on her thin cotton robe with a glance back at Jill. A glance that shot daggers through her.

Jill ignored it. "I didn't mean to interrupt you, but I really need to . . . I just wanted to talk to you." She looked down at the floor, took a breath, and closed her eyes for a moment and tried to steady her nerves.

Both of Marc's hands were coated in wet, flesh-toned paint. One still held a brush. "It's okay. We were just about to wrap up for today anyway." Marc bent his knees, bringing his eyes level with Jill's. "Hey. What's up?" He reached a hand up for her shoulder, then, apparently thinking better of it, wiped it on his paint-covered jeans. "What's the matter?" He tried to get her to look him in the eyes.

"I need to . . . I . . ." Jill was on the verge of tears.

Marc stood up and turned around. "Cinnamon?"

She'd been watching them, her blue eyes not missing a thing. "Yeah?"

"We're done for today. You can go ahead and get dressed."

Cinnamon stood still for a moment, as if she hadn't quite heard him, before she turned and languidly walked toward the Japanese screen at the back of Marc's studio. The wool sweater that had been hanging over the top of the screen slid down and disappeared on the other side when she stepped behind it. The pair of jeans disappeared next.

Cinnamon was back on their side of the screen so quickly, it occurred to Jill she must not be the kind of woman who bothered with the tedium of underwear. The way her nipples flounced under her sweater seemed to confirm it.

"We can pick this up tomorrow. Ten o'clock again?" Marc said.

Cinnamon replied with a slow tilt of her head. "Sure."

"See you tomorrow, then."

She walked passed Marc, her eyes boring into Jill's.

Jill hadn't interrupted anything, but clearly Cinnamon wanted to imply that she had.

When they were alone, Marc asked her again, "What's the matter, Jilly?"

Jill hesitated. She wasn't so sure, now that she was here, that she really wanted to go through with it, confess to him.

"I'm stuck," she said finally. "I'm totally blocked. My show is in less than two weeks and I've got so much to finish and I can't . . ." It felt as if her eyes might start to well up again. She looked up at the ceiling to stop them. "I feel like I'm going crazy. I'm so . . . so upset. I've never had anything like this happen to me before—ever."

"You've never been blocked before?"

Jill shook her head and sniffed.

"Jeez, Jilly girl. Where've you been? Everyone gets blocked. Especially before a show."

Jill had to admit there were times, and usually right before her shows, when her nerves seemed to get the best of her. Sometimes she'd fuss and fuss with a painting, trying to get it just right, until she'd add that one final stroke—the one that just ruined it. But that wasn't being blocked. That was nerves. This was different.

"I can't paint a thing. I just stare at the canvas. I—"

"You are putting wa-a-a-y too much pressure on yourself. You need to re-lax." He walked over to his sink and started washing his hands. "C'mon. Have a seat. We'll talk this through." He nodded at his couch under the window.

Jill gave him a look. It's where they usually had sex.

"Not that kind of re-laxing." He smiled and held up two dripping hands, palms out. "I promise. Just talking. We'll fix this for you, get you back on track."

"Okay, so you've gotten a lot of good advanced publicity, right?" Marc said, sitting down on the couch next to her after he'd finished washing his hands. "And that's a good thing, isn't it?"

Jill shrugged, looked up at him with a frown.

"Well, it is usually, anyway. Okay, sure, I know it adds a little pressure, but you're my Jilly girl . . ." He gave her his disarming smile, but Jill couldn't bring herself to smile back. "Hey . . . c'mon. This isn't as dark as you think. You still have enough for a show, right? Even if Gretel—"

"Greta."

"—if Greta says it'll be a little thin, so what? What's the trouble? The show's gonna go on. And if you don't break out—then you don't break out this time. No biggie. You do it next time. Right?

"So here's the thing," he continued. "Here's what you need to try. It's what I do when I get stuck. I *pretend* there's no pressure." He leaned back and raised his eyebrows at her as if to say, *brilliant, huh?*

Jill just looked at him. *What's he talking about?* He seemed somehow younger to her right then.

"I pull out a canvas with no plan and just paint. No pressure. It's not *for* anything, I tell myself—it's *not* for a show or even for anyone to see. It's just to paint. It's for the alley. The landfill. Nothing. No pressure. Just get something down. And you know what happens?"

Jill shook her head.

"No, c'mon. You *know* what happens."

"It's good."

"It's good," he said.

Jill nodded her head as though she liked his idea, but what Marc didn't seem to understand was just how stuck she was. She didn't even think she could *pretend*. Especially knowing that a spell was behind it. That witchcraft had brought her to this point. *Should I tell him about that?* No. That was not the answer. That wouldn't help anything and it would probably just make things worse.

"I don't think I could even pretend; I just feel so stuck."

"Okay, here's what we're going to do. Tonight. Right now, we're going to leave here and stop by Rick and Dave's Lakeview Liquors, where we're going to pick up some Crown Royal. Then we're going to Blockbuster to rent, what, *Casablanca*? *Caddyshack*? Whatever. Then we're going to go back to my place and get drunk while we watch it. Because tonight it's just about loosening up and forgetting. Then tomorrow, I'm going to bring you back here with me at ten and you're going to lock yourself in your studio and you're going to paint some nonsense for the landfill. And by noon, when you've broken through this block, you're going to come down here and we're going to piss Cinnamon off again by kicking her out," he smiled.

So he *had* noticed.

"And you're going to thank me for my wonderful advice that helped you so very much by taking me to Sally's for coffee."

Jill couldn't help but smile at him. He was being so sweet, like he really cared. And he seemed so eager to help her. Maybe his plan *would* work. Maybe she would be unblocked by noon tomorrow. He said it worked for him. And she still had two weeks. There were no laws saying her paintings couldn't be drying on the walls of Eleventh House when her show opened. She should at least be open to trying his idea. Hell, if she was open to thinking a spell had caused her painter's block, then she should at least be open to Marc's wacky *pretending* plan to break through it.

Maybe her plan to talk to him had been a good one after all.

"So? Whaddya think?" he asked. "Is it a plan? Is it good?"

"It's good," she said.

Chapter Twenty

✦

Claudia could feel fifty eyes boring holes into her back. She couldn't bring herself to turn around. *What was going on?* She'd been tapping a marker on the Dry Erase board in her classroom, trying her darndest to write the words "Heart of Darkness," but she was unable to control the marker and make it do what she wanted. After a few odd squiggles, the felt tip kept hitting the board with irritatingly calm thuds. Claudia couldn't make her fingers move the marker across the board to form anything legible.

"Dang things," Claudia finally said, shaking the marker, "always running out of ink." She turned around and smiled stupidly at them. "Well, anyway. Heart of Darkness."

"There's a red one on the ledge," one of the students offered, pointing.

Claudia grimaced at it. "Oh. Thanks. Well. Anyway. I don't care for red. Too much like grading." She laughed. "Besides, I don't—we don't have to have the title on the board. This once I think we can get away without it." Claudia smiled and pushed her glasses up her nose. "I think we can all remember that we're reading *Heart of Darkness* for the next forty-five minutes."

Their eyes were boring into her face now. "Oohkaay," she said, picking up her book and walking around to sit on the front of her desk. She crossed her legs and put her *Norton Anthology of Short Fiction* on her lap.

"Who can tell me who the protagonist is?"

"I love the smell of napalm in the morning, *man.*"

"That's right, Tom. Conrad's novella was the basis for the movie." She paused. "But now, since you brought it up, I'd like you to tell me who the protagonist is in *Heart of Darkness* and in *Apocalypse Now.*"

"Oh, maan." Tom groaned at the cost of his mistake while the class shared a laugh at his expense. He stuttered and fumbled through an explanation—getting it completely wrong.

Claudia seemed to have as good a grasp on what was going on in her life as Tom did in English Literature. *What is wrong with me? I can't write.* Oh no. Oh God please no. Not her wish—not again. Not like this. She'd even crossed out the one about writing a novel—and she had wished *to* write. But now she *couldn't* write. "*No.*"

Fifty eyes bore into her own now, questioning. Tom had fallen silent. *Uh-oh.* She'd said "*No*" out loud—and probably too harshly. Claudia shook her head. "No," she said it again, drawing the word out, trying to make it sound normal this time, in context, like something she *meant* to say out loud, "but you're sort of on the right track. Let's get back to what the difference is between an antagonist and a protagonist, shall we? Who can explain it for us? April—go ahead."

April brought her hand down with a smug smile as she launched into her explanation. What if this problem got worse? What if Claudia couldn't write—ever again? How could she teach? Take a message? Copy an address? *The horror, the horror!*

Something clattered to the floor at the back of the room. A compass. The kind they used for making circles in geometry in the math lab. It was resting in the aisle between the last two rows. No one claimed it. But if Claudia had to guess, it belonged to Tom.

"Where'd that come from?" Claudia interrupted April's antagonist/protagonist explanation.

No answer.

Claudia searched *their* eyes this time. What had the world come to, she thought, when kids weren't allowed to carry compasses in school anymore? The zero-tolerance policy covering weapons and drugs covered an age-old tool used to make circles in math class, and therefore compasses weren't allowed out of the math lab. *It's as if we've dropped our moral compass.*

She was surprised someone on the school board hadn't suggested they change the name of the math lab as well—it sounded way too much like meth lab—and well, goodness only knows where that might lead. Besides, math *lab* was a stupid name anyway. It wasn't as if they were cooking cosines over Bunsen burners in there.

The fifty eyes revealed nothing to her. No one would snitch. Claudia sighed.

"Well, I have to take that."

She walked back and picked up the compass. "Zero-tolerance, and all," she said. Claudia pointed at the sharp tip, ready to make a point about how ridiculous the policy was, until her finger accidentally touched it. She pulled it quickly back, a spot of bright red blood blossoming on the end of her finger. She hoped no one had noticed.

Claudia went around to the other side of her desk, opened the bottom drawer, and dropped the compass into her purse. She made a mental note to take the compass back to the math lab later in the day. She certainly didn't want to try writing herself a *real* note.

It figured that, instead of finding a compass to show her the way, she had found one that just went around in circles—and drew blood to boot.

Claudia sucked on her index finger for a moment while she leaned over, then she stood up and moved back around to the front of her desk. She sat down and crossed her legs, returned the *Norton Anthology* to her lap, and tried her best to ignore the taste of blood in her mouth.

"Dr. Seeley's office." Mara sang it into the phone, in a tone of voice way more cheerful than she felt. This had been happening more and more often lately. It had started toward the end the previous week, her voice taking on a mind of its own, some of her sentences coming out in a cheery, singsong way. It was especially noticeable over the phone.

"He's here Mondays and Wednesdays from eight to five, Tuesdays and Thursdays from nine to seven." To Mara's ears, it sounded like a nursery rhyme. "And Fridays from seven to noon." New—oon. The word chimed out of her mouth like a doorbell. *What the hell is going on?*

At least the person on the other end of the line thought it was sweet. The old woman seemed impressed by Mara's cheerfulness. "I've never heard a doctor's receptionist like you before. Most of them are so rude."

Mara wanted to tell the woman that she wasn't the receptionist, but that would be rude—and it would probably come out in her new singsong voice, which only seemed to make the woman chattier. She'd been nattering on about what she thought was wrong with her gums and Mara had let her, a little distrustful of her new voice, hesitant to use it. The woman wanted an appointment this week—the second week of March—and Mara had almost laughed out loud. But then, that would have been rude, too. Instead, she said, "Our next opening isn't until April thirtieth."

The woman was silent on the other end of the line for a long time. She finally said, "You give me that appointment on the thirtieth of April. You sound so nice. And Dr. Seeley has come so highly recommended by the other women at the Foundation. I think I'm going to like him."

Mara couldn't wait to see the expression on the woman's face when she actually met Dr. Seeley. Although, a lot of these older women seemed to like him, especially the ones from the Women's Foundation. It was so weird that he was the preferred dentist of Chicago's aged society women. His office was no great shakes, and he didn't have a fancy address. Those fussy old ladies probably liked his lack of personality and cold manner for some strange reason. Maybe he reminded them of their wealthy husbands or ex-husbands. Although it was more probable they liked Dr. Seeley for the way he dished out gossip—in a manner that made it seem like he wasn't dishing out gossip. "*How's Ann Batista?* Why, she's fine. *Oh, I was just wondering, worried about her really, what with the way she was so poorly treated in the divorce settlement.*" And then Mara could see the woman's eyes light up. *Poorly treated in the divorce settlement? I knew the new Mercedes was a front!*

Mara shifted the phone to her other ear and wrote the woman's appointment down in the book. She took some of her other pertinent information as well. She should start the file now, so it would be ready when the woman came in, but Mara was hungry. She reached into her bottom desk drawer for a snack. When it was open, Mara stared at it for quite a while. Everything was—albeit very slightly—out of place. As if it had been searched through. Dr. Seeley must have been in here, she thought. Probably couldn't find an envelope or a stamp, or his ass with both hands. Mara grabbed the box of Fig Newtons. At least he hadn't said anything to her about keeping snacks in her desk. Maybe he was afraid to— afraid that her husband might come down here and punch him in the nose, give *him* two black eyes.

The cellophane on the Fig Newton packet crinkled over the soothing sounds of Lite FM. Mara hummed along with the song, "You Are the Wind Beneath My Wings." She couldn't help herself, even though she hated that song. With fig seeds cracking between her teeth, Mara rolled her chair back to the filing cabinet behind her desk to get to the stock of new files. The stock drawer looked messed with, too, as if it had been clumsily searched through and then put back together again, with everything just a little out of place.

What had he been looking for? He should know by now where I keep most everything.

Mara stopped chewing. The books. Mara had two witchcraft books in her desk. A Wiccan spell book—*Everyday Magick for Everyday People* and *The Basic Principles of Wicca*. Mara opened the top middle drawer of her desk—the one she could lock, but never bothered to. Both books were still there. This drawer didn't seem to have been disturbed. Well, whatever he'd been looking for, he must have found it before he got here. She took another Fig Newton from the packet.

Did you ever know that you're my heeee-roh?

What has gotten into me? She hated this song—and now she couldn't stop singing it. Mara turned the radio off and shivered. Ugh.

The song kept running through her head. She couldn't stop humming it. She couldn't stop herself from *singing*.

I want you to know I know the truth, of course I know it.

Oh no. Mara swallowed a lump of Fig Newton, forcing it down the back of her throat, then picked up the phone and dialed Claudia.

*A*s soon as her class was over and all her students had left, Claudia sat at her desk with a pen and paper and tried to write out her name. She couldn't do it. No matter how she tried, her hand couldn't make the pen move the way she willed it to. Claudia tried a few other words but all she ended up with was a paper with a hieroglyphic-like mix of scribbles and dashes and dots.

What the hell was she going to do? *I can't write.* Her thoughts ran from arthritis to Alzheimer's—to all sorts of horrible autoimmune diseases due to which your body starts to attack itself, rendering you unable to control even the simplest motor functions. Just this morning she'd been able to type to check her e-mail, and she'd been able to get coffee in the break room without spilling. She'd tied her shoelaces before class. What could be so wrong with her hands now that she couldn't write?

Claudia leaned over her desk and put her head in her hands. She pulled her glasses off her face and rubbed the bridge of her nose for a moment, then absently started chewing on the frame of her glasses. When Claudia realized what she was doing, she pulled them from her mouth. *Just what I need. Another nervous habit.*

What she really needed was to talk to someone from Book Club, Lindsay or Gail, but she couldn't use her cell phone in the classroom and she didn't have time to run down to the faculty lounge before her next class. She thought about closing the door—but with her luck, someone like April or Nurse Marion or Headmaster Peterson would barge in and catch her in the act of *departing from school policy.*

She didn't know what a call to either of her friends would do for her now, anyway. Lindsay had been so dismissive two weeks earlier when Claudia had told her she thought her wish had caused her to find an abandoned baby. Lindsay had the most amazing ability to skew reality to her point of view. When she was losing weight and her butt was getting smaller by the day, the wishes were working. But when Claudia found an abandoned baby in the trash after wishing for a baby—*without delay*—well, that was just a curious coincidence.

"These kinds of things happen all the time, Claude. You don't think your wish had anything to do with this? How could it? We wished for you to get pregnant—not to find any old baby lying around."

"It wasn't any old baby lying around; it was a baby at my school. In the bathroom on the floor where my classroom is—"

"Honey, I don't think—"

"—I know you don't think so. But what if the wish-gods are, I don't know, really literal? What if you have to be careful how you ask for something?"

Lindsay hadn't budged, so Claudia had called Gail, who had barely let her talk. She hadn't needed to convince Gail that their wishes were backfiring. "Claudia, I think we did this to Andrew. I think this was our wishing—my wish."

Claudia had called Gail to find comfort for herself, an ally in thinking that the whole wish-making process was going all wrong, but now . . . now that Gail was on her side, suddenly, Claudia didn't want her to be. She wanted to stop Gail's pain, stop her tears before they started. If Gail thought she'd done anything to hurt her kids, it would kill her.

Claudia had no idea how she, the woman who didn't believe in coincidences, the woman who believed that everything happens for a reason, was going to convince Gail they hadn't had anything to do with hurting Andrew.

But when she really thought about it, where *was* the proof that they had done it? Where was the proof that her wish had made her find Elliot, that Gail's wish had started a fire? Seriously—this was crazy talk. If she'd been having this conversation with anyone else they'd have thought she was completely bonkers.

How'd that old saying go? Something like, *For those who believe, no proof is necessary. For those who don't believe, no proof is possible.* Well, where was their *proof* here, either way?

"You know, Gail—I have a hard time, you know, now that I think about it . . . I have a hard time really believing that a candle and some chanting and hand-holding can alter the world like this. When you step back for just a minute, it seems a little ridiculous— don't you think?"

And so, Claudia had allowed herself to believe that maybe—in the case of *wishes gone wrong*—it was all in their heads.

Until today. Until two weeks after making her second wish and she couldn't even write her own name. She hadn't even *made* the writing wish. Something spooky was going on.

Claudia looked down at the undecipherable scribbles in front of her. She and her friends had tapped into something they couldn't control anymore. She crunched the paper into a tight ball in her fist, then threw it into the garbage can in the corner.

Their wishes *were* working and they *were* going haywire and now, no matter what Lindsay said, no matter what Gail wanted to believe, no matter what she'd tried to convince herself, Claudia knew they needed to do something about fixing them. If that were even possible.

In the attic, surrounded by dozens of dusty, opened boxes, Gail was as angry with John as she'd ever been in all the years she'd known him. Probably angrier than she'd ever been at him in any past lives, too. He'd looked for *their video* and told her he couldn't find it. Deep down, she'd known she was going to be the one to have to search for it anyway, John being a man who couldn't find ketchup in the refrigerator. He liked to quote Voltaire on the subject: "I hate women because they always know where things are." Voltaire had said that in the eighteenth century. Gail thought that somehow over the past three hundred years, men's searching skills should have evolved.

The missing video was making her start to despair. She'd searched the house, taking all the unlabeled videos to the small TV and VCR in their master bedroom for screening after the kids went to sleep. Nothing.

Today she'd started in the attic, the only place she hadn't looked. It had to be somewhere—but where? Could it have gotten mixed in with some other stuff and somehow mistakenly given away to charity? Thrown out?

With her hands blackened with dust, Gail left the attic in disarray and went down to her second-floor office. She locked the door and, on a dark whim, googled "tall naked blondes."

She was shocked at what she found. *My God. How many sites are there?* She had over a million hits. She clicked on a site. Gail glanced back at the door to her office to make sure it was still shut. Some of these girls looked so young.

She looked at the window behind her, checking again, even though she already knew no one could see in. *Oh, this is ridiculous.* She wasn't going to find herself here. The video was simply missing—destroyed. Taped over maybe, with a soap opera.

These sites were unbelievable. She'd never checked out porn on the Web before. Did John know all this was here? They had stuff here for every type of perversion and fetish. Some of the pictures? Eeuw. They needed to get parental controls on their computers—stat. Page after page; she'd had no idea Internet porn was such an industry. *Amateur Site. Home videos—Hot sex from our house to yours.* Gail clicked. You had to pay to enter the site, but the home-page Web photos were enough, she thought. Dear God.

Gail clicked on another link.

What was she doing? She was not going to find evidence of an eleven-year-old videotape here. But now she was pruriently curious. Some of these pictures—even just the ones on the home pages. To think, anyone could just click and find photos of men and women having sex any time of the day or night. She and John should have a computer in their bedroom instead of a VCR. Gail clicked on "Dirty Housewives at Home."

And there she was.

Her whole world dropped out from under her. Her heart began to race and she could feel the intense heat in her cheeks as she blushed. The panic rose up. She couldn't swallow. She could only stare.

No. No no no! I'm a mom. I'm someone's mom. I can't—this isn't happening . . .

Gail kept staring with disbelief and then, when she thought the nightmare playing out in her head couldn't get any worse, she asked herself, *who else has seen this?* Anyone who clicked on this site. *Oh dear God.* All the people in her life that could have stumbled upon this. But there were so many millions of sites; the chances of someone she knew running across it were so slim, right? Gail flashed back over the last decade or so of her life, scanning for any knowing looks she might have received from former coworkers or cashiers. In the photo her face was mostly in shadow—and she had had long hair then. John was in profile; actually, he was a little more recognizable, well, if you knew him back then, before he'd put on the weight.

What a nightmare. This was terrible. A disaster. What was she going to do? She needed to call John. She needed to get these photos back, get them off the Net. But how do you do that? Call the Web-site operator? She wanted to sue. Who could they sue?

At least I had nice thighs back then. Was it normal to have a thought like that, Gail wondered, while looking at a picture of yourself having sex on the Internet? She wanted to bury herself. She wanted to cover the monitor with her hands. But she kept clicking, checking around the site to see if she would find more pictures.

Chapter Twenty-One

$\mathcal{S}ome$ indeterminate substance had adhered to Gail's couch, melted crayon or maybe a hardened crust of food. Claudia absently picked at it with her fingernail, waiting for the rest of the women to arrive.

Gail had called Claudia last night, and her voice had been so unsteady. It was rare to hear Gail so upset, and Claudia had known the news would be bad; for a moment she feared it was something about Andrew. When Gail told her about the Internet pictures, Claudia had tried her best to console her, eventually convincing Gail that even though it might be hugely embarassing for her, they needed to get everyone together. For the first-ever Emergency Meeting of Wish Club.

Gail's great room had been an addition onto the back of her house, and it always felt a little cooler than the rest of her home during winter. Today, even though it was mid-March, it felt cold. Claudia grabbed the zippered front edges of her sweater and overlapped them on top of her chest, hugging herself as she looked out the window. The wind was strong today, and it pushed the swings hanging from Gail's backyard swing set, making it look as if two ghosts were idly swaying there.

Gail walked in, with a slight limp, carrying two mugs. She'd insisted on making tea.

"How's Andrew?" Claudia asked.

"Better." Andrew was with Ellen upstairs, and Gail glanced toward the stairway. "He scoots around on those crutches amazingly fast. I thought—well, I don't know what I thought. I guess I figured he would struggle with them." Gail set the mugs down on the table. "I guess it's me who's struggling with everything, way more than he is. It's the inhaler that bothers me the most. His ankle will heal. The crutches will go away. But it'll be a while before we know about the inhaler. One doctor said he might need it forever."

"Forever? Oh God—"

Gail's mouth pulled into a thin straight line.

"Well, let's hope he's wrong," Claudia added.

Gail nodded as she sat down on the couch next to Claudia. She lifted her right leg up onto a pillow that had been lying on the coffee table, apparently for that purpose.

Claudia picked up her mug of tea. "It looks like you could use some crutches, too. When are you going to get that taken care of?"

"Oh, it's not too bad—the pain comes and goes. It's sporadic. Today's just a bad day."

Claudia looked at her.

"As soon as everything settles down I'll get the MRI. My doctor thinks it's just a torn meniscus. Nothing serious."

"Sounds serious to me."

Claudia took a sip of tea, not sure where to put her eyes. She *so* did not want to believe their wishing had caused any of it. That it had made Andrew suffer, or Gail. But there seemed to be too much of a connection for everything to just be coincidence—especially now, with all the new developments, everything else that was going wrong, for all of them.

Well, for all of them except Lindsay. "I can't believe Lindsay agreed to an emergency meeting," Claudia said. "She's been so adamant about how none of these bad things have had anything to do with the wishing."

"I think that's why she's coming. To convince us they don't. Have you seen her lately? She looks like a lollipop. She wasn't even overweight before. That's the thing that kills me. Why would anyone with her figure feel like they needed to lose so much weight?"

"I guess that's easy for you to say, always looking like a supermodel. I personally don't know a woman alive who isn't trying to lose five pounds, or ten—or more."

"Yeah, well. Even I just realized my thighs aren't what they used to be."

Claudia offered a weak smile, because what was she supposed to say to that? *I'm sure your thighs still look great—even if you're not a twenty-two-year-old porn star anymore.*

Gail turned to look out the window. She sipped her tea, instantly lost in thought.

Claudia studied the side of her face, the tightened jaw, the way the lines were starting to splay out at the corner of her eye. Gail looked afraid. And Claudia had never known Gail to look afraid before.

There's got to be a way to fix this, Claudia thought. *There's got to be a way to turn these wishes around.*

The doorbell rang and Gail set down her mug.

Claudia set hers down quickly and stood up. "Don't you even think about it. I've got it."

Lindsay walked into the great room ahead of Claudia, carrying a box from Dinkel's. "I brought some cookies. Do you want me to get a plate for these or should we just eat them right out of the box?" She set them on the table and answered her own question. "Let's just eat them right out of the box." She pulled the stack of napkins out from under the twine and started to open it.

Just who is she trying to fool? Claudia thought. Lindsay and her big box of cookies. Showing off for them. *Look at me eating. See? No dieting here. Just pure magic.* Claudia watched her undo the string. *Right.*

And she looked so thin—too thin. "Lindsay, how much weight have you lost?"

"Oh, I don't know." *Bullshit.* "Maybe ten or fifteen pounds." *This is the same woman who has been calling me with ounce-by-ounce updates—and now she doesn't know?*

"Looks like closer to twenty if you ask me." Gail leaned over and reached for the Dinkel's box.

Lindsay bit into a cookie and shrugged, a few crumbs tumbling from her lower lip. She pinched them out of her lap and sprinkled them over a napkin on the coffee table. "Where are Mara and Jill?"

"Not to change the subject or anything," Claudia said.

"Mara's coming later." Gail's words were goopy with cookie. She swallowed. "She has to work until seven. And Jill finally got back to me like an hour ago. She can't make it, said she had plans with Marc tonight." Gail deepened her voice and did a silky imitation of Jill's. "He's just been so fabulous." Gail returned to her regular voice. "She also said she was way behind at work and that she needed to get ready for the opening. She made it sound as if she needed to work all night."

"Work all night with Marc, is my guess." Lindsay gave them a wink. "See? This is what I've been trying to tell you. Jill is doing great. She's busy painting. Hanging out with Marc. Now she's spending so much time with him she's starting to abandon us. Not that I blame her—have you seen him? Wow."

"But Lindsay—"

"Let me finish." Lindsay held up her hand, the *wait, wait* gesture. "You guys are so down on these wishes, trying to blame them for all of your troubles; but, well, look at me. My whole life I've been trying and now I've finally been able to lose weight, and now—" Lindsay stopped suddenly.

"And now what?" Claudia asked.

"And . . . and, now everything is great."

"That's not what you were going to say."

"No . . . I. Yes, it was."

"What is it, Lindsay?" Gail asked.

"Out with it."

"Oh, all right." Lindsay exhaled. A huge grin spread across her face when she looked at them. "I've been asked to be in the Foundation fashion show."

Lindsay was two for two. No wonder she didn't want to quit. No wonder she didn't want anyone finding fault with the wishing process.

"I almost didn't want to say anything. Everything's been going so well for me—and for Jill—and it just . . . Well, it just seems like the results have been the opposite for you guys."

"Aha! You admit it. You *do* think our wishes have gone bad."
Claudia was waving a finger at Lindsay. "You just didn't want to
ruin it for yourself. Everything is going great for Lindsay, so Lindsay
doesn't want to change it. Never mind that everyone else's life is a
mess. You're going to be in the fashion show. You're a size four. But
exactly how small are you planning to get? A size two? A zero?
Every time I look at you these days, I feel like I want to feed you a
sandwich." Claudia was breathing hard, her heart pounding.

Lindsay's mouth hung open. She looked at Gail, then back at
Claudia. "I don't deserve this. Just because your wishes have backfired and mine haven't doesn't mean you get to lay into me about
my . . . my weight loss."

Lindsay was yelling now. "It's not my fault your wishes are going
wrong. You can't blame me for everything. You don't even know
for sure the wishes are what's really behind all your troubles in the
first place. It's just easier for you to blame me. Take potshots at
Lindsay—the obvious target, the easy target."

"What?" Claudia was incredulous. "I can't believe what I'm
hearing—you always think it's about you. Well, it's not always about
you—it's . . . it's . . ." Claudia could feel one of her verbal stumbles
coming on. She breathed hard in silence, glaring at Lindsay.

The anger swirled between them like a cloud, as if waiting for
either of them to utter one more word, one more sentence to make
their anger sublimate into something solid, a wall they couldn't get
through.

"Maybe," Gail's voice was gentle, "it's not as black and white
as y— as we're trying to make it. Maybe some of our wishes have
succeeded and some of them have gone wrong, and some of the
bad things that seem like results are just coincidences; maybe even
some of the good things, too. But I think the most important thing
is that we have to stick together. Be here for one another; support
each other. And then maybe somehow we can try to find a way to
fix the wishes that have gone wrong."

Lindsay took a deep breath. "Well, as I was trying to say." She
glared at Claudia as if to say, *before I was interrupted.* "I was trying to

say, that I just couldn't see how half of our wishes could be working and the other half could not. Like what Gail said. It didn't make any sense, especially because we'd had such huge success and everything had been going so great. It made me think all the bad things were unrelated. A coincidence. Until this week. With everything that's happened after that second set of wishes—you not being able to write at all and you and the whole, um," Lindsay cleared her throat, "and the whole Internet thing. Well, I decided to do some research."

"So you really do believe," Claudia asked, "that maybe a few of our wishes have backfired?"

Lindsay gave Claudia an impatient look. "*Yes.* Now I think maybe some of them did. But here's the good news. We can fix them. I've been reading in my books there are ways to reverse spells." Lindsay started to revert back to her take-charge self again. Enthusiastic and positive. "There's a whole section in the *Modern Witches' Grimoire,* which I suppose if we'd read it more thoroughly, we would have known about, but there's a whole part on how to fix bad spells—"

The phone rang, interrupting her, and Gail reached over to pick it up.

She set it back down on the end table. "Mara's on her way. She got off work a little early. Sounded really cheerful about it, practically sang into the phone."

Gail looked over at the box of Dinkel's on the coffee table. "Guess we'd better hide the cookies."

"I just thought it would be worth a try." Mara sat on the edge of Gail's couch, a pained, slightly embarrassed expression on her face. "I just thought, how much more harm could I do?"

When Mara had joined them in Gail's great room, they'd tried not to act startled by her appearance. Claudia had already tried not to act startled at the front door. Mara's jeans strained under the pressure of (at least) an additional twenty-five pounds. Her face, always full and round, had added the beginnings of an extra chin, which was more apparent whenever she opened her mouth to talk or smile.

"It's just so horrible." Mara closed her eyes and shook her head. "Henry was shaving again when I left." The pitch of each word dipped and climbed as Mara spoke.

"How come . . . what's the matter with your voice?" Gail asked.

"I don't know. It's like I can't help it. Every now and then, when I'm talking, my words just come out like . . . like singing."

"Oh my God—your second wish."

Mara nodded, but she didn't speak.

"Okay," Claudia said, "we have got to do something. Maybe trying to fix these wishes ourselves isn't the best idea, but there has to be a way. We've got to . . ." She paused, then flashed her eyes up at them. "I know, we should get outside help. We should try to find help from a real witch."

"Oh, sure," Gail said. "Let's see, would that be in the Yellow Pages under Witches for Hire?"

"Yeah." Mara giggled. "Spell-Breakers Я Us—We reverse spells so you don't have to." She giggled again.

"I'm serious, you guys. Look, we just saw with Mara what could happen if we try to get out of this ourselves."

"I think my mistake was doing it by myself." Mara's eyes were on the Dinkel's box on the table; her voice was relatively stable now. "I should have waited, gotten together with you guys." She reached in and pulled out a butter cookie, the kind with a candied cherry in the center.

"Do you really want to take the chance that we'll make things even worse?" Claudia tried to look at Lindsay and Gail, but her eyes were drawn to the way Mara was eating the cookie, in about a dozen small bites, as if she were trying to tell herself she could put it down at any moment.

Claudia tore her eyes away. "Can you imagine how much more we could mess things up if we tried to break these spells as *a group*? The same way we got ourselves into trouble in the first place? Face it. We need outside help. We need an expert."

They were listening to her now. Claudia took a breath. "Maybe we could find someone at a New Age bookstore, or there might be information about witches on the Internet." She hesitated. "There's this woman I've run into a couple of times. I keep seeing her around and . . . I don't know, but I get the impression she may be able to help us."

"Some woman you've been seeing around?" Gail asked.

"I saw her at the bookstore. She said she'd read *The Sacredness of the Wiccan Way* a long time ago. She had a crystal. And I saw her at the juice bar at Wild Prairie and, oh, hell, I don't know. I just think she might be able to help us somehow."

"You saw this woman at a bookstore and a juice bar and you think she can help us fix our spells, *somehow*?" Gail shook her head.

"I'm still not convinced we even need help." Lindsay held up the grimoire. "I'm not so sure a lot of it isn't going to resolve on its own. It says in here if we—"

Claudia tilted her head at Mara and widened her eyes. "You think *this* is resolving? Just look at her."

Mara put a hand to her chest and pressed her back deeper into the couch, a defensive look on her face.

"I'm afraid to mess with this again, Lindsay. Can't you see? There's got to be someone out there who can help us."

"How do we know we're not going to find some crackpot?" Gail asked. "How can we be sure we wouldn't find someone that would put us under a psychic attack—"

"—make us his zombie-witch slaves?" Mara finished.

"Oh, please." Claudia sank back into the couch. "I think we're the crackpots. I think the hardest part is going to be finding someone who's willing to help us once they hear the stupid things we've done."

"We didn't do stupid things." Lindsay was angry again. "We wished for things. We asked for our wishes to come true, to make our dreams real." She frowned, the anger in her face dissipated. She tilted her head to one side. "Okay, so maybe our wishes were a little self-serving. Maybe the dabbling-with-witchcraft part was stupid. I'll give you that. And we probably should have done more research, or more homework, or been more literal, or something, but you'll never convince me that making a wish is a stupid thing to do."

They looked around at each other and it was apparent that everyone agreed with her.

Lindsay popped her eyebrows once in triumph. Finally, she had won an argument.

Chapter Twenty-Two

✦

Claudia pulled the envelope from her mailbox, thinking it strange; the school didn't usually get the faculty mail out until the afternoon. The envelope had Strawn letterhead. Her name, Claudia Dubois, was hand printed in black ink on the front. She tore it open. The letter was written in the same black ink.

> Claudia,
>   Please stop by my office this afternoon after classes.
>   Headmaster Charles Peterson

Well, shit. Here it comes. This has to be about Elliot. Claudia looked down at the letter. Headmaster Charles Peterson. *Who signs their title?*

She read it again, looking for clues, but found none. Great. Now she had something else she could worry about all day. Something to keep her distracted. Maybe April had confessed to the whole thing and now that Peterson knew Elliot was his grandnephew, he was going to tell Claudia to halt the fostering procedure. The memory of Elliot's warm body filled her arms. Claudia looked at her watch. No, she was not going to sweat this out all day. Classes didn't start for nearly forty-five minutes. April and her class could wait one more day for the results of their *Heart of Darkness* quizzes. She was going to go talk with Peterson right now.

Claudia left the faculty break room and hurried to Peterson's office. The halls were dark and empty. She turned right at the main entrance and went down another hallway, but when she got to the end, his office was dark and so was the glass-enclosed reception area. *He must be here. He left the note.*

Claudia walked back down the hall and turned left down the office corridor at the front of the school, heading back toward the faculty break room. *I suppose he could have dropped the note in there last night, but I left so late . . .*

Light peeked out from under the door to the nurse's waiting area. Marion might know what the letter was all about. She might even know what was going on with Elliot, the way she and Peterson were always whispering to each other, sharing their little looks. And she'd been involved since the day they'd found Elliot, too.

Claudia pushed open the door to the nurse's waiting room and held it open, but the lights in the interior office were dark through the smoked glass. *Hmm. That's strange.* Claudia turned to go, putting her hand on the light switch to turn it off on her way out, when she heard the distinct sound of paper crinkling, the sound the sheet of paper on a doctor's examining table makes when you adjust yourself on it. *Someone's in there? A burglar? A student looking for drugs?*

"Hello? Is someone there?"

The crinkling sound grew frantic and she heard more movement, a dull thud, a whisper.

"Who's in there? Marion, is that you? Answer me now or I'm calling the cops."

The light inside the interior office switched on. "It's just me— Marion," Marion called through the closed door, her voice cracking and breathless. "Don't call the cops." Now she was trying to sound lighthearted, but lighthearted coming out of Marion sounded just plain weird.

Marion opened the door and stood there, trying on an innocent smile. Her usually crisp white uniform was a tad crumpled, and the buttons down the front veered off to her left as they descended, the bottom button hanging open over her knee. Marion's frantic curls looked even more frantic than usual, perhaps because they contrasted so vividly with the classic white nurse's cap perched on top of her head.

She sleeps here?

Claudia's eyes dropped to Marion's conspicuously absent white hose, her legs a mottled red, two plump stalks growing out of her white nurse's shoes. But it was the shoes underneath the examining table behind her, tucked under the flat metal step, that caught Claudia's attention: a gleaming black pair of Salvatore Ferragamo oxfords.

The first indication that maybe things weren't going to go as well as planned was the yelling and screaming in Greek. Lindsay stepped from the elevator into the top-floor banquet hall at the Metron Hotel and could hear shouting all the way from the kitchen.

The circular room was set up for the fashion show, a two-foot-high runway platform jutting out into the middle of it from the curtains and stage at the far end. The room could rotate slowly around, giving everyone, eventually, a three-hundred-and-sixty-degree view of the lake and city. It was left over from when the top floor of the Metron had been a restaurant in the late 1970s, back when rotating restaurants were hip and trendy. All the tables had been arranged in a circular fashion in harmony with the shape of the room and they were supposed to be covered with ecru tablecloths to evoke the beaches of Lake Michigan, visible far below from the floor-to-ceiling windows.

But the tablecloths were not sand-colored. They were mauve, a color so embarrassingly 1980s that it made Lindsay's jaw drop open when she stepped into the room. *Mauve.* When she got closer, the color made her wince. She panted out little "ha's" of disbelief. *What in the world are they thinking?* This horrid shade of pink was causing her pain—real physical pain in the center of her chest. Lindsay took a breath and shook her head. She would have to deal with that later. Right now, she needed to find out what the trouble was in the kitchen.

As she walked along the curved aisle to the kitchen, the yelling grew louder. Just before she got to the double doors in the back, she could see a toque coming toward her, growing rapidly larger in the high round window. The doors burst open with such force that Lindsay had to ram her back against the wall to avoid being run over. A large, cursing chef charged by.

After he'd passed, Lindsay reached around to rub her back where it was throbbing. She'd jammed it into a panel of switches. She could see the large one in the middle that had poked her. Most of the switches were for lights, all labeled: "front rear," "front center," and so forth, but the switch that had jabbed her was the one under a square plastic cover labeled "floor rotation." The switch was larger than the rest, with a little red light above it. How odd that they'd put *that* switch here, right out in the open. It seemed that switch should require a key, or should have been placed in a back room somewhere. At least it was under a plastic cover—even if it was a hard one with pointed corners.

Through the swinging doors Lindsay could still hear a voice yelling—probably cursing, she couldn't tell, it was still in Greek—getting louder and softer as the doors swung back and forth. Rubbing her bruised back, Lindsay strode into the kitchen.

Nikki, the hotel catering staff member with whom Lindsay had been working, had her back to Lindsay and was still yelling and screaming, slapping both of her arms out in the air, as if she were repeatedly saying, *and another thing.*

"Nikki?"

Nikki stopped her gesturing and turned around, an embarrassed look on her face.

"Is everything okay?" Lindsay asked.

"Yes. It is fine. Everything will be fine."

"Good. I hope everything is okay because lunch is in three hours, and if we don't have anyone to make it—"

"He was just the dessert chef. He is very arrogant. He wants to make what he wants to make and not what is called for by the order."

Lindsay nodded that she understood.

Nikki continued. "He wants the apple cake with preserved lemon and cinnamon streusel for your dessert, Miss Lindsay. He says this is better complement to the chilled seafood salad entrée. He says he doesn't like the looks of the berries today, either. He says, to him, they are not ready. But I point to the order, show him, 'minted seasonal berries, with Grand Marnier cream sauce.' He says the basil vinaigrette will stay on the palate from the poached shrimp and calamari, and that will make the minted berries taste strange. He says he is trained chef and so he should be one to decide. It is hard to argue with that, but I tell him we need to follow the order, because it is these same people who pay the bill. For him, it is hard to argue with that. So, he storms out because he cannot have his way."

Nikki held a hopeful expression on her face, like maybe Lindsay would acquiesce to the apple cake streusel.

Lindsay smiled back at Nikki, a smile that said "minted berries."

"We'll have a delicious dessert for your luncheon, Miss Lindsay." Nikki's face betrayed her uncertainty.

"Thank you, Nikki." Lindsay gave her a bubbly smile now. "You know I'm counting on you." She paused, the smile still plastered on her face. "Well," she exhaled, "I'll leave you to your work. I have got to get these tablecloths taken care of."

And Lindsay spun out of the kitchen to find some help with that.

She knew tablecloths were the kind of detail that no one paid much attention to. It fell under what she called her Wedding Cake Theory, her personal philosophy concerning *all the little details*. Lindsay believed that when it came right down to it, no one ever really paid much attention to the cake at a wedding. They all look the same, essentially, if you ever get around to seeing them up close before they get cut up. They just need to be there. But still, brides spent hours and days agonizing over finding the perfect cake and getting all the details right—three tiers vs. two tiers, white vs. pink flowers. But why? The cake will end up looking just like every other wedding cake in the eyes of the people who are there to eat it.

But this was her big break. She was coordinating the luncheon and modeling in the show. If she could pull all of this off, the sky was the limit. So, in spite of her Wedding Cake Theory, Lindsay still wanted everything to be perfect. It would be disastrous for her to go forward with *mauve* tablecloths and a pedestrian dessert like apple cake streusel. *Streusel.* Honestly. Why didn't they suggest Rice Krispie treats, for crying out loud? *Next thing you know they'll be trying to sell me on a Jell-O mold.*

The visual assault of mauve was less of an ambush the second time Lindsay walked through the dining room. There were forty pink tables in the room, each seating eight. Lindsay thought perhaps she could go through and remove the tablecloths completely, letting the natural wood-tone of the tables provide her with her ecru. It would have been a simple solution, but she would need some help. A magician would have been nice, the kind who can slide tablecloths out from under plates and silverware without spilling a water glass, because the tables had already been set. Lindsay lifted a tablecloth to check the color of the wood, so she could make this suggestion, but was greeted by a metal leg underneath. She dropped the tablecloth in frustration.

Lindsay stormed out of the room and back to the elevator bank. She jammed her thumb onto the down arrow. She was going downstairs to have a little talk with the hotel events coordinator. Mauve tablecloths indeed.

Chapter Twenty-Three

Something in the jacket of the yellow Hermès skirt-suit Lindsay was wearing was cutting into the back of her neck, and she kept reaching her hand around to smooth it down while she waited backstage for her turn on the runway. A lot of the models were milling around with her, many of them looking just as nervous as she felt.

All Lindsay had been able to eat today were a few bites of toast, her whole body fraught with tension. It didn't help that, in order to make her suit fit, she'd been pinned and taped into it so haphazardly that now she was afraid to take deep breaths. Apparently she was even more of a skinny-binny than Nancy Blades.

But, at least so far, the luncheon seemed to be going off without a hitch. And Lindsay had only overheard a few snide comments on the mauve tablecloths—although one of them had been from Evelyn Cantwell.

"Who thought mauve was a good idea?" Evelyn had laughed.

Lindsay stopped and turned around, then walked back to explain. "The mauve was no one's idea. It was a total mix-up on the Metron's part." But when she looked at the expression on Evelyn's face, Lindsay was reminded too late of the saying that said explaining was the same thing as losing.

What's that about? Does she really despise mauve that much? At the time, Lindsay might have worried more about Evelyn's disapproving look, but she'd needed to hurry backstage.

Now, Lindsay had plenty of time to mull over the day's events while she paced backstage, and she fretted over what Evelyn's odd expression could have meant. This was supposed to have been such a happy event for her, but her mood matched the gloom outside.

The morning had begun with a light rain that had faded into a drizzly fog, and the top floor of the Metron was still encased in it. There was no view at all, except for the inside of a cloud, which was a shame because the view from up here was usually so spectacular. One of her earlier worries had been that the turnout might suffer because of the rotten weather, but it didn't seem to have had any effect. So far, so good. If things could just keep going smoothly, the women might be extra generous when they pulled out their check-books, raising more money for the adult literacy campaign, which might get Lindsay her hoped-for mention in Ann Gerber's column.

"I thought witches only wore black." Jocelyn Cantwell had come up behind Lindsay. She was Evelyn Cantwell's sister-in-law, her brother's second wife, the trophy wife. Her old-money status obtained via marriage and plastic surgery.

"Witches? What are you talking about?"

"Oh, I think you know what I'm talking about," Jocelyn said, and the woman standing next to her, whom Lindsay didn't know, tittered.

"I'm sure I haven't the foggiest idea."

"We know all about your little book group." Jocelyn shared a look with her friend. "We know you like to pretend to be witches."

Lindsay tried to brush the tag or whatever it was away from the back of her neck, but it fell back into place, rubbing into the raw spot at her nape. When she'd reached her arm up, she'd felt one of the safety pins at the back of her skirt pop, poking into her hip. "My book group? Where did you hear such a preposterous thing?"

"Everyone's talking about it." Jocelyn smiled—a smile reminiscent of Molly Bonner from the Forest Woods High School cafeteria. "Everyone's talking about how your book club has gone . . . *supernatural.*"

"Supernatural? That is so ridiculous. What would make people think something like that?"

Jocelyn shrugged. "You know what they say about a kernel of truth behind every rumor." She grinned again, revealing two extremely white rows of impressive cosmetic dentistry.

Lindsay hesitated. *What on earth am I going to say?* She should deny it completely. *No, too defensive.* Throw them a bone to chew on with their perfect little teeth. "Well, we did read a book about witches last fall—in October. You know, for Halloween. And we did that finger-lifting thing—you know, like in junior high, 'Light as a feather, stiff as a board.'" *Why am I making stuff up? Because it sounds better than the truth.* "But that's all it was—a bunch of drunken silliness. Do you think that's how such a silly rumor got started? I mean, witchcraft? Honestly."

Jocelyn shrugged and gave Lindsay a mysterious look before she and her tittery friend walked away. *Well, that would explain that look from Evelyn. Which means I'm ruined. Oh dear God no, I'm ruined.* Lindsay felt nauseous.

The stage manager was waving her out. From the look on her face, and the fact that the other model was more than halfway up the aisle on her way back, Lindsay knew she had missed her first cue. She wiped the sweat from her upper lip, took a deep breath, and stepped out into the floodlights.

The lights added another ten degrees to the temperature on the stage and Lindsay was already covered in a light film of sweat. She walked the way they'd taught her to, one leg crossing in front of the other, and it took all of her concentration. The pin on her hip poked her with every step, and she wanted to look down to check that her skirt wasn't crooked, or worse, about to fall off, but she resisted. Her whole being felt wobbly, her nerves on edge. She attempted to get her bearings. She looked at all the smiling faces staring up at her, watching her, judging her—wondering if she was a witch.

She tried instead to focus down at the tables, where the waitstaff was handing out the plates of dessert. *Oh, this is too much. No!* Lindsay quickly lifted her eyes, but there was nothing solid for them to grab on to, nothing but cloud-filled windows.

She made it to the end of the runway and was turning around when she heard a low-pitched grinding noise and felt the room begin to lurch out from under her. She took another wobbly step down the runway. The whole room felt like it was moving. *Oh my God, I'm going to be sick.*

Lindsay looked at the floor-to-ceiling windows and the tables inside the room. Wait. The whole room *was* moving. She tried to find something to focus on, to establish in her mind that this wasn't a trick and that the room was really rotating, that the spinning wasn't just in her head. Near the doors to the kitchen Jocelyn and her tittery friend stood grinning by the panel of light switches, the large red bulb in the center glowing like a one-eyed monster in a horror movie.

The runway platform no longer lined up with the exit. There was no way out. The outbound model had just passed her. They were, essentially, trapped out there. Trapped in the center of a room filled with women, all baring their teeth at her. A science-show factoid popped into Lindsay's head: humans are the only animals that bare their teeth in greeting.

The heat and the stress and the fear of being outed as a witch welled up in her stomach like a noxious bubbling potion of newt-filled brew. She felt the bile rise in her throat. She tried to steady herself, but between the rotating tables and the horizonless windows her eyes found nothing stable to focus on. Every time she moved her gaze, she felt a wave of vertigo.

Lindsay wiped more sweat from her upper lip—a big fashion-show no, no, which only brought on more panic. She felt the room spinning, her whole world spinning right out of control. She took a shaky step down off the runway and hobbled a few more paces toward a table. Then, in the middle of the Chicago Women's Foundation Spring Fashion Show Extravaganza, Lindsay fainted on Evelyn Cantwell's streusel.

A truck's horn blared in her ear. Gail lurched, her heart racing, and slammed her foot on the brakes—before realizing she wasn't driving at all, but sitting inside her parked minivan, outside of her sons' school. She must have fallen asleep.

The truck was trying to get by all the SUVs and minivans parked and double-parked outside the school. It looked to Gail as if the Hummer in front of her was the sticking point.

She swallowed and tried to breathe. Stupid natural-birth breathing exercises. They'd failed her three times; she didn't know why she thought they would calm her now. Emily was still sitting contentedly in the back seat, watching the moms parade by outside her window. "C'mon Em. Let's go get the boys."

A couple of kindergarten moms stood outside the gate, and Gail walked down to join them. When she got close, she saw them whisper to each other and close ranks. Two of them picked up their toddlers, who had been running around on the sidewalk.

That's weird. What would they be upset with me for?

A voice called from behind her. "Gail Preskill! We haven't seen you in ages." Ugh. Susie Schaeffer. Craft mom. *Probably wants me on another committee.* "Have you been hiding?"

Hiding is the impossible dream. "No, I've just been busy. Andrew—"

"Well, we thought you might be hiding." Susie ended most sentences with the same two tones. One high-pitched. One low. She alternated the pattern from low-high to high-low and it made her sound as if she were caught in some eternal playground-taunt hell.

"Why would I be hiding?" Gail tried to sound calm. *She knows about the porn.*

"Well, when I heard, I just couldn't believe it. I said, 'Not Gail Preskill. Our kids play together.'"

"Couldn't believe what?" Gail's pulse was racing and her mouth had gone dry. *I'm holding my two-year-old's hand. Would she say something about the porn in front of a two-year-old?*

"About your book club. You know, the *witchcraft.*"

Gail didn't know whether to be relieved or irritated that she now had something else to worry about. "Witchcraft?"

"Just say it's not true. Because no one wants to believe it—so just say the word, and we will back you up one hundred *percent.*" Susie smiled, waiting. "It's not true, is it? Because," she laughed nervously, "if it were, I of course couldn't let Connor—"

"It's not true," Gail said.

———

*W*hen Claudia entered the reception area of Peterson's office after classes, his secretary glanced up and then continued typing, not making eye contact, appearing to be very interested in her computer screen. Claudia thought this was a very bad sign. The woman leaned in a little closer to her computer and squinted without taking her eyes from it as she told Claudia, "Go ahead in. He's expecting you."

Claudia pushed open the door and found Peterson waiting behind his desk, his fingers intertwined, elbows resting on top of it.

Shouldn't he, really, be busier?

Claudia had wondered if he would display any hint of embarrassment at what he certainly by now must know she'd seen evidence of this morning in Marion's office. But no, he seemed to be in complete denial—or could he honestly think she hadn't seen anything? That she was so unobservant as to not notice his shoes, or Marion's unusually ravaged condition? The ridiculous little nurse's hat on her head? She would have liked to have seen him right then, seeing as how he always looked so *pressed*. Not in the *pressed for time* sense, but in the *my clothes are perfectly pressed* sense. What was that term Mara used for something like this? *Precious.* That was it. Peterson was like the male version of "precious." *Pressed.*

"Claudia, hello. Sit down please." *Uh-oh. Pressed and professional. This was* not *good.*

"Claudia, I'm afraid it's come to our attention . . . Some very serious accusations have been made about you, and"—he cleared his throat—"and I wanted to discuss them with you, first."

Accusations? First? Before what?

"Accusations?" *Are they going to accuse me of planting babies in garbage cans? In teenage girls? Oh God, this is the last thing Dan and I need.*

"It's come to our attention that you've become involved in some sort of a—a witchcraft cult. A coven."

"A coven?" Claudia was stunned. She'd thought for sure Peterson had called her in here to talk about Elliot and the whole baby-in-the-bathroom incident. "Witchcraft?" Claudia repeated. "Who's making these accusations?"

"Well, I'm afraid I'm not at liberty to discuss—"

"Not at liberty? Of all the ridiculous . . . a coven? Is this about my Book Club?"

"The information we were given suggests that your book club is more than just a book club—that your group has become involved in more *unseemly* activities. I wanted to give you the opportunity to explain yourself, here. These are very serious allegations to be raised against one of our teachers. If something like this were to get out into the community, why it could—"

If something like this were to get back to the DCFS social worker . . . Shit. Who did this? Damn. Think, Claudia, think. Pull yourself together, just this once. Don't panic. Don't get defensive.

"Mr. Peterson," Claudia paused, then changed her tack. "Charles." She smiled at him. "I've been teaching here for how many years now? Almost eight? I'd have to say by now that you must know me pretty well—"

"I was pretty shocked when I heard the allegations were against *you.*"

Claudia gave him another smile, *thank you.* "I'm not a big fan of conspiracy theories, Oliver Stone and all that, but do you think that maybe someone could be . . . out to get me? I hate to sound paranoid, but with all that's been going on, the baby and everything, maybe someone is trying to muck it up for me."

"So you're saying you're not involved in any sort of witchcraft-type, coven thing?"

"No. Of course not. I mean, my book club read a novel about witchcraft a while back—but that's about as close as we've come to witches of any type." *Who is his source? How much does he know?* "We also sometimes do group . . . meditations, to send positive, healing energy to each other. It's a good-karma thing." Claudia saw a look of concern appear on Peterson's face. *Ooh, "karma" bad choice of word. He's one of those people that fears stuff like this, thinks yoga is a religion.* "It's just about channeling"—*shit*—"happy thoughts for each other. Giving ourselves a little positive energy boost."

Peterson nodded as if he understood, but Claudia was pretty sure her New Age jargon had stumped him as much as quantum physics theory would have.

"Well, I hope you appreciate my position here," he said, "the necessity for me to investigate these types of things. I have to make sure all my teachers are on the up and up—no Satan worship or animal sacrifices." He smiled at Claudia, but his eyebrows asked her, *none of that, right?*

"Mr. Peterson, I assure you, the only crime my Book Club is guilty of is picking a few bad books."

Chapter Twenty-Four

✦

The juice machine raged in the background, and the milk steamer seethed in the foreground, but Claudia was oblivious to the noise. She wasn't trying to read the book she'd brought, a first edition of a John Irving novel, *A Son of the Circus*. She'd read it last year; now it was a prop. She looked over the top of it, scanning the store, looking for her mystery woman, the woman whom she hoped would help the members of Wish Club find their way out of their respective messes. The woman whom Claudia presumed was an Irving fan, since she'd been reading him the last time Claudia had seen her here.

Claudia had also tried to find her crystal, with no luck. It would be a way to break the ice. She'd looked everywhere for it—in her desk at school, in drawers and pockets, at home—but it had never turned up. Just like this woman.

This was the sixth or seventh time since the Emergency Meeting that Claudia had been in the Wild Prairie Market Café. She'd also been going to the Barnes & Noble on Clybourn after school. In both places she sat and drank coffee and kept a lookout. After so many espresso drinks a day, she was experiencing the alert exhaustion that only too much caffeine can bring on: her lungs felt close to hyperventilating, her jaw was tense, and her eyes felt too wide open. The combination would make her appear insane, she thought, should she ever actually find this woman she was looking for.

Her Internet search was proving fruitless, too. There were so many Web pages under witches and covens, tons of sites, and only a few of them had pictures of actual witches—and so far none of them matched. What were the odds she'd ever find her online? (Then again, what had been the odds that Gail would find herself?) But with the wishes going haywire and the allegations of witchcraft springing up, Claudia simply had to find her—or another witch, or someone that could help them.

And now Dan was starting to complain, voicing his disapproval with her for having been gone almost every night for the past week and a half. After she'd made her rounds at the café or the bookstore, or some days both, she would stop by the hospital to cuddle Elliot for a while. Most nights, when she got home, she continued searching on the computer for an hour or two, before getting into bed late.

Sleep eluded her, and all her switching from side to side was disturbing Dan—but she couldn't stop her mind from racing. *Am I just wasting my time on the stupidest quest in the world? Who is this woman? Where is she? What if I actually find her and then she doesn't want to help—or worse, can't? What then?* The coffee only made it worse, but she'd fallen into the vicious caffeine cycle—not falling asleep at night because of it, then needing it twice as much the next day.

The previous night she had been so exhausted and had gotten to bed so late that she'd been certain she would fall asleep right away. She had tossed and turned a couple of times, then opened her eyes, immediately realizing she was so charged up that it had been foolish to try to force them closed. *How come I can't capture this feeling at three in the afternoon?*

During her next eyes-wide-open toss, she was surprised to see that Dan's eyes were wide open, too.

"Hmm, you look familiar," he said. "Didn't you used to live here?" He reached an arm out and pulled her closer. "Am I going to have to hang out at the Wild Prairie Café if I want to see you in the daylight?"

"It's not going to be for too much longer," Claudia said. "At least I don't think so. I'm starting to feel a little ridiculous about this whole *searching for the mystery woman* thing. I'm either going to find her soon or give it up."

"Well, that's good news," Dan gave her a squeeze, "because I miss my wife." He kissed her on her forehead before rolling back onto his other side, mumbling a comment about preferring a different type of tossing and turning in bed.

Claudia wondered if the other women were going through the same thing as she was—struggling unsuccessfully to find a witch during the day and then getting the third degree at night. She doubted it. Mara still hadn't told Henry anything about the witchcraft stuff and Lindsay had just started *really* trying to help them search. Claudia was pretty sure she wouldn't tell James anything about spell reversals, it being tantamount to admitting failure. Gail wanted to help, but didn't have the time. Would she have mentioned it to John? Probably not. He was so skeptical about the wishing causing any of their troubles in the first place, he certainly wouldn't be sympathetic to their trying to find a witch now. As for Jill, who knew what was up with her anymore? She'd practically disappeared.

Now at the Wild Prairie Café, Claudia lowered her book and rested her face in her hands. This was all so silly. She couldn't spend all her time sitting in coffee shops and bookstores hoping some stranger would show up.

All the muscles in her face and neck were tight. She relaxed them into her hands, and the artificial alertness she'd been feeling evaporated instantly. She felt she could just fall asleep right there. All she had to do was lower her head onto the table and she would doze right off, like a baby. Like Elliot.

Watching Elliot sleep; that's what she should be doing now. Holding that little baby, watching his face, had convinced her that babies are the real angels, or at least the inspiration from which the idea for angels had come—straight from heaven, precious gifts. How could anyone have done what his mother had?

The search for her had focused mostly on a few students at Strawn, but it was still ongoing. For Claudia and Dan, the fostering process had been proceeding pretty smoothly. The DCFS home-study interviews had gone well, she thought. Claudia was torn between not wanting to find his mother (perhaps bettering her chances of keeping Elliot) and wanting the opportunity to smack her squarely in her jaw. It was a strange sensation, this mama-bear feeling. She'd never known anything like it before.

Claudia lifted her head out of her hands and scanned for the witch-woman again out of habit. She should go home—or to the hospital. All she'd wanted was a baby and now it was starting to look more and more like that might actually happen. And not just any baby, but Elliot. What was going to happen if she found this witch? What if they undid the wishing and then Elliot's mother or father turned up and wanted him back?

The realization that maybe she shouldn't be doing this crept over her slowly. *If I really want to get Elliot, why am I trying to undo my wish?* Oh, stop being so selfish. She needed to do this; she had to. Their wishes needed fixing.

But maybe not necessarily. Maybe all the wishes would fix themselves on their own, like Lindsay had said. Claudia could write again, although not very well. Earlier in the week, while watching for the woman at Barnes & Noble, she'd spent the better part of her time working on her handwriting. Now she could do a pretty good job of signing her name. Most everything else she wrote was illegible to anyone but her, however, and she still couldn't put lesson outlines on the board. Typing up Post-it notes on her old typewriter in order to grade her papers was getting old, fast.

No, they needed a witch and Claudia was pretty sure this woman was the one. She looked around the Wild Prairie Café one more time. Then she looked at her watch; she really should get going now. She *was* exhausted.

She closed her book and tucked it in her bag and told herself it was common sense and exhaustion, not her realization about wanting to keep Elliot, that had curbed her enthusiasm for her quest.

Claudia maneuvered her car into a cramped space with a minimum of bumper thumping, happy she'd found a place to park on her block. She was so tired, she decided not to go to the hospital tonight so she could get home a little earlier than usual, a maneuver intended to placate Dan.

Her cell phone rang and Claudia fumbled through her purse to find it, her finger narrowly missing the point of the compass that had been in there for over a week now. One of these days she'd remember to return it to the math lab.

The phone flashed red as she pulled it out, flipping it open without checking the caller ID. It was Mara, frustrated with her search for a witch.

"Have *you* had any luck?" Mara's voice rose up an entire major scale with the question. The singsonginess was getting worse.

"Nope." Claudia leaned back into the seat of her car.

"I'm at my wit's end. I don't know what else to do." Mara sounded horribly panicked, in spite of her musical voice. "Henry's got so much hair—on his back, and his arms. He has to wear long-sleeved shirts all the time, even at practice, and it just keeps getting thicker."

Claudia knew. She'd seen him at school.

"And I've gained so much weight—I can't stop eating."

"Mara, we're going to find someone."

"It can't happen soon enough. I thought I had a lead, a tarot reader at the Chakra Shoppe. I had a reading with her last week and then I went back a couple of times, but I couldn't do it. I couldn't bring myself to ask her, you know, if she was a witch. And then, and then yesterday, when I walked in, they asked me to leave." Mara's voice was in an extremely high-pitched range now. "They said I was making Star Raven nervous. I got kicked out of a New Age bookstore. For stalking! These people—the New Age woo-hoos—they're the most tolerant, accepting people in the universe and they kicked me out. I've been banned from the store like on that Seinfeld episode!"

Claudia tried not to sound alarmed at the odd ululations and gyrations Mara's voice was taking. "At least Dr. Seeley isn't starting an investigation into you because he thinks you're a witch."

"What? Who's doing that?"

"Strawn."

"I should have guessed. They're so freakin' uptight. Peterson already had a talk with Henry about shaving—making a nice,

clean-cut impression on the young men and all that. Yeah, right."
Mara paused. "Wait. How did they know? Who snitched?"

"I have no idea, but Gail's been accused, too. Another mom at
her kids' school just walked right up to her at pickup last week and
straight-out accused her of being a witch. Right there in front of
all the kids. Told Gail she wouldn't let her son play with Andrew
anymore."

"No."

"Yes." A car had pulled up alongside Claudia and the driver was
asking via sign language if she was leaving her space. Claudia
shook her head and turned off her lights.

"I wish I could have been there to hear Gail's comeback."

"Gail said she couldn't think of a thing to say—it had taken her
so off guard. She said at first she thought it was about the Internet
thing . . . you know, the pictures." Another car had pulled up
alongside Claudia and was waiting for her to pull out. Claudia
decided to get out of the car and walk home. "Gail denied everything, of course." When Claudia opened the door, the car sped
past, the driver giving her the finger.

"Jeez. Some people."

"I know. They have a lot of nerve, coming up and accusing
someone to their face, based on a rumor."

"Huh? Oh, I know." Claudia didn't feel like explaining someone
had just flipped her off. "You heard what happened with Lindsay?"

"The fainting thing? Yeah. I feel so sorry for her."

"At least now she's *really* trying to find someone to help us. She's
been to Transitions twice and yesterday she drove out to Insight in
Naperville. I got the impression her heart wasn't in it before."

They fell silent on the line for a moment as Claudia walked
toward her building. The fresh air felt good in her overcaffeinated
lungs.

Mara spoke first. "You know, you don't think Jill could have
started the rumors?"

"Funny you should say that, because she's the first person I
thought of, too, even though it would be completely irrational. It
doesn't make any sense. I mean, why would she do it? She was

right there along with us, even when she was so against the wishing. And the wishing helped her meet this Marc guy, who she's so involved with no one's seen or heard from her since before she blew us off at the emergency meeting. But I don't know why she would spread rumors. Like I said, it doesn't make sense. It is a little weird, though, that both of us thought of her first."

"I still wouldn't put it past her," Mara said. "Maybe it is irrational . . . she'd be implicating herself, too. But who *else* knows about all of it and would talk? Besides, I've never gotten any warm fuzzies from Jill. I don't care how *misunderstood* Lindsay says she is. I think it would be right up her alley to try to put a stop to it by spreading nasty rumors about us and witchcraft. And now it's like she's totally avoiding us.

"And what about this Marc guy?" Mara continued. "What if she told him about the wishing and he made her quit? All it would take would be for either one of them to mention it to a few people. This town can be pretty small sometimes.

"She's still seeing him, right?" Mara tried to imitate Jill's smooth voice when she said, "Is it still *going fabulously*?" but her words came out in a descending minor scale. Decidedly un-Jill-like.

"I think so, but I don't know for sure. Like I said, no one's heard from her. As far as I know she's still seeing him. As far as anyone knows, it's still fabulous. Lindsay's been trying to call her for days, trying to figure out what's up, but Jill won't return her calls. Lindsay's hoping it's just because Jill's busy, between Marc and the opening on Friday."

"I'm telling you she's avoiding us." Mara paused. "Hey. We can talk to her on Friday. Why didn't I think of that before? We're all going to be there anyway and we can ask her about everything. The rumors. Why she blew us off."

"At her opening? With all those other people there? Don't you think that'll really piss her off?"

"Not if she isn't behind the rumors. Not if she really has just been busy."

"It's at five-thirty, right?"

"See you then."

✦

J*ill's* phone rang again. It was the doorman downstairs. Someone was trying desperately to come up and see her, or he wouldn't have tried twice. She had only one friend with that sort of tenacity.

Jill reached her arm out and patted the other side of the bed, but Marc had already left. She lifted her head and looked at the clock. It was nearly noon. Her head ached: too much to drink again last night. Mercifully, the phone stopped ringing.

Why were they making this so hard? Everyone from Book Club kept calling her, trying to find out if she was okay. Leaving all these messages. And now Lindsay was downstairs trying to barge in on her morning—what was left of it. Couldn't they just leave her alone? She'd made up every excuse in the book. You'd think they'd get the hint by now.

Jill got up out of bed and went to the bathroom. The phone rang again. *Ugh. Give it a rest.* The phone was still ringing when Jill went into the kitchen.

She picked it up. "A Lindsay McDermott here to see you."

"I know." Jill sighed. "Send her up."

A few minutes later Lindsay was striding around her condo. "This place is a mess. I knew something was up. I knew things weren't all fabulous with you."

Jill stood behind the kitchen counter in her bathrobe. She lit a cigarette, defiantly blowing the smoke out through her mouth.

"And look at you. It's twelve noon and you've just now gotten out of bed."

"I would have slept later, but someone kept calling."

"I'm worried about you. We're all worried about you. I know you're busy with this new Marc guy, but the least you could do is return our calls, especially in light of everything that's going on."

"I've been busy." Jill pulled on her cigarette again. *She must have lost at least twenty pounds,* Jill thought. *She doesn't look good.* Jill fought down an emotion: worry. She exhaled with a sigh. "Listen. I'm not trying to blow you guys off . . ."

Lindsay raised her eyebrows.

"Okay. Maybe a little bit. It's just all this wishing stuff and then all the creepy things that have been happening. I . . . I don't want to be a part of it anymore. We can still be friends. I just don't want to go to Book Club anymore."

"And you couldn't just tell us that? You couldn't pick up the phone and call *me* and tell me that you want out?"

Jill shrugged. "Marc said"—she could sense Lindsay's nerves heighten at the mention of Marc's name. "I just want out." Jill shrugged again, *Okay? I'm telling you now.*

"What did Marc say?"

Jill hesitated. "Oh, he . . . he just says I should focus on my work—on the show. That I didn't have time for a big social life right now."

"A big social life? Since when is Book Club a big social life? Did you tell him he wouldn't be in your life now if it hadn't been for Book Club?"

Jill tapped some ash into the ashtray in silence.

"No. Of course you didn't tell him. Jill, I'm not so sure I like this guy; I don't care how charming and sweet you say he is. Look what he's doing. He's isolating you from your friends. He's turning you against us."

Jill stomped her cigarette out. "He's not turning me against anyone. In case you don't remember, I never really cared for all the wishing in the first place. I hated it, remember? But you guys just kept pressing along and pressing along. And we made all these wishes. Well, maybe Marc did come into my life because of a wish. I don't know. But I'm certainly not going to tell *him* that. He'll think I'm a lunatic and I don't want to risk losing the best thing that's happened to me in ages.

"I know I was going along with all the witchcraft stuff, but that doesn't mean I ever liked it. And horrible things have started to happen because of those wishes, too. Weird, horrible things have started happening to all of us." Jill paused and ran her eyes up and down Lindsay. "Look at you. How much weight have you lost? You look terrible."

Lindsay's mouth hung open. *Terrible?*

"And I haven't been able to paint a thing since my last wish. Not one thing. I can't work anymore—at all. My second wish has completely backfired: I wished for inspiration and now I'm totally blocked! My opening is tomorrow night and it's going to be awful."

Lindsay's eyes flashed. "I knew it. I knew something was wrong. I knew there was a reason why you were blowing us off. This is why we've been so worried about you. Don't you see? We care about you. With all the bad things that have been happening, I just couldn't believe that you were the only one whose wishes were going fine. Maybe your Marc wish is going fine, but your creative inspiration wish has . . ." Lindsay's voice faded out. She snapped her head up. "You don't think Marc is behind your inability to paint, do you? He came into your life right about the same time. Maybe he's like . . . like a psychic vampire or something."

"Listen to you. Can you just hear yourself? Psychic vampires now?"

"Well, I don't know what you want to call it, but if he's behind—"

"He's not behind anything. He's the one person in my life right now that's normal."

Lindsay put her hands on her hips. "Will you at least think about coming to the next meeting? We want to help you." Lindsay gestured at Jill's messy apartment.

"I don't need help." She looked across the housekeeping disaster that was her living room. "I've always been a little sloppy, you should know—"

"Sloppy is one thing. But this?" Now Lindsay waved her hand up and down at Jill.

"I don't need any help." Jill crossed her arms over her bathrobe.

"We're going to try to fix all the wishes that are going wrong. We're going to get help. We're trying to find a real witch."

"A real witch? Good Lord. Are you guys nuts? Haven't you learned your lesson?" Jill shook her head. "You're just not getting it. You need to leave it alone. All of it. Just drop it."

"Don't you want to paint again? Don't you want to help the rest of your friends with their wish troubles? The least you could do—"

"I don't want Marc to know. He'll—" Jill closed her eyes and took a breath. "The least *you* could do is respect my wishes. I told you, I don't want anything to do with wishes and witchcraft or Wicca or whatever you want to call it. I'm done with it. All of it. And, unless you guys agree to keep me out of it, stop bothering me with all of this witchy nonsense, then maybe we shouldn't . . . Maybe we can't . . ."

But Jill couldn't bring herself to say the words out loud.

Chapter Twenty-Five

The 10 duck hung in shreds from the big canvas. Jill was breathing hard, her heart pounding. The X-acto knife she'd used to shred it was still gripped in her left hand. Her chest heaved in and out with the exertion. She was covered in sweat. She stood back and looked at it. *There, take that, you fucker. I hate you. I hate you!*

Her opening was tonight, and there would be no breaking out or big canvas. The more she'd thought about it, the more she was sure it was going to be a disaster. She would be lucky not to be made a laughing stock.

The anger and frustration had surged up inside her, like nothing she'd ever known before. She laid into the canvas with the knife, shocked at how good the release felt. She hadn't had a tantrum like this since she was a kid.

The shreds hung from the stretcher bars in ragged strips, torn every which way. Gesso dust covered the floor. Jill glared at her handiwork. It was exactly how she felt. She felt torn to shreds. She looked down at the knife in her hands, the purple lines of veins in her wrists. She started to cry.

The tears hurt at first, breaking their way through ducts constricted from years of disuse. It's not that she wanted to die. She didn't. She wasn't suicidal. It just felt like she didn't know how to live.

What's wrong with me? The tears came streaming faster now.

I'm lost. The thought brought on a fresh round of sobs. *Look at that canvas. Look at what I've done. I'm crazy. Crazy and alone.* Her show was ruined. She'd abandoned all of her friends.

Someone knocked on the door to her studio and Jill jumped. It was probably Marc. She should ignore it. She didn't want him to see her like this. Jill looked down. The blade of the knife glistened under the fluorescent light. She dropped it on the table and ran to get the door.

"Hey, hey, hey babe. What's the matter?" He grabbed Jill and held her, confused by so much emotion pouring out of her. His eyes took in the big canvas—or what was left of it.

"What happened here?"

"I'm falling apart. My whole life is falling apart. I—I—"

"Hey. It's okay. Everything's going to be okay." He paused. "Except for maybe the big canvas."

Jill allowed herself a brief smile through her tears. "I don't know what got into me. I destroyed it—I was so mad. At everything. My show is ruined." Jill sniffed and wiped her eyes.

"Your show is not ruined. It's going to be great—just a little smaller than you wanted, that's all. Which, in the great scheme of things, is no big deal, huh? You can't be Picasso every time, right?"

She looked up at him, trying to gauge his expression. It was the first clichéd thing she'd ever heard him say.

He was staring over her shoulder at her studio. His eyes lit up. "Let's go to New York."

"What?"

"I mean now. Let's go right now. Spend the weekend, just the two of us."

"Leave now? My show opens tonight."

"Forget your show, nobody goes to those anymore, it's so . . . bourgeois."

Bourgeois?

"C'mon, be crazy. Let's have some fun. We can go check out some galleries there, watch someone else stress out at *their* opening. If we leave for the airport right now, we'll be there by dinner. Let's go, with just the clothes on our back, what do you say?"

It was the craziest, most careless, impetuous idea she'd ever heard.

Of course, she loved it.

"*I*'ve never seen Jill looking the way she did yesterday, not in my whole life." Lindsay spoke into her pink Razr phone as she walked down Diversey Parkway, talking to Gail. "Her hair was a mess, eyes all puffy and bloodshot. The apartment was a train wreck. I know from college she was never a neatnik, but it looked like a bomb had gone off in there."

"And you think talking with her tonight is going to help with any of that?" Gail asked.

"It's this Marc guy. I think he's bad for her. When I was there I got the impression that he was the one turning her against us. As soon as he came into her life, she started to shut us all out. We just think it would be a good opportunity for all of us to talk to her about him—"

"We?"

"Claudia called me. She and Mara think it's a good idea."

"Well, I don't think Jill's going to appreciate you guys ganging up on her at her opening."

"We're not going to gang up on her. We just want to talk to her—get her to let us help her."

"Help her? How? By cleaning her apartment?"

"No, not that. Did you know she can't paint anymore? We can reverse her spell, too, when we reverse ours."

"If we can reverse ours."

"Yeah, well, we're all working on that. Anyway, she needs to know we're still her friends."

"It sounds like she really likes this Marc guy and doesn't want any help. I think it's pretty normal when you first start seeing someone, to ignore all your friends for a while."

"You should have seen her, is all I can say. Plus," Lindsay continued, "Mara and Claudia think she might be the one who started the rumors."

"The rumors?"

"They suspect Jill's the one who told the Women's Foundation."

"But that doesn't make any sense. Why would she do that?"

"Well, I don't know. Mara and Claudia think maybe she did. I guess I don't know why she would. She'd end up incriminating herself, too. But she really does want us to stop the wishing." Lindsay paused, then said, "So, anyway, will you be there?"

"Believe me, nothing sounds better than a girls' night out at a gallery opening; but I just can't now. I've already got Ellen working all day so I can get this MRI taken care of and John's flight doesn't get in until like nine or something."

"Isn't there anyone who can watch the kids?"

"Lindsay!"

"Well, I think this is important. I want to show a united front."

"I'm sorry, Linds, but you'll have to show your united front without me."

"I'll have the Pad Thai and a Thai iced coffee," Lindsay said.

"What?"

"I stopped into Penny's Noodle Shop. I'm having lunch."

"And you couldn't wait until we were off the phone? Are you being one of those irritating restaurant cell phone people?"

"I'm starving and I'm going to eat a huge bowl of fat- and carb-laden rice noodles. Those prissy Foundation bitches didn't want to be my friend when I was fat, so I—"

"Lindsay, you were never fat."

"Maybe. Maybe not. I wasn't very happy either way. Now that I'm thin, I don't want to be their friend, either. But I do want to be happy. And today, right now, that means Pad Thai."

Claudia stood outside of the nursery window on Friday afternoon after school, trying to find Elliot in his bassinette. Maybe it was feeding time or something. She walked to the nurses' station to ask, but the nurse looked mortified when she saw Claudia. It was the same nurse who'd helped Claudia hold and feed Elliot the first time. She dashed out of the room before Claudia could speak, saying, "Wait here, hon. I'll get Nurse Galt."

Oh my God. Something terrible has happened to Elliot. Why else would she be going to get the supervisor? Claudia felt panicked.

Elliot had been in the hospital now for a little over three weeks, but he was out of the NICU now. His weight had been building. His lungs, and the rest of him for that matter, were growing stronger. He'd been doing very well, especially lately, and Claudia had a hard time believing that all of a sudden—

"Claudia?" Nurse Galt had entered the reception area behind her. "I thought that was you. Why don't we come sit down over here?" Her voice was warm and sympathetic. She pointed at three molded plastic chairs that lined the wall near the door.

Sit down? Claudia eyed the chairs with fear. "*Sit down*" *is never good.*

"I'm okay. I don't need to sit."

Nurse Galt's eyes were full of compassion. She managed a gentle smile.

"What's happened?" Claudia said. It wasn't right that Nurse Galt was oozing warmth. "What's the matter with Elliot?"

"I'm so sorry to be the one to have to tell you this," she paused, "but Elliot is gone."

It felt to Claudia as if the earth were tilting off its axis. *He's gone?* She hadn't even said good-bye. She didn't even get the chance. She'd wasted all that time at a coffee shop and a bookstore and now Elliot was gone and all the time she should have been spending with him was gone, too. She could never get it back. Claudia felt weak, as if the floor were angling up toward her. Nurse Galt reached out a hand to steady her.

"I am so sorry, I know how much he meant to you, honey. But we just couldn't keep him here any longer. DCFS came this morning and took him home, to his foster family."

They took—"They took him?" *He's* gone, *not* gone. Claudia's relief slowly turned to sorrow. *But no. Wait. I'm his foster family. Me and Dan. He's not home. I'm his home.* Claudia looked up at the ceiling, rolled her lips under her teeth and closed her eyes, but the tears started falling anyway. All the nurses at the station had made themselves scarce and the room was unusually dead for this time of the afternoon. Claudia looked off in the direction of the nursery, where Elliot used to be. *Gone.*

"Why don't you sit for a while, give yourself a minute or two."

Claudia shook her head, slid a finger underneath her glasses to wipe away her tears. She pressed the back of her hand to her nose. "No. It's okay." She sniffed. "I'm okay. I'm just going to go home, too."

The water was eerily calm today, not a ripple, and a light fog was settling in right at the shore. This is perfect, Claudia thought; I'm in a fog, too. She hadn't gone home; she'd gone down to the lake instead.

There were days when she could walk along the lakefront and the fresh air and beauty of it, rain or snow or shine, would reenergize her and melt away anything that might be troubling her. Today wasn't one of those days.

She sat on a bench facing Belmont Harbor, staring at the reflections of the floating docks like inverted photographs on the surface. No boats in the water yet—too early in the season. The fog was growing so thick now it obscured the position lights out on the peninsulas, where the harbor opened out onto the lake beyond.

Elliot is gone, I can't write, my boss thinks I'm a witch, I can't get pregnant, my husband is irritated with me and doesn't want a baby anyway, all my friends are in trouble in a creepy supernatural way and I can't help them. Oh, and did I mention I'm clumsy and far-sighted, too?

Damn, her life was a mess. She'd lost Elliot, she might lose her job—and for what? Because she'd wanted to make her wishes come true? What kind of world was this, anyway? Maybe it *was* a big steaming pile of shit, where rich assholes chase ambulances and others flip you off just because you're not leaving your parking space. Where trying to get what you wish for makes your whole life turn into a mess, with everything upside down.

Claudia's thoughts were as dark and black as the lake. If she closed her eyes, she could feel the blackness envelope her, taking her deeper and deeper, farther and farther down. She wanted to curl up on the bench and sleep.

She hugged herself instead. The air had turned cold with the setting sun. Claudia sat frozen to the bench, watching her breath unfurl out of her nostrils when she exhaled. She didn't know what to do anymore. She'd always had a plan and now, nothing in her life was going according to her plans. What the hell was she supposed to do?

The lights in the park flicked on, one at a time, taking a long time to brighten. Claudia stared at the darkening lakefront before she finally stood up, her butt and legs aching with cold, and started walking back to her apartment in the gloom.

It was dark by the time she turned onto her street, and she was still lost in her miserable thoughts when a man appeared in front of her, stepping out from the alley.

Claudia cried out in alarm, thinking at first he was going to rob her, but he didn't threaten her. He looked homeless.

"I'm sorry," she said. "I didn't mean to . . . you surprised me, that's all."

He didn't seem surprised at her response; he seemed used to startling people. He asked her for change. Claudia was about to refuse, but then she reached into her wallet and handed him a twenty-dollar bill. He stared at it in disbelief.

"Are you serious?" he said. He didn't smile. He looked at it as if he was curious, holding it out in two fingers of each filthy hand.

"Take it." She almost started to tell him she was having a bad day, that it would make her feel better to do something nice, but instead she said, "Just take it. Please. It'll make me feel better."

And it did.

Good grief, she thought as she was walking away; she'd come close to telling someone who slept under viaducts that *she* was having a bad day. Nothing like having a little perspective dropped on your head like an anvil. She looked down her street. It was a nice street. Maybe they didn't own a condo or a house—but they had a nice place. Her life wasn't so bad.

She had Dan. She had her friends. And so far, she still had her job. Who knows why things with Elliot hadn't worked out? Maybe there was a bigger reason behind it that she couldn't see yet. Maybe it could *still* work out. All the wishes could end up resolving themselves even if they never found a witch to help them.

By the time Claudia got to her front door, she was feeling better, about life, the universe, and everything.

But it wasn't long after Claudia got home, that this new-found optimism shattered around her.

"He didn't say what he wanted," Dan repeated. "He just said he would talk to you on Monday." Dan sounded frustrated. He'd already explained it to her twice.

"Peterson called here." Claudia was thinking out loud. "Charles Peterson, Headmaster at the Arthur G. Strawn Academy of Arts and Sciences calls here, to talk to me, in my home, and then doesn't leave a message?"

"Right."

"Oh, God, no. I just know it's the witchcraft thing. Or the Elliot thing. Oh God, whatever it is, it's not good." Claudia started to whine, "Oh man oh man oh man, I just know this is bad."

"Maybe it's not." Dan sounded hopeful, as if he was trying to sound like *her*. "Maybe you're getting a promotion."

Claudia laughed. "Peterson doesn't hand out promotions over the phone. He likes to make big productions out of them at staff meetings. Besides, what is he going to promote me to? Assistant Assistant Head of the English Department? C'mon. This is not good. He has never called here before."

"What happened to my Claudia? The girl for whom the glass is always half full?"

For the first time in her marriage, Claudia wanted to slug him. Her emotions had been wobbling on the edge between anger and melancholy ever since she'd left the hospital. And now this. This was how he was going to make her feel better? By poking fun at her? Next thing she knew, he was gonna snort.

What could Peterson want that is so important he's calling me at home? Was it the witchcraft thing? Was Jill going around—? "Shit." Claudia looked at her watch. "Shit. Jill. I'm supposed to—"

"Maybe I shouldn't have told you he called. There's nothing you can do about it till Monday, and he didn't leave a number for you to reach him—"

"I have his number. It's not that, it's Jill. I'm supposed to be at the gallery. I'm supposed to be with Lindsay and Mara; we were going to talk to Jill." Claudia started to get up off the couch.

Dan grabbed her hand. "I know you're upset about Elliot. I'm disappointed, too." He squeezed her hand. When she looked into his eyes, she could have sworn he looked as if he meant it. She put her weight back down onto the couch.

"He was . . . I don't know, a cute kid." Dan shrugged, then continued. "It would have been fun for us to be a family. And now you've got this thing with Peterson, and you promised your friends about the opening . . . but why don't you take a break for one night? You've been completely stressed out lately. Maybe you should take a night off this once, forget about everyone else and what you *should* be doing and just stay here with me. We've hardly seen each other all week. We could order in some food. I could go rent a movie . . . or, hey, maybe you'd rather go out instead?"

Claudia sighed. It really did sound great. Better than some uptight gallery opening anyway.

"I'm sure we can find something to do that'll make you feel better." Dan smiled a wicked smile.

Claudia sniffed, looked up at the ceiling, the beginnings of a smile on her lips. *How was he always able to do that?* "So, you're saying I should stay home? Just forget about my friends?"

He inhaled a deep breath through his teeth and held it in while he said, "That would be my advice." He exhaled after the last word, his tone full of a fake bravado that suggested she'd be a fool not to take it.

"Really? And there's nothing in it for you?"

"In it for me?" Dan smiled, innocent and boyish. A fake Indian accent now, "No, no. All my advice is purely selfless." He scooched over closer to her on the couch.

"Is that right? And what else does The Great Wise One advise?"

Dan put his hands into prayer position and closed his eyes. After a brief pause, he said, "For you, I think sex. Tantric sex—all weekend long."

"Hmm. I don't know, seems a little self-serving to me . . . maybe I should go to the next mountain over, seek out different counsel . . ."

"Hey." Dan grabbed her around the waist.

" —although this guru's pretty cute." Claudia let herself dissolve into his arms. She really couldn't think of a better escape from the tensions of the week.

"All right, Great Wise One," she said. "I'll take your advice." She tilted her head up, threw her arms around his neck and her legs over his. "Let's order some Indian food and then see what this guru knows about the Kama Sutra."

And with an uncharacteristic lack of guilt, Claudia blew off her friends.

Chapter Twenty-Six

The washing machine started its spin cycle with a click, and Mara checked her watch. She knew Jill's opening lasted until eight, but they'd agreed to meet there at five-thirty. It was almost five, but if the washer finished her pants in the next ten minutes, allowing twenty minutes to dry, she would be less than twenty minutes late—which, if you were an airline, was practically on time.

She knew she really should have planned her outfit earlier, but she couldn't possibly have predicted that she wouldn't have *anything* to wear. And this was not the standard pre-social-engagement, female predicament of *I don't have a thing to wear*. It was the more unusual, yet more prevalent, predicament for her lately, the *I don't have a thing to wear that fits over my new thighs*. She truly didn't have a thing she *could* wear.

Mara's bed and dresser were strewn with cast-off clothes, pants, skirts, and dresses that didn't fit. There'd been one other pair of pants she had thought she might be able to get away with, if she didn't button the top button and wore a long sweater over them, but the zipper wouldn't stay up and they kept falling down. Which left her with the pants she'd worn at work all day, but they had two ketchup spots on the right knee, from the cheeseburger she'd eaten in the car on the way home.

In a moment of hopeless desperation, she'd walked over to Henry's closet for a look. That's when she'd started crying. *What is happening to me? I'm so fat.*

It was horrible, *horrible,* the way she felt, the way people stared at her now. She could feel them whispering behind her back, their words sinking into her flesh the way sound penetrates through water, the way *whales* communicated. Every time she passed a mirror she felt disgusted and swore she would never eat another bite of food as long as she lived. But every time she passed the refrigerator, she did.

And poor Henry. His whole back and chest were covered with hair. His bald spot had filled in and he was shaving so many times in a day she'd lost track. The hair on his arms and legs was thickening more and more. Dr. Bernstein had been little help. He'd run some hormone tests but they were still waiting for the results. Henry had joked at dinner last night that the boys on the baseball team were teasing him, saying they were worried Coach O'Connor was going to leave his coaching position to take the mascot job for the Strawn Academy Wolverines. He'd rubbed the top of his head when he told her the story and she could tell he loved the feel of hair up there; it was the hair everywhere else that was getting to him.

The washing machine started to wobble out of balance and she had to reach in and even out the load. She checked her watch again. It was after five now; the spin cycle was taking longer than she'd thought. But what was she supposed to do? By the time she'd realized she only had one pair of pants she could wear, it was already too late. She'd put them into the washing machine and watched them disappear under the suds.

Now her slacks spun around and around. *I should call them—but I'll only be a little bit late, and besides it's Lindsay and Claudia. They won't mind if I get there at six.* Mara walked upstairs to the kitchen, to get the phone. *I should call, really. It's only polite.* But when she got upstairs, she passed up the phone on the counter and headed for the refrigerator instead.

Everyone was talking, their voices loud and animated. Now and then laughter rose up from a group. Jill's paintings lined the raw brick walls and several display walls on the interior of the gallery. The track lights beamed down from the ceiling with perfect intensity, illuminating the art and the people and casting a nice glow on the hardwood floors. With wineglasses and canapés in hand, all the guests were mingling happily, and Lindsay had to wonder if she would be tormented forever by the sights and sounds of a successful party.

Her husband, James, had found someone to talk real estate with, and they'd been going on and on about all the loft conversions in the neighborhood while Lindsay sipped her wine and tried to look interested.

Normally, she enjoyed a nice gallery opening, a chance to see and be seen, to shop and chat, and she usually always ran into someone she knew. But tonight she couldn't help but search the crowd, trying to find Jill, who so far was nowhere to be seen. The same for Claudia and Mara. *Where are those guys?*

Lindsay checked her watch. Six-fifteen. The opening only lasted until eight. What could be keeping them?

The front door opened, and Lindsay's head snapped around as it had the last several times, but it was just a young, twentysomething couple wearing their trendy 1970s clothes.

"I think I'm going to go shopping," Lindsay said to James. But she wasn't really interested in buying any art; she wanted another glass of wine, something to help take the edge off.

"Just save us some money for cab fare," James said before turning back to his loft-condo conversation.

It wasn't unusual for Claudia to be late. Lindsay didn't know why it was upsetting her so much. But where was Mara? Lindsay worked her way around the groups of people, looking for anyone she might know. She glanced over Jill's paintings while taking little sips of her wine, then went to refill her wineglass.

A few sculptures, not Jill's, were placed here and there, and Lindsay was intrigued by them. The one she'd spotted when she walked in the door had raised her eyebrows. She thought it might be fun, a lesson in psychology, to stake out that "flower" all night, to watch the reactions of those who went by, to see who saw it for what it was—and who didn't.

"I don't know where Jill is. I can't believe she's missing it," Lindsay overheard a woman's voice behind her.

"Maybe she wants to make a dramatic entrance," a tall, dark-haired man answered, "or maybe she's not coming at all."

Lindsay pretended to be admiring another of the glass flower sculptures, walking around it slowly, trying to make it appear that she was more interested in seeing the sculpture from all sides, than in overhearing the conversation going on behind her.

"No way. She'd never missed an opening. She loves the attention. Maybe I should try to call her, to see if she's okay."

The man shrugged. "If you must."

"Oh, Davis, you're probably right. I'm being silly." The woman was laughing now. "Jill's probably just being moody. Her father used to tell me her mother was difficult like that."

The couple drifted away and Lindsay was tempted to follow them, but that would be *too* obvious. *Is Jill not coming at all? Blowing off her own opening night? What is going on with her?*

Lindsay looked back toward the front of the gallery, scanning the crowd for Claudia or Mara. *I am going to kill those two, talking me into showing up here to confront Jill, and then both of them just blow it off without so much as a phone call.* At that thought, Lindsay flipped open the top of her purse to check her cell phone. Nothing.

She continued her wandering and found several small paintings hanging on the back wall. They weren't abstracts and obviously weren't part of Jill's show, which had turned out to be surprisingly small. Lindsay walked slowly past them, contemplating each one absently with a sip of wine.

A narrow hallway led to an office in the back. A solitary artwork hung on the brick wall at the end of it. Lindsay edged closer, turning down into the hallway to get a better look at it, sensing somehow that this area was off limits. It was a painting—and strangely quite a lovely one—of factories. Its palette was gray and black and rust, but there was something in the way the smoke rose from the chimneys and in the color of the sky, with the stars. It was compelling. *I wish I could go there,* Lindsay thought while staring at it, and at the moment she had that thought, much to her surprise, she swore the paint shifted around—almost playfully—making stars twinkle and smoke waft up. She shook her head and looked into her wineglass to see if maybe someone had slipped something in there when she hadn't been looking. Perhaps she simply had drunk too much.

When she looked back at the painting, the paint was, of course, very still. She stared at it for a while longer, waiting to see if it would happen again, wondering how a painting could make her want to go visit a factory.

"That one's not for sale," a woman's voice said from behind her, and the soothing tone of the words let Lindsay know she wasn't in too much trouble for being back here.

"Oh. It just caught my eye. I hope you don't mind. I wanted a closer look."

"Not at all," the woman said calmly. "I just wanted you to know, it's not for sale."

"It's very unusual."

The woman's expression carried a hint of a smile, as if she *knew* Lindsay had just hallucinated moving paint. "Oh, it is indeed. My mother was the artist. She was an unusual lady," she paused. "Magical."

"You know, this is going to sound crazy," Lindsay decided to confess, the wine loosening up her judgment. Plus it already seemed to her that this lady knew anyway. "But I swear I thought I saw the paint move."

The woman's expression was serene. She made no comment and appeared to be waiting for Lindsay to continue.

"There isn't some special kind of, I don't know, holographic paint in it, is there?" Lindsay asked, turning back to look at the painting.

"Holograms? No."

Okay, I guess I won't be able to come back to this gallery. Lindsay tried to console herself with the thought that she probably wasn't the first guest here who'd had one too many Chardonnays at an opening.

"There's magic in it, though," the woman said. And when Lindsay turned around to see if she had heard her right, the woman's serene expression had changed into a smile.

Chapter Twenty-Seven

✦

"So the paint *moves*?" Lindsay asked.

"It can. But not everyone sees it."

Lindsay was speechless for a moment.

Then, for lack of anything else to say, she held out her right hand. "I'm Lindsay. Lindsay McDermott."

"Tate," the woman said, shaking her hand.

Lindsay was confused. Was the woman's name Tate? Because that was Lindsay's maiden name, but it had sounded like she was being corrected. "*Your* name is Tate?" she asked when they had shaken hands.

"No dear," the woman replied, "*yours* is."

Lindsay's eyes narrowed on this odd person. Mentally she was trying to shrug it off. A lot of people knew who she was. After all, Lindsay Tate-McDermott was a woman about town. A person could have heard of her, could know her maiden name was Tate, that she often went by Tate-McDermott.

"Where are my manners?" The woman laughed at herself. "I'm Greta Craven."

"Pleased to meet you, Greta." Lindsay thought about asking how Greta knew her name, but instead asked, "Are you the owner?"

"I am."

Lindsay turned around to look at the painting again, watching it closely. "Well, like I said, it's a most unusual painting." Lindsay stared hard at the stars. "How often does it, uh . . . move?"

"It only moves for those who are willing to see it move."

"Oh? And who can see it? Anyone?"

"So far, the only other person I know of that has seen it, besides me, is you."

Lindsay was unused to being rendered speechless twice in one evening. She kept her back to Greta as her mouth went dry. She tried to swallow but couldn't make the back of her throat close. A nervous smile had frozen on her face as she stared at the painted factories. When she realized she still had some wine in her glass, she took a drink and it helped bring her voice back.

Lindsay turned to face Greta. "Just me?"

Greta nodded.

She was a slippery one, this Greta. A woman of few words. Her silences reminded Lindsay of an interviewing technique James used, just nodding silently at the end of an interviewee's response. He said they always felt compelled to fill the silence and that it was always amazing to him the disparaging details with which they chose to fill it.

Well, Lindsay was not going to fall for that trick. She turned and quietly watched the painting even though she was dying to pump this woman for more information, ask a million questions, such as, *How come I'm the only one who's ever seen it move?* Or, *What do you put in your Chardonnay here, anyway?*

"I think only people who believe in magic are willing to or able to see it," Greta answered her thoughts. "They're the ones who are able to recognize it when it's right in front of them. It's rather sad, really. There's so much magic in the world and not many can see it for what it is, preferring to believe in luck instead, or maybe in nothing at all."

Lindsay was flattered. "Oh, I absolutely believe in magic. I think I've always believed. In fact, sometimes I think we all have the ability to do magic, to make our wishes come true."

"Do you now?" Greta sounded mildly amused.

"Some of my friends and I have been able to do it. We've gotten together and helped each other wish for things. At first we had just amazing results—" Lindsay stopped there, realizing too late that the Chardonnay had started talking again and she shouldn't have blabbed so much about Wish Club to a complete stranger. She felt the beginnings of a headache coming on.

"What sort of things have you *wished* for?" Greta asked. Now she seemed seriously interested, her brows scrunched together over the thick plastic frame of her reading glasses.

Pick something lame, Lindsay thought to herself. *Think of a little one.* But for some reason the only wish that came to her mind was the one for the rain.

"Well, one time we made the rain stop."

Greta's eyes closed, her shoulders dropped abruptly, and she exhaled while a look of complete understanding washed over her face.

When Greta opened her eyes, the expression on her face said *this explains everything.* She looked at Lindsay, gently shaking her head up and down. "Of course you did."

The door buzzer blared in the hallway and it startled both of them awake. Granted, it was three in the afternoon on a Saturday, and they probably shouldn't have been sleeping, but it was a much-needed recess from their weekend of sex and they hadn't been expecting company.

"Don't answer it," Dan said.

Claudia sat up on both elbows and looked out the bedroom door toward the buzzer. He wrapped an arm around her and tried to pull her back down under the covers. The door buzzed again.

"I don't know," Claudia said. "It might be Lindsay."

"All the more reason not to answer it."

"She's already called twice today. It might be urgent."

Dan flopped his face down into his pillow. Claudia picked up her jeans and sweater from the floor and put them on, grateful that the pillow had made the last thing he'd said about Lindsay unintelligible.

"You'd better get some clothes on, too," she said. "Just in case."

Lindsay and Claudia were on the couch when Dan finally emerged from the bedroom, his hair sticking out in odd directions. Apparently, it wasn't until she saw Dan and his hair that Lindsay realized she'd interrupted something.

"So anyway," Lindsay continued, watching Dan walk across the hall to the bathroom, "I really am sorry to barge in on you like this." She said that a little louder, Claudia knew, so that Dan would hear it.

Lindsay touched her finger to the tip of her nose and popped her eyes at Claudia, who felt herself flush ten shades of red.

Lindsay lowered her voice before continuing, "Claude, I'm sorry—I didn't realize."

"It's okay, never mind." Claudia looked down the hallway toward the bathroom with a smile. She turned back to Lindsay. "What else did she say?"

"She said we need to get everyone who was there both nights back together at the next meeting, in order to undo the spells." Lindsay contorted her face into a wry smile. "And what that means is—"

"We need Jill." Claudia groaned. "Great. How are we going to get her back? She didn't even show up last night—"

Lindsay just looked at Claudia. She didn't need to say that wasn't her problem. She'd already complained ad nauseum about how none of them had shown up at the gallery.

Great, Claudia thought. *I get stuck with Mission Impossible.* She was already having second thoughts about even trying to undo the spells. And now she was supposed to somehow make Jill show up at the next meeting? How was she going to do that? What was in it for Jill?

"What reason could Jill possibly have for wanting to come back?"

"Well, for one thing, Greta is going to make us promise not to do our wishing thing anymore."

Claudia raised her eyebrows.

"That's one of the conditions she has for helping us. She said if we still want to make wishes or do magic, she'll teach us. She'll train us in the Craft, show us how to be real witches."

"Oh, that'll get Jill to the meeting," Claudia said, but her mind had already started turning. *Real witches? Making wishes come true—successfully? No more turning lives upside down. No more chaos? Hmm.* Now *that* could make trying to talk Jill into coming back for one more meeting a challenge worth accepting.

Everyone told Lindsay they'd be able to make tonight's meeting, the second Emergency Meeting of Wish Club. For whatever *that* was worth, Lindsay thought. They'd told her they were going to be at Jill's opening three days earlier, too.

She put the cookies in the oven and was rinsing her hands in the sink when the door chimes started ringing. Lindsay carried the dish towel with her to the front hall, drying her hands as she went. She looked through the peephole. It was Greta, right on time.

In the time it took Lindsay to hang up Greta's cape-like coat, she'd already entered the living room and was taking a look around. Greta's outfit was a cross between professional gallery owner and hippie-witch. She wore a long, dark, almost black, purple velvet skirt and a long-sleeved black silk T-shirt. Her gray hair was pulled back into a bun and held together with a black velvet scrunchie.

When Lindsay turned around, Greta had her head tilted up, as if she were trying to get a sense of the place, as if she were sniffing it. "What a lovely home you have," she said, and it gave Lindsay a pleasant chill to think this woman thought her home was lovely.

"Oatmeal raisin cookies?" Greta asked.

"Yes, how—?"

"There is nothing else that smells quite the same as homemade oatmeal raisin cookies. They're my favorite."

Lindsay was not much of a baker, but this afternoon she'd decided to make something for Wish Club, as a way to keep herself busy, to calm her nerves until the meeting. She'd pulled out her cookbooks, settling on oatmeal raisin cookies. Plopping scoops of dough onto the metal sheet, she'd tried to tell herself it wasn't *that* strange that she'd suddenly felt compelled to bake something. Now she wasn't so sure it wasn't so strange.

Greta bent over the coffee table to examine a book. "I've always been a fan of Mapplethorpe." She quickly moved on from the table and the Mapplethorpe book, over to the bookshelves.

"Me, too . . . well, obviously." Lindsay wrung the dish towel in her hands. *Now I'm acting as confounded as Claudia when she's in one of her states.*

Greta scanned the bookshelves, running her hand along the spines on a shelf that was at about chest height, and Lindsay got chills again.

"Oh my, such loss. Such terrible loss," Greta said, never taking her eyes off the bookshelves. "It must have been a very difficult time for you."

What? Could she know? I never told anyone. Lindsay did a quick scan of the bookshelves herself. She felt dizzy, almost faint. *Not again!* Her heart thumped in her chest.

"I suppose by now you realize your destiny lies elsewhere," Greta said.

Lindsay opened her mouth to reply, but just closed it again. What on earth would she say? *Are you talking about what I think you're talking about?*

Greta slowly finished her scan of the bookshelves, then turned her attention to the rest of the room. She moved around gradually, checking out a few paintings on the walls, the view from the windows, the bric-a-brac on an end table. Lindsay got chills again when she watched Greta pick up a small paperweight from the table and gaze inside its bubbled glass.

Then suddenly Greta was finished. She put the paperweight down and turned back around to face Lindsay, raising her watch and her eyebrows simultaneously. "I suppose everyone is always fashionably late to these things?" She walked over and sat in the middle of the couch, folding her hands in the middle of her purple lap. She sighed, looking straight ahead, a resolved expression on her face.

"I still have a little finishing up to do in the kitchen." Lindsay pointed over her shoulder with the dish towel. The timer from the oven buzzed as if on cue.

Greta looked at her and smiled, but didn't say anything.

"I'm just going to go take care of that, then."

"Oh yes, of course, dear. Go right ahead." Greta didn't move from the couch, made no offer to help. She spoke as though she knew Lindsay had a lot to think about.

Mara stabbed the point of the wine opener into the waxed top of another cork. "Now, that was just weird." She tried to keep her voice low, even though there was a good distance between Lindsay's kitchen and the living room, where Greta was still sitting alone on the couch.

She pushed the opener farther down into the cork and began to twist it, while Lindsay arranged vegetables on a tray. "How did she know about Dr. Seeley? That he's so mean? Did you tell her?" The little silver wings of the wine opener rose up crankily.

"Of course not," Lindsay said. "I get the impression that Greta is just like that. She knows things sometimes."

"She's psychic?"

"I don't know, maybe. She just knows things."

The cork popped as Mara pulled it from the bottle.

"She just knows things," Mara repeated. She twisted the frayed cork from the opener.

"I don't know . . . maybe she *is* psychic. She certainly seemed able to read my mind at the gallery. And earlier tonight, she mentioned some things she couldn't possibly have known about—" Lindsay stopped abruptly, picked up a celery stick, and examined it.

Mara had just stabbed the corkscrew into another bottle. She let its wings drop with a clack. She stared at Lindsay. "You can't just leave it at that."

Lindsay started to raise the celery up to her lips, then lowered it. She was silent for a very long moment, as though she were debating whether or not she should tell Mara. She took a deep breath.

"Right after James and I got married," Lindsay's voice was quiet, her eyes examining the celery as she rolled it between her fingers, "we'd only been married like two months—and we found out I was pregnant. It was a huge shock. We were planning to wait a year or two at the very least. Maybe not even have any children at all. I don't know; we still hadn't decided then. But the more we thought about it, the more we started to, you know, just roll with the idea we were going to have a kid. There wasn't much else we could do, and we actually started to get pretty excited about it.

"Well, I lost the baby just prior to the end of the first trimester, right about the time we were going to start telling people I was pregnant. For two people who hadn't really wanted a baby right then, we were devastated. It totally wrecked us.

"So we tried again. And again and again. I had five miscarriages. Five—" Lindsay stopped. Her eyes glassed over and she touched her other index finger and thumb to the bridge of her nose.

Mara's hand left the corkscrew, which she'd been holding motionless in the cork for the last few minutes. She walked around to the other side of the counter and gave Lindsay a hug.

Lindsay softened against her.

"Aw, honey. Why didn't you ever tell us?"

"It was too hard to talk about. I just . . . couldn't. And then after so much time had passed . . ." Lindsay sniffed and stepped back out of Mara's embrace. "Well, anyway. Earlier tonight, it was like Greta knew about it. She said something like, 'Oh, such terrible loss' and 'It must have been so hard on you.' It's the only thing that's happened to us like that, and I don't know how she could have known about it." She looked up at Mara. "I've never told anyone before—not even Claudia."

"I won't tell a soul."

Lindsay nodded and sniffed again. "You know, it doesn't matter. Now I think it would be okay if you did." She walked to the other side of the kitchen and grabbed a tissue. "I feel better for talking about it. It's almost a relief." She blew her nose.

Lindsay pulled the Kleenex away from her face. She furrowed her forehead and pointed the tissue at the counter behind Mara's back. "Just how much wine do you think we're going to drink?"

Six open bottles were sitting out.

Mara turned around and surveyed the bottles behind her with both hands on her hips. "Tonight," she said, "I think we're going to drink a lot."

Chapter Twenty-Eight

"*There* are many ways to make your wishes come true, dear. Just ask any motivational speaker."

Lindsay thought Greta would smile after she said that. But she didn't. She just continued talking. "The Craft is just one of them. The difference is that the power inherent in witchcraft is incredibly potent, and when you start using it without the proper precautions . . . I guess I don't need to explain the ramifications to you." Greta looked over her reading glasses at her. Lindsay nodded. Mara and Gail nodded, too.

"You must understand that witchcraft isn't a bad thing. It's a very powerful thing, not to be taken lightly and never to be underestimated. There's some new thinking in some of the witchcraft circles out there, that magic is powerful because we believe it's powerful. Well, that may be true in those circles, but the magic I know is powerful because it *is*.

"And this concept—making wishes come true, creating your own reality—it isn't anything new. In fact, it's very, very old. It's *thought*, *word*, and *deed*. The Bible mentions it, the Bhagavad Gita, the three doors of Buddhism. The *Conversations with God* series of books discusses them at length; variations exist in the writings of Richard Bach—and of course they're the basis for the Witches' Pyramid."

They looked back at her blankly. *Huh?*

"The Witches' Pyramid. To know, to dare, to will, to be. . . . Did you *read* any of those witchcraft books you had or did you just skip to the good parts?" Greta gave them a matronly glare, as if to say, *what kind of book club is this?*

"Well, I see," she said, "we just skipped to the good bits. Well, I hope we learned our lesson about doing *that*."

"What's the Witches' Pyramid?" Mara asked.

"It's a formula, a way of creating your reality—of making things happen for you. To know, to dare, to will, to be. Another form of *thought, word,* and *deed.* It starts with *thought,* in your mind: *To know.* To know that whatever it is you want can happen for you. *To dare* is to put it into words, to say it or write it, as you would a spell. That, of course, would be the *word* part. And then *To will:* to do what you need to do to make it happen, the *deed* part. The *to be* part completes the circle back to thought: it means to be certain, to have the certainty that what you want to happen *will* happen. It's faith. The same faith all the religions talk about—but in the Craft, and for many other enlightened folks, the faith you need isn't in some white-haired god off sitting on a throne somewhere who has the ability to grant your wishes. The faith is in yourself. Unwavering belief in yourself."

Greta looked at the women staring up at her. "It's what *you* did. It's how you managed such success in making your wishes manifest."

"Success?" Mara asked.

"Well certainly, success. Every single wish you made manifested in some way—albeit not all of them in the way you intended. And that's the thing. The tricky thing. You know the old saying about being careful about what you wish for? Well, it's an old saying for a reason. Especially when you start dropping in magical tools, such as candles and herbs, which are themselves infused with properties that can . . . but I think I'm getting ahead of myself here. What I'm saying is this: I know women who've practiced Wicca for twenty years who've had less success getting spells to manifest than you ladies have had. You wanted some things so badly, had such faith you would get them, that you *deserved* them. Well. Voilà. Success. Just like Anthony Robbins." And this time, she did smile.

Lindsay's front door chimes sounded, snapping the women out of their *whoa* moment, and Lindsay jumped up to get it. "I hope that's Claudia and Jill so we can get started."

"Jill?" Mara asked.

"Yeah," Gail said. "Speaking of *A Course in Miracles.*"

Lindsay opened the door and looked out past Claudia into the night. "Where's Jill?"

"Hell if I know." Claudia shrugged off Lindsay's comment and her coat. She opened the front hall closet and took out a hanger.

"She's not coming?"

Claudia hung her coat and turned to face Lindsay. "I did my best, but what was I supposed to do? She didn't answer her phone. I must have called her twenty times. I tried her at home, her studio, her cell phone. I don't know what else I could have done. Wait outside her building to kidnap her? Face it, she's finished with us."

They walked down the short hall, Claudia leading the way. Lindsay followed, complaining, "But if she's not here, then Greta says the energy won't be—"

Claudia turned into the living room and froze in the doorway. "It's you." She stared at Greta.

"You know each other?" Lindsay looked back and forth between them.

"I remember you from the bookstore," Claudia said, "and from Wild Prairie that one time."

"Oh yes, yes. Of course." Greta nodded her head in recognition. "Did you enjoy the books?"

Claudia's mouth hung open for a moment. Her lips started to move, as if she were trying to form the right question.

"It's okay, Claude," Mara said. "She's been doing that all night."

Claudia turned to look at Mara, as if noticing for the first time there were other people in the room. "I . . ."

"Where's Jill?" Gail asked.

"I don't know." Claudia started to snap out of her shock. "She wouldn't answer my calls or return my messages. I mean you have to realize this is the same woman who blew off her own gallery opening." Claudia glared at Lindsay. "I don't know how anyone expected *me* to get her here."

Now it was Greta's turn to look surprised. "Jill Trebelmeier? *My* Jill?"

"Didn't I tell you?" Lindsay turned to Greta. "I thought I told you. She's our Jill too. She's the whole reason I was at the opening Friday. We were a little concerned about her and this Marc guy. Well, that and the rumors," Lindsay conceded with a roll of her eyes. "We just wanted to talk to her, but it's as if she's shutting us all out. When I saw her last Thursday, I guess maybe I laid into her a little too hard, because she said she didn't want to come back . . . but you should have seen her. She looked like a wreck and the place was trashed."

"And no one's talked to her since?" Greta looked around the room. The women shook their heads no. "I sure would like to know the reason she wasn't there Friday." Greta stared off into space for a moment. "I'm still having a hard time believing Jill Trebelmeier was a part of all this."

"She was," Gail said. "Reluctantly, though. She never really liked the wishing that much. Too much like witchcraft for her Catholic upbringing, I guess."

"You look like you could use a drink." Lindsay gestured to Greta. "Why don't you grab a glass of wine? You too, Claudia. Grab a drink."

At the suggestion of a drink, Greta stood up immediately.

"There's red wine on the breakfront in the library. The white's in the kitchen." Lindsay pointed toward the hallway. Claudia was already on her way.

But Greta remained where she stood, smoothing the front of her skirt. "Wine and candles and wishes and chants. I can understand why you feel like you need a drink now, but my goodness, you ladies and your wine. It should be the first thing you take off your list."

Claudia stopped and turned around. The others stared over their wineglasses at Greta.

"All that drinking—it clouds the brain. Leaves big holes in your mind. Not to mention what it does to your energy field. Have you no idea? It could be the single greatest factor as to why all your wishes went awry."

Greta clucked and sighed, apparently recovered from her shock at discovering Jill was a member of Wish Club, brought back to her purpose for coming here in the first place. "Wishes. Wishes. All these backfiring wishes. Well, then." She picked up her big black bag, set it on the coffee table, and slid her sleeves up her arms. "We're not going to be able to get the energy exactly right without Jill here." She started pulling what apparently were wish-fixing supplies out of her bag. "But I don't think we can afford any more delay. We need to get started fixing them."

Two white pillar candles glowed on Lindsay's coffee table. The room was dark and silent. With the exception of a thunderstorm raging outside, it was eerily reminiscent of their first witchy meeting. Claudia felt her stomach roll with nerves—or was it fear?

Greta stood over the candles, their light shining up under her chin in a most unflattering way. "I suppose we didn't bother to use the Wiccan creed with any of our wishes? *Do what thou will, may it harm no one?* 'Harm no one' being the operative words there." She reached into the bag and pulled out more candles. "I don't suppose we did any binding with our wishes, either? Same general idea, binding. Insisting we don't want the spell to go forward if anyone is going to get hurt along the way." She placed some gray metallic plates on the table. They had a rainbow sheen on their surface, like oil in a puddle, which seemed to indicate a lot of use, although Claudia couldn't even begin to guess what *kind* of use.

Crystals, stones, vials, and small bowls cluttered the top of the table as Greta scanned it. She frowned, still searching with her eyes, apparently not finding what she was looking for. She reached back into her bag and pulled out a knife. The women drew backward. Mara let out a musical whimper.

The mother-of-pearl handle of the knife flashed in the candlelight as Greta held it in her fist. She used the same fist to hold up one side of her bag, while she continued to root around inside of it. A few seconds later she finished searching and set a stack of three-by-five note cards on the table, dark flowing writing on the top of each. She looked up at the women, surprised at their surprise.

She looked down at the knife, then back at the women. "You really don't know anything, do you?" Greta took a deep breath and exhaled. Holding the knife in front of her, she rested the tip of the blade against the fingertips of her left hand. "This is an athame. Yes, it's a knife, but it's been blessed and consecrated. It's used in the practice of magic for things such as casting a sacred circle. It's not even sharp." She poked it into her left index finger, then ran it over the back of her left hand several times. "Hardly an effective weapon if I was trying to *off* a roomful of people." She turned around and placed her carpetbag on the floor. They exchanged nervous smiles behind her back.

"When practicing magic, you need to create a protected, sacred space. It helps your spells from being interfered with from outside—well, let's just say, unfriendly—sources. I am going to consecrate a protective circle around our group. From the time I put the circle into place until the time I remove it, no one will be allowed to pass in or out of it. So, what I'm saying is, if you need to use the bathroom, you should get that taken care of now."

No one moved from her seat.

"Are you sure? After all that wine? This whole process could take quite a while." Still no one moved. "All right then, if you're certain. Here we go."

Greta held the knife in her right hand, elbow bent, and pointed the blade out from the center of her waist at a ninety-degree angle to the floor. She walked with the knife pointed out in front of her this way, first toward the wall of bookshelves. She paused there for a moment, and then, with her neck still bent toward the ground, turned her head abruptly to the left to look at the front windows. Nodding, she stood up straight again, then walked over to stand facing the windows. "Right, right, *this* is north, compass north."

She brought the knife down with both hands grasping the shining mother-of-pearl handle, her elbows straight, arms extended, and pointed it at the floor. After a big breath, she began walking around the room in a clockwise direction, casting an imaginary circle on the floor. She talked quietly to herself while she did it and

Claudia caught snippets of her whispered words as she made her way around the room: ". . . with the earthen power of North, let our blessed ritual go forth . . . with blessed air that comes from East . . . force of fire, from the South transpire . . . from the West with water be blessed."

Their heads turned in unison as she moved around them. On the couch, Gail, Mara, and Claudia leaned away from Greta and into each other when she walked around to the western side of the sofa.

When Greta completed her circle at the windows, she moved back to the table in the center of the room and raised both arms toward the sky in a V. "Our circle has opened. For nothing be it broken."

Claudia watched Greta with awe. Should they have been doing this every time they wished? Claudia's stomach calmed, her fear starting to subside as she gained more confidence in Greta; maybe she really could fix everything they'd messed up.

Greta put the knife down and leaned over the table. She picked up the stack of index cards. "Lindsay was so kind as to write down your wishes for me, with as much as she could remember of the wording and ingredients that you used," she paused, "and the results." Greta gave them an admonishing look. "I have two cards here for each of you." She looked up at the women. "So, unless there are any objections, we should begin."

When Greta looked back down at the card on top, her face contorted into a frown. "Oh dear," she said.

The women exchanged worried glances. *Oh, no. She can't fix them! I hope that one isn't mine.*

Still looking flustered, Greta started searching around the table. She picked up her reading glasses and put them on. "There now, that's better." She bent her head back down to read the card, while once again the women exchanged embarrassed looks.

She picked up a large three-ring binder from the table and started flipping through it. The binder was stuffed full of pages that displayed varying levels of wear. Some sections appeared new, others had browned with age, their edges frayed from use. Handwriting filled entire sections, others were typeset, some both. Greta held it balanced out on her forearm and the palm of her hand as she searched its pages. She flipped and she flipped and she continued flipping until she found what she wanted. Running her fingers along a page, she read silently for a long time, oblivious to her audience; then she finally set the book down.

"It's always a good idea to write down your spells, to keep a magical logbook, if you will, of everything you do. It makes it so much easier if anything ever misfires, and believe me, even the best of us can cast a doozie every now and again. That's my record book, my grimoire." Greta pointed to the book on the table. "But, since you didn't know this before, we don't have an exact record of what your spells were. It will make it a challenge to reverse them, certainly, but hopefully one we'll be able to overcome. Now. Claudia. You first. How's Dan? Happy yet?"

"He's fine, but . . ." Claudia was ready to launch into how she couldn't write, but now that she thought about her wish for Dan, she realized he really did seem happier now. "You know, I think he *is* happier. It's like, there's this new lightness about him that I haven't seen in a while. Like he's funnier now." She remembered his joking on the couch the other night—the fake accents, how he'd tried to cheer her up. "I've been so preoccupied with the fact I can barely write my name, I guess I hadn't paid too much attention."

"You can't write your name?" Greta asked.

"Well, actually now I can sort of write my name."

Greta watched her silently. Waiting. As though she knew Claudia wasn't telling her the whole truth.

Claudia squirmed a little in her seat. "You see, I started to write down another wish . . ." Claudia stopped, took a deep breath, and then started again. "The first wish I wrote was about writing—about me wanting to write again, a novel. But I chickened out. So I scribbled it out and wrote the one for Dan instead. And now, somehow I can't write anymore. Well, not very legibly, anyway. Which isn't . . . it isn't going over very well at school. I'm already in so much trouble there. They're talking about . . . it's like my job's already on the line and this not-writing situation isn't helping."

Claudia shook her head and paused for a long moment. She shrugged and gave a short laugh. "But at least now it seems like Dan is, well, I guess he's acting happier."

Greta held her eyes on Claudia for a moment, then crunched her lips together. "Needs fixing, this one. The trick is going to be getting you writing again without making Dan unhappy. Plus, without any physical components left from the wish-making itself, it's going to be even more of a challenge." Greta furrowed her face in thought.

"We're just going to have to do a general outing and hope for the best." Greta picked up the black binder again. She studied the page for a long time and then made quite a few notes in it. When she finished she said, "What I need from you, Miss Claudia, is for you to visualize your wish as it was when you made it, when you first wrote it down—the one about writing, not Dan's. Imagine yourself tearing it to little bits in your mind. Can you do that?"

Claudia nodded. "I'll try."

"No. No trying."

Huh?

"Just do it, the best you can. In your head."

"I'll—Okay," Claudia said.

Greta set out one of the gray metallic plates. She took a small blue vial, uncapped the stopper, and began.

> *For our Claudia who can produce no written verse,*
> *We ask the Goddess our spell to reverse.*
> *Allow the words and prose to move freely*
> *Make sure all writing will now flow easily*
> *And in the end lift away the curse.*
> *It is our will, it is our plea and harm it no one, so mote it be.*

Greta sprinkled the water from the vial on the plate. She lit a black candle, and when the wax had melted a little, she let a drop of it fall, sizzling onto the plate. After pinching out the black candle, she repeated the same procedure with a red and then a white candle.

"Okay now. That should take care of that." Greta capped the blue vial and set it onto the table next to the plate. She picked up the three-by-five cards.

"Now then." She adjusted her glasses down onto the bridge of her nose. "You also wanted the baby, the brand new life right away? Then you found a baby in a garbage can.

"You see, the thing about spell-casting, ladies—and it was spell-casting you were up to, not simply *wishing*—is that it doesn't mess around. And it takes you quite literally." She looked directly at Claudia. "Well, what's going on with the baby now?"

"Dan and I were trying to be his foster parents. I was hoping we could adopt him some day, but they took him away on Friday. He's already in foster care with another family. And I didn't even get a chance to say good-bye to him." Claudia could feel her tears starting to swell.

"I see." Greta paused, considered for a moment. "What about the child's mother?"

"They still haven't found her. They think she's one of the students at my school, but they don't have any real suspects. Or if they do, they're keeping it pretty quiet. They don't want to bring any embarrassment to her . . . well, mostly they don't want any bad publicity for the school."

"Bad publicity. Yes. Well." Greta coughed. "And you and your husband, you both wanted to foster him?"

"We did. Well, I did. Dan was never quite as sure about the whole thing as I was. I would visit Elliot in the hospital. He was so precious. So beautiful." Claudia sighed, then, thinking maybe Greta could help her case by pulling some magical strings over at the Department of Children and Family Services, kept talking. "I didn't think it was possible I could fall so much in love with a baby that wasn't mine, but I'm so in love with that boy. I just want to protect him, take care of him. He's so amazing, so perfect . . . and Dan, he softened up too when he was there. I could see it in his face, around his eyes. He looked so beautiful holding him, it took my breath away. . . ."

Claudia looked up. *I'm rambling.* She sat back into the couch and crossed her arms over her chest. "I still can't believe someone just threw him away." She reached a hand down from her chest to nervously brush away some imaginary lint from her lap.

"I don't think asking the DCFS to make you the foster parents is the way we should proceed here," Greta said. "At the risk of sounding trite, you need to know that everything happens for a reason, that things have a way of working out the way they are meant to be. . . ."

Greta slowed on the last sentence, sounding a little preoccupied. She stared at Claudia's lap for a long awkward moment, as if trying to see if Claudia had missed any imaginary lint. It was the same kind of pause as when she'd read from her book, on and on, oblivious to everyone else in the room, as if she'd just dropped off-line for a while.

"I think," she finally snapped out of it and looked up at Claudia's face. "I think that baby has already worked some magic on you . . . a little good to come out of your debacle. Let's just do a blessing for the child's good health and happy future." She nodded to herself. "Yes. I think that would be the best thing."

Greta reached for the blue vial again and picked up a small stone, which she held in her right hand. She faced Claudia. "We'll do a blessing. Just in case."

Just in case what? Claudia figured Greta had the power to help her, to work some magic for her, and she didn't understand what she'd meant when she said the baby already had. A baby couldn't work magic—not the kind she wanted, anyway. Claudia wanted to protest, to scream out, *Wait! Aren't you going to help me get Elliot? What about my wish for a baby?* Her heart was pounding. She listened to Greta do the blessing in disbelief.

> *Spirit of Brighid join us here,*
> *Bring to baby Elliot a life free and clear,*
> *Clear of dis-ease, of hunger and strife,*
> *May happiness and joy stay with him through life.*

She dabbed some of the water from the vial onto the stone using her thumb and waved it over Claudia in the pattern of a five-pointed star.

"With our free will, we bind this plea and harm it no one, so mote it be."

This had been Claudia's worst fear. She'd been afraid that by bringing in a real witch and reversing the spell, not only would she end up not pregnant, she would end up without Elliot as well.

When Greta finished, she returned to the table, picked up her note cards, and slid the top card onto the bottom of the stack. "Okay now. On to Mara."

"Wait," Claudia yelled, then more quietly, she said, "Wait. Please. I mean, is that it? We're not going to try to— Isn't there something—? I really wanted to be Elliot's mother." Claudia closed her eyes. *Damn these stupid tears.* She opened them.

Greta's face was full of compassion when she looked back down at Claudia.

"I know you did, dear. I know what that little boy is to you, but there are some things that are best not interfered with. They're best left alone, to work out their own course. This is one of those things. Your love for that little boy, well, it's pretty powerful. I think you'll see it has a magic all its own.

"There are times in our lives when we want something so badly; we want it so much for ourselves, and it's not until later, when we look back and . . . and then we can see, we can see *the why*, the reason everything happened the way it did."

Claudia swallowed hard. What was Greta saying? That she couldn't have Elliot? That she couldn't have a baby *ever*?

Everything happens for a reason. She'd heard all those New Age platitudes before—hell, she'd even *used* them—but she didn't really like having them tossed out to her like some sort of consolation prize. *I'm sorry Ms. Dubois, you didn't win the baby, but here are some lovely parting gifts.* She'd rather have Turtle Wax and a case of Rice A Roni than some trite blather about the way things were meant to be.

"You should keep that crystal with you, at any rate," Greta said.

Claudia looked at her blankly.

"My crystal. The one you found?" Greta paused, waiting for some recognition in Claudia's eyes. "You *were* right about it, you know. It will bring you answers, and good luck, and maybe even courage, if and when you have the courage to let it."

Claudia couldn't help but think she'd be better off with the Rice A Roni. All that crystal seemed able to do was disappear. And now, Greta was standing here telling her she needed something she didn't have or couldn't find in order to get what she wanted.

Figures, Claudia thought. *Why didn't she just tell me to click my ruby slippers together?* Greta looked away and Claudia watched helplessly, sinking back into the couch again as Greta raised the stack of cards and began reading silently. *Is this my penance? A childless life filled with yoga and decorators and the Chicago Women's Foundation? I'm going to turn into Lindsay? All because of a misguided spell—cast with only the best of intentions—and some stupid crystal I can't find?*

Greta looked down at the cards in her hand. "All right then, on to Mara and that abundance wish."

"Please." Claudia's lips were quivering. "Why won't you help me? I know you can. I know you can help me get Elliot. You could make his foster family give him back. Why won't you try?"

"Because that would be black magic, dear, and we don't mess with that. Ever." Greta's face had grown deadly serious. "We should talk about it now. I hadn't mentioned it before, but I think now might be the time.

"Black magic is any type of witchcraft that is performed to get someone else to do something against their will. Arguments vary, but most Wiccans would even consider love spells black magic. No good, really, can come of forcing something that isn't meant to be. Wishes need to be about you—what's best for you—not bending someone else's will to your own. As I looked over your wishes, I was relieved to see you ladies were amazingly self-centered. Had you stumbled, even unintentionally, into black magic, the repercussions could have been terribly disastrous. Much worse." Greta looked at Claudia.

Claudia wanted to argue that her wish for Dan had been selfless. But if she was being brutally honest, she couldn't. She knew if

Dan were happier, if he felt more secure or had his career on a better track, he'd be more inclined to want a baby as much as she did. Her inability to write might be the backlash for trying to bend his will to her own, but the oddest part of all of it was that *Dan was happier.* The one wish they'd made for someone else had seemingly come true, without disastrous repercussions.

Claudia looked up at Greta, a new understanding in her eyes.

Greta held her stare briefly and nodded once. "Okay, now for Mara's abundance wish."

Mara shifted her weight in her chair. "I just wanted to be financially secure. Now look at me." She'd gained nearly thirty pounds. "I keep eating and eating. I can't help myself and I've gained so much weight. And Henry—he's become *hairy.*" Mara looked genuinely afraid. "It's like he has *fur.*"

Most of the women grimaced at this revelation, even Greta.

"Like I said, you will be taken quite literally when you cast your spells," Greta said. "If it was financial abundance you wanted, that's the way you should have asked for it. You need to be very careful."

"When I tried to fix it, I was careful."

"You tried to fix it?"

Mara nodded and explained the whole episode with the myrrh.

"We need to break this one, definitely," Greta said. "Same for you as for Claudia. Since we don't have any physical remnants from your wish, you're going to need to visualize it as you made it. For you, no tearing it up in your head, though. I want you to see yourself jumping up and down on top of it. Can you do this?"

"I . . . sure," Mara looked over at Claudia.

Claudia gave Mara a silent, open-mouthed shrug.

Greta flipped through her book again, dropping off-line in the way in which they'd now become accustomed. After making a few notes, she set the book on the table, then picked up one black and one white candle. Greta held the bottom of each one, one at a time, over a burning candle to melt a bit of wax on the bottom, using the melted wax to glue them onto two of the metallic plates.

The two candles were placed on either side of a large piece of purple amethyst. She cleared her throat and began.

> *Seven weeks ago a spell was cast with our verse,*
> *The results of which we must now reverse.*

Greta lit a small white birthday cake candle, then used it to light first the large white candle and then the black. She pinched out the flame of the birthday candle between her fingers.

> *For Mara and Henry abundance was sought.*
> *Let the spell be undone and the results it has wrought.*
> *We lift this spell, and ask all be well,*
> *And any harms done their negativity quell.*
> *It is our will, it is our plea*
> *And harm it no one, so mote it be.*

"All right." Greta picked up the stack of cards and put Mara's card on the bottom. "That should take care of that one now."

Mara looked up at Greta as if to say, "shouldn't there be more?" She shifted in her chair again and tugged out on a belt loop of her pants, loosening their grip on her waist, then crossed her arms over her stomach, resting her forearms on the soft rise of her belly, as if she were trying to press it out of the way.

"And now for your second wish. The singing career."

Mara rolled her eyes. "My voice is getting so bad now, I'm becoming afraid to use it at all. It's almost cost me my job. Although I'm not so sure Dr. Seeley doesn't like the new, quieter me in the examining room."

"If you choose this new path you've all started down, you're going to see changes—huge, magnificent, life-altering changes—not so easy, always, but good. Mostly good. Tonight, as we attempt to reverse these spells, we need to understand that if we're going to have even a little success at reversing any of them, especially since Jill—"

Everyone's questions burst out at once, interrupting her.

Lindsay: "A little success? You mean you aren't sure?"

Mara: "*Attempt* to reverse the spells? "

Gail: "What path?"

Claudia: "We may *not* be successful?"

Greta calmly held up one hand. "I don't remember giving out any guarantees that this was going to work. You see, you are all coming into your own power, a new kind of power, and it's not necessarily about the witchcraft as much as it is about controlling your own destiny and taking charge of your life. *Thought, word, deed.* It's like an unconscious use of the Witches' Pyramid. Can't you see the connection between your wishes and what's been happening? And it's not all about spells and potions.

"Lindsay, you wanted to lose weight. To obtain the *perfect body*, whatever that might be. Was it really your wish, or your belief that you'd finally found something that would work for you, that made the weight loss easier this time? How many times this time around did you sneak down to the kitchen for a midnight snack?"

Lindsay looked around nervously.

"Mara," Greta continued. "You asked for a chance to sing again. What kind of singing did you mean?"

"I don't know, I guess a small jazz club or something like that, once in a while. That's sort of what I had in mind."

"But really, wasn't that just a wish to be heard? You wanted someone to *listen* to you—to your voice. How much does your husband—Henry, is it?—how much does he listen to you with the game on all the time? And two teenage boys? That boss of yours? Forget it. So you wanted to sing. And now you do sing—and believe me, when you do, people listen.

"Gail, you wanted time to yourself. I don't think your wish was so nefarious that it started your sons' school on fire, but I guess I really don't know. But didn't all of it make you stop and think? Did you imagine for even a second what your life would be like without your children? And what was the final result? Aren't you an even better mother now? The fire couldn't be all that bad if it strengthened you as a parent. Yes, your son was hurt, but he's going to be fine. However, you ended up with a torn meniscus in your knee.

"Ladies, the Universe even has a sense of humor, it's a witty wordsmith. *Pay attention to your own knee—your own needs.* You've been ignoring them for years, Gail, and now as soon as you pay them some attention the Universe hands you not only a pun, but a pun that forces you to slow down for a change. How can you care for others when you aren't even caring for yourself? It's the old *put on your own oxygen mask first.* These other wishes are just the same: you wrote them down and gave them credence, and before too long they started happening.

"And the creativity wishes—Claudia's wish to write, and Jill's wish for inspiration. I think you must understand those are in a league of their own. That's why they backfired with results in complete opposition to their intention. You see, magic is really just another form of creativity, and *creativity is life.* Think about it: what is *creation?* It's making something, producing something, up to and including your own reality. How we live our lives, what we do with the gift of life is, essentially, our own personal magic. Claudia, you couldn't honestly expect the Universe to grant you a novel if you never sat down in a chair to write one. And so when you tried to ask, and even when you chickened out, the Universe gave you the *what for.* As far as Jill is concerned, if you look at the way she's lived, the way she's treated her gift, the gift of life . . ." Greta stopped there. She didn't need to explain Jill's history of self-destructive behavior to them.

The women sat in stunned silence.

"It's all just so complicated," Lindsay spoke first. "I don't understand how—I mean, how come all of our first wishes—for the candle and the rain, for Tippy—how come they went so well and most of the rest of them went so wrong? Well, all of them except one: Jill's wish for the perfect man."

"Those first wishes weren't quite so selfish," Greta answered. "Or maybe it was just beginner's luck. I don't have a definitive answer other than to say the Universe works in mysterious ways."

Greta stopped talking suddenly and tilted her head, a puzzled expression on her face. Again she stayed frozen that way, thinking, for a length of time most would consider inappropriate to take while holding the floor without talking.

When she finally looked up again, her eyebrows were furrowed together. "I'm starting to think Jill's first wish may have backfired, too. Maybe worst of all."

Chapter Twenty-Nine

✦

"**I** need you. Please come over." Marc's voice had cracked when he'd pleaded with her on the phone, and Jill finally had relented, driving over to his apartment to be with him. He hadn't sounded like himself. He'd sounded, well, desperate. "I don't know what's wrong, I . . . I just want to be with you tonight. Will you come? I miss you."

I miss you? She'd seen him just yesterday, Sunday. They'd returned from New York around noon. He'd dropped her off at her building and had been angling to get invited up, but she'd shut him down. "I'm tired. And I have a lot to catch up on around the house. I'll see you tomorrow, okay?" Which meant today.

Jill didn't really want to see him today, either, but she'd been unable to come up with a good enough excuse. He'd changed. Something about him was different, and she couldn't put her finger on what.

He'd started acting weird on the flight out to New York. For one thing, he'd just sat there. He hadn't read. He hadn't watched the short video segment. He hadn't scanned the in-flight shopping magazine. He sat. Looking straight ahead. Sometimes he shut his eyes, but mostly he just sat. And he had seemed very content to be doing it. He hadn't wanted to talk. At all. She'd thought it was the queerest behavior.

Oka-a-ay, maybe he's a nervous flier, she'd rationalized. A lot of people still got nervous on airplanes—as hard as that was for her to believe. It probably led to all sorts of strange behavior. She should be grateful all he was doing was staring straight ahead.

But during the entire trip she was troubled by a low-grade sense of something irretrievably wrong. She felt she was irritating him somehow, but not in the leaving-the-cap-off-the-toothpaste way; in a much more dangerous way. There was a darkness to his irritation, a sense of imminent rage.

Jill feared the reason for his irritation might be that her feelings toward him had changed, deepened, and that somehow he'd sensed it. On Saturday morning, the day after she and Marc had arrived in New York, they were walking in Central Park and had stopped on a bridge to admire the view. While spending several moments in comfortable silence, Jill was close to bringing up mutual exclusivity for their relationship. She was just about to tell him she thought she was falling in love with him, but right before she was ready to speak the words, he abruptly reached down and picked up a handful of gravel and began pelting the water below with small rocks.

"People talk too much," he said. "They just talk, talk, talk." He punctuated his words with harshly thrown pebbles. "I like that you're not like that, Jilly girl." Jill smiled and nodded silently, relieved that she hadn't spoken. Marc threw the remaining rocks down into the water with a violent snap of his arm. "I like that you're not like that," he repeated.

And just as these strange snapshots of Marc would suddenly appear—on the airplane, in the park—they would disappear, and Marc would return to his normal charming self. Jill tried to explain it away: *maybe he just doesn't travel well.*

On the flight back, he'd started talking with one of the flight attendants. The cute brunette one. With blue eyes. The one who looked like Jill. During the conversation he once again seemed to be back to his old self, the one she was falling in love with. But Jill hadn't known if she should be relieved he was getting over whatever it was that had been disturbing him, or if she should be bothered even more. And then she started feeling like she didn't really want to see him so much anymore, maybe take a break for a while. A complete turn-around from her previous line of thought about him—from her line of thought the previous day, even.

Tonight, Jill dragged herself up the front steps to his building. She held her finger on the buzzer for a moment before pressing it down.

Marc greeted her at the door, and the minute she saw his face she knew she'd made a mistake coming there. Something had tipped. It felt as if she were looking at a completely different person. She sensed she was looking at the strange Marc, the one with the odd behavior, the one who whipped small rocks down into black water. Only now, she didn't get the impression this latent anger would suddenly dissipate.

She sat down on the couch, nervous now. She wanted to leave even though she'd just arrived. But she tried to appear normal, to act normal—and not like she wanted to bolt for the door.

"What's up, hon?" she asked, taking a seat on the couch. "What's bothering you that couldn't wait until tomorrow?"

"I'm glad you're here . . ." He started walking back and forth in front of her, simultaneously pulling his hands through his hair. It was fluffed up in front and on the right side from the abuse. "I'm glad you came . . . I . . ."

It was like watching a big cat pacing back and forth at the zoo. Gorgeous. Regal. The word *crazy* came to mind.

"I thought you'd be more of a challenge." He sighed. "It's weird, you know what I mean, when it doesn't work out the way you think. I usually have a better instinct for these kinds of things. But I was wa-a-a-y wrong with you."

He continued pacing up and down the living room and pulling his hand through his hair over and over. "It's just not that fun," he said, "you know, when it's *too* easy. I really thought you'd be tougher. As soon as I started the portrait, I knew you would be too easy. I wanted a challenge. I was ready for a challenge.

"When you looked at it, that's when I knew. I really thought you wouldn't—I thought, not Jill, she's too cool for that—but I was wrong again." He shook his head, his mouth in a line, his expression extremely confused, as if to say, *how could I have been so wrong?* "You know how I could tell that you looked?"

What is he talking about? He's acting nuts. Jill smiled silently, nervously, from her seat on the couch.

"I could tell because of your hands," Marc continued. "Did you ever notice that? When people lie, they never know where to put their hands. Sometimes they look at you too hard—try to maintain too much eye contact. Other times they don't look at you at all. That's another way to tell. But the hands—that's the key. Yours were flailing all over the place."

Jill tried to remember the day of the first portrait sitting, if her hands had been *flailing all over the place.* She did remember peeking at the portrait. It hadn't been very good, she recalled. Her first impression was "outsider," and not the university background he'd claimed.

She'd peeked. *So what?* He'd had sex with her right afterward. How upset could he have been? That day she'd explained away his Outsider Art technique as just that, technique; but today she wasn't so sure. *Had he not studied at the University of Nebraska like he told me?*

Jill continued to sit silently on the couch, watching Marc pace up and down his apartment. It figures that just when she got to the point in a relationship where she thought everything was damned close to perfect, where *she* was the one ready for a commitment, the other person turned into someone else.

On the flight back from New York, she'd started to entertain the idea it might be best if they just took a break. A little time apart might be what they needed to recapture the way they'd felt before. Kind of like the break she was taking from Wish Club. Which now got her thinking some more.

She'd only been dating him for two months, but in such a short time, she'd isolated herself from all of her friends. She hardly saw anyone else anymore, didn't even talk to them on the phone. Her painting had gone down the shitter. She'd blown off her own gallery opening at his suggestion. Now that she thought about it, he didn't have any friends of his own, at least none that she'd met. And wasn't that strange? His rationale had been that he'd just moved to Chicago from Nebraska, where he'd kept a studio in Lincoln, but she never heard him talk much about Lincoln or the art community there. She really didn't know anything about him or his past, not even where he grew up. Nothing about his family. They'd never talked about it. She'd liked that, at first, how he didn't need to know what kind of cereal she used to eat for breakfast when she was in the second grade or what the name of her first boyfriend was. He was just letting the relationship unfold. But, by now, shouldn't she at least know where he was *from*?

Suddenly the course of their relationship seemed to be littered with red flags she'd failed to see earlier, like a slalom course in the middle of a straight run that she'd somehow managed to miss. She really didn't know this man. And now he was acting very strange.

Jill realized she was watching her wish for the perfect man unravel right before her eyes. Lindsay had been right. Something was very wrong with him.

And Jill wanted out of his apartment. Now.

"Maybe you're just tired, honey," she said. "I know I am—the trip and all. I think if you just get a good night's sleep then maybe everything will seem better in the morning."

"Who the fuck are you? My mother?" His face had turned dark. No more fun sexy boy. His look was menacing.

Jill's heart started to race, but she tried to keep her face calm. *Why did I come here? I should have listened to that little voice.*

"No, I . . ." Jill stammered. "I just don't understand what you're talking about, hon, and I thought maybe that if you . . ."

She looked past him at the door. He caught her glance.

He smiled at her now. The old smile. The sexy one. "I'm sorry, Jilly. I'm sorry. I don't know what gets into me. I . . . I'm. Maybe I am tired." He shook his head, flustered. Then he flashed a smile at her, the kind of smile an adult gives a child when they don't mean it, before the adult starts screaming.

And then he burst out laughing. A laugh so loud Jill jumped in place on the couch.

"Portraits? Why portraits?" He imitated her voice with a mock falsetto. "Oh, God. That was . . . that was funny." He looked down at her on the couch. "I'll tell you *why portraits*. Because the portraits are my souvenirs."

Fear chilled her blood, made the palms of her hands grow cold with sweat. She forced a smile, still trying to pretend everything was normal. She stood up. "It's okay. I'll come back tomorrow. We can talk tomorrow."

"No, you should stay. I think I'd like it very much for you to stay."

"I really think I should go." Her voice cracked.

He blocked her path to the door.

Jill tried to laugh it off, even though she knew he wasn't playing. "Come on, Marc. I want to leave."

She tried to brush past him, and again he moved to block her. The door was only a couple of feet behind him, but he stood in her way.

Jill held a fake smile on her face while she contemplated her options. After many nights in his apartment, she knew how poor the soundproofing was. Some mornings she could actually hear the guy upstairs peeing. She should try to bolt for the door—and yell.

She leaned to the right and then quickly went left and tried to pass him. Her left hand touched the doorknob as she fell. She didn't know what he'd used to hit her, maybe just his fist. She didn't get a chance to yell.

Claudia had never met Marc. She didn't know what he looked like or much of anything about him, except that he was *fabulous*, according to Jill. And *gorgeous*, according to Lindsay. But it had occurred to her before that maybe he really wasn't any of that. If all of their wishes had backfired so stupidly, then certainly there was the possibility that this Marc guy wasn't who they thought he was.

From the center of Lindsay's living room, Greta was continuing with her spell-reversing, wish-cleansing ritual. After finishing up a guilt-washing and privacy spell for Gail, she was now working on Lindsay, who was still insisting that most of her weight loss had been due to the success of her first wish and not due to any change in her eating or exercising habits.

Duct tape. An image of a roll of duct tape came into Claudia's head, like a movie, running past her eyes even though they were

open. An odd thing to occur to anybody—well, maybe not anybody who was listening to Lindsay—but the way it had just floated
into her head. She saw Jill now, too. Jill *and* duct tape. She got the
feeling something was wrong with Jill and that it involved duct
tape. The thought was so vivid, Claudia couldn't shake it, as much
as she wanted to clear it out of her head. It was all so—dumb. *Who
gets visions of duct tape?*

Greta was leaning over, lighting a red candle on the coffee table.
Suddenly she snapped her back up straight. "Lindsay, you saw Jill
last Thursday? At home?"

Lindsay nodded. Claudia could practically hear her thought,
What does this have to do with fixing my wish?

"And Marc wasn't there?" Greta asked.

"No."

Greta nodded, silently thinking in that way she had. "Did you . . .
I don't know how much of their, well, *private* life you knew about,
but did you happen to know if they liked to use," Greta swallowed,
appearing uncomfortable for the first time ever, "duct tape?"

Claudia's leg knocked the underside of the table. Everything on
top of it was sent straight up a fraction of an inch, before landing
back down in disarray, herbs spilled, crystals tumbled to the floor.
Wax sloshed.

"Did you say duct tape?" Claudia said.

"Yes, dear." Greta looked at her calmly, as if she weren't wondering, like everybody else in the room surely was, why Claudia had
just spazzed out for no apparent reason. "What is it?"

"Because I just saw duct tape, too. Like a vision, kind of. I saw a
roll of duct tape, and I saw Jill and I . . . I got the impression something was wrong, but I didn't want to say anything. Because you
were working on Lindsay's butt—I mean, her weight spell . . . and
I thought I would wait to say something . . . because it seemed
nuts, you know. Until you said something."

Greta continued to watch her calmly. She closed her eyes and
held very still. She sniffed. "I think Jill might be in some trouble."

"Did you see something? Did you have a vision?" Lindsay asked.

"What's the matter with Jill?" Gail asked.

"You saw duct tape, too?" Claudia asked her. Maybe her vision hadn't been so dumb after all.

Greta shook her head. "Yes, and I sensed danger, too. It's not clear," she said, "but we need to close our circle and find her. Especially since two of us received the message. And the sooner the better."

The women started to stand up before Greta motioned them back into their seats. "Wait, wait. I need to close up the circle. It'll only take a moment."

They sat back down and Greta picked up the athame, this time without any adverse reaction from the women. She held it out in front of her the same way she had when she had drawn the circle, only now she walked in the opposite, counterclockwise direction. She didn't say, chant, or whisper anything as she walked. When she arrived at the place she'd started, Greta loudly stomped her foot, startling them. "The circle unbroken, even as it is opened. So mote it be." And then, quite unceremoniously, Greta put the knife back in the large bag and began collecting the rest of her things.

The lake sped by on the right, a black abyss, the light from the highway soaked up by the water in the first few yards before darkness prevailed. Black sky and black water met at some imperceptible horizon, one continuous flow of unending night.

Gail raced her minivan toward the exit ramp at Belmont and headed for the inner drive. A few moments later, all of them— Gail, Claudia, Mara, Lindsay, and Greta—pulled into the circular driveway of Jill's building. Claudia jumped out and hurried inside.

Breathing hard, she huffed up to the doorman, the same arrogant doorman who'd made her wait before. "I'm here to see Jill Trebelmeier."

"One moment please, I'll try her." He eyed Claudia closely and ran his finger over his mustache as he held the phone to his ear.

Claudia eyed him back.

After about twenty seconds had passed, he said, "I'm sorry, she's not answering."

"Could you keep trying—just a while longer?"

He nodded and said "sure," politely enough, but the corners of his mouth had turned down into a frown.

"I'm sorry, still no answer."

"Do you know if she's here? I'm a little worried about her."

"No, ma'am," he said. "I don't know."

"Has she had any other visitors tonight? Do you know if Marc is here? Or was here?"

The doorman frowned at her again. "You know I'm not allowed to tell you that."

Claudia glared at him for a moment before saying "thank you," politely enough.

"No luck," she said as she opened the door to the van and sat down.

"Had he seen her tonight? Did he think she was out?" Gail said.

"He wouldn't say."

"Perhaps we should try the studio?" Greta asked.

"Marc keeps a studio in the same building," Lindsay said. "Maybe if there's a directory, we could get his last name, use it to find out where he lives."

"Do you know how to get there?" Gail looked at Greta in the rearview mirror.

"Yes, dear. Get on Addison westbound. It's up on Ravenswood."

$Gail$ drove north on Ravenswood Avenue. Extinct factories loomed on the west side of the street. The Metra tracks high up on their berm formed the other side of a dark tunnel. A train went by, all of its cars empty, its lights casting an eerie green glow. Gail turned the van onto a side street and parked in front of 4400 North.

Between Ravenswood and the El tracks, this end of the one-way street was deserted. There were only two other cars parked here besides Gail's van, which is where they sat, looking at the front of Jill's studio building. A dog barked in the distance.

"What should we do?" Lindsay asked.

"Find Jill." Claudia started to open the passenger-side door. "Let's go inside. Which studio is hers?"

"She's in 2W." Greta pointed to the corner of the building, but no lights were on on the second floor.

"His studio is right below hers," Claudia said. "Isn't that right? Lindsay, didn't she tell you that Marc had moved in right below her?"

Their heads all turned back to the building. The lights in the studio below Jill's were on. The only sign of life on this entire end of the street.

The women looked at each other and nodded. Emboldened now, they would find Marc and get some answers. But instead of jumping out of the van, dramatically slamming doors and marching up to the front of the building, they had to wait for Gail to very undramatically slide the minivan doors open electronically. While they were humming closed, the light in 1W went out.

The women stood outside the van, unsure of their next move. After a moment, the front door swung open and a tall man in baggy jeans and an oversized T-shirt hurried out, carrying what looked like several canvases rolled together into a tube.

"That's him," Lindsay whispered.

As he approached the sidewalk, Gail called out, "Hey, Marc?"

When he looked up, she continued, "We'd like to talk with you for a minute."

He stared at them gathered together on the grass between the sidewalk and the curb, and appeared to be sizing them up. Five women of all shapes and sizes, standing in front of a minivan.

He smiled at them, a warm sexy smile.

Wow. Claudia could feel all five of them gasp internally. Lindsay hadn't been kidding. He *was* gorgeous.

"What can I do for you ladies?" he asked. "Do I know you?"

"Hi Marc," Lindsay stepped forward. "It's me, Lindsay—from Jill's book club."

He deepened his smile, just for her. "Oh, hey."

His smile had the desired effect. Lindsay paused briefly before she smiled back, a little flustered. "We're trying to find Jill. We haven't seen her in a while and we're a little worried about her. We know she's been seeing you; we were wondering if maybe you can help us."

Marc kept smiling, his face expectant as if he were waiting for more. "Help you with what?"

"Help us find Jill. We want to talk to her." Claudia slid her glasses up her nose, holding the side of the frames, instead of shoving her index finger up the bridge of her nose the way she usually did.

"I haven't seen Jill since we got back yesterday."

"Got back from where?"

"New York. We took a little trip over the weekend."

"New York? She didn't mention she was going to New York," Lindsay said.

"It was *spontaneous*." He said it in a tone of voice that suggested Lindsay wouldn't understand *spontaneous*. "We got back yesterday. Did you try her apartment?"

"She wasn't there," Mara said.

Claudia was standing at the front of the van, next to the curb, behind a silver Hyundai Elantra. Marc started making his way toward it, tucking the tube of canvases under his arm and pulling out a fistful of keys from his front pocket. "I haven't seen her since yesterday, but you know how she is, needing her alone time. I'm sure she's fine." He smiled at them again, but now no one was smiling back. "If she calls, or if I see her, I'll tell her you're all looking for her."

"We'd sure appreciate that, Marc." Greta stepped out from her place next to Lindsay. When she spoke, his head snapped toward her, as if he were caught off guard by her voice. He smiled and nodded nervously, like a boy being chastised by his mother.

Claudia noticed the Hyundai was full. Boxes filled the backseat, a canvas next to them on the floor. More clutter and a boom box littered the rear window ledge. An open box sat on top of the pile, some books and other debris stacked hastily inside. Claudia looked at the trunk, her vision of duct tape and Jill coming back. Making sense.

"Did you drive to New York?" Claudia asked.

"No. We flew. Listen. I'd love to help you ladies more, but I really need to get going."

"No one, not one of her friends, anyway, has seen Jill in days," Claudia continued. "We're worried about her. You say you took her to New York, but nobody, not even Greta, knew about the trip. Why would she leave town when her show was opening at the gallery?"

His voice turned chillier now, irritated with them. "Listen, I don't know what she did or did not tell you. Like I said, the trip was spontaneous. I dropped her off at her building yesterday afternoon and that is the last I saw of her. I wish I could help you nice ladies, but I am in a bit of a hurry and I really would like to get going."

"Looks like you're leaving town." Claudia patted her hand on the trunk of his car and his eyes flashed at her, first fear, then rage. His eyes bore into hers. She held them.

The El thundered by, its loud metallic clatter obliterating all other sound. Without answering her, Marc looked down and started sorting through his keys. White flashes of light splashed off the tracks as the El finished speeding past.

Lindsay looked at Claudia with a bewildered expression.

Claudia tugged twice on her right ear. She motioned with her eyes at the trunk of the Hyundai. Lindsay's eyes got huge.

Lindsay looked up at Marc. "Are you leaving? On another trip?" she asked. She moved over farther, to stand in front of the driver's-side door.

"I need to get back to Nebraska for a couple of days. My dad's sick." He tried his sexy smile again.

"A couple of days?" Lindsay looked down at the back seat of the Hyundai. "Even I can't pack like that for a couple of days."

"Listen," he said, angry again. "I don't need to stand here and put up with the third degree. I told you, I don't know where Jill is. And now I'm going. And where I'm going and for how long is none of your business."

"Somehow," Claudia moved to stand next to Lindsay, "we all think it is."

"You ladies are crazy." Marc pushed Claudia aside brusquely, bumping her with his shoulder, knocking her purse to the ground, all of its contents spilling.

Claudia ignored the clutter around her feet. "I think you know where she is. I think she's in trouble. And I think you're the reason."

"What have you done to her?" Lindsay asked.

"Where is she?" Mara said.

Marc stepped forward again and roughly pushed Lindsay out of his way. She stumbled off to the side.

He leaned over to unlock the door to the car and Claudia leaped onto his back, her arms encircling his neck. "You're not leaving until you tell us where she is!"

"Jesus Christ!" Marc hissed out the words as they spun around a couple of times, sending the tube of canvases tumbling to the ground, before he was able to wrestle her arms from his neck. He twisted his body and, with a lurch, sent Claudia flying to the ground as well.

He turned around to face them, while reaching an arm behind his back and pulling a switchblade from his rear pocket, springing the blade out as he did so. It flashed at them in the dim light. This time there would be no demonstration on the knife's harmlessness.

"Okay, ladies. Now that I have your attention."

They held their breath in silence, statues on the grass.

"No more questions. No more accusations. I'm going to leave now. And you're going to let me." No one moved. "That's better." He held the knife up and walked backward a few steps, then crouched down to pick up the roll of canvases. When he stood back up he held a smug smile on his face.

Claudia looked up at him from where she was lying frozen on the ground. *Did I really just jump on his back? Put my butt right on top of that knife? Good grief.*

Never taking his eyes from them, he opened the door to the car, threw the canvases inside, and sat down. "Good luck finding your little friend Jill."

The last of his words were trampled by the thunder of the El flying by again, sending off more white sparks. A silver glint on the ground flashed up in its light, catching Claudia's attention. As Marc slammed the door of his car, she dove for it.

The car rumbled to life. Claudia grabbed the compass from the ground and jammed it into the rear tire of his car just as he started to speed away from the curb.

From her stomach, Claudia watched his car fly around the corner at the far end of the block without stopping at the stop sign, tires squealing, the tail lights blurring out of sight.

"Oh my God. Are you okay?" Mara came over to where Claudia was lying, no music in her voice now.

"What are we going to do now? I think he has Jill. Is he going to kill her?" Lindsay looked from Greta down to Claudia and then back. "Did he kill her already?"

Gail had her cell phone out and was dialing. "I got the plate number. I'm calling the police. Hopefully, he won't get far."

Lindsay rubbed her arm where Marc had pushed her. "Claudia, what are you doing?" She looked back down at Claudia, still lying prone on the ground, as though implying she really should be more productive during these times of crisis.

"Claudia was busy saving the day," Greta said.

They all looked at Greta, puzzled. Lindsay most of all.

"He won't get very far." Claudia was still looking down the street where Marc had just driven away. "I have a zero-tolerance policy, too."

Chapter Thirty

✦

Jill woke to the smell of motor oil. Her mouth had been taped shut and her hands were bound so tightly she couldn't feel her fingers anymore. She was cold, and her feet felt even colder, not just because they were tied together tightly as well, but also because she wasn't wearing any shoes. It hurt to breathe.

She was in the trunk of Marc's car, of that she was fairly certain. The side of her face was pressed into what felt like indoor-outdoor carpeting, and she could hear road noises under her ear, traffic sounds around her. The car dropped into a pothole, which sent a spasm of pain through her chest. At least she could be fairly certain she was still in Chicago.

The car slowed to a stop and the engine idled roughly, the muffler's rugged vibration jarring the length of her right side. He'd beaten her pretty badly. It must have happened after the first blow because she didn't remember any of it. Judging from the stabbing pain in her chest, he'd broken a rib or two. Jill tried to roll onto her back to relieve some of the pressure, but the pain was excruciating. There wasn't much room in the trunk anyway. The car lurched and started moving forward again.

Where is he taking me? What's he going to do? Jill had never known this kind of fear before. *He's going to kill you, Jill. That's what he's going to do—if he doesn't think you're already dead.* She tried inhaling larger breaths of air to calm herself, without success.

If she'd listened to Lindsay, she thought, then she'd be at Wish

Club right now instead of waiting to die in the trunk of her crazy boyfriend's Hyundai Elantra. Why hadn't she noticed all the signs? Why hadn't she listened? She could only hope there'd be time for berating herself later. Right now, she needed to come up with a plan. She tried the bindings at her hands and feet again. They wouldn't budge.

Jill closed her eyes. For the first time in recent memory, she started to pray.

"Let's go," Claudia said, getting to her feet.

"Go where?" Lindsay asked.

"We have to follow him." Claudia pointed down the street. "C'mon, Gail, let's get in the van. We have to follow him. Jill's in that trunk. I know it. I just know it! We have to save her. And we need to hurry."

"I think Claudia's right." Greta was nodding. "I sensed it too."

Gail pointed her remote at the van and the doors started to slide open. She handed her phone to Mara. "Here. When they answer, tell them I got the plate number. That he had a knife and he threatened us—and tell them which way he went."

The women piled into Gail's van. She pulled away from the curb before the doors had slid completely shut, while the little warning beeps were still sounding.

The sound under her ear had changed to slow tires over gravel, and Jill realized she must have passed out again. The car leaned to one side, her body angling down toward her feet now. The waterfall noise of the gravel was accompanied by a soft thwump thwump thwump. The traffic noise was gone, just the hiss of a highway in the distance.

Where are we? They came to a stop. Silence. She could feel him moving in the front seat. The car door opened and slammed shut. Footsteps headed toward Jill. They stopped.

"Fucking goddamned bitches."

His boots scraped the gravel, kicking some up to pelt the car, startling Jill when it loudly pinged against the side of the trunk. More silence.

"How the fuck am I going to—" Marc stopped abruptly.

Jill heard the sound of tires on gravel. Another car approaching. It stopped. *Thank God.*

"Hey. What are you doing down here?" a male voice called out. "This area's off limits."

"I got a flat. I just pulled off the drive to take a look."

Lake Shore Drive? The lakefront reconstruction project had gravel roads going all through it. *Are we down by the lake?*

Jill heard a car door slam and footsteps come closer, while Marc's walked toward the front of the car.

"I wanted to get off the highway, get someplace safer to change it," Marc said.

She could practically see the expression on Marc's face, just from the tone of his voice, the way he tilted his head when he turned on the charm. She'd seen it work on men, too.

"I didn't want to drive too far on it," Marc added.

"You got a spare?"

"Yeah, in the trunk."

"You know how to change it?"

"Yeah."

Jill tried to make noise, to yell, but the duct tape over her mouth turned the sound in her throat to a moan. She tried lifting her feet to kick the hood of the trunk, but the pain was unbearable. She managed one soft thump, tried to lift her legs again, then relaxed them in defeat.

"All right then." The man hadn't heard her. "Get it fixed, then get on out of here. You should have used one of the pull-offs. You're not supposed to be down here with the construction going on."

Jill heard his footsteps walk away, and her panic rose as hope fell.

✦

"He'd leaving!" Lindsay was shocked. "He's just driving away! What do we do now?" She was whispering even though they were still inside the van on the other side of the park, far from Marc's Elantra.

"The police said we shouldn't approach him." Mara held up Gail's cell phone. "They were adamant about it—because of the knife."

"But why didn't the cop grab Marc?" Gail asked. "Didn't they put the word out yet? Should we call them back?"

"We have to do something!" Claudia said.

"All right, ladies," Greta said. "School's in session a little early. Keep your minds open and your brain waves clear."

They looked at each other. *Whatever you say.* And with that, Greta started their first lesson in the Craft.

"Sorry, officer," Marc said. "Thank you," he called after him.

Jill could hear the footsteps retreating.

Oh God, it was a cop. He was right here and now he's leaving. Jill tried to yell, to lift her feet again. She rolled onto her back, her chest in agony.

Marc didn't move outside the car and she knew he was plotting his next move, just like she was.

The sound of the other car's tires crunching the gravel retreated as it drove slowly away.

"Thanks for fucking nothing, officer." Marc was still near the front of the car.

He'd need to open the trunk to get out the spare, but what was she going to do? She couldn't attack him. She couldn't yell, not loud enough for anyone to hear her anyway. Not if they were really down by the lake. Had Marc heard her make noise? Did it matter?

His footsteps came around to the back of the trunk. The key slid into the lock. *C'mon Jill, think. Think!* But the only plan she could come up with was to close her eyes and play dead. The trunk opened and a rush of air swept in.

"Well, well, well. My Jilly girl. Are we napping now?" He paused. "Knock off the act. I heard you."

Jill opened her eyes. The light hurt but she held his gaze.

"Thought you were in for the big rescue, didn't you? 'Mmmpggph. Mmmpggph.'" His voice went high to imitate hers. "Did you really think some fat old deaf cop was gonna hear that shit? Lazy bastard never took five steps from his cruiser." Marc had both hands up on the hood of the trunk, one hip cocked to the side.

He laughed. "Your pathetic little Book Club friends tried to save your sorry ass. One dumb bitch even slashed my tire. But, I'd have to say, all in all, it didn't work out so bad. You see, it gave me this really great idea. And now it's time for me to get you out of there, 'cuz you're going for a little swim."

Marc lifted a few plastic bags out from in front of her and set them on the ground. She rolled away from him when he reached in to grab her but she was up against the rear of the trunk. He pulled her by the arms, sliding her backward across the floor before he reached under her armpits and lifted her out. She crunched her eyes closed with the pain. Her ribs hurt so much it made it nearly impossible for her to breathe, but she still tried to squirm out of his grip.

He's going to throw me in the lake here? What kind of moron is he? The cop saw him here and there'll be traces of my hair and clothes in his trunk. Didn't he watch any of those CSI shows?

Jill kept squirming. "Steady, Jilly. Steady now. Such a fighter."

The lakefront was deserted. *Where are the crazy midnight joggers?* A construction trailer sat in the dark to her left. Piles of gravel, stacks of pipes and cinder blocks littered the gravel lot. The lake loomed about thirty yards to her right. "'*Cuz you're going for a little swim.*"

Jill prayed again: *God, please send a jogger, a homeless person. Someone. Anyone. I promise I'll be good from now on.* When the answer to her prayer wasn't instantaneous, she started another prayer, to Saint Jude.

———◆———

They held hands in as close of an approximation of a circle as they could manage in the back of Gail's van. In their minds' eye, they held the image of Marc, his legs bogging down, walking through molten lead, unable to move with speed or coordination.

Greta conducted the visualization. "Freeze him. Keep imagining his legs seizing up, as if he were slogging through wet cement."

Isn't this black magic? Claudia wanted to ask, but then, fearful she might disrupt the spell to save Jill, she refocused her thoughts and kept her mouth shut. Perhaps later they could find time to discuss the finer points of witchcraft ethics. Right now, they needed to stop Marc from hurting Jill.

"Take the energy through yourself," Greta continued, "draw it up from the center of the earth, through your feet. Make it a cold beam, a laser of ice-blue light coming from each of you—joining together at the center of us and then shooting out and into Marc. Shoot it into his core. Have the beam of icy light hit him and envelope him. Focus on the legs now. That's it. That's it . . . Mmm-hmm. Mmm-hmm. Very good. That's very good."

Can she see it? Can she see a beam of light? Claudia had been trying to focus for all she was worth, but still, it seemed too beyond belief to consider. She allowed herself a peek at Greta's face. Her eyes were closed, a hint of a smile on her face.

She seemed very pleased.

Marc carried Jill half over his shoulders as he hurried her toward the water, every step sending a shooting pain through her ribs. Jill started to cry. She didn't want to die. Not like this.

The water's dank fish smell grew stronger, and he started to slow down. They must be getting close.

Jill opened her eyes. Marc had slowed to a walk, but they were still about twenty feet from the edge of the lake. She felt him waver underneath her, as if he'd lost his balance for a moment. He weaved in place, like a drunk, then put a foot forward. It seemed to be taking a lot of effort on his part. He put his other foot forward with a grunt. He was walking as if his legs were encased in cement, like in those dreams where you need to run but can't make your legs move at all.

Jill started to squirm again, and she could feel his arms try to wrap more tightly around her thighs, but there was no pressure behind them, no strength.

He'd had to stop his strained walking while he struggled to get control of her, and she started writhing again, trying to get away. Marc groaned and tried to take a step. He couldn't move! Jill twisted off his shoulder, her hands still bound behind her, unable to break her fall. He flailed a hand against her as she slid down, brushing it against the side of her face as she fell. His hand felt like ice.

Jill hit the ground just as tires squealed behind her in the lot, accompanied by the sound of gravel spraying. She tried to lift her head but didn't have the strength. She managed to open one eye. A police cruiser barreled toward them.

Marc turned around to see it, too. His eyes filled with fear. He looked down at her and seemed to have a moment of indecision, his legs rooted to their position on the ground. Then he took a step, his eyes filled with surprise. He took another step, a brief smile flashing across his face as he started a doubled-over trot along the lake.

One of the cops got out of the squad car and ran after Marc, both of them disappearing quickly in the dark.

An older, larger cop had gotten out of the car at the same time and he was hurrying over to Jill. Behind him she could see a minivan racing into the gravel lot, pulling up right next to the squad car.

"Sweet Jesus," the cop said when he bent down next to Jill. He reached over and touched her forehead with a gesture more gentle than would be expected from such a burly man. He spoke into the radio microphone on his shoulder and called for an ambulance, giving their location, Montrose Harbor.

Claudia, Lindsay, Mara, Greta, and Gail came running out of the van and up to them, encircling Jill and the cop, kneeling down, reaching out, embracing her with their presence.

"Is she okay?"

"Will she be all right?"

"Don't let that bastard get away."

Jill could sense the cop reeling back for a moment, overwhelmed by the sudden rush of female energy and emotion. He made a patting motion with his hand, the standard male "calm down" gesture.

"She's beat up pretty bad, but she's still breathing and alert. There's an ambulance on the way."

Gail knelt down next to her, putting a finger to the tape over her mouth. "Can I take this off?" she asked both the cop and Jill.

Jill closed her eyes and gave a brief nod.

The cop nodded, too. Gail slowly peeled the duct tape away. It didn't hurt, but Jill moaned anyway. Her head had hit the ground when she had fallen off Marc's shoulder. Blood was seeping into the corner of one eye. Her lips felt swollen. She ran her tongue around the inside of her mouth and noticed several of her teeth had been chipped, and the inside of her lower lip was bleeding.

Claudia sat on the other side of Jill, resting a hand on her shoulder. She touched Jill so lightly, it was as though she were trying very hard not to hurt her any more, yet she used just enough pressure to let her know that they were all still there, that she wasn't alone.

"The ambulance'll be here any minute now," Claudia said. "You're going to be okay."

Jill ran her tongue over the newly rough interior of her mouth before whispering, "I know."

Chapter Thirty-One

"*I* feel like such an idiot." Jill's huge blue eyes flicked up at Claudia briefly before she returned her gaze to her lap.

The Wish Club women encircled Jill's hospital bed. Everyone must have had a hard time hearing her, because, like Claudia, they all moved in a little more closely now.

"An idiot?" Gail asked.

"Because you loved somebody? That should never make you feel like an idiot," Mara said.

"Love always makes me feel like an idiot." Claudia rolled her eyes and made her *silly me* face for Jill.

"I . . ." Jill took a shallow, obviously painful breath. "I feel like I should have seen it coming . . . somehow. That I shouldn't have been . . . so blind. Looking back, there were so many signs."

"Honey, haven't you heard the old saying that love is always blind?" Lindsay adjusted Jill's thin hospital blanket while she spoke. "You're being too hard on yourself. You need to focus on getting better, not stuff like that."

"They say a plane crash is never caused by one mistake." Greta sat in one of the chairs by the window, her back to a view of Lincoln Park. "They say it's always a series of errors, a chain, created by more than one person. Life is just the same. Most terrible mistakes are the result of a series of errors."

"Yeah," Gail said. "Marc may be a murderous lunatic, but how did he get that way? And why hadn't anyone caught him up until now? You can't blame yourself for being the final link in the chain."

It turned out Marc was actually John Latham from Rice Lake, Wisconsin, wanted for questioning in Wichita, Kansas, and Lincoln, Nebraska, in conjunction with the disappearances of two blue-eyed, dark-haired women.

The police suspected the other two women were dead.

A tear slid from the outside corner of Jill's eye, down the side of her purple cheek. "I just can't believe that . . . that the first time I get close to someone . . . to really letting someone in," she took another shallow breath, which made her wince, "he turns out to be a psycho."

"Well, psycho or not," Greta said, "he helped you to realize you were capable of it. Of giving love. As crazy as this may sound, he helped you find a way to let someone in. It wasn't the best way, or the only way, but it was *a* way. And that's a start. For you, dear, that's a very good start."

Tears streamed down Jill's cheeks. She looked down again at the blanket covering her legs, then said, as if apologizing, "Everything just hurts."

Marc had beaten Jill pretty badly. She had three broken ribs, a broken wrist, and a concussion, along with some severe bruising. And two chipped teeth.

"Of course it does, dear." Greta got up from her chair and stood next to the bed. "And it will for a while. But now, you need to take care of yourself and try to get well. Learn to give *yourself* a little love."

Jill brought her eyes back up to look at Greta; she looked completely bewildered.

"I know *that* idea may sound a little strange to you," Greta said, "but in all honesty, you've never been very loving to yourself. In fact, you've been rather the opposite. I'd suggest you try it. I think you'll be surprised. I think you'll find when you're successful, there'll be a whole stable of *perfect men* lining up to sweep you away."

"And in the meantime," Lindsay spread her arms, palms up, "you've got us."

Jill smiled through her tears. "My own personal coven." She looked at Greta. "You never said anything about being a witch."

"Dear, it's not the first thing I think of to trot out there when I meet someone. Most people are . . . well, very uncomfortable with it. Although I have begun to notice lately that people seem less and less freaked out by it. More likely to ask questions, or to ask for help. But I did get the sense, as I got to know you, that perhaps you were one who wouldn't be so open to it."

Jill nodded. "I never would have believed witchcraft would save me." Jill shook her head and looked down at her lap again, silent for a while. "I don't know what . . ." She took a breath, her face contorting with it. "I don't know what I did to deserve you guys. I really don't." Jill paused and sniffed, then tried another smile, her face a full spectrum of emotion. "But thank you." The tears flowed freely now. "Thanks for saving me."

Gail leaned into the door of John's office. "Hey," she said, "I'm home." She was just getting back from the May Book Club meeting.

"Well, if it isn't Samantha Stephens." John swiveled his chair around to look at her. "I didn't hear you sneak up. Are you sure that old witch isn't teaching you her secrets?"

Gail limped into the room, her knee still recovering from the arthroscopy she'd had earlier in the week. "She's not teaching us anything. She's just another member of Book Club. Your hearing's just shot from listening to Yes albums too loud."

John looked skeptical, as if he couldn't believe Book Club could simply revert back to being Book Club again, especially with Greta in it now. "At least my Yes albums are better than your Talking Heads." He patted the top of his lap and Gail sat down. He wrapped his arms around her hips. "So who was there? The usual suspects?"

"Yeah. Everyone except Jill. She wasn't up to it, Lindsay said. But I don't know if she meant Jill wasn't up to it yet physically, or if she wasn't up to it, period."

"I wouldn't blame her if she didn't want to come back."

Gail nodded.

"So?" John asked, "Everyone like the book?"

"Yep. But we always like Claudia's picks. I can't wait to read the one she's working on. And you should see her. She cut her hair! Just to her shoulders, but it looks great—so much more flattering."

John smiled, acting as though he were actually interested in Claudia's new hairstyle. "So . . . there was no more, umm . . ."

"No. Nothing like that." Gail twitched her lips back and forth. Paused. Did it again.

John was looking at her with suspicion, as if maybe he thought she was actually expecting something to happen when she twitched her lips.

"Oh c'mon. I'm just goofin' on you," Gail said, and John smiled, relieved. Gail took a breath and became more serious. "You know, I never thanked you for putting up with all the Wish Club stuff. It must have sounded so crazy to you."

"No. Not so crazy. Not from you." He paused. "But now I am starting to get lonely around here. First your theater workshop, now back to Book Club. What's next? Are you going to sign up for archery lessons with Lindsay?"

Gail laughed. "No. Nothing more on my plate for now. And I saw the pizza box downstairs. Was it two or three hours of Super Mario Brothers? You guys aren't suffering in my absence."

John threw a hand over his chest as if to say, *Super Mario Brothers? Moi?*

Gail was smiling as she looked up and saw her Clio on the bookshelf over John's desk. She knew she wasn't ready to go back to work yet, or maybe ever. This workshop she'd joined at the Wisdom Bridge Theater seemed just the thing for her right now. It gave her a chance to do something she loved and have adult contact and conversation. Maybe it would lead to something, or maybe not. Either way, she tried not to feel guilty taking the time. She knew it was better for everyone. If she was happy, then everyone would be happy. And as far as her family and everyone else was concerned, at least the theater workshop wouldn't involve witchcraft. Unless they decided to take a stab at *Macbeth*.

"It's weird, but lately I've been thinking a lot about that whole thing with the wish and Andrew and the fire. And now . . . now that I absolutely believe in the power of those wishes, the thing is, I'm not so sure anymore that we didn't have anything to do with it."

"You think you guys *did* start the fire?"

Gail shrugged. After a moment she said, "No . . . I don't know. For a while I was so certain we hadn't, that it wasn't possible; but now I just don't know anymore." She looked hard at John, to see if he was following her, half expecting another *Bewitched* joke.

His tone was serious, though, when he held her a little tighter and said, "You know, hon, it could just be one of those things. One of those things you never know the answer to."

Mara found herself staring at the sailboat watercolor that hung on the wall opposite her desk. Lately, she found herself staring at it almost every day. The print was behind a glass frame and she had to hold her head just right to see past the glare from the office lights. The sail on the boat billowed out large and white. The artist had gotten the light just right: the sun screamed bright off the edge of the sail. It had the number 365 painted on it next to a small blue and white flag. Mara often wondered at the number, what it meant. Something nautical, the number of the boat, or the number of days in a year? Whatever it meant, she knew every single day she stared at it like this, she was dreaming about sailing away.

Dr. Seeley approached her desk in his awkward way, lips pursed out before he spoke. "You know Jill Trebelmeier, don't you?"

"Yeah."

"Terrible what happened to her. Terrible."

"Yes, it was terrible." Mara knew for a fact it was terrible.

Dr. Seeley looked hard at Mara. She looked back at him calmly. Waiting.

"They say that John Latham character is a suspect in another disappearance now, too. A girl in Wisconsin."

Mara nodded. "I'd read that."

"I also heard something rather disturbing about your book group being involved in, with . . . er, witchcraft. I . . . well, you wouldn't happen to know anything about that?" Dr. Seeley tilted his chin up after he asked.

Mara blinked. "Oh, that?" She smiled, lightened her voice a little for effect. "Those rumors got just so out of hand." She shook her head and shot some air out of her nose. "It was just parlor games, you know, like Ouija boards and stuff. We read a book about witches, a long time ago, and, well, it was just all in fun. You couldn't say we were practicing witchcraft or anything like that." She looked at him and changed her expression to concern. "Is that what you heard?" And now she made her face say, *because that's crazy.*

"Well, I couldn't help but notice some of your reading material, that it had to do with witchcraft, spells and such."

Couldn't help but notice books hidden inside my desk?

Dr. Seeley continued. "And when the police were here for the investigation into Marc, I couldn't help but overhear them asking about it."

Couldn't help but overhear after you cracked your door open!

And then it all became clear.

Dr. Seeley was the snitch. He was the one who had started the rumors. He'd seen the books she'd been reading when he'd rifled through her desk. He knew the names of a few members of her book club. And he had clients at the Women's Foundation as well. Once that group got wind of something, there was no slowing it down.

Mara stared up at him with a look of complete disgust, to which Dr. Seeley seemed oblivious.

"Well. Anyway. I was just wondering." He waited for a moment, as if hoping Mara would confess to him her involvement in a coven. When it seemed apparent to him she wouldn't, he said, "It's good they got him. Good that the Trebelmeier girl is going to be all right. She is recovered, isn't she?"

"Yes, yes. She'll be back over a bubbling cauldron with us in no time."

Dr. Seeley's eyes got wide.

"She'll be back casting spells and putting curses on bad guys before you know it." Mara flipped down a wrist. She pretended to just notice Dr. Seeley's startled expression. "Oh, you know I'm only kidding." She laughed.

Dr. Seeley smiled uncertainly along with Mara. She was surprised the gesture didn't make his face creak.

"Well, anyway." He coughed. "Carry on." He backed away from her toward his office.

Carry on? That man could be so annoying. The way he talked down to her sometimes. Snooping around her desk. Listening in on conversations. And she'd had it with his condescending, judgmental manner.

She checked her watch. She'd better get to work soon or he'd be back over here growling at her. At least her stomach wasn't growling all the time anymore. It was almost lunchtime, but Mara decided to finish up the filing before she ate.

Thank goodness Greta's spell reversal had been a success. Mara wasn't singing spontaneously anymore either, and she'd lost four pounds of the weight she'd gained. One pound a week. If only the weight loss would happen for her as effortlessly as it had seemed to happen for Lindsay. But Mara didn't dare ask for that. A diet was small penance.

Her appetite was back to normal: no more downing entire boxes of Girl Scout cookies in one session. And Henry had returned to shaving once a day, his extra hair falling out. She'd found a small clump of it on the bathroom floor and had immediately begun to chastise Tippy for leaving bits of himself lying about, until she picked up the clump and realized, after closer analysis, that it must have come from Henry's back.

Dr. Bernstein said the results of the hormone tests he'd done were inconclusive. The only explanation he could offer for the onset of Henry's hairiness—and then its subsequent loss—was *stress.*

Mara had never told Henry anything about the wishing and he hadn't heard any of the early rumors floating around the Strawn Academy about himself or his wife, either. He had, however, noticed the silences that fell over the faculty break room when he entered, and the strained smiles he got in the halls, but he'd thought it was because of all his new hair. He'd never suspected it was because of a rumor that his witchy wife and her book group had turned him into some sort of werewolf. It wasn't until he'd come up behind a group of boys at baseball practice three weeks earlier that he'd learned the truth.

"Yeah—his wife and Ms. Dubois are in the same book club. They're witches," one of the boys was saying.

"Shut up."

"No, really. Just look at the guy; they've turned him into a were-wolf. And then Ms. Dubois finds that baby in the bathroom. I'm tellin' you, this school is like an episode of *Supernatural*."

"Shut up," the other boy had said again, a harsh whisper this time, because Coach O'Connor was now standing right behind them.

Henry had confronted Mara that night. It was only a few days after Jill's abduction and at first Mara had started to deny it, giving him the parlor-game /Ouija-board routine, but she'd stopped mid-sentence.

"Henry, I'm sorry. The truth is, I think we did this to you." And then she told him everything.

It was true, she thought, about the truth setting you free. As soon as she'd told him she felt better, and he hadn't reacted the way she'd thought he would. He'd actually seemed oddly support-ive. Like he kinda wouldn't have minded a wife that was a witch. "Maybe turn some of the more horrid students of mine into frogs." He'd laughed.

She'd thought that's what would happen, that they'd start learn-ing witchcraft with Greta, but in the end everyone had chickened out. Even Lindsay. They'd all realized that they could get the things they wanted from life without lighting candles, chanting chants, or putting herbs in a bucket.

But mostly, nobody wanted to risk casting another doozie.

As much as Mara had been charmed by the idea of casting spells, she'd decided that she'd be better off without that particular brand of *wishing*. In fact, half the battle of getting what you wanted was just realizing *what* that was—and not even witchcraft could help her with that.

Instead, Mara had asked Henry if he would mind if she took some voice lessons, maybe eventually get a job at a piano lounge somewhere. "You know, someplace nice."

"I always wondered if maybe someday you'd go back to singing," he'd said. "I was hoping, actually. I always felt like I was the one who took it away from you."

"You didn't take anything away. You gave me everything." And as soon as she had said it, she realized how very much it was true.

Mara now picked up a file and pushed it into its proper place on the shelf. "Ow. Damn it." She watched blood seep into the white line on her finger. A paper cut. Mara put her finger into her mouth.

This sucked. The truth was, she hated this job. The truth was, she didn't *need* this job. Her boys could work during college. They could take out loans. *They* didn't need for her to have this job. What was it that she and Henry didn't have that she couldn't live without? Nothing. She had everything she needed. *Life is way too short*, she thought. *I could go at any minute. Just look at what almost happened to Jill.* And suddenly she had a great idea.

Mara dropped the stack of files she'd been holding onto the top of her desk. She looked at the sailboat watercolor. *Only 365 days in a year and I'm not wasting another one of them.*

Mara walked down the short hall and knocked on the door to Dr. Seeley's office, a brief courtesy, and then she just opened it.

He looked up, completely taken aback at her audacity. He hadn't granted her permission to enter. His fat lips were pursed out dangerously far.

"Dr. Seeley," Mara said. "I quit."

Dandayamana Dhanurasana. Sanskrit for Standing Bow Pulling Pose. Lindsay stood on one leg, with one hand holding an ankle and the other reaching for her reflection in the mirror, palm to the ground, her arm stretching forward solid and strong—a laser.

Sweat trickled down her back, under the palm of the hand holding her ankle, down the side of her face. Fabulous! Her skin had never felt so young. The balancing series in Bikram yoga was hard, but after a couple months, she'd begun to master it. She didn't fall out as much as she used to.

"Kick, kick, kick," the instructor was saying. "Play with it. If I don't see you guys falling out in the second set, I know you're not pushing hard enough."

In the end it was all about balance. Lindsay stood in rest position, her heart racing. Strong. That's how she felt now. Strong. She set up for Balancing Stick.

Her reputation at the foundation hadn't been as tainted as she'd expected after her fainting episode and the witch rumors. Lindsay was now cochairing a silent auction that was coming up in the fall. Even Evelyn Cantwell seemed to have forgiven her for passing out on her dessert. She'd asked Lindsay to join the guidance committee on the redecorating of the ladies' lounge at foundation headquarters. Lindsay had heard that when it got back to Evelyn that Lindsay had suggested mauve as the main color scheme, Evelyn hadn't been sure if Lindsay was serious or if somehow she was making Evelyn the brunt of a joke.

Some of the women had even approached her about the rumors later, to ask her if they might be true, and Lindsay had surprised herself by not vehemently denying them. In fact, she'd practically encouraged them.

"A witch? Of course. And I can't wait until everyone sees me on my new Versace broom." The interesting thing was the women seemed really curious about it, as though it were something they'd always been interested in or wanted to pursue themselves.

Deep down, Lindsay thought, every woman knows she's a witch. But they could have it. Lindsay had decided against witchcraft as a means of achieving what she wanted out of life. She glanced at her butt in the mirror as she turned for Standing Separate Leg Stretching. *Thank goodness it's not growing back too much.* She'd been keeping up her fitness routine, although not as rigorously as before. But she had added Bikram yoga.

It was like what Greta had told them: the Universe is a witty wordsmith. Her pun, the message for her, had been to get off her butt. Quite literally. It wasn't so much her wish as her decision, her commitment to it, that finally helped her lose the weight. And now Lindsay realized that if she wanted to change the world, she should just get off her butt and do it, with or without the Chicago Women's Foundation.

Lindsay stood, legs wide apart. She bent at the waist, putting her butt in the air, and tried to touch her forehead to the floor. One of the more ridiculous positions she'd found herself in, but really no more ridiculous than fainting on streusel after being accused of being a witch.

With her arms spread wide, Lindsay held her own eyes in the mirror as her upper body did a swan dive. *I look beautiful.* The thought floated through her head. It shocked her to have such a lovely thought about herself, and she decided it would be her own secret; no one else would have to know.

Her hands found her heels and she pulled her head close, close, closer to the floor. Perhaps today, her forehead would finally touch it. She snuck a peek at the woman behind her, whose forearms paralleled her calves.

This yoga, it *was* invigorating, in spite of the heat and the sweat, which she didn't seem to notice anymore. It was something she could see doing for a long, long time. Lindsay smiled, relaxed a little more, and the burning in her hamstrings started to subside.

Much to her surprise she felt her forehead bump the floor, and a laugh escaped her. Saltwater filled her eyes.

Chapter Thirty-Two

C*laudia* sat at the long mahogany table, watching the water condense on the outside of her glass. Everyone had a glass of ice water in front of them and several pitchers were placed strategically around the table. The tiny dots of water on the outside of her glass grew larger and larger, some of them joining together with others to form rivulets that rolled down the side, gathering steam as they picked up more and more followers on their cascade to the bottom. They hadn't given her a coaster. *Fine, they can accuse me of leaving a watermark, too.*

Claudia was in a lot of trouble. The Strawn Academy frowned on its teachers getting themselves involved in anything that might bring notoriety to the school. And Claudia's life the past several months had been fraught with notoriety. It was why Peterson had called her at home. He'd wanted—in his transparent, ingratiating way—to tell her the school board was going to put her questionable conduct on the agenda of their next meeting.

So now, here she sat at her own personal Salem witch trial: the Strawn Academy school board's annual spring meeting.

Instead of taking the word of some adolescent girls, as had the elders of Salem, the accusers here at Strawn were taking the word of some mysterious, unnamed informant. It seemed worse than the Salem witch trials to Claudia, because, as one look at Marion confirmed, the same kind of self-serving hysterics portrayed in *The Crucible* were still in operation now, more than three hundred years later.

Claudia would be required to defend herself against the board's many "concerns" about her. She had found an abandoned baby in a school bathroom, and then she had had the audacity to try to foster the child. She was, and continued to be, involved in a book group that was rumored to be practicing witchcraft. And there were strange reports coming from her classroom: her teaching ability had been called into question by a reported unwillingness or inability to write on the board.

Outside the window of the conference room, the buds on the trees had started to open into leaves. The lilacs lining the circular drive were in full bloom on the south lawn, and, if the windows had been open, their rich scent would have wafted in. The sun was shining in a beautiful blue sky dotted with fluffy white clouds, and on this bright May morning, the outside air finally felt warm, a hope-filled hint of the coming summer. Claudia wanted to throw up.

Ever since she'd peed on that First Response stick and watched her urine soak into the scientific paper, turning both lines pink—in seconds, not minutes like the package said—she was no longer able to discount her morning nausea as nerves. She'd been stunned at the result. She'd been so caught up in losing Elliot, in Book Club's errant wishes, in Jill, and in this hearing, that her quest to have a baby had taken a backseat.

The complete unexpectedness of a positive pregnancy test blew her mind. Her period had been over a week late and she hadn't even noticed! When Claudia finally had looked over her neglected sheet of graph paper, she'd been more convinced of the possibility that she'd misplaced an entire week of her life than the possibility she could actually be that late. After she'd taken the test, she'd sat down straddling the toilet, trying to get her head to stop spinning. The little plastic stick rested on the ceramic lid and Claudia sat there staring at the two pink lines.

The real shock had come when she told Dan. She'd wrapped the pregnancy test in wrapping paper and ribbon and nervously handed it to him when he got home from work.

He'd looked at her, puzzled.

Claudia had been purposefully cagey. "I hope you like it," she said. "You're going to have it for a long, long time."

After he opened it and realized what he was looking at, he picked her up in a big bear hug and spun her around, then set her back down, a terrified look on his face, as if he were afraid he'd hurt her or the baby somehow. He was so happy, so excited. His eyes glazed up. Pure joy. She hadn't really known what to expect, but she hadn't expected that. He had told her that losing Elliot had changed his mind about wanting a baby of his own.

"I thought I would be more relieved, you know?" Dan said. "But it made me sad. I felt disappointed. It was weird. Totally not what I'd expected. That's when I knew if we got pregnant, it would be okay. More than okay. It would be great."

And then what she liked to refer to as the "New Dan," the new, happier Dan, had started to appear more and more. He had talked about buying a condo. *We've got a ton saved up, when you really think about it. More than enough for a down payment, and a little bit of a cushion.* He had begun talking about starting his business soon. *I don't really know why I've been putting it off for so long. Fear, I guess. It's like having a baby. You never feel like you're ready, so you might as well just jump right in and hope for the best.* And he'd started scheduling his Structures tests and formulating his business plan, just like that. It was as though her pregnancy had become his inspiration.

The wish for Dan, to make him happy, had been an overwhelming success. It was ironic, Claudia thought, that the most unselfish wish she'd made was the one that brought her the most happiness. Then again, maybe that wasn't irony at all.

Claudia turned her attention back inside the conference room.

"But now that the grandparents have come forward, I think it's really out of our hands," one of the board members was saying.

Elliot's mother had left Strawn a few weeks earlier, when her identity had been made known. Her family was moving *back east* so she would be able to *put all that nastiness behind her.* The fact that they didn't want custody of Elliot simultaneously surprised Claudia— and didn't surprise her. She couldn't imagine a family not wanting to keep their own grandchild, no matter what the circumstances of his conception. Then again, she'd been watching these Strawn families for so many years now, she really should have learned not to be surprised at anything.

Elliot's mother had been a senior at Strawn and the identity of Elliot's father, when Claudia learned it, had helped to explain, at least partially, why Elliot's family had not wanted custody of him. Elliot's teenage mother had been having an affair with her father's middle-aged business partner.

So, April Sibley was not Elliot's mother. Although she had been in the bathroom at the same time as the mother. In fact, she'd been there while the mother had been giving birth, but April, in her naïveté, had assumed the girl had just been constipated. The mother had the added misfortune of having worn very cool shoes that day, which April had noted, because she had thought it would be fun to *out* the girl for taking such a vociferous dump. Her brand-new pair of Skechers were what had given her away.

It had, however, taken April a while to admit she had this information—more likely because of her embarrassment at not having realized what she'd witnessed rather than because of any desire on her part to protect a slacker or a wanna-be.

Elliot's other grandparents—his father's parents—wanted custody of him now. A rumored quote from the grandmother ran something to the effect of, "Elliot couldn't possibly be any more of a screw-up than our son." Which made Claudia like them instantly.

It made her happier to know that Elliot was going to be with his family, but that didn't take away from the hurt she felt at losing him. Perhaps it was a small price to pay for dabbling in witchcraft. And she should be grateful that at least she'd had Elliot in her life long enough for him to work his own kind of magic on her and Dan.

Now Peterson was talking about what implicitly condoning witchcraft could mean for the school.

At least he wasn't talking about the "warning signs" of teen pregnancy anymore. *What a moron.* Claudia tuned him out. She was finding it hard to concentrate on anything these days, with all the hormones coursing through her. She really needed something to eat, to settle her stomach, and she opened a packet of crackers she took from her purse, rattling the cellophane below the edge of the table, hoping it wouldn't disturb anyone. A few of the board members closest to her looked her way.

What are they going to do now, she thought, *kick me out for eating crackers?*

The water droplets on the outside of her glass had become huge; they looked like bubbles floating in midair. She took a drink and set the glass back on the table, feeling she'd committed another crime somehow, that maybe the water wasn't there to actually drink.

Claudia was due in December and she thought this was a good sign; her baby would be home for the holidays. Even if she did get to keep her job, she wouldn't be able to finish out the school year that would start the next fall. The following spring semester would be void of April Sibley and spit-wad fights and Marion Chutterman and Peterson. No more inquiries into found babies. No more ice water at Strawn school board meetings. Claudia had a vision of herself sitting on a blanket on her living-room floor, playing with the baby, waving one of those black-and-white toys in the air, both of them smiling.

Perhaps if I take a long enough maternity leave, I could finish my book.

Claudia looked up at the faces seated around the table. Most everyone's eyes held the same zombie-like expression. This meeting was ridiculous. It had gone on long enough, and Claudia was ready for it to be over. These idiots talking didn't know what they were talking about, what they thought the implications of having such a disreputable teacher at their school would be—what the parents' reaction would be, what it would do to enrollment and perhaps, more importantly, donations.

Marion Chutterman kept looking at her with disgust, as if she'd just witnessed Claudia downing a whole box of Munchkins. She kept shaking her frazzled curls and thinning her lips.

Claudia was hungry. She wished she *could* pull a box of Munchkins out of her purse. She felt around in it again, hoping for another packet of crackers. Instead she felt something familiar in her fingers. Claudia looked down into the depths of her purse and caught a glimmer of something sparkling partially buried at the bottom. She probed again, moving her keys out of the way, and pulled out the crystal she'd thought she had lost. *It was in here the whole time?* It looked like a small sword, and Claudia thought this was a good sign, too.

Holding her miniature crystal sword in her hand, Claudia let her mind wander to Greta and the things she'd said about wishes and witchcraft and how Greta had told them that the Wiccan tools they'd used were powerful because *they were* powerful, and not just because *they believed* they had power. It was Greta's belief that things like myrrh and crystals and bloodstone actually contained magic.

Claudia had a realization right then, that maybe these things were magical because they'd been empowered with the energy and belief of thousands of women over thousands of years. Maybe that's the way their power had become "real." Maybe it was just like the ruby slippers: the power is with you all along; you just have to believe.

"Ms. Dubois? Is there anything you'd like to say on the matter?" It was Peterson, snapping Claudia back into the room, the expression on his face his version of a "wink-wink," as if to say, *Here's your chance to say your piece—aren't I a clever and generous boss?*

"Yes," Claudia said, "I do have something to say."

Peterson's face darkened rapidly. Clearly he wasn't expecting Claudia to be so eager.

"I think you need to watch where you park your Ferragamos."

Peterson's face twitched, quite inadvertently. Marion's hand flew up to her chest.

Anyone who, like Claudia, had not been giving the meeting their full attention previously was giving it all of their attention now.

"I've sat and listened to you all long enough to realize that, although you've been able to talk extensively about it for the past forty-five minutes, you clearly know nothing about the Craft. It's the practice of Wicca and it's a religion based on the worship and preservation of Earth and nature. Wiccans celebrate the seasons and the cycles of life and don't believe in Satan or bite the heads off chickens. It sort of sounds like that's what you think, and if that's true, then you've been watching too many movies and are even more misinformed that I thought."

Claudia paused and took a breath. *I should deny everything . . . or maybe explain that I'm not . . . No. Wait. Remember what Lindsay says, about explaining being the same as losing? Let 'em wonder,* she thought, forcing back a grin, before she continued. "You may choose to have me suspended or even have me fired," she paused again for effect. "I do think a public hanging would be a bit over-the-top. But if you choose to do anything to me, it will be considered discrimination based on religion, and Wicca *is* a religion and if I'm not mistaken, religious persecution is against the law. I think even a mediocre attorney could prove that in court."

Marion looked positively horrified. In fact, most of them looked positively horrified . . . but no one more so than Peterson. His thought process had been evident on his face. *She knows? Claudia knows about me and Marion?* Now his face was full of fear. More than fear. Terror.

"Religious discrimination? Why, that's a very serious accusation." A less hairy Henry O'Connor spoke from his place at the table. "That would certainly bring discredit to Strawn. We *pride* ourselves here on our openness to everyone, our ability to embrace differences. Wicca *is* a religion. It's recognized by the government. People in the military get holidays and such for it."

Bravo, Henry! Mara must have told him.

He continued, "The last thing Strawn needs right now is any more bad publicity." Henry paused for a moment, letting his words sink in. "And Ms. Dubois has indicated a lawsuit would be concomitant with any action on the school's part—and I think she's within her rights. If I had to guess, I'd say she would be successful in her pursuit of this in a court.

"Personally, I say we drop this whole thing. Adopt that new *don't ask, don't tell* policy. We are actively engaging in a real-life witch hunt here and I think it sets a terrible," he made eye contact with everyone around the table for emphasis as he spoke, "terrible precedent. This is a career we're talking about. A livelihood. We all know Claudia. We know she's not satanic. She helped that poor baby she found. Maybe saved his life. She's so kind that she even tried to be his foster mother. She fell in love with him right away. That's not the mark of an evil person.

"Come on, everybody. Claudia's not a bad influence on our students; you know that. I don't know if I could exercise such self-restraint if I had the ability to turn some of them into frogs." Henry laughed quietly. Some of the other teachers looked at Claudia a little more fearfully. They'd seen what Henry's wife had done to *him*.

The room was silent. Some ice settled in a glass. Peterson cleared his throat.

"Well, I think that we could take this under"—he cleared his throat again—"under advisement," he said. He looked very pale. He and Marion kept exchanging nervous glances. "I think, maybe . . ."

Peterson rubbed his chin, then a lightness washed over his face, as though he were trying to make his face all happy and friendly again. "Actually, in light of this new information, about this, er, this Wicker religion, perhaps we should drop all the charges against Ms. Dubois immediately." Marion was bobbing her head slightly, encouragingly. "I see no reason why we need to go forward with any further hearings or termination proceedings—"

"Great," Claudia said, pushing her chair away from the table. She stood up, even though she knew Peterson was only warming up, that his little speech was just getting under way. "But if it'll make your decision process any easier, I'd like you all to know that I'm pregnant and will be starting my maternity leave immediately. I'll be taking next year off as well. So, you see," she smiled, "there's no hurry for you to decide my fate."

They stared at her, some with their mouths agape.

Claudia smiled back, a smile of pure glee. She picked up her purse and started for the door.

When she passed Marion, Claudia stopped. She cast her right index finger at her, snapping it down as if it were a wand.

Marion leaned back in her chair, where she remained momentarily frozen, pinned to her seat, only her eyes moving from side to side, as if pleading, *Please don't turn me into a frog.*

"I think congratulations are in order," Claudia said to Marion, bringing her hand slowly and dramatically back to pat her belly, where her baby's beating heart was nestled inside.

Epilogue

———✦———

$\mathcal{G}$reta stepped out onto the fire escape and inhaled a breath of fresh air. A thunderstorm had just rumbled through, and the sun to the west was now breaking through the clouds as it descended toward the horizon, lighting up the sky with an explosion of gold and pink.

To the south, the storm still raged in the distance; she could see occasional flashes of lightning and dark shafts of virga. If she could look to the east, most likely there would be a rainbow, but Greta didn't lean around the corner to look; she just held her gaze steady at the horizon, watching the streetlights start to flick on.

The storm had sprung up quite suddenly. It hadn't lasted very long, but the wind had been fierce, rattling her windowpanes, pelting them with rain, making the same sound marbles make when they're dropped to the floor. Hail had created even more of a commotion on the fire escape when it had hammered down, its melting remains still on the railing.

Now the air was thick with moisture, but instead of the wormy odor of a spring shower, the air smelled clean and fresh. Like summer was here. Greta inhaled the warm air and a sense of calm filled her. The air felt peaceful.

Greta put both hands on her hips and took in another breath before she turned to head inside. Maybe everything wasn't exactly right in the world, maybe it wasn't perfect; but at least the storm was over.

Acknowledgments

✦

Wish Club never would have found its way into print without the help of many, many people to whom I'm forever indebted. There's a special place in heaven for my very first readers, Martin Madden and Lauren Peck, who took my baby, my lame beginning of a story and, with honesty, love, and encouragement, helped me keep going. Thanks to all the following readers for their insight, keen eyes, and support: Inga Hoffman, Kristen Guggeis, Jomarie Fredericks, Patty and John Henek, Alan Maass, Rick and Bridget Kaempfer, David Stern, Michelle Halle-Stern, Mike and Mary Bogumill, Homa Shojaie, Chris Rice, Janet Joseph, Adrienne Walker, Annie Barclay, Gretchen Hirsch, Charlotte Shreck Burns, Livia Gaffield, Amir Rakha, Neil Turner, John Swift, Lon Wehrle, and everyone else at the Chicago Writer's Bloc Writing Workshop, and a big shout-out to Theresa Rizzo for the final spit and polish, the one that made it happen.

I would like to thank my agent extraordinaire, Sha-Shana Crichton, for her words of encouragement, for somehow seeing in my manuscript a diamond in the rough, and for sticking with me every step of the way as we tried to polish it into something that might sparkle. Thank you to Shana Drehs for being the one to pick Wish Club from the pile, and for the ensuing brilliant editorial guidance. Great big thanks to Lindsey Moore for so enthusiastically jumping on board, and for additional sage advice, brilliant guidance, and insight, and to Janet McDonald for making me look smarter than I am.

For help with research and technical advice, I'm indebted to: Silver RavenWolf for all of her many books on witchcraft (and for one amazing tarot reading at BEA 2004); Dorothy Morrison for her book on spells, *Everyday Magic*; Evidence Technician Brigid Cronin, Sergeant Christopher Ferraro and Officer Matthew Jackson—all Chicago's Finest; Sandra Tapia-Colon, Maria Prassas, Dr. Stefanie R. Spanier Mingolelli, Dr. Audrey Chang, Vicki Poplin, Stephen Grant, Kris LaCerda, and Dr. Joan Burkhart. Any errors, exaggeration, or omissions are purely my own.

So many others have helped along the way, with support and encouragement, or a shoulder to cry on. Thanks goes to: Linda Howe, Christina Cross, Deanne Lozano, April Miller, Starbuck O'Dwyer, Liz McGarry, Kelly James-Enger, Sheryl Curcio, Charlie Meyerson, Cara Lockwood, Ellen Karas, Karen Coons and Jim Karas; Mason Green—for the place of inspiration; Deb Claflin, Lois Keller, Pam McGaan, Georgy Ann Peluchiwski, Kirsten Rider, Anne Rossley, Stacey Saunders, Cynthia Scazzero, Nancy Shields, Meghan Strubel, and Vicky Tesmer—all the fabulous ladies in my book club, which never, not ever, practiced witchcraft. Thank you also to Hanna Dabrowska, because of you I never worried.

I would like to thank my mom and dad, Anne and Rick Strickland, for, among other things, teaching me to never quit.

Ethan and Kyle, I am eternally grateful for all of your loving support. Kyle gets a special thank you for the ending, which made me think. Ethan gets a special thank you for his itchy tongue and other excuses, all of which made me laugh. Both of you so unbegrudgingly gave me the time for *Wish Club*, time that so rightfully belonged to you. You are the heroes of my story.

And finally, I'd like to thank my best friend, Jeff. For pushing me. For always being brutally honest, even when I didn't want you to be. For slogging through countless drafts, and being the best natural-born editor I've ever met. For believing in me when I stopped believing in myself. For you, the words *thank you* are not enough. I love you, my darling. When you came along, everything started to hum.

Still, it's a real good bet, the best is yet to come.